MOTIVE

~by~

Alan McDermott

For Del.
Sorry you didn't get to read this one, bro.

Also by Alan McDermott

Gray Justice
Gray Resurrection
Gray Redemption
Gray Retribution
Gray Vengeance
Gray Salvation
Gray Genesis
Trojan
Run and Hide
Seek and Destroy
Fight to Survive

Chapter 1

In many of life's pursuits, location is key. Where to buy a house, where to take a holiday, where to find work.

But never more so than where to kill a man.

She drove around the back of what had once been a thriving industrial estate to open space. Today, most of the buildings had no roofs, and the remaining walls were covered with graffiti. It was perfect because few people came here.

The last thing she wanted was an audience.

She parked a few feet behind the only other vehicle in the area, a silver BMW belonging to Sean Conte, and got out. She'd seen him leave his house twenty minutes earlier, but hadn't followed him. There was no need. He was going to take the dog for a walk, just as he did every day. Always the same spot, rain or shine. All she had to do was be there when he returned to his car.

The derelict estate had an unwelcoming feel to it, like it knew it was about to host an evil deed, even in the gorgeous July sunshine. The wild grass was at least knee high, but a trail cut through the yellowing weeds and down a slight incline towards a clump of oaks. That was where Conte would come from. She'd see the top of his head while he was still a hundred yards away, and that was when she'd get into character. Until then, she had little to do but set the scene and wait.

She opened the boot of the car and put the jack, portable compressor and X-shaped wheel brace next to the rear tyre, then let most of the air out.

She was ready.

The dog in the back seat of her car pawed at the window, but she didn't let it out. It was just there for show. She'd borrowed it from a neighbour who'd been unfortunate enough to sprain her ankle a few days earlier, offering to take it for a walk. She could have completed her task without it, but her presence would arouse less suspicion with a canine in the vehicle. She'd cranked the windows a few inches to make the Labrador more comfortable, not because she hated to see an innocent animal suffer, but to avoid having to explain to its owner why it was either dead or seriously dehydrated.

A wave of excitement washed over her when she saw the top of Conte's head appear twenty minutes later. His hair was dark, not a sign of grey even though he was in his mid-fifties, but his daily walks seemed to be his only form of exercise. His stomach had long ago turned to flab, and she could almost hear him panting as he made his way up the shallow incline, even from a hundred yards away.

His poor condition was a bonus, but she couldn't be complacent. At six feet, he was four inches taller than her, but she didn't anticipate that being a problem.

She forced herself to relax, then leaned into the open boot of the Honda and began tugging at the spare wheel in its well. It wouldn't move, but that was because she hadn't removed the wing nut securing it in place. In fact, she'd tightened it as much as she could.

"Oh, for the love of…"

She stood upright, kicked the boot of the Honda and stood with one hand on her hip and the other against her forehead.

"Need a hand?"

Her eyes flashed open and she saw Conte standing close by. A small white Yorkshire terrier strained at the lead to get to her, its tongue lolling, but the man easily held it in check.

"If you could, that would be great," she said, offering a tired smile while moving away from the car. "I've got a flat but can't get the spare wheel out."

Conte handed her the dog's lead and rolled up his sleeves. "It's probably just caught on something." He leaned into the boot, then laughed. "You haven't removed the restraining nut."

She smacked herself on the forehead and groaned. "I am *so* stupid."

Conte chuckled. "It's easily done…wow, this is on tight."

As he leaned into the boot and struggled with the wing nut, she dropped the terrier's lead and took two items from her handbag. The first was a stun gun, and she jammed it up against his rib cage and pressed the button. Conte's body spasmed as electric current shot through his body. She felt as if some of the charge was coursing through her own body, but she knew it was just the adrenaline that came with each kill.

After five seconds, she released the button and Conte slumped forward into the boot, a low groan emanating from him. She leaned over him and stuck the second item from her handbag, a hypodermic needle, into his carotid artery. She pushed the plunger down, emptying the sodium thiopental into his bloodstream. It would take around thirty seconds for the drug to take effect, so she put her hands on his shoulders and pushed down hard, pinning him inside the car. He struggled initially, but soon his efforts petered out and he lost consciousness.

She had no time to lose. The drug would wear off in minutes, and she still had work to do. She pushed his upper body as far into the boot as she could, then lifted his legs and swung them inside. Once he was in, she pulled a plastic bag over his head and used a thick elastic tie with hooks on either end to secure it around his neck.

She angled his head so that she could look into his eyes, but they were closed. Still, she stood looking at him for a moment, a sensation of power rushing through her that was better than any sex she'd ever had.

The terrier shattered the moment by barking, darting towards her before backing off sharply and repeating the dance again and again. She picked up the tyre iron and waited for the dog to get close enough, then swung. She missed, so she planted her foot on the dog's lead for a second attempt. The terrier had nowhere to go. She raised the tool once more and brought it crashing down, catching the dog on the side of the head. It yelped, took a couple of uneasy steps sideways, then collapsed. She hit it a few more times for good measure, then picked up the limp body and threw it into the boot beside its owner.

She lowered the lid, then used the compressor to inflate the tyre once more. When she was done, she tossed the equipment on top of the two bodies. It had been almost four minutes since she'd put the bag over Conte's head, and when she checked his pulse she knew it had served its purpose.

It was almost anticlimactic, but it wasn't just the killing that gave her the rush. The knowledge that she would get away with it was the main driver.

She slammed the boot lid and got behind the wheel. The hard part was behind her, but she still had plenty to do. First, she would take the Labrador for a walk at another place—one that was busier—and then return it to her neighbour. It wouldn't hurt to establish an alibi, though she didn't expect to need one. She'd killed twice before and suspicion had never pointed her way.

It wouldn't this time, either. She was refining her methods with each kill, and so far this one was going as planned.

She drove out of the abandoned industrial estate and made her way to Richmond park, where she let the neighbour's dog chase a ball for half an hour. She bagged up two piles of its crap like a good citizen, then dropped the mutt off with its owner. She declined the offer of a cup of tea, saying she was running late for a lunch appointment. Ten minutes later she was on the M3 heading west.

"...but if the sun ain't shinin', then I ain't smilin', and I hate to—"

She turned off the radio to concentrate on her driving. When her speed read sixty-eight miles an hour she engaged the cruise control, sticking to the inside lane and maintaining a good distance between herself and the car in front. If she was stopped by the police, she'd have a hard time explaining away the bodies in the boot.

It wasn't easy to stay focused on the road. The feeling of elation was still with her, her muscles tingling and her pulse racing. She drove on autopilot, barely noticing the road or her surroundings as she recalled the moment she'd hit Conte with the stun gun and his body shuddered.

There was even better to come.

She left the motorway at junction five and took the first exit at the roundabout, then a right onto a country lane. She'd been down here twice in the last month, scoping out a suitable place to dump Conte's body.

After fifteen minutes on the quiet roads, she found the spot she'd chosen on her last visit. It was a small dirt track that led into five hectares of dense woodland. She was able to drive fifty yards through the trees before the track ended abruptly, where she turned off the engine and got out.

The only sounds were bird calls and the ticking of the car's engine as it cooled down, but the little red wallet she'd left behind ensured her that she was alone and that her hiding place hadn't been visited in the past two weeks. She picked it up, and apart from a little rain damage from a downpour days earlier, it seemed untouched. The twenty-pound note was still inside, which meant no one had seen it.

Satisfied that she could work uninterrupted, she popped the boot and took out a canvas holdall. Inside was a full-body, disposable coverall. She put it on, making sure her blonde hair was tucked inside the hood. She took off her shoes and put on another pair, which she would dispose of later.

Once she was dressed appropriately, she took a portable vacuum from the back seat and ran it over Conte's body to remove any of her hairs that might have fallen on him. She spent ten minutes on the task, minutes that would save her from years in prison, then picked up the bag and walked ten yards west of the car until she found the spade. It was leaning against the tree, exactly where she'd left it.

She took a polythene sheet from the holdall and laid it out on the ground, then started digging, carefully placing each shovelful on the plastic sheet. To make the hole big enough to accommodate Conte and his dog, she had to stop a few times for water breaks due to the heat.

As she finished off her third bottle of water, she sat at the edge of the hole and caught her breath. The exertion had taken it out of her, but she was only halfway through. She gave herself a few minutes' rest, then walked back to the car to gather the dead.

As she opened the boot, a putrid stench enveloped her. Conte's bowel had given way. She made a mental note not to leave the next one so long as she fought past her revulsion and pulled him out feet first. She dragged him over to the hole and dumped him in so that he was lying on his back, then knelt down to remove the plastic hood and elastic tie.

She got the shock of her life when he groaned. She jumped back and picked up the spade, poised to strike, but he didn't move.

She waited a minute, frozen in the same pose, before relaxing and dropping the spade.

It's just gases escaping, she told herself.

She put the plastic bag and tie into her holdall and took out a facemask, a pair of gloves, a hammer and a cloth. Also inside was a see-through Ziploc bag containing a few hairs and a pair of tweezers. She used the implement to place the hairs on Conte's body. She wedged two under his fingernails, with others placed on the legs of his trousers. After planting the evidence, she put the gloves on carefully and used the cloth to wipe down the shovel and hammer to remove her fingerprints, then put the rag back in the bag. She then put the mask over her face and picked up the hammer.

You won't feel this, but it has to be done.

4

She brought the hammer down on his forehead with all her strength, then his cheek, his temple, his lips, eyes, the side of his neck. With each impact, she thought about her very first kill, and the strength of the blows intensified. She was no longer looking at Sean Conte, but Colin Harper, the man who had set her on this path. She'd seen his face last time, too, but she hadn't beaten the previous victim with a hammer; she had stabbed him repeatedly, instead. She was careful not to use the same *modus operandi* in case the killings were linked. That was the last thing she wanted. Anyone investigating this crime had to see it as a one-off.

The main reason for the unnecessary violence was to obliterate all signs of the hood and tie as well as the injection site. Research had told her that death by asphyxiation caused tell-tale petechiae to form, and these little red spots would be a red flag at an autopsy. She wanted the cause of death to look like a savage beating; otherwise, the evidence she was about to leave would be for nothing. The police would establish that the attack was carried out in the shallow grave post-mortem, which would add to the mystery.

The kick she got out of inflicting the damage was secondary.

Once his face was reduced to a bloody pulp, she dropped the hammer next to his body and took out his wallet. It contained fifty pounds in cash and several bank cards. She put the money aside and tossed the wallet onto Conte's chest, then went back to the car and dragged the dog's corpse by its lead to let it rest with its owner.

Filling in the hole was a lot easier than digging it, and fifteen minutes later she was done. She threw the spade to one side of the unmarked grave, then took off her paper suit and mask and put them in the holdall, followed by the plastic sheet. Her last act was to remove the gloves she'd spent weeks creating. They were a work of art, but she knew she couldn't keep them. Reluctantly, they went into the canvas bag, which she zipped closed.

When she got back to the car, the smell from Conte's evacuation had almost gone. She fetched a couple of air fresheners from her glove box, the kind designed to hang from the rearview mirror, and tossed them into the boot before slamming it shut. She changed shoes once more and put the other pair back in the bag, then put the holdall on the passenger seat and reversed back to the road. In all the time she'd been there, she'd heard no more than a dozen vehicles pass by, so she felt it safe to cover up the tyre tracks she'd left. She backed out onto the road, then pulled onto the grass verge and walked back into the woods, where she pulled a branch off a tree and used it to scrub the ground the car had passed over.

With her penultimate task completed, she allowed herself a smile. It would be a nervous few weeks before she would find out whether her latest venture had paid off, but it had all gone to plan. All she had to do now was dispose of the evidence in the holdall, and she would take care of that later in the evening.

As she drove back to the motorway, she was buzzing. She imagined it was what people who took cocaine felt like after a couple of lines, though she'd never touched drugs of any kind.

Killing was the only high she needed.

Chapter 2

After two in the morning, the streets of Manchester were surprisingly busy.

Ryan Anderson thought so, anyway. It had been a long time since he'd had a Saturday night out in the town, but not a lot had changed in his absence. The scores of teenagers in short skirts and boob tubes had been replaced by even younger girls in shorter skirts, but for the most part, it was the same town he'd visited briefly seven years earlier.

He walked toward a group clearly celebrating something. There were six women and three men, all wearing fancy dress costumes. One of them was dressed as a French maid, complete with short black outfit and fishnet stockings. Others included a vicar and a cavewoman, and the three young men looked like extras from the Rocky Horror movie. They were all making the most of the heatwave.

Ryan angled his walk to avoid them, but the maid stepped into his path. She had black hair in a high ponytail, and the costume hugged her trim figure.

"Hey, handsome," she said, waving a feather duster at his crotch. "Want me to polish your bed knob?"

Her friends howled with laughter, and Ryan had to admit that it was a unique chat-up line. However, he had more important things to do. He smiled politely and tried to walk past, but she stepped in front of him once more.

"What's wrong," she mewed as she stroked the two days of stubble on his cheek. "You prefer boys, is that it? Then you're in luck. Jason here loves his meat injections, don't you, Jase?"

One of the boys turned red and averted his eyes, while the rest of group whooped and cheered. "Go on, Jase, you like 'em tall and rugged!"

Ryan was already bored with the banter, and time wasn't on his side. He took a big step to the left, and when the maid copied him, he shimmied to the right and past her. She lost her balance as one of her high heels caught in a crack in the pavement, and her friends rushed to help her up as Ryan continued on his way, calls and jeers ringing in his ears.

A younger Ryan Anderson would have been flattered at the attention from the maid and would have probably accepted her offer, but he'd done a lot of growing up in the last decade. These days he preferred women with a mature outlook, not drunk twenty-somethings who'd take anything with a cock and a pulse.

He left the partygoers behind as he walked towards the Vine, one of many nightclubs in the city centre. From a distance, he could see the bouncers at the door were dealing with a couple of drunks who seemed desperate to get in but not having much success. He could hear their shouts from seventy yards away.

Two men leaving the club saw the commotion and stepped in to end it. One of them, a tall blond wearing a black leather jacket, jabbed out an arm. From his viewpoint, it looked like a fun tap to Ryan, but the recipient didn't think so. He collapsed like someone had turned off his central nervous system. His friend didn't fare much better. The blond's companion, similarly dressed but squat and bulldog-shaped, launched into him with a flurry of blows to the body and then to the face. He looked like a boxer gently sparring, but the effect was devastating.

The two attackers spoke to the doormen, sharing a laugh, then turned to the door as a short, thin man left the club. Even from afar Ryan could tell his dark suit was tailor-made and expensive. The trio walked toward Ryan, who took his phone from his pocket, looked at the screen, then put it to his ear.

"Hi, what's up?"

The trio was still approaching, with blond and bulldog flanking the suit.

Ryan was on an intercept course with them, but he wasn't about to step aside.

The collision was inevitable. The bulldog hit Ryan in the chest with his shoulder and the phone shot from his hand, crashing to the ground.

"Oi!"

The three men ignored Ryan's shout. He stooped to pick up the handset, then jogged after them.

When he got to within five yards, they turned. The two in leather jackets stood slightly in front of the suit.

"You broke my phone," Ryan said.

"Piss off," was the terse reply from the one in the middle. He was considerably older than the two goons, at least fifty-five, with short grey hair combed in a side parting.

"Sure, just as soon as you pay for my phone."

The old man's face remained placid, but his voice dripped with venom. "I'm feeling generous tonight, so I'll give you one last chance to fuck off before I set the dogs on you."

Ryan couldn't help but smirk. He pointed at the leather jackets in turn. "You mean these two? Are these your bitches? 'Cos they look like bitches."

The tall blond took a step towards Ryan. "Watch your mouth. Do you know who you're talking to?"

"Well, gee, I've only been in town a few days," Ryan said, sarcastically, "so I haven't had a chance to meet everyone yet. Tell you what, though. Pay for my phone and we can be best mates. You can come round my house and fuck my dog."

The bulldog looked at the old man pleadingly. He got a nod in response. "Make it quick. I want to get home."

Bulldog took two steps toward Ryan and pulled his arm back.

That was as far as he got.

Ryan feigned with a low left to the stomach, but all his weight was behind the right hand that hit bulldog in the temple. The stocky man staggered and shook his head, desperate to stay in the fight, but Ryan pirouetted on his left foot and his right connected with bulldog's cheek.

Ryan didn't even watch him fall. His attention was now with the blond, who had adopted a fighter's pose and was bouncing on the balls of his feet. He seemed calm, focused, sizing Ryan up as he danced to his left. Ryan stood his ground, waiting for the attack to come.

It was surprisingly swift.

The blond's fist flashed towards Ryan's head, but he jinked right just in time, the attacker's knuckles grazing his scalp. Ryan had never faced anyone so quick, but he wasn't fazed. He just had to make sure he landed the first telling blow.

Blond kicked out at Ryan's groin, but he deftly blocked it and lashed out with a backhand to his opponent's face. Blood erupted from blond's lip, but he barely seemed to notice. He started dancing once more, looking for the opportunity to strike, but Ryan wanted this over quickly. He lashed out at the other man's crotch with his left foot, and when blond instinctively crouched to protect his sensitive region, Ryan switched his stance and brought his right foot under blond's chin. His head snapped backwards and he fell to the ground face first.

Ryan turned to face the suit. "As I was saying, I need someone to pay for my phone. You're the only one left, so you're it."

The older man stared at him for a moment, then surprised Ryan by laughing. "You've got some balls, I'll give you that." He pulled out a roll of banknotes, counted a few fifty-pound notes and handed them to Ryan. "There's three hundred."

"My phone cost five."

"Don't push your luck," the suit told him. "Out of curiosity, where did you learn to fight like that?"

"I grew up in a rough place, but mostly my time in the army." He looked down at the two unconscious bodyguards. "The tall guy's good, but the short one really is a bitch. I'm guessing they work for you?"

The suit nodded.

"I'll take the bitch's place," Ryan said, "but I want two grand a week, minimum."

"You're a presumptuous little bastard, aren't you."

Ryan shrugged. "I need a job. I've got the skills you want, and if you can afford to hire muscle you've obviously got the money I want. It's a no-brainer."

The older man studied Ryan for a moment, then gestured over his shoulder with his thumb. "Come to the club tomorrow night at six. There's a door 'round the back. Press the top buzzer."

Ryan nodded. "Need a hand with these two?"

"Yeah. Help me get 'em up."

The suit kicked bulldog in the thigh. "Wake up, you malingering shit. I ain't paying you to sleep."

Ryan slapped the blond a couple of times and was rewarded with a groan. "Come on, up you get."

Blond opened his eyes and blinked a few times, then pulled away from Ryan and scrambled to his feet, his fists up ready to continue the fight."

"Pull your neck in, George," the suit told him. "He's golden."

George looked confused, but relaxed his stance.

"Help me get sleeping ugly here back to the motor."

George helped the groggy bulldog to his feet and half-dragged him towards a black Jaguar that was parked down the street.

"What's your name?" the suit asked.

"Ryan. Ryan Anderson."

He mulled the name over for a moment, then turned and followed his bodyguards. "See you tomorrow, Ryan Anderson," he said over his shoulder.

Ryan watched them leave, then tried to hail a passing taxi, but it was full and ignored him. At this time of night, he knew he'd have more luck tripping over a unicorn nest than finding an empty cab. It was a two-mile walk back to his bedsit, most of it through the busy city centre. The distance didn't bother him, but he didn't fancy running into any more hen parties on the way.

He'd had enough excitement for one night.

Chapter 3

"I'd never have picked France for a holiday location, but I have to admit, this place is beautiful," Scott Davison said.

His companion, a man in his thirties dressed appropriately in a Hawaiian shirt and cargo shorts, agreed.

The café was one of four situated on one of Auxerre's narrow, pedestrianised side streets. Whether by design or good fortune, the street ran east to west, so the sun was always above them.

"Think you'll settle here?" the man sitting opposite asked in his public-schoolboy accent.

Scott sipped his coffee. "Probably. It's quiet, the food's good, plenty of sunshine." He got up gingerly, using his cane to support his weight. "I need a piss."

He hobbled inside the café, past a dozen tables covered with the obligatory red gingham cloth, and into the toilet. After relieving himself, he washed his hands, then took off his glasses and smoothed down his salt and pepper hair in the mirror. It was time to get it cut again. He'd never worn it this long, and it didn't really suit his facial features. Short hair accentuated his good looks, whereas his current style and dark beard made him feel like a bum.

He put his glasses back on and returned to his table outside the Café Antonia. His companion was just settling the bill when Scott collapsed into his seat. The elderly couple who had been occupying the next table had left, and in their place was a young woman with dark hair who was swiping away on her phone. Scott noticed her red nail polish and gold watch on her left wrist, as well as the absence of a wedding ring.

Picking up little details like this had always been second nature to Scott, but since his injuries, he paid even closer attention to his surroundings.

Especially people.

This woman didn't appear to be a threat of any kind, though. He pegged her as middle management because of her pencil skirt and white blouse, probably still working as she took an early lunch. She was rather attractive in an unconventional way. A year ago he might have approached her, but the events of the last twelve months had changed him.

"I've got to head back," Scott's friend said, breaking his concentration. "Are you sure you're going to be okay? Can I drop you home?"

"I'm fine," Scott assured him, though it was as far from the truth as he could stray. The nightmares were relentless, and although he was close to full mobility once more, progress had been slower than he would have liked. There had been days when he'd wondered if he'd ever walk again without the cane, but he'd persisted nonetheless. The alternative was to use the walking aid for the rest of his life, and Scott wasn't going to let that happen. He would keep up his exercise routine of gentle walking and cycling, eventually upping the intensity levels until he was back to his former self.

"Well, you've got my number. If you need anything, give me a bell."

Scott watched him walk away, then took out his phone. He opened a browser and clicked the bookmark to open the BBC news website. Catching up with the latest developments on the go was the only reason he had the device. The contacts list comprised two numbers: his old boss; and the man who'd just left. He'd never used it to call either of them.

Scott navigated to the sports page but was interrupted as a shadow fell over him. His head snapped up, his body tense as it entered fight-or-flight mode.

It was the woman from the next table, smiling down at him. She was much shorter than Scott, and her body had been looked after. Not the most striking woman Scott had ever seen, but there was something…mysterious about her. She pushed aside a few strands of mahogany hair

"Hi," she said. "I heard you and your friend speaking English. Mind if I join you?"

Her accent was home counties, maybe Berkshire or Buckinghamshire. Scott relaxed and pointed to the empty seat opposite him. "Please do."

He could have done without the company, but there was nothing to be gained by being rude. It wasn't as if he had a pressing engagement. His schedule for the rest of the day consisted of three periods of boredom, followed by a long evening of doing bugger all.

"I'm so glad I finally found someone I can talk to," she said as she carried her laptop case over from the next table, and Scott immediately regretted his decision. She sounded like she had a lot to get off her chest, and he had a feeling very little of it was going to be of interest to him.

"I'm Scott," he said, offering his hand.

"Oh, sorry, I'm Kelly."

Her handshake was strong, confident. She took a seat and put her phone in her purse.

"I've been here for five days and you're the first person I've heard speaking English. None of the shopkeepers can, so I've had to rely on my high school French lessons to get by. I got a C minus, so that tells you how well I've fared."

Scott couldn't help smiling. He knew for a fact that many of them spoke acceptable English but chose not to.

He asked the obvious question. "So what brings you to France?"

"Work," Kelly said. She saw a waiter walk by and grabbed his attention. "You want another coffee?" she asked Scott.

He didn't, but she would probably feel uncomfortable if she was the only one drinking. "Yes, please A latte."

Kelly ordered, mostly through sign language. Fortunately, cappuccino and latte were internationally recognised beverages.

"What work takes you to a country where you can't speak the language?"

"Graphic design," Kelly said. "The advertising company I work for is based in London but has offices around the world. They landed a contract with the wine board of Burgundy to boost tourism. It's based in Chablis, about twenty minutes from here."

Scott knew of the place, though he hadn't been there, and his knowledge of wine was limited to passing it on the supermarket shelf on his way to the beer section.

"It must be hard to understand their requirements if you don't speak French," Scott noted. "Doesn't your company have anyone local?"

"They do, but the wine board saw a campaign I did for one of the Gulf airlines and asked for me specifically. They have a couple of English speakers on the team, but I only get to chat with them once every few days. Our next meeting is on Monday."

"So for the next four days, you'll have no one to talk to? No relatives to call? No boyfriend back in England?"

He didn't know why, but he was curious as to how she would answer the last question.

"Of course I'll chat to my parents, but it's not the same as having a conversation in person, is it?"

Scott wasn't sure if she'd deflected the boyfriend question or if it simply wasn't relevant. It certainly wasn't worth pressing her on it.

"How long do you think you'll be here?" he asked.

"Anywhere from three weeks to a few months. It all depends how happy they are with the original set of designs."

"That's a long time to be away from your loved ones," Scott said.

Kelly laughed. "I left home years ago. My parents are used to me not being around, and vice versa."

Still no mention of a boyfriend.

"What about you?" she asked. "Here on holiday?"

Not quite.

"Recuperating," he said, holding up the cane. "I had an accident."

"I'm sorry. What was it? A car crash?"

I wish.

"Yeah," he lied. "I T-boned a guy when he pulled out of a side street without looking. I broke both kneecaps and lost a couple of toes. My parents own a holiday home here and they let me have it for a few months 'til I'm back on my feet—no pun intended."

The injuries he'd described were accurate, but not the circumstances, and it wasn't something he wanted to discuss with a stranger.

"So, what do you do when you're not recovering from major accidents?" Kelly smiled.

"Actually, it saved me from a rather boring office job. In the last few weeks, I've had the chance to re-evaluate my life. I might start my own business using the insurance money."

"That's a great idea!"

Scott liked her enthusiasm. Her face lit up when she smiled, and there was a mischievous twinkle in her eye. Despite his desire to be alone, he was warming to her.

Having gone a year without close female companionship could also be a factor, he realised.

"As I said, I might. Nothing's set in stone. I'm just toying with a few ideas."

"Well, I think you should stop toying and start doing," Kelly said as the waiter arrived with their drinks. "I'm going to work for myself one day. All I need is the capital to pay the bills until the money starts rolling in, then I'm through being just a number on a corporation's spreadsheet. No one ever got rich working for someone else, unless they're the CEO of a multinational."

Scott was barely listening to her. Alarm bells went off in his mind when he spotted a man walking down the narrow lane toward the café. He was muscular, strode confidently, and was wearing a leather jacket in spite of the heat. Scott shifted his leg so that the holster strapped to his ankle was within reach.

The man walked past the table without looking Scott's way. Ten yards farther on, he met another man and they embraced, then kissed.

Scott relaxed and breathed out audibly, but Kelly had obviously seen his reaction.

"You have an issue with gay men?" she asked, her brow furrowed.

"Not at all. I thought I recognised the guy in the leather jacket. He looks a lot like the man whose car I hit."

Her frown was gone, instantly replaced by that captivating smile.

"Where are you staying?" Scott asked, wanting to steer the conversation away from his past.

"A hotel here in town. It's cheaper than Chablis and the buses are regular..."

While she spoke, Scott sipped his coffee as fast as he could. He wanted out of this situation. As he'd told his companion before she'd turned up, he wanted to be alone. He needed time to reflect, and he couldn't do it with people dribbling in his ear. Much as she intrigued him, Scott wanted rid of her. For one thing, she asked too many questions, and while innocuous, there was no telling what she would want to know if they spent more time together.

He finished off the last of his drink and looked at his watch in a not-too-subtle fashion. "I'm afraid I have to go," he told her, dropping a few euros on the table to cover the bill. "Sorry I couldn't stay longer, but I have an appointment with my physio."

Kelly looked a little disappointed, but that was the least of Scott's concerns. He eased himself out of the chair once more and picked up his cane.

"Best of luck with the contract," he said, offering his most sincere smile.

Kelly picked up her coffee. "This might sound like a corny line, but do you come here often?"

Scott couldn't help but laugh. "Yes, it does. And, no, this is my first time here. I like variety, so next time I'll find another café."

She dug into her purse and handed him a card. "If you ever feel like talking, give me a call. My hours are flexible, so I'm available any time."

Scott looked at the card, then put it in his back pocket. "Will do," he said, though he knew the chances of contacting her were slim. Under different circumstances he would have stayed with her all day, but right now he needed his space.

He walked away, still reluctant to put his full weight on his new knees. He reckoned that with another four weeks of twice-daily exercise, his gait would be back to normal, but only if he pushed himself. Until then, he'd rely on the cane to get him about.

Scott sneaked a look back at the café and instantly regretted it. Kelly was looking at him, her elbow leaning on the table and her chin cradled in her palm. She wiggled a few fingers in his direction, and he returned the gesture with a feeble wave. She had a longing look in her eyes, and he asked himself what the hell he was doing. She was harmless, just a young woman looking for some company on a gorgeous day in a beautiful setting, and he'd blown her off for no good reason.

Scott turned and hobbled to the end of the street, her eyes burning into his back all the way. Once he was out of sight, he relaxed a little. It was a ten-minute walk to the Place des Cordeliers where he'd parked his three-year-old Citroen, then a fifteen-minute drive home.

His two-bedroom bungalow was owned not by his parents, but his old employer. They'd given him use of it until he was mended, both physically and mentally, with no set timeframe for recovery. They'd made the gesture with the hope that one day he would return to work, but Scott knew that wasn't going to happen.

He tossed the keys on the kitchen table, then went into the bedroom to change into his workout gear. With his shorts and t-shirt on, he went into the other bedroom, which had been kitted out as a gym. He did half an hour on the bike, then did fifty pull-ups and fifty sit-ups.

Scott was drenched by the time he finished, and after taking a shower, he took three bottles of beer from the fridge and dumped himself in front of the TV, where he searched for a suitable box set to watch. He'd tried Game of Thrones, about as far from real life as he could wish to get, but some of the scenes brought back too many memories. Cop shows were also out, so he tended to binge on comedies.

He was halfway through an episode of the American version of The Office when one phrase catapulted him back to that fateful day months earlier. His body shivered involuntarily as a ball of ice gathered in his chest and spread down to his abdomen. He was tempted to turn off the television, but that would have left him alone with his thoughts. Instead, he turned up the volume and sank his first beer in one go.

Get a grip, you soft twat!

He couldn't get back into it. The memory refused to leave him, so he tried to picture something less traumatic.

Kelly popped into his head unannounced, and he once again asked himself why he'd behaved in such an offhand manner. All she'd wanted was a little conversation, and it wasn't as if he had been pressed for time.

Scott hobbled through to the bedroom and found her card in the back pocket of his trousers. It was far too soon to call her; he'd look desperate. Instead, he took it through to the living room, opened his laptop and did a search for the company she worked for.

Chapter 4

The Vine looked a lot different in daylight. The twelve-foot neon sign was off, and in the bright summer sunshine, Ryan Anderson could see that it was covered in a couple of years' worth of soot from a billion passing vehicles. The garish bruise-coloured façade, normally illuminated with a black light, looked like it hadn't seen a paintbrush in a decade.

Curriculum vitae in hand, Ryan walked around the back via an alleyway piled high with black bin liners and empty boxes that once held a variety of spirits. There was no name over the door, just a buzzer attached to the frame. He ran his finger through his short, dark hair, then pressed the bell and waited.

He still couldn't believe he was here. It might be a genuine job offer, or it could be a way of isolating him so that the two goons he'd floored the night before could exact their revenge. He regretted not tooling up, but before he could change his mind, the metal door creaked open on squeaky hinges.

The man facing him was Ryan's height, with dark brown hair cut close to his scalp. A tattoo of a red rose clung to his thick neck, but it was his eyes that caught Ryan's attention. They were a little too close together, and they seemed to look right through him. He was wearing dark slacks and a white Hugo Boss jumper.

"I was told to be here at six," Ryan said. "For a job."

The man said nothing. He stared at Ryan for a few seconds, then stepped aside, holding the door open. Ryan walked into the building and found himself in a kitchen. Not restaurant standard, but large enough to provide pizza and burgers for the night crowd.

"Stand still, arms out by your side."

Ryan stopped and turned around, then put his arms out. Rough hands patted him down, from his neck down to his ankles. Rose Neck took his mobile phone and placed it on a countertop, then directed Ryan through a door and along a dimly lit corridor.

"I want that phone back. I only got it today."

At the end of the hallway was a set of double doors that led onto the dance floor. Ryan had never been inside the club during normal hours, when it would have been wall to wall with youngsters strutting their stuff while spaced out on whatever synthetic drug was in fashion these days. Maybe it was still ecstasy, or perhaps something new had come along.

The guy with the rose tattoo gestured to a seating area consisting of round tables and chairs, where two men were sipping from coffee mugs. One was the suit from the previous night, the other the blond he'd beaten up. There was no sign of the bulldog. Ryan walked over, Rose Neck not far behind.

"Have a seat," the suit said, pointing at a comfortable armchair.

Ryan would have preferred to stand, but the words were a command, not an offer. He undid the buttons on his jacket, rucked up his trousers and sat down. The suit he was wearing cost just under two hundred pounds, a fraction of the price of the one opposite him.

"My name's Franklin Marsh," the older man said, smoothing his already immaculate hair. Even in the dim light of the nightclub, his eyes shone green. "This is George, that's Paul."

George was the one Ryan had fought with the previous evening. Paul had the rose tattoo.

Ryan nodded at George and was met with a malevolent stare. He clearly hadn't forgotten his humiliation when they'd last met.

Marsh picked up a clipboard from the table in front of him and held it up. Paul took it from his hand and gave it to Ryan.

"Fill that out," Marsh said. "George, fetch some more coffee."

Ryan unhooked the pen from the top of the clipboard and looked at the document. It appeared to be a standard application form, and he started filling in the blanks. Name, date of birth, address and national insurance number were all expected, but the form asked for his family history as well as his last five addresses, which seemed a bit extreme. It also wanted details of his last five employments. Ryan referred to his CV for that information, then handed the form back to Paul, who had been hovering by his side.

"Where did you learn to fight like that?" Marsh asked, sipping the coffee George had made.

Ryan dropped a sugar cube into his own cup and stirred it. "A combination of growing up on a council estate in Leeds and five years in Two Para."

"Whereabouts in Leeds?"

"Halton Moor. I lived on Kendal Drive."

Marsh nodded slowly. "I know Halton Moor. Did some business there a few years ago. It was the arse-end of the world, rough as fuck."

Ryan smiled. "My thoughts exactly. I got into a few scrapes, but back then, you didn't call the police, you handled things yourself. Most times, you have an argument with one guy, you had to take on his whole family. If you live there, you have to know how to look after yourself."

"What about Two Para?"

"I lived in Halton Moor for four years until I was fourteen," Ryan said, "then moved to Colchester. My old man was in the army, so we moved around a lot. He wanted me to join up as soon as I left school, so I did. Pissed him off that I chose Two Para, though. He was REME—Royal Electrical and Mechanical engineers— and wanted me to follow in his footsteps, but I joined the army to fight, not sit behind the lines fixing tractors.

"Why'd you leave?"

"Got shit-canned for fighting. I'd made corporal and was up for sergeant, but so was this other guy. He knew I'd get it, so he took a pop at me one day. I beat the shit out of him and he told the brass I started it. The lying bastard even got a couple of his mates to say they saw the whole thing."

"So they kicked you out."

"No. After the court-martial, they said they were going to demote me back to private, but that didn't matter. What really hurt was when they blocked my application to join the SAS. That was the only reason I chose the paras, as a stepping stone. After that, there was no point staying in. I asked for a discharge instead, and they gave me one. That was a year ago."

"You reckon you could have made the SAS?" Marsh asked.

"Hard to tell. Maybe I could, maybe I couldn't, but I wanted to find out. Now I'll never know."

Marsh chewed on that for a few seconds.

"What have you been up to since you left?"

"This and that," Ryan said. "I worked a building site for a couple of months, labouring. I also worked in a packaging factory, but that only lasted a couple of days."

"How come?"

"My supervisor was a dick. He was only about twenty-two, but thought that because he earned twenty pence an hour more than me, he was some kind of god. Told me he wasn't taking any shit from me, but it turns out he did. On the second day, I asked for a toilet break and went to the staff room instead. I took a dump in his lunchbox. You should have seen his face at lunchtime. Priceless."

"Why not just slap him about a bit?"

It was Paul with the red rose who'd spoken, and Marsh didn't seem to mind the interruption.

"I did consider it," Ryan said, "but it wasn't the best way to deal with him. Instead of everyone sympathising with poor Johnny for getting his head kicked in, they're all laughing about him and his turd sandwiches."

That brought a smile to Marsh's face, but only briefly.

"If you work for me, I'll expect more than just shitting on peoples' dinners. I have a reputation to uphold, and that means sometimes you have to show your nasty side. I don't want people who over-think, I need people who do what the fuck they're told."

"I spent five years in the army doing as I was told. I'm sure it won't be a problem."

"Even if what you're told to do isn't strictly legit?"

"What are my alternatives? Work for Johnny shit-box or carry bricks for minimum wage? No thanks. I left the army with these"—he held up his fists—"and nothing else. Might as well make good use of them."

Marsh drank the last of his coffee and swirled it around his mouth for a few moments. He swallowed as he came to a decision. "I'll call you in a couple of days." He pointed towards the exit, and Paul stood over Ryan, ushering him to his feet.

Ryan took the hint: interview terminated. He got up and walked back the way he'd come, with Paul always a couple of steps behind him. His phone was where he'd left it.

At the back door, Paul grabbed Ryan's elbow in a powerful grip. "The boss is gonna check you out. If you're not who you say you are, I'll come for you."

He let go, and Ryan resisted the urge to rub his arm. "No worries. It's all kosher."

"It better be. You'll be working under me, and I don't like fuck-ups."

Ryan thought about answering, but simply nodded and walked away.

Everything he'd told Marsh had been the truth, so he had no concerns on that score.

He just hoped he knew what he was getting himself into.

* * *

When Ryan left, Franklin Marsh picked up his coffee and walked through a door marked Staff Only. His office was the first door on the right, and once he was settled behind his desk he turned on the CCTV monitors. He saw Ryan walking down the alley, and when he disappeared out of sight, Marsh switched to another camera and watched him make his way down the main road. Ryan had his hands in his pockets.

"What d'ya reckon?" Paul asked. He'd followed Marsh into the office and was sitting on the leather sofa.

"Hard to be sure. His story seems plausible."

"And you say he didn't smell of booze last night?"

"No, he didn't," Marsh said. "So why was he walking the streets of Manchester at two in the morning?"

"I can't answer that one, Franklin, but I'll tell you one thing: he's trouble."

On the screen, Ryan crossed the road and turned a corner. Marsh turned the monitor off. Ryan hadn't used his phone to call anyone, which fit in with his story that he didn't have family to speak of. According to the application form, Ryan was an only child, his mother was in a nursing home, and his father had died of cancer five years earlier.

"I'll get Billy to look into him," Marsh said.

Billy Marsden was a police sergeant with a passion for the bookmakers. Marsh funded Billy's gambling habit, and the copper paid him back with information

Marsh took a pack of cigarettes from his pocket and popped one in his mouth. Paul got up from his seat and lit it.

"You think he's plod?"

"Maybe," Marsh conceded.

The police had tried before to infiltrate his organisation, and it hadn't ended well. At least, not for the undercover officer. The police never did find his body, but the episode had forced Marsh to pare back his operations for a while. He was, after all, the prime suspect in the undercover officer's disappearance, and though nobody ever questioned him about his involvement, Marsh knew the cops would be keeping him under intense scrutiny.

Not that it would have done them any good. There were always three layers of separation between Marsh and the goods he dealt in. He never got close to the money, either, which was laundered by a Greek accountant and hidden in offshore holdings so complex that not even Marsh knew how they worked. He'd told Paul many times that he was looking forward to the day he could quit England's shores, retire to the Caribbean and enjoy his millions. He was fifty-seven now, and Paul reckoned on three more years. By that time Marsh's youngest would be seventeen and Marsh senior would have spent thirty years as one of Manchester's most notorious criminals.

Paul assumed Marsh had enough to retire on already—close to seventy million sterling accruing interest at a decent rate, apparently—but the boss wanted his son to finish his education first. There was no point sending him to university, though. *Degrees are pointless if you use them to work for someone else.* Marsh believed that the only way to make money was to have people work for you, and he planned to teach his kids his business acumen, though not his villainy. Charlie was fourteen and Debbie was seventeen, and Marsh made a point of not spoiling them. They knew that they had to work hard if they wanted something, and that would stand them in good stead for adulthood.

"I'll send Billy a text, get him to meet me in the pub," Paul said.

"Okay. And give him a copy of Ryan's application form. I want every detail checked and double-checked."

Paul tapped out a message on a phone he used solely for communicating with the policeman in Marsh's pocket and hit Send. He got a reply less than a minute later.

"He's heading to the Pig and Whistle now. I'll be back soon."

Marsh stubbed out his cigarette and picked up the till receipts from the previous night, signalling the end of the meeting.

Paul left, his mind focused on Ryan Anderson. Was he a cop, hoping to destroy everything Marsh had built up over the last thirty years, or just a kid out to make some money?

He hoped the lad was everything he claimed to be.

For his own sake.

Chapter 5

Detective Inspector John Latimer stopped on the stairwell between the third and fourth floors of the police station and stared out over a sun-washed Lewisham High Street.

The pub across the road looked awfully inviting.

As ever, the thought was fleeting. After his scare three years earlier, he'd gone from drinking every day to just twice a month, and only when he went out with his wife.

He could do with a drink right now.

The Higson case had been one of the worst he'd worked on, and he was glad to have wrapped it up. In his fifteen years in the force, five with Murder Investigation Team 14, he had never been so haunted by a crime scene. It was always harder when a child was the victim, but this one had been especially disturbing. Now that the suspect had been charged, he could take down the photos from the briefing room wall, but the innocent face would stay with him for a long time.

It was at times like this that Latimer was almost thankful that he didn't have children of his own. He couldn't imagine the anguish Carrie Higson's parents had gone through, or how they would ever get their lives back on track. They were victims just as much as the little girl, but their pain would last a lifetime.

Two punters left the pub and lit cigarettes. Yet another vice Latimer had kicked since the result of his echocardiogram. Being diagnosed with coronary artery disease had felt like a death sentence when the doctor had sat him down to explain the results, but he'd been assured that with a change in lifestyle he could live a long and fruitful life. That meant an end to his nightly visits to the boozer and no more fags. The new diet was just as hard.

"You okay, boss?" DS Paul Benson joined Latimer on the stairs. At six-one, he was a couple of inches taller than Latimer. He was also ten years younger.

"I'm fine," Latimer said. He took his vape stick from his pocket and took a deep drag, blowing an aniseed-flavoured cloud towards the floor, where it hung around like a bad memory.

"MAC-10 will go apeshit if she sees you using that in the building."

The moniker had been given to Detective Chief Inspector Carole Ingram within minutes of her posting to MIT 14, partly due to her sharing the same name as the weapon's creator, Gordon B. Ingram. Few realised at the time that she could be just as deadly as the machine pistol if they were caught in her sights. One sure way to get in her bad books was to use the nickname in her presence.

"Walls have ears," Latimer warned him, and Benson looked up and down the stairs to see whether anyone was within earshot.

Latimer had no issues with her. While many considered Ingram a promotion-chasing megalomaniac, he saw her for what she was: a competent officer who didn't suffer fools gladly.

"The lads want to know if you'll be joining us tonight," the DS said, changing the subject. "Even if it's just one."

Latimer put his vape stick away. "Not this time," he said. "I'm gonna go 'round and see Carrie's parents, give them the good news, then I'm heading home."

"Good news" was definitely not the right phrase, but at least it would offer them closure.

"No worries. I'm off to get some lunch."

Latimer watched Benson walk away, a spring in his step as he skipped down the stairs, and he envied the younger man's emotional detachment. Latimer had been like that once, able to leave work at the office once it was time to clock off. That had changed in recent months, and Latimer wondered if the alcohol had been suppressing his emotions all along. Wake up with a hangover, recover throughout the day, hit the pub as soon as the shift was over. The routine had been the same for at least a decade, leaving him little time to think of anything else but chasing down criminals.

Even his wife had played second fiddle to the booze, but he'd always been able to justify his actions. If a case was particularly frustrating, he needed a beer after work. If the team solved one within twenty-four hours, it was celebration time. Any excuse would do, and if he had none, he fell back on the idea that his wife, who worked from home, needed the time alone.

It was the heart murmur that first warned him something was wrong. Actually, not so much a murmur as an earthquake inside his chest.

He vividly remembered sitting at his desk, enjoying his fourth coffee of the morning when it felt like everything inside his rib cage had disappeared, leaving a huge vacuum. It lasted for a couple of seconds, then his heart started acting like a golf ball in a tumble dryer. The beats were erratic, sometimes two close together, then a worrying gap before the next one. He waited for it to pass, but after a couple of minutes, a colleague came up to him, concerned.

"You okay, boss? Want me to call you an ambulance?"

Latimer waved him away. "It's nothing." *It's just stress*, he thought. *A couple of days off and I'll be right as rain.* Ten minutes, later his heartbeat was back to normal, but an hour later, it happened again.

Latimer took the advice and went to Accident & Emergency. After a long wait for an electrocardiogram, he was asked a few lifestyle questions.

"Yes, I drink."

"How many a week?" the doctor asked.

Latimer was honest with his answer. "Five or six pints, maybe six times a week.",

"That's rather a lot."

"Is it?" Latimer asked. He'd been drinking that much for the last ten years and had never thought much of it. His wife, Fiona, clearly had. She was always on his back for him to cut down, but he always for an excuse to sink a beer: celebrating when his team solved a case; consoling himself when he couldn't solve a case; the fact that it was his day off…

"Yes, that's a lot for a rugby team, never mind one person. I'm going to monitor you for the next hour, but I suggest cutting down to fourteen units of alcohol a week, and maybe lay off the coffee, too."

Latimer took the advice with a pinch of salt. By lunchtime he was discharged, and before returning to work, he stopped off at a café for a fry-up. That night, he was in the pub three minutes after clocking off.

The murmur returned the next morning, though it wasn't so pronounced. He shook that one off, but when it happened twice more that day, he started to get worried.

Latimer resorted to self-help. He went to the local shop and purchased a jar of decaf coffee—he hated the fancy ground stuff that came out of a machine and always insisted on instant—and that night he went straight home after work. His wife was surprised to see him completely sober, so much so that she asked what the matter was. He laughed it off, saying he just fancied an early night.

The next day, the tremors started. He was in the bathroom, trying to shave, but felt like he was strapped to a washing machine on max spin. He managed to nick himself half a dozen times, and as he stood in front of the mirror waiting for the bleeding to stop, he looked at his reflection. The face staring back was unrecognisable. His hair used to be dark brown, but grey was starting to take root, and the broken capillaries on his face gave him an unhealthy ruddy complexion. The bags under his eyes looked like they belonged to a sixty-year-old, not someone just turning forty.

Still, it hadn't been enough of a wake-up call. That night, thinking the day of sobriety had given his liver the rest it desperately needed, he was back in the pub.

He was on his second pint when it struck.

The episode he'd experienced the previous day was back with a vengeance, only this time there was what he could only describe as a total reset. He was sitting at the table with his hand over his heart when everything shut down. There was a split-second of complete darkness and silence, then he was back. Latimer stared at his pint for five minutes, waiting for something else to happen and praying it wouldn't. He eventually got up and walked the few hundred yards home.

The next morning, on his way to work, he phoned the doctor and booked an appointment.

They performed a battery of tests over the following year, culminating in the echocardiogram. That had shown him to have an extremely high total coronary calcium score.

He still remembered the meeting with the doctor as if it had been that morning. The result had been cc'd to him and arrived the day before, and on reading it Latimer thought he had seconds left to live. He'd phoned his GP and arranged an urgent appointment for later that day, wondering if he'd still be alive by the time he got to the surgery.

"Your age and gender-adjusted calcium score is above the 90th percentile, which would indicate a high future cardiovascular risk," the doctor had told him. It was the lack of concern that struck Latimer first.

"I read that. It sounds bad."

"Actually, it's not uncommon for people with your lifestyle." The doctor checked Latimer's health history. "It says here you consume in excess of seventy units of alcohol a week. When it's that high, it's usually a conservative estimate and more like a hundred."

Latimer had confessed that he perhaps might have missed off a few here and there. "So how long have I got?" he'd asked.

"Hard to say. If you're willing to cut out the cigarettes and reduce your alcohol intake to less than fourteen units a week, plus get plenty of exercise and eat a healthy diet, I'd say around thirty to forty years. If you carry on as you are, five, maybe ten."

Latimer had opted for option A. He'd dumped his cigarettes and lighter in the doctor's waste bin and stopped off at a vape shop on the way home. He thought it would be a simple process involving buying a stick, some juice and away he went, but he'd spent an hour listening to the salesman explaining all the various configurations and sampling dozens of flavours.

"One stick is fine, but what are you going to do while it's charging for four hours?"

Latimer knew he wouldn't be able to go without his nicotine fix that long, so he'd bought a second stick to use while the other was charging. His purchases, which included thirty different varieties of vape juice, numerous spare coils and expansion kits, had set him back almost three hundred pounds. When he considered how much he spent on cigarettes each month, it was a bargain.

After picking up his prescription for statins and aspirin, pills he'd take daily for the rest of his life, he'd gone home, removed the dozen beers from the fridge and put them in a box in the garage. He could still drink, but would limit it to once a week to start with. He already exercised by playing golf every Sunday, but decided to step that up and bought a bicycle to get to work and back. As it was a short journey, he took a circuitous route in each morning.

"Sir, the DCI's looking for you."

Latimer looked at the constable who'd stuck his head out of the door. He nodded, took out his vape stick for one more puff, then walked up to the fourth floor and along to Ingram's office.

He knocked and waited for her to answer. Too many people had made the mistake of entering before being beckoned.

"Come."

Latimer entered and stopped in front of her desk. It was police issue, functional chipboard with a laminate finish. Some senior officers like personal touches and the odd little luxury—family photos, hardwood desks, recliner chairs. Not Ingram.

"You wanted to see me," Latimer said, a statement more than a question.

"Yes. Take a seat."

He sat in the chair opposite her and wondered why so many were scared of her. She wasn't physically intimidating. In fact, if he weren't married, he might have been interested. She was the same height as Latimer, with short, dyed platinum hair cut in a side parting. She wore minimal make-up and no jewellery, apart from a pair of stud earrings.

Certainly no wedding ring.

There were rumours that she was a lesbian, but Latimer doubted their veracity. He didn't care either way.

"Hampshire Constabulary has asked us to bring in a murder suspect. A body was found near Hook and his prints were found on the murder weapon and the victim's wallet."

"Can't you send the…uniformed officers?" He'd almost said "wooden tops," the derogatory term used by plain-clothed officers for their uniformed colleagues. He knew from experience that Ingram hated the term. "I have to go round and let Carrie Higson's parents know that we've charged the suspect."

"I'll visit the Higsons," Ingram said. "I want you to handle this transfer. You know the suspect."

Latimer frowned. "Someone I've banged up before?"

"Hardly. It's James Knight."

A face jumped into Latimer's head, but he quickly dismissed it.

"You can't mean my first DCI." He couldn't think of anyone less likely to commit a crime.

Knight had been promoted to Ingram's grade four years before taking early retirement in his late fifties. Latimer had stayed in touch with him in the last four years, and they played golf together once a month.

"The very same," Ingram said. "I must admit, I was shocked when it was suggested he could have been involved with a murder, but the evidence they presented makes for a pretty solid case."

Latimer was stunned. "You say they have prints? You mean a partial, something that could be discredited?"

"When I say prints, I mean lots of them." She turned to her computer and tapped at her keyboard. "A full set on the handle of the hammer, another—"

"A hammer!?"

"Yes. It was found on top of the body, along with the victim's dog and his wallet. They lifted another set of prints from that, too."

"That doesn't make sense," Latimer told her. "James was one of the best cops I've worked with. Even if by some incredible stretch of the imagination I believed he would kill someone, there's no way he'd behave like an amateur and leave his prints all over the crime scene."

"My thoughts, too, but it appears that's what he did. They also found a few hairs and are waiting to get a DNA sample from James so that they can verify that they belong to him. They also want you to pick up a pair of shoes."

"Don't tell me, they found shoe prints at the scene."

Ingram's expression was all the answer Latimer needed.

"This sounds like a setup," Latimer said.

"Or James wanted to be caught," Ingram suggested. "Either way, I want you to deliver him to Basingstoke today."

She turned back to the computer and clicked the mouse a couple of times. The printer to Latimer's left spewed out a few sheets of paper. "That's what Hampshire sent over. Take a look before you pick him up."

Latimer nodded, retrieved the documents and walked out without another word. What could he say?

He went to his office and closed the door, a sign that he didn't want to be disturbed. Once he'd made himself a cup of instant decaf, he sat down and looked through the information Hampshire had sent over.

It made for worrying reading.

The victim had been identified as Sean Conte, aged fifty-five, from Wimbledon. The name rang a bell. Latimer searched his mental database and came up with a conversation he'd had a year earlier.

It had taken place on the golf course.

With James Knight.

And while it was a stretch, Latimer knew that what Knight had told him could be seen as a motive.

Another tick in the guilty box, yet Latimer still found it hard to believe his old boss could have done it.

He read through the rest of the information. Conte had been found two days earlier in woods near Hook, Hampshire, following a tip-off. It didn't say how that had been communicated, so it could have been a phone call or email. Latimer made a note to follow that up with Hampshire CID. He'd also request permission to visit the crime scene. A shovel had been left next to the shallow grave, and several prints had been lifted from it. On exhuming the body they'd found a blood-stained folding wallet with another good set of prints on the inside. Even more had been found on the hammer that was on Conte's chest. The preliminary cause of death had been recorded as blunt trauma to the head, though the autopsy report would provide a definitive answer.

Latimer sipped his coffee, and one question kept rearing its head: *why would an experienced police officer, even a retired one, leave so much evidence behind?*

The hairs found underneath the victim's fingernails were still being analysed, but Latimer knew that they would belong to James Knight.

It was time to find out what his old boss had to say.

Chapter 6

John Latimer signed for a pool car and began the twelve miles to James Knight's house in Merton Park. Protocol dictated that he take another officer with him, so he'd chosen DS Benson.

He'd have much preferred to go alone.

"What did the guy do?" the younger officer asked.

Latimer had told him they were to pick up a suspect and deliver him to Basingstoke, but hadn't given a name.

"Hopefully, nothing."

Benson looked over at Latimer. "You've lost me."

Latimer pulled onto the A20. "A body was found in Hampshire and the prime suspect lives in London. His name's James Knight."

"As in DCI James Knight?"

"The very same."

Benson looked the way Latimer had felt on hearing the news. "He's the last guy I'd have pegged as a killer. What do they have on him?"

"Prints on the murder weapon, possibly DNA, shoe prints, motive, you name it."

"Wow. I mean…wow!"

"My thoughts exactly," Latimer said. He wound the window down, took a long drag on his vape stick and blew out a white cloud. "It just doesn't make any sense."

He spent the next few minutes explaining exactly what was in the document Hampshire had provided, from the tip-off to locating the body and the mountain of evidence gathered from the scene.

"I see what you mean. Even a moron would know not to leave prints behind. I can only imagine—if he did it, that is—that Knight wanted to be caught."

"Then why not just kill Conte and hand himself in?" Latimer asked. "Why go to all the trouble of taking him to Hampshire and burying him? They lived next door to each other. He could have just popped round, killed him and called it in."

Like Latimer, Benson had no answer for that one.

They drove the rest of the way in silence, and Latimer tried once more to make sense of the situation. If he hadn't known the suspect for so long, one look at the evidence against him would have been enough to convince him that Knight was guilty. The only explanation he could come up with was that his friendship with the old DCI was clouding his judgement.

It took fifty minutes to reach Knight's house, a 1930s semi-detached on a tree-lined street. Latimer had been there many times before, and he recognised Knight's

Volvo in the driveway. He pulled in behind it and turned the engine off, then took a couple of drags on his vape stick.

Keen as he was to hear his old friend's side of the story, Latimer wasn't looking forward to the conversation. He sat for over a minute, his hands on the wheel as he stared at the front door.

"You okay, boss?"

Latimer looked over at Benson, his face blank. He was far from okay, but he wasn't about to reveal his feelings to a subordinate. He liked Paul. He was a good copper, but that was as far as the relationship went. He was still the detective sergeant's boss and had to maintain that professional distance.

"I'll do the talking," Latimer said. He got out and walked to the front door, which had been painted in recent weeks. Now retired, Knight had plenty of time on his hands, and he'd clearly been using some of it to get the house up to scratch. The last time Latimer had been there, the door had been a faded red, the paint peeling in a couple of places. It was now a shiny royal blue.

Latimer took a deep breath and rang the bell. After thirty seconds and no response, he rang it again.

The door opened and James Knight smiled when he saw Latimer. He was in his late fifties but looked younger, with a blue jumper and beige slacks covering his thin frame. His hair was black with a few flecks of grey, and thinning on top.

"Hello, John! What brings you here? I thought we weren't due to play until the end of the month."

DS Benson stepped into view, and the smile disappeared from Knight's face. "This looks official," he said.

"Can we come in?" Latimer asked.

Knight stepped aside and held the door open. Both officers wiped their feet and went inside. Latimer led the way through to the spacious living room, the décor neutral tones of whites and light greys.

"Should I offer you coffee?" Knight asked as he stood by the French windows that overlooked the neatly manicured garden, but Latimer shook his head.

"Take a seat, James."

Knight remained standing. "Is this about Jenny? Has something happened to her?"

"Jenny's fine, I'm sure," Latimer said. Jenny was Knight's wife. She was a couple of years older than the ex-DCI and worked in an insurance office in the city.

Knight relaxed a little at the news, but was clearly anxious.

Latimer put him out of his misery. "We're here regarding Sean Conte."

Knight exhaled loudly and took a seat in his armchair. "You had me worried for a moment." He took a pack of Marlboro from his pocket and lit one. "As I told the officers who came round a couple of weeks ago, I haven't seen him for some time."

"We found him," Latimer said.

Knight blew a grey cloud towards the ceiling. "That's good. Where was he? Shacked up with his mistress?"

"Lying in a shallow grave with his head caved in," Latimer told him, and watched for a reaction. What he saw was genuine shock. Either Knight was a good actor and had been prepared for this line of questioning, or it really was news to him. Latimer suspected the latter; there would be no point leaving incriminating evidence near the body, then being surprised when the police came calling.

"I'm sorry to hear that," Knight said, stubbing out his cigarette in a glass ashtray. "We had our differences, but I wouldn't wish that on anyone."

"What differences?" Benson asked, earning a glare from Latimer.

"The whole business with the extension," Knight said. "I'm surprised you didn't know about it. It was in the Evening Standard and even made the London section of the BBC news website."

"I'm not one for newspapers," Benson told him.

"Well, three years ago I applied for planning permission to extend the kitchen by three metres and put a ground floor office on the side of the house. It was granted despite objections from Conte, and work began a few months later. A week after the build started I saw Conte leaving his house and he had a smirk on his face. I had no idea what his problem was until the extensions were completed. That's when he contacted the council and claimed that the building work had encroached on his property by two inches. They sent surveyors round and confirmed that he was right. He demanded that the whole thing be torn down and the planning officers agreed with him. I tried applying for retrospective planning permission but it was denied. I even offered to buy the strip of land from him but he wanted thirty grand for it. That worked out at seven thousand pounds a square foot. I wasn't going to give the smug bastard the satisfaction, especially as he must have known that I'd encroached on his property when the build started. He waited until it was done before doing anything about it, knowing it would cost me an arm and a leg to resolve."

"What did you do?" Benson asked.

"I exhausted every legal means, but it was no good. The council finally gave me an order to take the extensions down. Both of them. I asked if I could just move the side wall in a few inches but they wouldn't have it. I had to re-mortgage the house to raise the funds to put everything back as it was. It cost me over a hundred and fifty grand all told, and I've got nothing to show for it but a bigger pile of debt. We thought about downsizing, but there's so little equity left in the place that it would mean leaving London for a tiny one-bed bungalow in the sticks."

"Where were you on July ninth, the day Conte disappeared?" Latimer asked.

"I was here, alone. Jenny was at work and…hang on, are you suggesting I might have killed him?"

Latimer sighed. This was going to be worse than any of the bereavement visits he'd made over the years. "Hampshire Constabulary found your fingerprints on what they believe to be the murder weapon. They also found hair follicles under his fingernails and want you to provide a DNA sample for a match. We've also been asked to bring in a pair of shoes." Latimer took a sheet of paper from his pocket and handed it to Knight. "This is an image of a shoe print found near the grave. I've been asked to secure any footwear you may have that has a matching sole pattern. As you can see, the tread is worn here, and there appear to be a couple of defects."

Knight stared at the paper, dumbstruck. He eventually looked up at Latimer. "This can't be happening. Is it some kind of joke?"

Latimer shook his head slowly. "I'm afraid not, James." He stood and faced his old friend. "I'm arresting you on suspicion of murder. I have to caution you that you do not have—"

"I know my rights!" Knight yelled, jumping to his feet. "I was a cop for thirty years, or have you forgotten that?"

"Of course I haven't," Latimer said.

"Then tell me, Sherlock, why I would leave my fingerprints on a murder weapon?"

"I didn't say I believed the charges are true," Latimer said, "but Hampshire have asked me to bring you in for questioning. You'll have a chance to present your case in Basingstoke. For the record, I had a hard time believing it, myself."

"I'm glad to hear it, because this is bullshit, and you know it."

Latimer finished reading Knight his rights. Any case against him could fall apart if that wasn't completed, even if the suspect knew the protocol and words verbatim.

Benson produced a pair of handcuffs, but Latimer waved him away. It was standard procedure not to allow a suspect into a police vehicle without restraints, but Latimer didn't think it necessary. James Knight wasn't a common thief. He was a highly respected former officer and would be treated as such.

"Can I at least phone Jenny before we go? She'll be worried sick if I'm not here when she gets home."

Latimer nodded, and Knight punched a couple of buttons on his phone. He spoke calmly, letting his wife know that he was going to Basingstoke to help out with an inquiry, and that he didn't know when he would be back. He said she shouldn't worry if he was away for a day or two, but he'd be in touch later.

"You can't smoke in the car, so have one now if you need one."

Knight thanked Latimer and lit up, holding the smoke in his lungs for ten seconds before slowly letting it out.

"Can you show me where your shoe cupboard is?" Benson asked, taking the sheet of paper from Knight.

"In the hall, under the stairs."

The DS went to look while the suspect finished his cigarette. He was back within a couple of minutes, and had a pair of black leather shoes in a transparent evidence bag. He held it up to let Latimer know he'd found what they were looking for.

"You know someone's fitting me up, don't you?"

"That was the first thought that crossed my mind," Latimer admitted, "but unless you can discredit the evidence they've gathered, I can't say it looks good, James."

Knight crushed his cigarette in the ashtray, then locked up the French windows and sighed. "Let's go."

Benson led them out of the house and held the rear door of the unmarked Ford open. Knight got in and Latimer climbed in beside him, sitting behind the driver's seat.

"Do me a favour when you get back to the station," Knight said. "Go through my file and get the names of everyone I've put away. One of them must be behind this."

"I can't act on this investigation," Latimer said. "It's Hampshire's. That's where the body was found. My involvement has to end when I hand you over."

"You can at least get the names so that my solicitor has something to give them. I also need you to find out who sells the brand and size of shoes I wear and match sales against debit and credit cards. It could provide a lead."

"That's something the guys in Basingstoke will do," Latimer said.

"It's not, and you know it. They'll be looking for reasons to charge me, not let me go."

Latimer knew his old boss was right. The investigation wouldn't look for evidence that Knight *hadn't* done it; they would want as much as they could to secure a conviction.

"Okay, I'll see what I can do. Were you really at home the day he disappeared?"

"I said I was, didn't I? I saw him leave in his car with that noisy mutt of his. Must have been around eleven in the morning."

"But Jenny was at work and you didn't leave the house, so no one can corroborate your story."

"I didn't think I'd be needing an alibi when I woke up that morning," Knight said angrily. He took a deep breath and let it out slowly. "Please tell me you believe me," he said.

"I do," Latimer said truthfully, "and any decent copper is going to see that this looks all wrong. DNA could be planted, the shoes might be explained away, the fact that you haven't got an alibi isn't uncommon. Is there any way you can explain your fingerprints at the scene, though?"

"What were they on?" Knight asked. "Maybe the murder weapon was stolen from my house."

"A hammer, which I admit could have been taken from your home, but they also found a good print on the inside of Conte's wallet. His bloodied wallet, which means the print was left there after he was killed."

Knight remained silent, and Latimer would probably have done the same in his situation. Until he had a lawyer present, Latimer wouldn't have said anything that might incriminate him.

"Fingerprints are not as infallible as everyone thinks," Knight eventually said.

Latimer agreed, but circumstances had to be taken into account. There had been the case of Shirley McKie, the Scottish DS who'd been charged with perjury when her thumb print had been found at a murder scene in Kilmarnock. Four members of staff at what had once been the Scottish Criminal Record Office had identified McKie from the print, and their testimony had ended her career. Pat Wertheim, a US specialist in fingerprint fabrication, was called in to verify the SCRO's results, and he and another expert testified at her trial that the print didn't belong to McKie. She was acquitted, but the damage had been done. The print had been misidentified by the SCRO team, though it hadn't been forged.

It also wasn't unknown for police officers to fabricate fingerprint evidence to secure a conviction. Four members of New York State Police's Troop C were jailed for planting evidence against those they believed to be guilty of crimes, including murder.

All Knight had to do was convince the right people that the evidence had either been incorrectly analysed or had been planted.

Neither was going to be easy.

"There's no way to sugar-coat this, James; they've got enough to charge you. If I were you, I'd arrange for an independent specialist to have the samples verified, then checked again."

"That won't be cheap," Knight sighed.

"I know, but if you can take fingerprints out of the equation—"

"—they still have motive, opportunity, and possibly DNA and shoe imprints."

"The first two are circumstantial, the others haven't been verified yet. This isn't a done deal."

"Well, someone went to a lot of trouble to make it look like I did this, so you can bet your life the DNA and shoes will match."

"They can be discredited," Latimer insisted. "Anyone could place a hair on a body, or wear similar shoes."

"Even shoes that are similarly worn, with the exact same defects in the sole pattern?"

Latimer looked out of the car window, but saw nothing. His mind was too busy trying to think of ways to prove Knight's innocence.

He came up empty.

Benson took them past Kempton Park racecourse and onto the M3, and Latimer stole a glance at Knight to see if the road they were taking elicited a reaction. Conte's killer would almost certainly have driven the same route to get to the murder scene.

There was nothing from the ex-DCI. No flicker of recognition, no increase in breathing rate. He simply looked out of the window, a shadow of his former self. The once-confident officer looked like a pale imposter, his hunched shoulders giving him the look of a beaten man.

An hour and twenty minutes after setting off, they arrived at Basingstoke Centre. They parked out front and Latimer let Knight have one last cigarette before going inside.

"It could be a cop," Knight said, sucking smoke into his lungs and releasing a cloud into the sky. "Someone I upset when they were serving under me."

"You were a respected officer," Latimer assured him. "If you did anything to make someone go this far, I'd have heard about it. As you said earlier, it must have been someone you banged up. I'll put together a list of all your collars and cross-reference them with shoe purchases."

"Thanks, John."

Knight finished his cigarette and dropped the butt on the ground, crushing it with his foot. "Let's get this over with."

Knight walked through the entrance first. At the desk, Latimer told the officer the reason for the visit.

After a couple of minutes, a door opened and a uniformed DCI walked through. He was Latimer's height, around five-eleven, with a gleaming bald head and sharp eyes. He ignored Latimer and Benson and went straight to Knight, his hand outstretched.

"James, sorry to see you here under these circumstances."

"You're not the only one. I'd like to get this cleared up as soon as possible so that I can get back to retirement." He gestured towards his escorts. "This is DI John Latimer and DS Paul Benson. They were good enough to give me a lift."

The DCI shook hands with both men. "DCI Terry Blakely. I'll take it from here, gentlemen."

Blakely held the door open for Knight to go through to the custody suite.

"If you need anything, James, you know where I am," Latimer said.

Knight offered a resigned smile, nodded, then turned and walked toward the cells.

Chapter 7

It was almost time to clock off when Latimer and Benson got back to Lewisham. While the DS went to fetch coffee, Latimer headed up to see Ingram. He'd spent the entire journey from Basingstoke wondering how someone could get access to Knight's hair and shoes, and had drawn a blank.

The simplest answer is often the right one.

James Knight had often repeated the principle of Occam's razor, and when Latimer applied it he came up to the obvious conclusion: James had murdered Sean Conte.

He knocked on Ingram's door and she shouted for him to enter.

"We just dropped James off," Latimer said, standing behind the chair that faced her desk. "Handed him over to DCI Blakely. They seem to know each other."

"And…?"

"I don't know. The idea of James killing someone is ludicrous, but it's going to be difficult proving otherwise. If the DNA turns out to be his, and the shoe prints match, they'll have enough to charge him. The thing that still doesn't make sense is why he would leave evidence at the scene."

"I've been thinking about that, too," Ingram said. She put her elbows on the desk and steepled her fingers. "Let's say the crime scene was sanitised. No prints, DNA or murder weapon. Who would you speak to first?"

"Conte's wife," Latimer said.

"Exactly. In the vast majority of murder cases, the killer was known to the victim. You'd ask if Conte had any enemies, and whose name would she give first?"

"James Knight."

"Correct. And if there was no physical evidence at the scene whatsoever, you might deduce that whoever committed the crime knew exactly what pitfalls to avoid. Someone like an experienced police officer."

"Are you suggesting Knight killed Conte and deliberately left incriminating evidence at the scene to throw us off the trail? That makes no sense. It doesn't help his cause, it puts him squarely in the frame."

"Not if he's lined up a competent brief who can discredit the evidence."

Latimer felt a headache coming on, the result of his brain going round in circles. Whichever train of thought he took, he always ended up at nonsense station. It would continue to frustrate him unless he took a step back and let the answer come to him.

"James asked if I could do a little groundwork for him," Latimer told his boss. He explained what had been asked of him, and Ingram gave him the green light.

"On one condition," she added. "You do it on your own time. This isn't our investigation, so I can't authorise the overtime."

Latimer thanked Ingram, then headed to his office. As he passed through the briefing room, he saw a DC removing the last of the Higson photographs from the wall and placing them in a file. The canvas had been stripped, ready to display the next major crime.

Latimer sat at his desk and looked up the name of the manufacturer of the shoes they'd taken from James Knight's home. He found a number for their head office and dialled. The clock on the wall showed it to be just after five in the afternoon, knocking-off time for most office workers, but Minster Footwear clearly kept different hours. His call was answered by a female receptionist, and he identified himself and asked to speak to the managing director, only to be told that he was in a meeting. He left his mobile number and asked that he be phoned back as soon as the man was available.

While he waited for the call to be returned, Latimer searched the police national computer for convictions where James Knight was the investigating officer. It wasn't a short list. With thirty years in the service, Knight had been involved in solving close to a thousand cases, averaging one every ten days.

"We're heading over to the pub now," Paul Benson said, sticking his head around the door. "Sure you don't want to join us?"

"You guys go ahead. I've got a few things I need to do first."

"Does that mean you're coming?"

"Maybe," Latimer said.

Benson hesitated, then walked into the office and closed the door.

Latimer knew what was coming. "Spit it out, Paul."

"It's about the information you shared with Knight," Benson said. "Are you sure that was a good idea?"

The DC had a good point. It was unusual for a copper to divulge the nature of the evidence they had against a suspect. That was usually held back until later in the questioning, aimed at tearing apart their story. More importantly, it was done when the interrogation was being recorded on audio, video, or both. It might even be given to the suspect's solicitor if requested, but it wasn't usually offered up by the arresting officer. Forearmed with the information, Knight would have the advantage over Hampshire's finest.

"You're right," Latimer acknowledged, "but I'm missing something, and I was hoping he could fill in the blanks."

"Unless he actually did it, in which case he'd steer you in the wrong direction."

Another valid argument, and Latimer would have expected nothing less. Paul Benson was one of the best coppers he'd worked with. His work ethic was exemplary, his attention to detail bordering on obsessive, and he knew the rule book inside-out.

But sometimes, the rules could be bent a little, and the appropriate moment to disclose evidence was more down to experience and best practices than inflexible directives.

"I made a judgement call," Latimer said. "I'm not sure it's going to make much of a difference in the long run. If you're worried that it'll become a habit, you can rest easy. James is a friend, and it was a one-off."

Benson nodded solemnly, then turned and opened the door. "Don't be too long, your beer'll get warm."

Latimer watched him leave, then sifted through the results of his PNC search. He discarded those who had been charged with non-violent offences, but that still left over eight hundred names. He then looked for those who had been incarcerated on the date of Conte's disappearance and that got rid of another three hundred. It still left around five hundred possibilities.

Latimer saved the results. There wasn't much he could do until he got a list of retailers from the footwear company. Once he had that, he would contact each one and ask for the details of anyone who had used a card to purchase a pair of the Wayfarer variant in size nine. From experience, he knew that could take a while. Companies were often happy to help the police with their enquiries, but profit came first.

Simon Ellis from Minster Footwear rang just before six. He sounded sceptical when Latimer asked for a list of companies that had ordered size nine Wayfarers in the last twelve months.

"How do I know you're the police and not one of my competitors?"

Latimer told him to call 101 and ask for him at Lewisham Central. He gave his name and warrant number and hung up before Ellis could object.

It was three minutes before the call came through on his desk phone.

"This is most inconvenient," Ellis moaned. "You could have just sent a Bobby round in the morning."

"Ten years ago I might have done, but funding cuts mean we have to work smarter. Now, how long before you can get the list to me?"

"I'll have my team prepare it first thing in the morning," Ellis said.

"Can't you get something to me this evening? It's part of a murder enquiry, and time is of the essence."

"I'm afraid not. Most of the staff has gone home. There's no one here to run that kind of report. Besides, don't you need a warrant for this kind of thing?"

"Only if we don't get co-operation," Latimer said. He'd dealt with many people like Ellis over the years, and one thing always brought them to heel. "Tell me, do you wear Minster shoes?"

"Of course," Ellis replied, affronted.

"That might explain why you appear to be so reticent. We're looking for a suspect who wears Minster shoes, and you seem to be doing everything you can to impede our investigation. It might be best if I send a couple of detectives over to pick you up and bring you back to the station. You can spend forty-eight hours in the cells while we pick your life apart."

"That's preposterous! I don't even wear the Wayfarer design, and I'm a size eight, not a nine."

"But you have easy access to the shoes, and a size nine would easily fit onto a size eight foot. It's not unusual for killers to wear oversized shoes to a murder to throw the police off the scent. And how did you know the killer wore a size nine? I don't recall mentioning that."

He had, and he knew it, but the lie was designed to get Ellis worked up.

"You did! I have it written down here, size nine Wayfarer and your warrant number!"

"I definitely recall saying Wayfarer, but not the size. Perhaps I should come down and pay you a visit myself."

Latimer smiled to himself as Ellis protested his innocence. He gave him a minute of silence, then apologised. "Sorry, I was arranging for a detective to join me."

"There's no need!" Ellis almost shouted. "There's a couple of people left in the office. I'll give them some overtime to stay and print out your report. It'll take a few hours, though."

"Well…okay, but you're still on my radar. If we don't get our man in the next seven days, I'll be round to speak to you."

He gave Ellis the email address to send the file to and asked that it be in CSV or Excel format, then ended the call.

There was no point hanging around the office waiting for Ellis to deliver. A couple of hours could stretch to four or five. Latimer decided to head home and make an early start in the morning.

As he walked down the stairs, he saw the pub through the glass wall that stretched from the first floor to the fourth. Two of his detective constables were standing outside with pints of beer, one smoking a cigarette and the other puffing on a vape stick.

It had been many months since Latimer had shared a beer with the team. He preferred to maintain a professional relationship with the men and women he worked with, and getting too close was a recipe for disaster. Going out with the guys had been fine in the days when he'd been a DC, but as he'd climbed the ranks, his socialising had waned. The last time he'd joined them had been January the previous year, a belated Christmas party. Since then, though, he'd left them to it.

It was time to show his face once more. The men and women of MIT 14 had done a sterling job in finding Carrie Higson's killer, putting in all the hours they could manage. The least he could do was get a round in to show his appreciation.

Latimer took the phone from his pocket, but hesitated before calling his wife. If he told Fiona he was going to the pub, she would try to talk him out of it. She was forever reminding him of his promise to drink just twice a month, especially if they were invited to social gatherings. She only had his best interests at heart, but Latimer thought she was being a tad over-protective. Fiona insisted that if he stuck to his new regimen, he'd live much longer. Latimer had seen things differently at first. He wouldn't live longer, he'd *exist* longer. Living meant enjoying life, eating the extra slice of cake, doing the bungee jump, having a couple of pints in the pub now and again. He didn't want to lie on his death bed, look back on his life and regret the things he could have done. Would he swap another thirty years of eat, sleep, work for ten or so years of doing what he enjoyed?

If he'd been single, the answer would have been easy.

But he'd made a promise to the woman he loved. And it wasn't as if he was the only one making the sacrifice. Fiona liked a drink, too, but when they'd found out about his coronary artery disease, she'd stopped buying wine with the weekly shopping. The few bottles they had in stock had been consumed over the next few weeks, until the house was alcohol-free. The first few months had been hard, but his wife had supported him every step of the way.

The prospect of spending the next three decades at her side was what kept him going.

Latimer put the phone away and walked out of the building, across the road and into the pub. The bar was busy, and his team had pulled a couple of tables together in the corner. A cheer went up as he walked over to them, mainly because most of their glasses were almost empty. He sat down, gave a DC a couple of twenties and told him to get a round in.

"What you having, sir?"

"Orange juice," Latimer told him.

"One pint won't kill you," Benson said. He put a fresh glass of Stella in front of Latimer and took a seat next to him.

"I guess it won't." He held up the pint and glasses clinked against it.

Five people worked under Latimer, and they were all present: Paul Benson, the only DS, and four detective constables. The newest of these was Simon Jones, who was standing at the bar with Latimer's money. At the table were the smoker, Gwen Harcourt, the vaper, Tom Adams, and Michael Whittaker. They were a good team to work with. All knew what was expected of them and got on with the job, giving him few reasons to complain. He allowed a little horsing around when appropriate, but otherwise Latimer ran a tight ship. No one had ever requested a transfer from under his command, which was a testament to his leadership skills.

Latimer was halfway through his pint when another appeared next to it.

"Nice try, but I'm not staying. I've got an early start in the morning."

"Looking into Conte's death?" Benson asked. "I'd like to ask you something about that."

"Sure, but outside. I need a vape."

The two men walked out into the warm evening, and Latimer took a long drag on his machine.

"It's about the victim," the DC said.

"What about him?"

"Why choose Conte? If it's really someone with a grudge against Knight, why murder Sean Conte? Why not Knight's wife? Most victims know their killers, and over forty per cent of female victims are killed by their partners or ex-partners. You know Knight well. What's his relationship like?"

"With Jenny? Great. Never heard a peep from either of them to suggest any problems."

"So he's hardly likely to kill her."

Latimer laughed. "No chance."

"But if someone wanted to frame Knight, she'd be the obvious target, wouldn't she?"

"Your point being?"

"Knight doesn't kill the woman he loves, he kills the man he hates, makes sure he leaves plenty of evidence that a DCI would never overlook, and tries to bluff his way out of it. I mean, who else even knew about the problems between Conte and Knight?"

"Anyone who had a copy of the Evening Standard," Latimer said. "About a million people."

"Okay, but how many of them have access to Knight's DNA? How many have the same fingerprints? How many have the motive? My point is, you might be too close to this one. Occam's razor, boss. Occam's razor."

Benson went back inside, leaving Latimer to his thoughts.

They weren't particularly cheerful.

Perhaps the DS was right. Perhaps he was letting his friendship cloud his judgement. Had it been any other suspect, Latimer would have charged them by now, yet he was prepared to dig to see whether anyone with a grudge against Knight could be tied to the case, no matter how flimsily.

He stepped towards the pub's door, then stopped, turned and walked back to the station. He unlocked his bike and took the shortest route home for a change.

He was still an hour late arriving home, most of that taken up with the Knight searches. Fiona would understand, though. No one stuck to regular office hours in Murder Investigation Team 14, and late nights were the norm by the time you reached DI.

Latimer took his bike around the back of the house and locked it in the shed, then went in through the back door. When he entered the kitchen, the lack of food smells told him something was wrong.

"Fiona?"

He heard faint sounds coming from the hallway. As he tip-toed past the sink, he considered taking a knife from the draining board, but chided himself for over-reacting.

The living room was the second door off the hallway, and as he approached, the sound grew louder. It was music. Latimer pushed the door open slowly and saw his wife sitting at her laptop, banging furiously at the keys. A glass of red wine was next to her, and the bottle it had come from was almost empty. Her YouTube favourite channel belted out hits from the television.

"What's wrong?"

Fiona looked up, startled. Her ginger hair normally flowed off her shoulders, but she had it tied up in a ponytail. She looked at her watch.

"I didn't realise it was so late," she said, and polished off the wine glass.

Latimer put his helmet on the sideboard. "What's with the wine?"

Fiona poured the last of the wine from the bottle. "Bethany Ambrose, that's what."

Latimer sighed. "I thought that was all done and dusted."

"So did I, but today I got a letter from her solicitor. She's demanding all the income I received for Truly Awful, and she wants me to take the book off the market."

That explained the wine.

Fiona had published her third book, Truly Awful, three years earlier. Her first two had sold in decent quantities, but the third had been a smash hit, selling well over two hundred thousand copies. That had led to an offer of a six-figure advance for her next work, but Bethany Ambrose had scuppered her plans.

Ambrose was an indie author. She'd self-published a thriller called Death By Opinion a year before Truly Awful hit the bookstores. Both books shared a similar theme, where an unhinged author has a hard time dealing with a one-star review and responds to it. A social media battle ensues and the author's darkest secrets are revealed online. The author then tracks the reviewer down and kills her.

Just as in the books, Ambrose had taken to social media, only this time to complain about the plagiarism of her work. She'd started a crowdfunding campaign to raise money for legal fees, and the indie community had filled her coffers.

As support for Ambrose grew, Fiona's star faded. The BBC news website picked up the story and asked to hear her side of it. Fiona had given them a six-hundred-word reply, but they'd taken just two sentences for the article, both of which simply said that the accusation was unfounded. When the backlash turned towards her publisher, they withdrew the offer of a new contract. Sales plummeted, and Fiona became a pariah. The only person to stand by her was her agent, and even he had told her that writing under her real name was no longer an option. She would have to start over, which meant re-inventing herself and forgetting about the following she'd built up. Fiona had taken the advice, laid low, and waited for it all to blow over.

A few months later, they'd gone to mediation. Fiona, John and their solicitor had met with Bethany Ambrose and her own counsel at the offices of a small law firm in the Hammersmith.

"I'm so nervous," Fiona said as they sat in the reception area.

"Don't be," Latimer told her, holding her hand for support. "You're in the right. You've done nothing wrong."

"Then why do I feel so guilty?"

"It's only natural. Most law-abiding people go to pieces when they're put in these situations." Latimer didn't know that for sure, but he had to say something to boost his wife's confidence. She wasn't one for confrontations, and this was as far outside her comfort zone as he could imagine.

A moment later, two more people entered the building. They spoke quietly to the receptionist, then took a seat opposite the Latimers and their lawyer. They both looked like solicitors, the dark-suited male in his forties, with prematurely greying hair cut short in a side parting. The woman was a head shorter, dressed in a black pencil skirt, black jacket over a white blouse. She looked a little younger, perhaps mid-thirties, with long blonde hair tied up.

"Where are they?" Fiona whispered.

Latimer checked his watch. The meeting was due to start at one, and it was already five past, yet there was still no sign of Ambrose.

An office door opened and a short, stout man with receding black hair stepped out. "Hello, I'm Donald Atkinson. I'll be chairing today's meeting. Where is the Latimer party?" he asked.

Fiona raised her hand, and the three of them stood.

"And the Ambrose party?"

The two solicitors were already on their feet, heading for the office Atkinson had emerged from.

The Latimer contingent followed them in. It was a boardroom, with a huge oak table and three walls lined with bookshelves. The other wall had a table full of cups, saucers, a coffee pot and pitchers of water underneath a large window.

Latimer took one of the five chairs on the left side of the table, sitting opposite team Ambrose.

"So," Atkinson began from the head of the table, "today we are here to—"

"Erm, shouldn't we wait for Bethany Ambrose?" Latimer asked.

The female solicitor opposite raised her hand slightly. "I'm Ambrose."

Latimer was confused. "You look nothing like your social media profile picture."

"I like the anonymity," she said.

Her demeanour was abrasive, and Latimer wondered why she would bring such an attitude to a mediation meeting. The whole point of the exercise was to find some common ground, yet Ambrose seemed determined to make waves from the start.

"I write under a pen name and my profile picture is used with permission," she added. "Do you have a problem with that?"

Latimer raised his hands in mock surrender. "None whatsoever."

Atkinson regained control of ceremonies, introducing the parties and outlining the case. "Miss Ambrose, it is your claim that Mrs Latimer plagiarised your work. What brought you to this conclusion?"

Ambrose took a manila folder from her bag and opened it. "I've noted twenty-four occasions where her title, Truly Awful, copies directly from my work Death by Opinion." She handed copies to all parties and waited for a response from Fiona.

Mrs Latimer?" Atkinson prompted after a few minutes.

"This is…ridiculous." She waved the paper at Ambrose. "It says both books have an unreliable narrator. Are you seriously telling me that you were the first person in history to use that technique in a novel? And…and this one, the protagonist is female and the villain is also female. Again, were you the first person in history to write about a woman going after another woman? This is pathetic."

Latimer was stunned at Fiona's outburst. He watched her throw the paper back across the table at Ambrose, who looked fit to burst. Fiona then took a sheet of paper from her own file and gave it to Atkinson.

"Bethany's book is self-published and only available on Amazon. That is a printout of all the books I have purchased from Amazon in the last two years. As you will see, Death by Opinion is not listed. How could I have stolen her ideas if I'd never read the book?"

"It's been found available for download on several pirate websites," Ambrose said. "You must have got a copy from one of them."

"A pirate website? Are you serious?"

"Oh, I'm serious, alright. It's up to you to prove otherwise."

"Actually, the burden of proof is on the plaintiff," Latimer broke in. "In this case, you, Miss Ambrose. But, if that's the way you want to play it, my wife saves a copy of her work in progress to the cloud after each writing session. She also sends a copy to herself via email each day. Prove to me that you don't have access to either her online storage or her email account. You could have read her first draft, made a few changes here and there and self-published it while her publisher was getting it ready for release."

"Are you suggesting Bethany stole your wife's idea?" Ambrose's solicitor asked.

"Why not? Does she have the monopoly on outlandish ideas? If it wasn't Miss Ambrose, then one of her friends, perhaps. I will contact my internet service provider and get a list of all websites visited in the last two years to prove that we haven't been to any pirate download websites. I'll let you decide how to refute my allegation."

Ambrose was almost purple with rage. She snatched up her papers and stuffed them into her bag. "I told you this was a terrible idea," she told her solicitor. "These people have no intention of settling this amicably. Let's go."

"Bethany, I strongly advise—"

Ambrose stood and left the room before her brief could finish his sentence. He apologised to those present, then joined her in the reception area.

"That went well," Latimer said.

"At least it's given her something to think about," his wife smiled. "When did you come up with that?"

"I don't know. I was just thinking her idea was preposterous, and how would she like it if we'd done the same to her." Latimer grinned. "Seemed to get her attention."

That mediation meeting had been eighteen months ago. Everything had gone quiet, and both Latimer and Fiona believed the entire episode was behind them.

It clearly wasn't.

Latimer went and put his arms around his wife. "Just write back to her solicitor and remind him—"

"Her. The solicitor's a woman."

She must have got a new one, Latimer thought. *Not surprising.* "Okay, remind *her* that the burden of proof is on Ambrose. She has to come up with evidence that you ever had a copy of her book. You've still got that list of purchases from Amazon. Send that to her."

Fiona nodded, but didn't look convinced.

"Look," Latimer pressed, "the books aren't word-for-word. In fact, most people said your version was vastly superior."

"It's not about who did it better, it's…it's…"

"It's time to knock off the wine," Latimer said, taking the glass from her hand. "You're working yourself into a state. Let me fix something to eat and we can discuss this tomorrow. Don't go responding to anything she says on Facebook or Twitter, and don't reply to the solicitor until you're calm enough to make sense."

"But what if she takes me to court and the judge awards her all of my royalties? That's over eighty thousand pounds! Where would we get that kind of money?"

It was indeed a formidable sum. The money hadn't come in all at once, and whenever she received a cheque, most of it went toward the mortgage. They'd spent twenty grand on a new car, and the rest on a couple of holidays.

"It won't come to that. British law says it's up to Ambrose to prove you did it."

"Yes, but not beyond a reasonable doubt. I looked into civil cases, and it says that Ambrose only has to prove her case on the balance of probabilities. That means if the judge has even the slightest doubt about my testimony, she'll win."

"Then we get you the best lawyer available and make sure the judge has no choice but to rule in your favour. You and I both know you didn't steal her idea. Anyway, it might not even get that far. Once you send her solicitor the evidence, she'll probably walk away from the case."

Fiona kissed his hand. "I hope so."

"Now, what's for dinner?"

"There's salmon in the fridge. I thought we'd do it with boiled potatoes, asparagus and cauliflower cheese."

Of all the aspects of his recent health transformation, the diet was the part he hated most. He'd never been a big lover of fish, but the plan the doctor had given him called for plenty of tuna, salmon and mackerel. He forced himself to eat them three times a week, as well as avocado and plenty of salads. Bacon and sausages were out, as were takeaways. No more curries, no more kebabs. It sometimes felt like his life was already over, especially at meal times.

The fact that Fiona was a great cook and could disguise the taste of the fish with subtle spices helped a great deal. He'd asked her to teach him a few simple recipes to give her a few nights off from the cooking, and the salmon dish was one of the easiest. The cheese sauce also hid the fish taste nicely.

Latimer chuckled. "You mean you thought *I'd* do it."

Latimer kissed Fiona and tried to walk away, but she grabbed his arm. "You've been drinking."

He'd expected her to fly off the handle, but she seemed calm, even sanguine. Latimer put it down to the bottle of wine she'd drunk.

"I only had a half. I went in for an orange juice to celebrate closing a case, but Paul bought me a beer. It would have been rude to say no. Besides, the last time I had a drink was eight days ago. It's not going to kill me."

"Maybe not, but when two weeks becomes eight days, then six, then four, you're back to where you started."

"It was a one-off," Latimer said. "I promise."

"Then you might as well make the most of it. I'll prepare the salmon, you nip to the shop and get some beer and another bottle of rose."

The twinkle in her eye told him that wasn't the only pleasure he was going to get that night.

Chapter 8

Ryan Anderson turned off the television when the doorbell rang.

"Who is it?" His voice easily carried from the cheap sofa to the hallway outside his bedsit.

"Paul. Open up."

Ryan went to the door and looked through the spyhole. The man who'd let him into the Vine two days earlier was there alone. Ryan opened the door and stood aside to let him in.

"How did you get past the front door?"

"Some fat bird let me in." Paul looked inside the room, but stayed where he was. "Get your coat."

"Where are we going?"

"Out."

Guessing he wasn't going to get anything more from Marsh's heavy, Ryan put on his jacket and walked out, closing the door behind him.

Paul told him to put his arms out, just as he had at their previous meeting. Ryan obliged, and Paul patted down every inch of his body, even checking inside his ears. When he came across Ryan's phone, he told him to leave it at home.

Ryan unlocked the door, tossed the phone on the bed, then locked it again.

"How come you live in that shithole?" Paul asked as they walked down the three flights of stairs to the entrance to the building.

"It's all I can afford," Ryan shrugged. "It's here or the streets, and the bedsit is slightly warmer."

That was the truth. Even though it was late summer, the single room leaked heat at night. It also made his clothes stink of the food he cooked, and the walls were so thin that he could hear conversations taking place two floors below him. The worst part was having to share the toilet and shower with five other tenants.

Outside, Paul led him to a black BMW and got in behind the wheel. Ryan took the front passenger seat.

"Nice motor," Ryan said as Paul started the car. "Does this mean I've got the job?"

"Not yet. Consider yourself on probation."

They pulled out into traffic and were soon heading south from Cheetham Hill toward the city centre.

"What's with the pat down?" Ryan asked. "Are you gonna do that every time we meet?"

"Pretty much," Paul said. "The boss likes you, but that doesn't mean he trusts you. The way you happened to bump into him last week was too much of a coincidence for his liking. Mine, too. Until we're both convinced you're not a copper, we'll take precautions."

"All you have you do is check my past," Ryan said. "I've got a full work history since I was seventeen."

"We're checking, don't you worry. The boss has got people looking into you as we speak."

"Well, when they get round to interviewing Johnny at the factory, tell them not to shake his hand. He was on his phone when he opened the lunchbox and he put his hand inside before the smell hit him."

The laugh surprised Ryan. It sounded like Paul was fighting for breath, a timid sound for such a big guy.

"Yeah, someone went round to visit him a couple of days ago. Johnny still hates you, by the way."

"I'm heartbroken," Ryan said, feigning sorrow.

Paul joined the ring road.

"So where are we going?"

"Salford," Paul told him, all humour gone from his voice. "Time to put your skills to good use."

Fifteen minutes later, Paul pulled up at the side of the road and nodded towards a side street. "Down there, number eleven. It's the fifth house from this end. I'll go in the front, you cover the back."

Ryan followed Paul's finger and saw a metal gate leading to a small alleyway that ran between two rows of terraced up-and-downs. They got out of the BMW and crossed the road.

"He's a slippery bastard, so watch yourself," Paul said. "And when we get inside, just do as I say. Got it?"

"No problem."

Paul walked down the road and turned right, out of sight. Ryan pushed the gate open and counted down the houses. They were all red brick with white lintels over the windows. The only differentiating features were the numbers on the back gates.

Ryan reached number eleven, one of the digits hanging askew, held in place by a single rusty screw. None of the houses looked in particularly good repair, but this one was exceptional. The wooden gate hadn't seen a coat of paint in years, and the bottom corner had rotted away. Beyond it, Ryan could see green mold growing on the wall where rainwater had run over the clogged guttering and down the side of the house.

Out of sight, a door opened. Ryan heard the footsteps of someone in a hurry, and the wooden gate flew open. A stick-thin man in his thirties, wearing tracksuit bottoms and a grubby t-shirt, ran into Ryan's arms.

His face was pasty-white and panic-stricken. "Lemme go, please!"

Ryan said nothing. He held on to the man's shoulders and pushed him back through the gate, toward the rear door of the house. The man resisted, and despite being six inches shorter than Ryan, he made progress difficult. Ryan adjusted his grip, and felt a searing pain as the scruff raked his foot down Ryan's right shin. As Ryan lifted his foot from the ground he was pushed backwards and lost his balance, clattering into a rusty metal barbecue that hadn't been used in years.

Ryan looked up as his quarry dashed through the gates. He cursed as he got to his feet to give chase, his shin still aching. He limped through the gate, and was relieved to see that Paul had followed him into the alley. He was gripping the man's throat and marching him back toward the house.

"I told you he was a slippery bastard," Paul said as he pushed past Ryan and forced the man inside the house. Ryan joined them in the gloomy living room just as Paul pushed the man backwards onto the fake-leather sofa.

The interior of the house was worse than the outside. Black mold clung to the walls, window frames and skirting boards, throwing off a putrid stench that made Ryan's stomach turn. The ill-fitting orange curtains were stained black, too, and probably hadn't been drawn in months. The carpet had been down for at least twenty years, and was marked with stains and cigarette burns. If there was a vacuum cleaner in the house, Ryan doubted the occupant knew how to use it. The only thing out of place was the fifty-inch television which sat on top of a dust-covered sideboard.

"Mickey, Mickey, Mickey. How come you always do a runner when I show up?"

"I didn't know it was you, Paul. I swear."

"You're a lying little shit."

Mickey fumbled through the drug paraphernalia on the cluttered table for his cigarettes and put one in his mouth with a trembling hand.

"Mickey here owes the boss some money," Paul said to Ryan.

"What for?"

"Never you mind. All you need to know is that he wants his grand, and Mickey is going to pay up or lose the use of some of his body parts." Paul turned to Mickey. "Where's the cash?"

"I…I ain't got it," Mickey said, and Ryan could see fear in his eyes. But also something else.

Deceit.

Paul must have spotted it, too, because he reached over and slapped Mickey's stubble-encrusted face. "I know when you're lying. I'll give you one last chance to tell me where the money is."

Mickey put his hands up to protect himself from the next onslaught. "I swear, Paul, I ain't got it. Drew Matthews screwed me over, honest."

"Then how come you got a new telly?"

"That was a present," Mickey said. "From me mum."

Paul picked up a heavy glass ashtray and threw it at the screen. It bounced off, leaving a crack that spiderwebbed out from the centre to the edges.

Mickey wailed, then put his head in his hands.

"We should have taken that and sold it," Ryan said. "Could have got a couple of hundred quid at least."

Paul thrust a finger in Ryan's face. "I told you to shut up and do what the fuck I said."

Ryan backed off and put his hands up in submission. "Just making a point, that's all."

"Well, don't." Paul kicked Mickey's shin to get his attention. "Last chance. Where is it?"

"If I had it—"

Paul silenced him with a slap to the head, then turned to Ryan. "I want you to fuck him up."

"Sure," Ryan said. He took off his jacket and handed it to his companion, then stood in front of the cowering Mickey. "Want me to break anything, or just kick the shit out of him?"

"Whatever floats your boat."

Ryan's fist connected with Mickey's face before the drug addict had time to react. His head snapped sideways and he fell off the couch, landing on the floor on his front. Ryan threw the coffee table aside and kicked Mickey in the kidneys, then stamped on his fingers.

"No more! Stop! It's in the kitchen!"

"Where in the kitchen?"

"The freezer. In the fish fingers."

Paul nodded toward the kitchen, and Ryan took the hint. It was as neglected as the rest of the house. Dishes piled high in the sink, and there was so much burnt food on the electric hob that it was impossible to tell whether it had once been enamel or stainless steel. Ryan opened the small fridge. It was almost empty, apart from some milk and half a block of cheese. The small freezer compartment at the top was stuffed full, though. He pulled everything out and found the box of fish fingers at the back. He emptied it out onto a greasy countertop, and after three dodgy-looking fingers fell out, he ripped open the box. A wad of notes fell out, and Ryan caught them before they hit the grimy floor. He did a quick count before returning to the living room. Mickey was sitting up, but still on the floor.

"There's four hundred," Ryan said, handing the money over.

"That's a start," Paul said. "You still owe me seven, though, Mickey."

"Six," the drug addict corrected him.

"No, seven. An extra hundred for lying to me."

"I didn't lie, I just forgot I had it in there…"

"Well then, my friend here is going to ensure you never forget anything else in future."

Ryan took his cue. He grabbed Mickey around the throat and pulled him to his feet, then punched him in the stomach. Mickey doubled over, gasping for breath, and Ryan delivered a left to the side of his head. He crumpled to the floor, and Ryan stamped on his ankle. He heard a bone snap, and Mickey let out a scream, throwing his hands in the air.

"That'll do," Paul said, throwing Ryan his jacket.

"At least we know he won't run next time we pop round," Ryan smiled.

He managed to draw a chuckle from Paul, who swung a leg and caught Mickey in the stomach.

"You've got one week."

Mickey just about managed a nod of acknowledgement, and Paul led Ryan out the back way.

"Where next?"

"Wherever you want. You're done for the day." Paul took the wad of money from his pocket and counted off a few notes. "There's a couple of hundred to keep you going."

Ryan took the cash. "Thanks, but I was hoping for something more permanent. I don't want to live in a bedsit forever, but I can't move until I've got a regular income. How long before Marsh makes up his mind?"

"It's *Mr* Marsh to you," Paul said, "and he'll offer you the job when he's ready, not before."

"Fair enough. Didn't mean to offend anyone, just wanted to know if I should carry on waiting or look for something else."

"It's up to you. If the boss wants to take you on, it'll be worth the wait. If you want to try your luck elsewhere, be my guest. No skin off my nose."

They reached the BMW and got in. Paul drove them back toward the city centre.

"You want me to drop you home, or do you wanna go buy some decent threads?"

Ryan compared his worn jeans, dirty trainers and cheap t-shirt to Paul's Lacoste polo and light brown chinos. He had a point.

"Home will do. Cheaper to get them off the internet."

They'd gone just a couple of streets when Paul swore quietly.

"What is it?"

"Behind us."

Ryan turned to face the rear window and saw the police car on their tail. Its blue lights were flashing.

"Shit! You think Mickey called them?"

"No chance," Paul said. "He's dumb, but he's not stupid. Just stay calm and don't piss them off. We'll be out of here in no time."

Paul pulled over and wound his window down, and the marked police car stopped behind them. Ryan adjusted his position so that he could see what was happening in the mirrors.

"Turn the engine off, please," the officer said as he approached the driver's side.

Paul did as he was told. "What's the problem?"

"You're not wearing your seat belt."

Paul checked, and swore under his breath. "Sorry about that. I wear it religiously. Can't understand why I didn't put it on today."

The copper, unmoved, had a notebook in his hand, and he started writing. He moved to the front of the BMW to note the licence plate, then back to the side. "Where are you coming from?"

"Just visiting a mate," Paul said.

The policeman leaned closer to the car and sniffed. "When was the last time you had a drink?"

"Last night."

"Anything in the vehicle that shouldn't be here? Drugs? Weapons?"

"Nothing," Paul told him.

The officer finished writing, then put his notepad away. "Step out of the vehicle, please. Both of you."

They got out, and Ryan noticed that a second cop had left the marked car and was standing at the rear of the BMW.

Both men were told to assume the position and the cops patted them down. It was becoming a regular occurrence for Ryan, but he held his tongue. They found his wallet and put it on the roof of the car. Paul's pockets contained just cash, his driving licence and his phone.

The cop with sergeant's stripes looked through Ryan's wallet and took out his driver's licence. "Long way from home, aren't you?"

"Just moved up here a couple of weeks ago," he replied. His licence had his old address in Colchester. "Looking for work."

The sergeant noted their names on his pad, while the other gave the inside a cursory search.

Satisfied that there was no contraband to be found, Paul was given a breathalyser test. He passed.

"It's a hundred pound fine for not wearing your seatbelt," the sergeant said to Paul as he handed him a fixed penalty notice. He explained how it could be paid, then walked back to his car.

Ryan and Paul got back in the BMW, and both made sure their seatbelts were fastened.

"Bastards," Paul swore as he pulled away slowly. "They only pulled me because I drive a nice motor. He's just jealous 'cos he's got to drive home tonight in a Fiat or some other piece of shit."

Ryan was just relieved that the stop hadn't been anything to do with their visit to Mickey's place.

"On second thoughts, drop me in town. I need a drink."

* * *

After dropping Ryan Anderson off on Princess Street, Paul Gardner drove to Hale Barns, one of the most exclusive areas in the north of England. Carrwood was home to a number of Premier League footballers and other multi-millionaires, among them Franklin Marsh.

His home boasted seven bedrooms, five bathrooms, four reception rooms and an indoor swimming pool, though it was one of the more modest properties in the area.

Paul pulled up to the gate that led to Marsh's home. He knew that a sensor in the road would have picked up the weight of his vehicle and sent an alert to the house, and he just had to wait until one of Marsh's staff checked him out through the CCTV camera mounted on the perimeter wall.

The gate eventually swung open, and Paul drove up the gravel-lined drive to the front of the house. It was a huge place, with white walls and grey roof tiles. The entrance was shaped like an arch, with two heavy wooden doors painted black. They opened as Paul got out of the car, and Marsh's Filipino housekeeper greeted him with a smile.

"Hello, sir, good afternoon."

"Hi, Camille. Where's Franklin?"

"In the garden, sir."

"I keep telling you, call me Paul."

Camille simply smiled, and Paul knew she would never agree to the arrangement. He'd been trying for two years now, but she was relentless.

He walked into the hallway, a space larger than his own apartment. Stairways curved up the walls on either side, meeting at the first-floor landing. The flooring was marble, and the walls were lined with oak panels.

Paul didn't care much for the décor. It reminded him of a stately home he'd once visited as a school boy. The old portraits on the wall had creeped him out, and the memory of the wax polish smell hit him every time he stepped inside Marsh's home Still, Franklin seemed to like it, and he was the one paying for it.

Paul walked through the drawing room to the kitchen, where floor to ceiling glass doors gave access to the rear garden, an area of tightly-mown grass the size of a football pitch. Marsh was sitting at a table reading a newspaper, a coffee mug and half-full ashtray in front of him.

Sonny and Cher, Marsh's golden retrievers, jumped up and ran over to Paul, their tails wagging with delight. He rubbed their heads, then walked over and took a seat next to his employer.

"How'd it go?" Marsh asked, folding his paper and putting it on the table.

"He had four hundred. I gave Ryan two, just like you said."

"I meant Ryan. How did he do?"

Paul shrugged. "He didn't hesitate when I told him to mess Mickey up. He asked how far to go, I said it was up to him, and he laid into Mickey like a good 'un. Smacked him with a right, kicked him in the back and stamped on his fingers. Might have broken a couple."

"That's it?" Marsh asked.

"No. Mickey suddenly remembered where he'd hidden his money, but after we counted it, I let Ryan have another go. He snapped Mickey's ankle like a twig. Even joked about it."

Marsh lit a cigarette and blew the smoke to one side, away from Paul. "What do you think?"

Paul sighed. "I have to admit, he didn't act like a copper. They have all that PACE bullshit to stick to. They wouldn't let him beat the crap out of anyone, not even a lowlife like Mickey Orton. Ryan didn't hesitate. He was like 'wham, bam, fuck you, man'."

The Police and Criminal Evidence Act 1984 dictated what police officers—even those undercover—were allowed to do, and kicking the shit out of druggies was a big no-no.

"When they're after someone like me, they'll use any tactics. I wanna wait to hear what Billy Marsden has to say."

"That's gonna be a couple of days. Billy pulled us over after we left Mickey's place. He got Ryan's name, so now he has a reason to look him up in the PNC."

The move had been Marsden's idea. Any searches done on the police national computer were logged, so whenever there was a need to do a background check for Marsh, Billy would pull the suspect over for some minor infraction and record the stop. If anyone questioned him, he would simply say he had a bad feeling about the person and wanted to check them out.

"Well, I hope he hurries the fuck up. In the meantime, I want you and Ryan to do the Dover run."

"Sure. Tomorrow?"

"Yeah, the sooner the better."

Charlie Marsh walked into the garden, his school bag over his shoulder. He went straight for Sonny and Cher and laughed as they licked his face.

"Hey, how about a hug for your old dad?"

Charlie pulled himself away from the dogs and ran to his father's waiting arms.

"I missed you. How was school?"

"Okay," the boy shrugged, pulling himself away from Marsh. The dogs continued to jump on him, and he knelt down to give them the attention they craved. "I made the rugby team. And don't forget, next term we're going skiing in Italy."

"It's all paid up, don't worry."

"Good. I'm gonna need spending money, though. Lots of it."

"You'll get five hundred quid, and that's it, you cheeky scamp!"

Charlie stood and scowled, but the smile on his father's face meant he couldn't hold it for long. "How about six?"

"You're worse than your mother. Go on, scoot. Unpack, put your dirty stuff in the laundry and get changed. We're going out to eat just as soon as your sister gets home."

Charlie took his bag inside, followed by the two hyper retrievers.

"The trip's costing me an arm and a leg, and that's on top of the astronomical boarding school fees. I wanted him to go to a local high school, but the wife won't have it. Says she doesn't want the kids growing up to be like me."

Paul waved a casual hand at the house. "I'd say you've done pretty well."

"Yeah, but she's got a point. I fell into this lark because it was all I knew. Growing up, we had nothing but what we could nick for ourselves. Most of the time me and me mates got caught, and back then, the cops gave you a kicking before they took you in. Never put me off, though. The others kept doing the same stupid shit, but I got smart. Instead of doing the nicking, I got the weak kids from the estate to do it for me. If they got caught, they knew not to mention my name. I was a real hard bastard, even back then, and if the cops came to question me about a job, I found the grass and made my displeasure known."

Paul had heard the speech a couple of times before, but wouldn't dream of interrupting.

"We moved on to cars," Marsh continued, "then houses. If my men got caught, they went down and did their time. While they were inside I looked after their families, and when they got out we'd have a big party for them. The best part was, inside they learned the tricks of the trade from the old lags and came out with fresh ideas. That's how I got into drugs."

Marsh's wife appeared with a tall glass of gin and tonic. "What are you two plotting?"

Anita Marsh was fifteen years Franklin's junior, and the body that had attracted him to her was the same as the day they'd met. She'd been a young model who was already making in-roads in the fashion industry, but Marsh turned her head with his smooth talk and bad-boy reputation. The shy 18-year-old had married Marsh within a year, and in all the time Paul had been working for Marsh, he hadn't heard a cross word between them.

"Nothing, Princess. Just reminiscing."

She looked at Gardner. "Poor Paul, he must have heard that 'I came from nothing' speech a thousand times."

"Rubbish! I hardly ever mention my past."

"Well, don't bend his ear too much. Young lad like him needs to be out with the girls, not babysitting an old man like you."

Marsh slapped her backside, and she leaned in and kissed him passionately before sauntering back into the house, her hips swaying for Marsh's benefit.

"She likes to play the dumb blonde sometimes, but she's a helluva smart woman, Anita is."

"I know," Paul agreed. He'd worked for the Marshes for ten years, and knew that she was the real brains behind the operation. Anita had been the one to suggest fronting his business empire with legitimate operations like the Vine and a series of restaurants and takeaways. The club wasn't a money maker on its own, but it did provide Marsh with a way to launder some of the cash he made from his other projects. Drugs were the main earners, and supplying arms made him a decent profit, too. He used to be into prostitution, but after the birth of his daughter, he'd had a change of heart. Perhaps it was becoming a father that had softened him, but Paul suspected Anita had been the one to make the decision. He'd sold the operation to the Turks and concentrated on his other two enterprises. His service empire had made him enough to buy the beautiful house and send his kids to boarding school, all under the watchful gaze of the police who were powerless to do anything about it.

"I don't want my kids growing up like me," Marsh said once more, lighting another cigarette.

Paul couldn't understand why not, but it wasn't his place to say it. Marsh was a great father, and kept his business and private lives separate. His reputation as a hard man was well-founded, but at home, with his family, he was a different person. He doted on his kids and loved his wife with a passion. Marsh had told him more than once how he disdained men who hit their wives. "They're asking for trouble. A wife who has reason to hate her husband will turn on him. But if he treats her well, she'll be happy to enjoy the benefits of his profession."

On the flip side, it would work out well for Paul. He was Marsh's right-hand man, and once the old man retired, someone needed to step up and assume command of the empire Marsh had built. Paul knew he'd be the one to take the reins.

Like his boss, he'd come from humble beginnings. He'd also grown up in a rough area, but unlike Marsh, Paul never got in trouble with the police. He wasn't into stealing or drugs, but being an only child, he had no-one to look out for him. He'd had to take care of himself, and when everyone in the neighbourhood was a hard man, that meant being willing and able to use his fists. He pretty much kept himself to himself, though, but the school bully singled him out for it.

Only once.

Paul had messed the kid up so much, the poor bastard had spent a month in hospital. With his reputation cemented, no one ever bothered him again until he left school. He began hitting the pubs at sixteen, getting into a few scrapes, until one of his friends mentioned that there was work available for someone with his particular skills. Paul had assumed it was bouncer work, but he was introduced to Franklin Marsh and hadn't looked back.

"You've taught them well," Paul said. "I'm sure they'll turn out great."

"That they will," Marsh agreed. "Now, go get things ready for tomorrow. If he does well in Dover, you can take him over to meet the Albanians."

"So soon? You don't want to dig a little more?"

"If all goes well tomorrow and Billy gives him a clean bill of health, that's good enough for me."

Paul wasn't going to argue his point any further. Jovial as Franklin Marsh was at that moment, Paul knew he could change in an instant, and second-guessing him was always a good way to provoke that reaction.

"I'll get everything set up and call you the moment we get back."

Paul got up and left, saying his goodbyes to the Marsh family on his way out. He needed to make a few phone calls to set up the Dover run, and then he'd see what Ryan Anderson was really all about.

Chapter 9

Ten minutes after taking the atenolol, Karen tied up her blonde hair and sat down at her workbench before checking her pulse. Thanks to the beta blocker, her heart rate was down to thirty beats per minute, and it would stay that way while she worked through the night. She placed her right forearm on the padded wooden block that had been screwed to the desk, then pulled the leather straps over it and pulled tight, securing the other end on the hooks under the table. She could now only move her fingers, but that was all she needed.

Karen hunched over the Kern OZC-5 microscope—a real bargain at three grand—and through the eyepiece, she could see the state of her current work in progress. It was a 24-carat gold ring, and on the inside of the band she was carving a scene from Cheltenham racecourse.

The piece had been commissioned by the wife of Toby Fordham, the owner of Dancing Folly. The horse had won the most prestigious race on the calendar, the Cheltenham Gold Cup, and to celebrate both the win and their thirtieth wedding anniversary, Celia Fordham had asked Karen to recreate the scene inside the gold ring. She'd given Karen a series of photographs taken on the day, some head-on shots, others taken from the stands. They'd settled on one showing Dancing Folly in mid-air as it leapt over the last fence to land two lengths clear of its nearest rival. The shot had been taken from right up against the far rail, the photographer obviously kneeling to get the perfect angle.

It was one of the easier pieces Karen had been asked to create, but she was still charging handsomely for it. Celia had initially baulked at the asking price of seventy thousand, but once Karen had explained that it would take several months to make, and that she was one of the cheapest and best on the market, they agreed to the deal. As soon as Celia signed the contract, Karen started work.

Seven weeks in, and she was still working on the fence. She'd completed the stand in the background, and the final addition would be the horse and jockey suspended in the air. That was where it would get tricky. One mistake, one muscle spasm at the wrong moment, and weeks of hard work would be gone, wasted.

Fortunately, that had only happened to her twice. Once when the power had tripped, plunging the workshop into darkness, and the other time when some pissed-up pranksters had rung her doorbell at three in the morning. She always worked late at night as there was less ambient noise and fewer vehicles on the street, but there was no accounting for drunken idiots.

Karen had to time her cuts to match her heartbeat, and could often wait minutes for the right moment to shift the graver less than a millimetre, which made for slow progress. After an hour and only seven strokes, she stopped and took a break. She walked past the piles of newspapers and through the door that led from her workshop annex to the kitchen of her detached house, where she took a bottle of water from the fridge. What she really wanted was a coffee, but the caffeine would interfere with her work. She didn't even trust decaf these days. She'd had one once and it had either been mislabelled or the manufacturer had tried to pass regular grounds off as decaffeinated. She'd lost a whole night's work because of that.

After checking her phone, Karen went back into the workshop and strapped herself in once more. She managed another sixteen strokes, then called it a day. She'd completed the front legs of the horse, but the rest could wait. She was already a few weeks ahead of schedule, and it wasn't the only piece she was working on. She carefully released the ring from its mount and set it aside in a cloth-lined box, then replaced it with the gold piece she'd been working on for the last few nights.

She wouldn't receive a penny for this work, but she wasn't doing it for the money. Pieces like the ring she was decorating for the Fordhams paid the bills, but this project was personal. No one would ever see the finished product. At least, not the block of gold she was working on.

Once it was secured in place, Karen took the photo she was working from and placed it next to the gold ingot. The picture had been taken with a high-resolution camera and was exactly the same size as the piece of precious metal she was working on. There were no horses, no buildings or people, just a series of lines that looped and whorled to create a pattern so unique that it could identify one person among the seven and a half billion on the planet.

While she was excited to get back to work on the latest set of fingerprints, her joy was tempered by the fact that she would have to destroy them once complete. She'd done so three times before, creating masterpieces and then obliterating them once finished, but that went with the territory. Only a fool would leave such evidence lying around for the police to find, though she never expected them to come calling. Up until now, each kill had gone as expected, including the latest one involving Sean Conte.

She got to work on the piece of art, for that was what it was. It might not be a Caravaggio or Monet, but it gave her as much pleasure as any landscape or still life she'd drawn at school.

Art had been the only class she'd enjoyed as a child. She'd done sufficiently well in her other topics to get Bs and Cs in her GCSEs, but her only A* had come in art. On leaving school at sixteen, she'd applied for jobs that would let her take advantage of her only skill, but there were few opportunities available. Karen had eventually found work in graphic design at an advertising agency, but it wasn't what she'd hoped for. Mostly she was told what to draw and had to work within strict parameters, which stifled her creativity. She put up with it, though, because she had bills to pay. In her spare time she'd created works of her own and set up an online shop, offering framed original works. They sold slowly at first, and with each sale she'd upped the price a little until she was commanding over three hundred pounds per picture. It had taken her over a year to get to that point, but even then, two sales a month wasn't close to what she needed to go solo.

Her break had come three years after leaving school. On visiting an art gallery in the hope of getting them to show her work, she'd seen a display of engravings. One piece, a silver shield four inches across, had a price tag of thirty thousand pounds, and Karen could see why. The intricate carving was perfect in every detail. The roses, castle, archers and lion told of a truly gifted hand, and she'd researched the artist. There wasn't much information online, but he did have his contact details on his website. She'd sent him an email asking to meet, expecting it to be ignored, but to her astonishment, he'd invited her around to his studio.

Damian Elsworth was not quite the man she'd expected. He was in his sixties, much older than Karen had envisioned. He was also frailer, and over glasses of orange juice, he'd answered her questions with enthusiasm. He'd invited her to try her hand, she suspected in an effort to prove how difficult a craft it was, but Karen had surprised both of them. She'd recreated one of his roses on a piece of scrap silver, and though the cuts were deeper than ideal and the shape a little off, Elsworth had declared it a fine first attempt. Karen had seized the moment and asked if he was looking for an apprentice, but Elsworth had shaken his head, telling her that he was close to retirement and couldn't afford to take anyone on. It was only when she offered to work for free two days a week that he relented.

Karen immediately informed her boss at the advertising agency that she had to go part-time, and spent every Tuesday and Friday for the next year under Elsworth's tutelage. The money she made from her own artwork more than made up for the cut in salary.

From her last year in high school to her twenty-second birthday, Karen hadn't stopped thinking about the man she'd murdered. She didn't often think about the deed, more the feeling of raw elation at getting away with it. She'd never once considered repeating the feat until the day she smudged the sheet of silver she was going to be working on.

Her first thought had been to wipe it clean, but something made her stop. She'd picked up her loupe and examined the smudge, clearly making out the individual ridges, loops and whorls. The seed of an idea was planted and when she got home that night, Karen began experimenting.

At first, she was disappointed. The work was too fine to be done with just a small magnifying glass, so she'd purchased a cheap second-hand microscope. Subsequent efforts were better, but it was clear that if she wanted to do this properly, she would have to invest in the right tools. She'd bought the Kern online, and paid good money for a set of micro-gravers, but the outlay had been well worth it. Within a month, she had an exact replica of her own fingerprint in silver. After cleaning the piece to remove every scrap of dirt and dust, she made a plaster cast of it, and once that was dry, she used the plaster mold to produce a rubber copy. She'd tested it out, but the rubber left no mark on the sheet of silver. She found that she had to rub it on her own palm first to get the oils from her skin to adhere to the rubber. Only then would it leave a print on the metal. Karen had spent three hours comparing her own print with the fake one, and it was flawless. She'd used superglue to attach the rubber prints to a pair of gloves, then tried it on her laptop, which had a biometric entry system that logged her in when she ran her finger over the scanner. That, too, had proven a success.

It was time to recreate the feeling she'd had when Dane Edwards had been convicted of murdering Colin Harper. However, research showed that her plan would backfire unless she took precautions. Several websites had mentioned that DNA could now be easily extracted from the oils in the skin that made up latent prints. Experimentation showed that most over-the-counter moisturisers left a decent enough impression on most surfaces, so she was able to use that as a workaround by smearing it on the gloves before putting them on.

Two kills later, and she hadn't made a single mistake. That was down to hours of research into forensic evidence. She'd purchased a pay-as-you-go mobile without registering it and created a new Gmail email account. The only time she used her disposable phone was when she was in the city, logging onto the internet at McDonald's or one of the other Wi-Fi hotspots. She would sit for hours learning about techniques used by police forces around the world, though she was under no illusion that everything was being divulged. It would make a criminal's life much easier if they could just look up the things to avoid when committing a robbery or murder, so much of it had been guesswork.

She'd done okay up to now, though.

The next one would be even better.

Karen had to take another break as the thought of the upcoming kill caused her heart rate to increase. It took half an hour of deep breathing exercises on the sofa to get it back to thirty beats per minutes, and then she walked back into the workshop and got back into the groove.

She'd started in the middle of the pattern and was working her way outwards. That way, if she made a mistake, it could be buffed out without having to start from scratch. It was painstaking work, but one mistake could scupper everything. Every ridge ending had to terminate at the right point, every bifurcation branching off at the correct angle.

It was worth the effort. DNA found at a crime scene could be explained away in most cases by a semi-competent defence lawyer: contamination; a deliberate planting of evidence; an innocent brush with the victim on a prior date.

Having DNA and fingerprints was a case-clincher, especially when complemented by her speciality.

Motive.

Chapter 10

Ryan Anderson woke ten minutes before his alarm was due to go off. Paul had told him to have an early night and be ready to go at six in the morning, though he hadn't been given any further details.

At least he wouldn't have to queue for the shower; none of the other residents were ever up at five in the morning.

After doing a hundred sit-ups and a hundred push-ups, he threw on a dressing gown and took his wash bag down two flights of stairs to the small shower room he shared with five others. It was barely big enough for him to wash in, and he'd lost count of the number of times he'd hit his elbows on the wall while scrubbing his body. Just how the large woman in room two managed to squeeze in, never mind wash, was beyond him.

Ryan swapped his slippers for plastic flip-flops and surveyed the tiled floor. No matter how clean he left the room after washing, it was always filthy the next time he used it. Today was no exception. Soap suds from the previous night had congealed into a green slime on the floor, and after putting a fifty pence coin into the meter, he used up half of his water allowance cleaning it away. He got under the tepid stream and washed as quickly as he could, forgoing the shampoo cycle.

He thought about leaving the shower as it was, but his years in the army had taught him self-discipline. He used the last of the water to wash down the walls and floor, then went back up to his bedsit and dressed.

Ryan was on his second coffee of the morning when the intercom buzzed. He grabbed his jacket and locked the room, then ran down the stairs. Paul was waiting on the doorstep.

Ryan offered him his phone, but Paul shook his head. "Keep it."

It promised to be another beautiful summer day, the sun already up and not a cloud in sight.

"So what's the plan?" Ryan asked as they got in the BMW. "Pay Mickey another visit?"

"No, we're off to Dover. A consignment came in and the boss wants us to fetch it."

"Dover? That's about three hundred miles away!"

"Two hundred and eighty, give or take. We can do it in about six hours if there's no traffic. And what's with the designer stubble? You forget to shave, or d'ya think you're the next George Michael?"

Ryan rubbed his chin. "I like the look. The girls dig it, too."

"Maybe twenty years ago," Paul laughed. "Word to the wise, Marsh likes his men smart, and that means shaving each morning."

"Got it. I'll buy an electric razor as soon as I get paid for this job. How much will I get, by the way?"

"Four hundred," Paul told him. "But if everything goes smoothly, you've got the job. A grand a week, cash in hand. You can get yourself a decent pad and some proper threads."

"I'll have to declare that if I want to rent somewhere," Ryan said. "They'll want payslips and all that."

"Nah, Marsh has a few properties dotted around. He's got a nice place up in Castlefield for eleven hundred a month, but if anyone asks, he's charging you six. He'll put you on the payroll at minimum wage, part-time, just enough that you don't pay tax or national insurance but enough to pay your rent if anyone starts digging. He'll make up the rest in cash."

"Sounds great. Can't wait to get out of that fucking bedsit."

Paul turned the air blue as he berated an old lady who'd waited a couple of seconds too long to pull away after the traffic lights changed.

"You got a surname?" Ryan asked.

"Gardner."

"And how long have you known Mar...Mr Marsh?"

"Ten years," Paul said as he indicated and changed lanes.

"So what are we picking up from Dover?"

Paul looked over at him. "You're a real nosy fucker this morning, ain't ya?"

"Sorry. I'm just used to being thoroughly briefed before an operation. That episode with Mickey was one thing, but this is different."

Paul honked his horn as a van driver slammed on the brakes in front of them. He spun the wheel to the right and drove around it, flipping the driver the finger as he passed.

"All you need to know is that Marsh has a personal interest in the cargo, so don't lose it."

"Me? You want me to drive it back?"

"Of course," Paul said, slapping the steering wheel. "Why the hell do you think I brought you along? You think I'm gonna drive two cars back by myself?"

"Yeah, I wasn't thinking," Ryan said.

"Good. Too much thinking will get you into trouble. Just do as you're told, and ask no questions. All you need to know is, the car has to be back in Manchester by midnight, and don't let anything stop you. Especially the police. If they seize his stuff, Marsh is gonna fuck you up big time."

Ryan remained silent as they drove through the centre of Manchester, heading south towards the M56 that would join up with the M6. If the police were likely to be interested in the consignment, it was safe to assume it was illegal.

Drugs? Guns?

This is what you signed up for, he told himself. *If you take money from a guy like Franklin Marsh, you're gonna have to do some dodgy shit.*

Paul pressed a button on the dashboard and music blared out of the speakers. He turned it down a couple of notches, and his head bobbed in time to the music. It was some techno beat, the kind of tune Ryan had never been able to get into. He much preferred songs from the late eighties and nineties, but knew that objecting to Paul's selection would do no good. He was still some way from winning the guy over, so criticising his taste in music wasn't a good idea.

Before they reached the motorway, Paul pulled into a petrol station and got out.

"Head inside and get something to eat for the journey. Take a piss while you're at it. We won't be stopping again."

Ryan went into the shop while Paul filled the BMW. He selected a couple of sandwiches for them both, plus crisps and chocolate bars. For drinks, he bought small bottles of water. If they weren't going to stop again, he didn't want a full bladder.

Ten minutes later they were on the motorway.

They talked very little on the way, mostly about Ryan's time in the army. There hadn't been any war stories to share as he'd never been called into action, but he did tell Paul about a couple of hilarious moments on exercise.

"One guy in my unit, a Geordie called Matt, was a real dick. Everyone hated him because he was a lazy sod, never chipping in to keep the barracks tidy. When we found out one summer that we were going to Germany for a week, one of the guys brought long a jar of chili powder. When Matt was sleeping, we poured it into the crotch of every pair of underpants he owned.

"Nothing happened for the first two days 'cos the dirty bastard didn't change his undies, but on day three it was hilarious. Out in the woods, marching for an hour in full kit, and suddenly we see him squirming as the sweat mixed with the chili. Every step he took, he was marinating his own bollocks. We were pissing ourselves, but the guy who'd bought the chili had decided to get the most potent blend he could. Matt ended up in hospital and was medically discharged a few weeks later. No one confessed to it, but the whole platoon got in a ton of shit for it. Worth it, though. Well worth it."

Paul's guess was correct. They reached Dover just after midday; the traffic on the M25 was kind to them. Once on the coast road, they headed west, then pulled into the car park of a housing estate. It was one huge building, and Ryan reckoned there must have been at least four hundred apartments in all. To the right was a row of lock-up garages, and a man in a black leather jacket was standing in front of one of them. Paul pulled up next to him and got out. Ryan joined him, glad of the opportunity to stretch his legs.

"This the new guy?" leather jacket asked.

"Yeah. Ryan, Terry."

They shook hands. Terry was a couple of inches taller than Ryan, and much thinner, but his handshake was firm. He had no visible tattoos, and shared the same taste in clothes as Paul.

Terry pushed the garage door up and over and the trio walked inside. There was a black Audi parked against one wall to allow the driver access, and according to the plates it was less than two years old.

Paul went to the back of the garage and picked up an old tin can. After emptying his bladder, he walked outside into the sunshine and threw the contents onto the ground. He went back inside and gave the can to Ryan. "You won't be stopping on the way home."

Ryan took the hint and filled the can. He emptied it in the same place, then put it inside the garage door.

Terry tossed a set of keys to Paul, who walked to the rear of the Audi and opened the boot. From the front of the garage, Ryan heard Paul unzip something, and guessed it was some kind of holdall. Paul studied the contents for a moment, then with a satisfied nod, he zipped it back up and slammed the boot shut.

"All yours," Paul said, handing the keys to Ryan.

"Where do you want me to take it?"

"Just follow the sat nav. I'll be behind you all the way, so don't even think about stopping to inspect the package."

"I wouldn't dream of it," Ryan assured him truthfully.

"Glad to hear it. And be warned, that baby's souped-up. It'll do close to one-eighty, but I want you to stick to the speed limit all the way. Don't draw attention to yourself. If you get nicked, Marsh will find you, no matter what prison they throw you in."

"Get home, live, get caught, die," Ryan smiled. "I think I got it."

"You better," Paul said flatly. He pulled open the door until it hit the wall of the garage and Ryan squeezed in behind the wheel.

"It's keyless entry," Paul said. "Just press the button next to the gear stick."

Ryan did so, and the engine responded immediately. "Nice."

The tank was full, and the satnav showed his current location with a blue line snaking up toward Manchester.

"Remember, no stopping."

Paul slapped the roof, and Ryan slowly pulled out of the tight space.

It was a nice motor, far better than anything Ryan had ever owned. He followed the sat nav's directions until he was on the A2, then merged onto the M2 towards London. Alone in the car, he turned on the radio and found a station that played his kind of music.

As Meatloaf blasted out of the speakers, Ryan was tempted to open the throttle to see what the car was capable of, but Paul's warning was still fresh in his mind.

Instead, he set the cruise control to sixty-eight miles per hour and tapped the wheel to the beat.

He cut across to the M20, then joined the M26 for the M25, which was back to business as usual. Two traffic jams between junctions five and sixteen held him up for over forty minutes, but eventually he got onto the M40 for the long run to Birmingham.

Ryan had eaten all of his food on the journey south, and by the time he reached the M42 he was famished. He was almost two-thirds of the way home, but he hit the outskirts of Birmingham at rush hour. After half an hour of crawling along, he got onto the M6, which was just as congested, and it was another ten miles before traffic started to thin. He managed to get back up to seventy, and that was when his heart almost stopped.

For the last two hundred miles he'd seen Paul's BMW—with Terry in the passenger seat—in his rear-view mirror, always within two or three vehicles of him. Now the only thing he could see was the blue flashing lights of a marked police car. It was twenty yards behind him, making no effort to overtake.

"Fuck!"

His first thought was to play it cool, pull over and see what they wanted, but if they decided to search the car, it would ruin his day big time. He looked back again. The cop car was a BMW, and he had no idea what speed it was capable of. The driver would certainly have chase experience, which put Ryan at a distinct disadvantage. Could the cop match the one-eighty of the Audi? There was only one way to find out.

Ryan indicated, pulled onto the hard shoulder and turned off the engine, leaving it in first gear. The cop stopped three yards behind him and the front passenger got out.

Breathe!

Ryan forced himself to relax. If he appeared nervous, it would make the cops nervous, and that was the last thing he wanted.

The cop walked up to the side of the Audi and Ryan spun down the window. "I don't think I was speeding, officer."

The cop stuck his head in the car and sniffed. "Step out of the veh—"

Ryan had been watching the traffic in his side mirror, his hand hovering over the Start button. As soon as he saw a gap, he pressed it, let the clutch out and hit the gas. The Audi shot forward, and the cop tried to grab hold of the door. He was dragged along for a few yards, then fell to the ground and rolled twice. Ryan watched in his mirror as the cop got up, ran back to the BMW and got in.

Ryan built up a lead of a few hundred yards, and he had to try to stretch that farther. He jinked into the outside lane and leant on the horn, but an obstinate Mondeo driver refused to get out of his way. Ryan undertook him and hit the accelerator, the needle quickly passing a hundred and twenty.

In his mirror, Ryan could see the cop car in pursuit. It was half a mile behind him, but had the advantage of the flashing blue lights to clear the traffic ahead of it. Ryan got back into the fast lane and leaned on the horn, flashing his lights at the cars ahead of him. They all got out of the way, and he put his foot to the floor. The needle crept past a hundred and eighty miles an hour as he flashed past the vehicles in the slower lanes, and the marked police car was having trouble keeping up with him.

His advantage wouldn't last long, though. They would call in support, which meant more patrol cars and possibly a helicopter. At that stage, he would be as good as caught. Outrunning the eye in the sky would be near impossible.

Get off the motorway.

The thought hit him as he saw the sign for junction fourteen for Stafford. He stayed in the outside lane until the last second, then darted left and just made the turn-off. He didn't slow until he saw the line of traffic held up by a set of red lights at the roundabout, but he couldn't afford to wait patiently in line. He slowed to thirty and took to the grass verge, the car bouncing on the uneven ground. He slowed even further, not wanting to damage the suspension, and at the lights he bounced back onto the road. Horns blared as he cut off two cars and a lorry, but Ryan ignored them. Getting away was all that counted, and he was already doing sixty when he reached the turnoff for the A34. The dual carriageway was mercifully quiet, and after cutting across a couple of roundabouts he continued to follow the A34 until he got to Newcastle-under-Lyme.

There had been no sign of the police since he'd left the motorway, but he was sure the car's details would have been passed to all units in the area. He decided to lay low for a while and let Paul know what had happened.

Ryan drove through the town centre, then turned off the dual carriageway and into a warren of residential streets. He eventually parked up and found his position on his phone's map, then called Paul.

"Where are you?" Ryan asked.

"Are you free to talk?"

Ryan guessed he was asking if the cops had pulled him over, and if they were listening in to the conversation. "Yeah. I'm just getting my bearings. How about you meet me." He gave Paul the postcode for the street he was parked on.

"I'll be there in twenty minutes."

"No rush. I'm not going anywhere."

Ryan noticed that his hands were still shaking slightly from the adrenaline that had flooded his body during the chase. He stayed where he was for a few minutes until his heart rate was back to normal, then started the car and drove to the next street. It wouldn't do to hang around in one place for too long, especially in an area with Neighbourhood Watch stickers on every lamppost. Some nosy sod was bound to take an interest in him eventually.

Eighteen minutes after calling Paul, he drove back to the first street and saw the black BMW cruising slowly down the road. Ryan pulled over and Paul stopped next to him, winding down his window.

"Follow me."

Ryan made a U-turn and tucked in behind him, and five minutes later they were in a business park. Paul drove around for a few minutes, then stopped on a quiet road. Ryan pulled up behind him and all three men got out of their cars.

"Nice bit of driving," Terry smiled.

Paul opened the BMW's boot and took out two licence plates. "Take the old ones off and put 'em under your seat." Ryan did as he was told, and two minutes later the Audi's makeover was complete.

"Is it safe to drive it with false plates?" Ryan asked. It was certainly risky to continue to Manchester with the originals, but this didn't make him feel much better.

"What do you think you've been doing for the last two hundred and thirty miles?" Paul asked. He tapped the front bumper with his foot. "These are the real plates."

"You bastard! You could have warned me!"

"What?" Paul laughed. "And miss a moment like this? No chance."

Terry was also grinning like an idiot. "We bought a spare pair of undies if you need 'em."

Ryan wasn't the least impressed. "This isn't funny! I could have been banged up! They could have taken Marsh's gear!"

"Relax. The other plates match an identical car that belongs to the boss. I called him and he'll pop into the local nick and report it stolen. That way, he's got an alibi. He can't be driving the car and be fifty miles away in Hale at the same time. The most that would have happened if you'd pulled over would be a breathalyser test that would prove negative."

"How do you know? What if they checked in the back?"

Paul gestured for Ryan to follow him to the back of the Audi and opened the boot. Inside was a black gym bag, and Paul unzipped it. "Take a look," he said, standing back.

Ryan peered inside, and anger rose in him like a tsunami reaching the shore. He picked up one of two-dozen toilet rolls and shoved it in Paul's face. "What the fuck is this?"

"Bog roll, comfy-bum, call it what you like. Marsh found it when he was on holiday in France and he can't get it over here, so he imports it. Softest, smoothest wipe he's ever had, apparently. Absorbent, too."

Ryan was beyond furious. "You had me drive all the way from Dover in a dodgy fucking motor for bog roll? Is this some kind of sick joke?"

"Not a joke, a test," Paul said, suddenly serious again. He nodded to Terry, who got behind the wheel of the BMW and drove away. "Get in, I'll explain."

Ryan climbed into the Audi's front passenger seat while Paul started the engine.

"A couple of years ago, the police tried to infiltrate Marsh's organisation. We got lucky when a Turk we were dealing with recognised the cop, and we dealt with him, but the boss has been paranoid ever since. Usually, he only recruits people if one of us has known them for years, but he took a liking to you. We couldn't be sure you weren't the filth, though, so he devised a couple of tests. The first was how you handled Mickey, and you passed that with flying colours."

"You mean you expected Mickey to be a challenge?"

Paul shook his head. "We wanted to see what you would do in that situation. A copper might have thought twice before laying into Mickey, but you didn't hesitate. And when the cop pulled you over earlier, you didn't try to call anyone to get them to back off."

Ryan frowned. "How do you know I didn't call anyone? I could have used hands-free."

"This says you didn't," Paul said. He tapped the satnav's plastic mount, and at the bottom there was a tiny hole. "That's a camera, and there's a microphone under your seat. We could hear you singing along to golden oldies all the way from Dover. Spandau Ballet? Seriously?"

"Gold's a classic," Ryan said defensively, but he was still angry about the way Paul had set him up. It was a lot of effort to go through just to see how he would handle being pulled over by the police. If the cops hadn't tried to stop him, it would have been a wasted journey. Unless…

"You put the cops onto me, didn't you."

Paul nodded, then looked over at Ryan and grinned. "Had to be done, mate. There's never a copper around when you need one, so I called the nines and told them a car was driving erratically on the motorway. Gave them your make and licence plate and sat back to watch the fun."

"You're a real prick," Ryan fumed.

"Calm down, you soppy bastard. You handled it well, and that means you get the job. As I said, Marsh liked you from the start. Me, not so much. But, you've proved yourself, so I'll admit I was wrong."

Ryan stared ahead. It made sense for Marsh to check him out thoroughly, and the two tests had been cleverly put together.

It didn't mean he had to like it.

"You said you dealt with the undercover cop. How?"

"Asked him to leave and never come back," Paul deadpanned. "No idea what happened to him."

Ryan knew a lie when he heard one, but he wasn't going to get anything more out of Paul.

"Is your passport up to date?"

"Yeah," Ryan said. "Got a couple of years left on it."

"Good. We're heading abroad in a few days. Pack for a week."

"Where're we going?"

"It'll be warm," Paul said. "Not shorts-and-flip-flops warm, but you shouldn't need an overcoat. A light jacket should be fine."

That could have applied to a hundred countries around the world, but Ryan suspected Paul wasn't going to reveal the destination until closer to the time.

They drove in silence for a couple of miles, then Paul ruined it by slotting a disc into the CD player. Techno music blasted out of the speakers, and Paul's head bobbed to the beat.

"You know, when we first met, I thought you were a wanker, too."

"And now?" Paul asked.

Ryan smirked. "I think I was right first time."

Chapter 11

It had been three weeks since Scott's first encounter with Kelly outside the café, and he'd barely stopped thinking about her. As he stepped aboard the treadmill in his home gym, the second meeting was still fresh in his mind.

Scott had waited three days before arranging to meet Kelly for a second time. He'd chosen a different venue, one that served lunch. He'd thought about just coffee, but this would allow the encounter to stretch beyond a brief conversation over lattes.

He tapped his fingers on the table nervously as he waited for her to arrive, scanning the passing crowd. When he saw her, his heart skipped a couple of beats.

She looked gorgeous. She was wearing a flowery knee-length skirt and white blouse with the top three buttons undone, and her hair was flowing over her shoulders as she walked towards him.

How could I believe she was in any way connected to the monster who'd almost killed me?

Such thoughts had threatened to overwhelm him in the lead up to the meeting. Could she be part of the man's gang, out to exact revenge? Was she waiting for the right moment to kill him, or hand him over to those who would?

She soon pushed such thoughts from his mind as she gave him one of her warm smiles and sat down.

"I'm so glad you called," she said. "I was going stir crazy in my hotel room."

"I know the feeling," Scott said truthfully. He handed her a menu. "I can recommend the pigeon."

Kelly made a face that suggested otherwise. "Not sure I could eat something like that. We used to feed the pigeons in the local park." She scanned the offerings, then settled for the seafood pasta.

Scott got the attention of a waiter and gave him their order, including a bottle of white wine and two coffees.

"So, this car crash of yours," Kelly said. "What exactly happened?"

"Like I said, I was driving down the road when some guy flew out of a junction and I hit him side on. Next thing I knew, I was in hospital."

"It must have been awful."

"It was," Scott said. "So, tell me about yourself."

"Well, I grew up in London, and that's about it. Mum and dad still live there, no brothers or sisters. I've had a couple of boyfriends over the years, but nothing serious. These days, I'm focusing on my career. One day I want my own design studio, but to do that I need to learn a lot more about the trade and cultivate my own contacts within the industry. I reckon another five years and I'll have enough money and experience to branch out on my own. How about you? Any family?"

"Well, my dad's in banking, mum's a sales executive, and my younger brother, Tom, lives in Canada."

The lies came easily, part of his training that now seemed so long ago. It pained him, though. Here he was, trying to get to know her better in the hope that something might blossom between them, and he was being deceitful with every breath. Not the most solid foundation for a long-term relationship. The alternative was to tell her the truth, but that was never going to happen. It would have made for an interesting conversation, but Scott didn't want to dig up the past. As far as he was concerned, that life belonged to another person.

"I tried looking you up on Facebook, but couldn't find you," he said.

She shook her head. "I don't do social media. Strange, I know, for someone in my profession. I'll set up accounts once I have my own business, but for now I can do without it. Who the hell wants to know what I had for dinner? Why would someone I haven't spoken to for five years want to know that I'm going to the cinema tonight? And which sane person announces that they're going on holiday for two weeks, leaving their house unattended?"

Scott felt exactly the same way. He saw no value in Facebook or Twitter, recognising them for what they were: advertising platforms that had become a sanctuary for the insecure and narcissistic.

The conversation turned to holidays—Scott hadn't had many, Kelly had—and then onto music and film. He was so engrossed in her that he didn't realise they'd finished their meal until the waiter brought the bill.

Scott finished his thirty-minute stint on the treadmill. It was his second of the day, and his determination to stick to the regimen set by his doctors had paid off. He hadn't used the cane in a week, and he believed he was ready to go from walking to a light jog within the next few days.

He finished off his routine with fifty pull-ups and fifty sit-ups, then took a shower and dressed. Kelly was due to arrive at his apartment at four, which left him with two hours to kill. The wine was already chilling, the chicken marinating in thyme, lemon juice, butter and garlic, and the house was spotless. With nothing left to do, Scott booted his laptop.

Since that first meeting, Scott had dug into Kelly's background as much as he could. It hadn't produced many results. If he'd had access to his old employers' network he could have found everything with a few key strokes, but there was no way he was going to contact them. They were the ones responsible for him being in this situation, and while he was happy to remain on the payroll, he wanted nothing else to do with them.

With little else to go on, he had to believe Kelly's story. Short of hacking into her school or university records, not something he knew how to do, he could only take her at face value.

What he saw, he liked.

Kelly had a mature outlook, yet could be reduced to fits of childish giggles with the corniest of puns. She knew what she wanted in life, was clearly intelligent, and while not stunningly beautiful, she was definitely easy on the eye.

There was a lot to like about her.

They'd been out a total of four times now. On the last two occasions she'd asked how his recovery was coming along, then thankfully switched the subject to her own work. It was something she was passionate about, and listening to her plan her future made him want to be a part of it.

He hadn't expected to feel that way about anyone, ever again. The ordeal he'd gone through had changed him. His self-confidence had been shattered, his trust in people severely eroded.

An episode six months earlier emerged unbidden in his mind.

Crutches beside in him his modified people carrier, he drove to his local supermarket and looked for a disabled bay. They were all occupied. He parked farther from the store, but as he hobbled nearer the entrance, he saw a beer-bellied builder get into a van. It didn't have the blue badge in the window and the driver didn't look handicapped in any way, so Scott asked him why he was parked in a disabled spot.

The large man got out of the van again, his face contorted in anger. The old Scott would have taken him down with a couple of punches, damaged knees or not. The new Scott just stood frozen, unable to kick his brain into gear.

"What the fuck has it got to do with you where I park, eh? Who are you, the fucking cripple police?" The man was in Scott's face, his breath stinking of cigarettes and last nights' beer. "What happened, someone run you over for being a nosey fucker? Go on, piss off before I give you a real kicking."

Before Scott could think of a response, the builder was back in his van and pulling away, flicking Scott the finger as he passed. Scott went straight home and ordered his food online, any plans to get back into the world abandoned.

That encounter had led to him moving to Auxerre, though not through choice. The entire episode had been recorded on someone's phone, and they'd thought it a great idea to upload it to Facebook; another reason he hated social media. The damn thing had gone viral, and one of the people who saw it was the man who'd first put Scott in a hospital bed for two months. Whoever had taken the video had followed Scott back to his car, and it was probably the plates that led them to him.

Scott began to sweat as he recalled what had happened a couple of weeks after the supermarket incident. He'd been in his ground-floor flat, staring out of the window as usual, when he'd seen two cars pull up in the street. He'd reached for his panic button, and by the time he'd looked back to the window, a number of hard-looking men in leather jackets were running up the path to his front door. He'd tried his best to get to the safe room under the stairs, which had a lock on the inside, but in his panic he couldn't get his arms and legs to work in unison. He was almost there, reaching forward for the handle, when the front door flew inwards and six men piled into the flat. They pushed Scott to the floor and dragged him into the living room by his ankles. One went to close the curtains, while another stuffed a rag into Scott's mouth and secured it in place with duct tape.

"Thought you could hide, did ya?"

Scott hadn't recognised any of the faces, but he knew who they worked for, and the next three minutes had been worse than the original beating that had put him on crutches in the first place. They stamped on his knees as he lay helpless on the floor, then one of them removed Scott's shoes as another took a pair of gardening secateurs from his pocket.

"Remember these?"

They'd used the same implement the first time around to remove two of Scott's toes, one from each foot.

"Time to finish the job," the heavy had grinned.

As the cutters bit into Scott's flesh, he'd passed out. When he'd come to, the face looking down at him was different, a mixture of concern and calm.

"Stay still. An ambulance is on its way."

Scott had no idea how the CO19 team had taken down his assailants, nor how the thugs had found him. It was only later, during his second extended stint in hospital, that his boss had mentioned the viral video of his supermarket encounter and he put the pieces together.

From that point on, Scott knew the UK wasn't a safe place, and he'd decided immediately to move overseas. After two weeks in the private hospital, with armed guards stationed outside his room 24/7, Scott had been flown to Paris, where a car had taken him to Auxerre. His personal possessions were already in the new apartment, and a nurse was on hand to help him through his convalescence.

Scott had made as little use of her as possible. He'd allowed her to shop for him and cook the occasional meal, but for the most part he spent his time alone, brooding. He'd slid down a six-month spiral of despair until Kelly had dropped into his life. Now, for the first time in a year, he had a reason to get up in the morning.

After an hour of listening to his playlist on YouTube, Scott went through to the kitchen and turned the oven on. It had just finished pre-heating when the doorbell rang. He looked at the clock.

Three-thirty.

Kelly wasn't due for another half an hour, which immediately set him on edge. Had they found him again?

Scott grabbed a knife from the block and tip-toed to the door in a crouch. When he reached it, he eased himself upright and looked through the peephole.

A distorted vision of Kelly's head looked back at him, and he realised he'd been holding his breath. He let it out, took a couple of deep ones, then opened the door.

"Hi," he said, hoping it hadn't come out as a squeak.

"I'm sorry I'm early," she said. "I got a cab but didn't realise he'd get here so quickly. I can come back if it's not convenient."

"No, no, come in. I was just about to put dinner on."

He held the door open for her and gestured towards the living room. She walked in and Scott stepped into the kitchen, where he deposited the knife he'd been holding by his side. He grabbed a bottle of wine from the fridge and two glasses, then joined her.

"Nice place."

"Thanks," Scott said. He uncorked the bottle and poured a couple of generous measures. "I'd give you the tour, but it's really just this, two bedrooms and the kitchen. You're welcome to see them."

"Show me the kitchen," she smiled. "I'll see the rest later."

He considered his answer for a long moment, but all that he could think to say was, "Sure."

He led her through to the kitchen. It wasn't fancy by any means, but it was enough for Scott. Just a simple four-hob stove, small oven underneath and a slim upright fridge/freezer. He usually cooked for one, though when she'd suggested a meal at his place, he'd jumped at the chance to show off his culinary skills.

He offered her a seat at the small dining table and took a gulp of wine before stuffing the marinated chicken with a lemon and sprigs of thyme and putting it in the oven.

"Smells divine," she said.

"Let's see what you think in two hours." He picked up his wine and sat down opposite her. "So, any news on the assignment?"

Kelly stared at her glass as she ran her finger around the rim. She finally looked up. "I'll be finished by the end of the week. I'm heading home on Friday."

Scott tried to hide his disappointment, and failed. "I'm sorry. I thought we had...more time."

"I did, too, but the vineyard contacted my boss to say they were happy with the package I've put together. The company wants me to head back to London tomorrow for my next assignment. I'll be staying overnight, then back here on Wednesday to finish up."

Scott's heart sank. Only four more days, and she'd be spending two of them on the other side of the channel.

"I was wondering...do you want to come with me? To London, I mean. For the two days."

It was the last thing Scott wanted, but didn't let it show. He'd vowed never to set foot in England ever again. Even here, in the middle of France, he felt too close to Britain's shore. His first choice would have been Australia, or failing that, the United States, but this was the only overseas safe house they had available at such short notice. Once he was fully mended, he could choose to settle anywhere in the world and the farther from England, the better.

All he could think of right now, though, was losing Kelly. They'd only met at cafes a handful of times, but Scott had never felt this way about a woman before. She was intelligent, kind, funny, and she knew what she wanted out of life. It was crazy and he knew it, but he didn't want to let her go. It was as if she was solely responsible for his escape from the misery that had engulfed him. How could he let someone that special slip from his grasp?

"I'd love to," he said. He doubted the people who had attacked him twice before would still be looking for him. Most were already behind bars. And with his new look, it was unlikely that anyone would spot him in the street. He hardly recognized himself when he looked in the mirror each morning.

Her face lit up. "Wonderful! I'll book a room at a hotel. Maybe we could take in a show."

"Sounds perfect." The more time they spent indoors, the happier he would be. And she'd mentioned one room, which sounded promising. Though one thing puzzled him.

"Can't we stay at your place?"

"It's being renovated," she said. "I'm having the small bedroom knocked through to expand the bathroom. They told me the water would be off for a few days while the work took place, so I thought I'd get it done while I was over here."

That was fair enough.

Scott got up and started preparing the vegetables for dinner. Kelly offered to help, but he insisted she remain seated and enjoy the wine. He part-boiled some potatoes and parsnips, then wrapped chipolatas in bacon before sitting back down at the table.

He asked about Kelly's next assignment, but she had no idea where it might be.

"The offices are international, so it could be anywhere in the world."

That wasn't a barrier for Scott.

"Though in all likelihood, it'll be in England."

That *was* a problem.

"Do you think you could ask for a transfer abroad?" he asked hopefully. "Somewhere with a warm climate, near a beach, with cheap wine?"

Kelly laughed, and the sound made his heart skip a beat. "I could, I suppose…if I had a good enough reason."

"I might be able to help you with that." Scott tried to top up her wine glass, but Kelly put her hand over the top.

"I'll have some more with my dinner. Too much on an empty stomach isn't good for you."

The next couple of hours flew by.

"That was the best chicken I've ever had," Kelly said as she mopped up the last of the gravy. "How did you get it so tender? Mine always dries out."

"The secret is the lemon. Prick it with a fork, then microwave it for thirty seconds and stuff it inside."

"I'll have to try that. And I definitely want to know how you got those roast potatoes so crisp but fluffy inside."

"I just part-boil them for seven minutes, drain and let them rest while the butter melts in the tray, then sprinkle with salt and pepper and a drizzle of olive oil and give them forty minutes in the oven."

"You have to invite me back," she said. "I can't wait to see what else you've got in your repertoire."

"Any time."

They retired to the living room, where Scott took a DVD from the TV cabinet.

"You told me your favourite film is Bridesmaids It just happens to be mine, too."

It wasn't, but a little white lie wouldn't hurt. He'd seen the film years earlier, and while it hadn't blown him away, he would happily sit through it again for Kelly's sake. He put it in the DVD player and sat down on the sofa next to her. Once he'd skipped past the previews, he put the remote on the table. Kelly picked up her wine glass, shifted closer to him and rested her head on his shoulder.

By the time Scott's favourite scene came on, he and Kelly were on the bed, a trail of clothes lying in their wake.

* * *

Scott took a sip of his coffee and sat back in his chair, enjoying the warmth of the mid-morning sun. This was a new café for him, set in a square surrounded by gothic buildings. The place as busy as tourists and locals mingled, none of them with a care in the world. Two children played with a ball, while others sat around eating ice cream. A woman who looked like she'd come straight from a Milan fashion show tip-tapped along on four-inch heels, a tiny dog on a lead galloping along in her wake.

Scott felt a calm like he'd never known. He couldn't even hear or feel his own heart beating, and he didn't seem to be breathing. It was as if he was watching the scene through a third person. He took another drink of the coffee, wondering what they'd put in it to produce such a soothing effect.

One of the children kicked the football across the square, and they both chased it gleefully. Scott's eyes followed the ball and saw it come to rest under the foot of a man who wasn't dressed for the occasion. He wore a long black coat and black fedora, and though Scott didn't recognise the clothes, he knew the face. It was the man who'd ended his career and left him in constant fear for his life. He smiled at Scott, then started walking towards him.

He wasn't alone.

Kelly, also dressed entirely in black, was striding next to him, and there was no warmth in her grin.

The sound of his heartbeat finally reached Scott's ears, and it felt like a jackhammer was going off in his chest. The crowd in the square seemed to fade away, until the only people he could see where the two figures in black, approaching relentlessly.

Scott was breathing heavily, like he'd run a marathon in record time. He tried to push himself out of the seat, but he couldn't move. He looked down and saw that his hands were gripping the arms of the chair, and the more he tried to push up, the tighter he held on. Scott attempted to stand, but his legs wouldn't obey his command.

Still they came closer.

Scott panicked, thrashing as much as he could but making no progress. It was as if his limbs were strapped to the chair by some unseen, unbreakable force.

"Hello again."

Scott's head snapped up and he looked into cold, dead eyes.

"Thought you could run, did you? Thought you could hide?"

Scott wanted to speak, to scream, but his mouth wouldn't work. He struggled once more against the invisible bonds, but it was no use. He was trapped, at their mercy.

Kelly leaned in, and her perfume filled his senses. "You shouldn't be so trusting, Scott." She produced a knife from her purse, a gleaming six-inch blade that seemed alive, glistening in the sunlight. Kelly smiled as she brought it up to his eye, closer and closer until all he could see was white-hot metal.

Scott jerked himself awake, his heart banging away like a heavy-metal drummer. He lay where he was, the dream still real in his head, until he was certain he was back in reality. He glanced over at Kelly, who was fast asleep, facing the other way. Her breathing was soft, contented. The clock next to the bed said it was just after four in the morning, and Scott knew he wouldn't be able to sleep again.

He got up and walked naked into the living room, picking up his boxer shorts on the way. He turned on the light and went through to the kitchen, the lingering smell of the evening meal making him hungry. He switched the coffee machine on and made himself a cheese sandwich, then sat at the table.

He'd had dreams about the man before, but they'd never involved anyone else. Why Kelly? Was his subconscious trying to tell him something, or was he just being irrational?

Scott saw Kelly's handbag hanging over the back of the chair opposite. Perhaps if he looked through, it might put his mind at ease. He went to the bedroom and opened the door a crack. Kelly was still snoring gently, so he closed it and returned to the kitchen.

The bag contained nothing to reveal her true intentions, though in truth he didn't know what he was expecting to find. A knife? Knuckledusters? He found a hairbrush, make-up, a keyring, receipts. The purse had fifty euros in it, along with her work ID and a debit card. No credit cards, but then not everyone carried them. Scott had never bothered, preferring cash.

He put the items back in the handbag, then took a bite of his sandwich.

You're just overthinking the situation, he told himself. Of course she wasn't a threat. If she were, she'd have done something by now. He'd be lying in bed with a knife sticking out of his chest, or poisoned, or...

If he allowed the past to rule his future, there was no hope. Living a life where everything scared him was no life at all.

You need to get your shit together, Davison.

* * *

They took the Eurostar through the tunnel later that morning. Scott had originally suggested flying to London, but as Kelly's office was just a couple of miles from St. Pancras station, it made more sense to take the train.

Scott felt apprehensive as they emerged from the station, his arm entwined with Kelly's. He needn't have worried. No one so much as glanced his way, and they made it into a black cab without being molested. It was a short ride to the office building in Oxford Circus, a glass edifice dumped in a Portland stone canyon. Scott paid the fare and they carried their overnight bags onto the street.

"Look, I'm probably going to be in there for a few hours. I've got to do a presentation to my department heads, then go through the upcoming projects to find a suitable fit. Why don't you go catch a film or something?"

That suited Scott. He'd much rather be in a dark cinema than out in the open. "Sure. What time shall I meet you?"

Kelly checked her watch. "It's almost noon, and my first meeting starts in half an hour. Shall we say five, in case things overrun?"

"Okay. I'll come and meet you here."

"No need. Check into the hotel and I'll meet you back there when I'm done. I won't be able to take calls or texts while I'm in meetings, so I can't let you know when I'll be out."

"That's fine," Scott smiled. "I'm sure I'll find something to keep me occupied."

Kelly stood on tip-toes and gave him a peck on the cheek, then threw her handbag over her shoulder and walked into the building. Through the glass façade, Scott watched her head straight towards the elevators, then he picked up the two bags and walked towards the Radisson.

Chapter 12

Life for Ryan Anderson had improved greatly since being added to Franklin Marsh's payroll. For one, he could now afford to eat more than just instant noodles. His new flat, too, was a vast improvement. Compared to the bedsit, it was a palace. It boasted one large bedroom, a shower room, and a large kitchen/diner, fitted with top-of-the-range appliances. It belonged to Marsh, one of dozens of properties in his portfolio, and because Ryan was only declaring a salary of around eight grand a year, the government was covering a large part of the rent. The rest of his pay was cash-in-hand.

Ryan was in the middle of washing the dishes when the doorbell rang.

He knew it would be Paul.

Ryan dried his hands and opened it, and Marsh's right-hand man walked in.

"Settled in?"

"Just about," Ryan said. He had only been in the place for three days, but already it felt like home. "Fancy a beer?"

"Nah, I'm not staying. Just wanted to give you a heads-up on your next job."

"Okay. When are we going?"

"An hour."

"Short notice," Ryan pointed out.

Paul merely shrugged. "You remember Terry?"

"Dover, the guy with the buzz cut."

Paul nodded. "He'll pick you up at six and give you the details."

"Still not gonna tell me where I'm going?"

"What's the point?" Paul said. "You'll find out when you get there, anyway."

Ryan sighed. "I was hoping you'd be done with the mushroom treatment by now."

"I said the other day that I was wrong about you being a tosser. I didn't say I completely trust you. That's gonna take time, and I've only known you a couple of weeks. You passed the tests, but it'll be months, even years, before you're one of us. Until then, you do as I say and stop with all the fucking questions. Got it?"

"Crystal," Ryan said, gesturing around the room. "No way I wanna give this up."

He was hoping to have won Paul round by now, but clearly he had work to do. He didn't know for sure what Paul's problem was, but Ryan guessed it had something to do with the story he'd told on the way back from Dover. Paul had been the one to do the background check on the guy who'd turned out to be a cop, and he blamed himself for not being thorough enough. It wasn't a mistake he was likely to make twice, which meant Ryan could expect severe scrutiny for some time to come.

With everything in his past laid bare, it shouldn't be a problem.

"Play your cards right and do as you're told, you'll look back on this and think it's a dump. You're on a good earner, now. Don't fuck it up."

Ryan had no intention of messing it up. "I'd better get packed, then. Seven days, you said?"

"Six, maybe seven. Best to take extra. And take a shower. It'll be your last one for a few days."

Ryan showered, then went to the bedroom and threw a weeks' worth of clothes into a holdall, adding his wash kit and a couple of paperbacks.

Paul had made coffee by the time Ryan reappeared. They made small talk for fifteen minutes until Paul received a text message.

"They're here."

Ryan pocketed his phone, but Paul told him to leave it. Ryan was about to argue a case for taking it, but thought better of it. To stay on Paul's good side, he would have to toe the line.

Ryan locked up and carried his bag outside. The transport wasn't what he'd been expecting.

"We're going to be in that for a week?"

"Pretty much," Paul said, smiling at Ryan's discomfort.

The Transit van looked to be quite new, but that was no guarantee of comfort.

Paul handed over a bundle of euros. "That'll cover your expenses. Terry's in charge, so do as he says."

"You're not coming?"

"Nah. This trip's a pain in the arse." Paul opened the rear door with a grin. "Have fun."

Ryan climbed in and immediately knew he was going to hate every second of the journey. The van stank of farts and sweat, and he guessed they'd come from the big guy in the passenger seat.

The cargo area contained a large inflatable mattress and two sleeping bags. There was also a wooden crate that had been turned upside down behind the driver's seat, and a petrol can. Ryan sat on the crate and Terry turned to face him.

"You drew the short straw, huh?"

"Looks like," Ryan said. "So where are we going?"

"Abroad," the big man replied. "Paul says that's all you get to know."

"This is Phil," Terry said. "He can't spell tractor but he can lift one."

"Fuck off, Tel" the heavily-tattooed Phil growled. He threw a meaty paw over the back of the seat, and Ryan shook it. The grip was powerful, just what Ryan had expected from a man with no neck and a body that appeared to be solid muscle under all the ink. He looked like he lived in a gym, and Ryan guessed his diet consisted solely of protein and steroids.

"I'm Ryan."

"I know," Phil said, and faced the front. Terry started the engine and Ryan grabbed on to the back of his seat as the van lurched forward.

"It's not going to be that bad," Terry said as he headed towards the motorway. "We'll be stopping at the services for petrol and something to eat, then taking a ferry. Until then, you might as well get your head down."

"I'm not tired," Ryan assured him. "Want me to share the driving?"

"You can take over once we get to Europe. Have you driven abroad before?"

"A couple of times, in the army."

"Oh yeah, you was a soldier," Phil said. Whenever he spoke, it sounded like he was seconds away from committing a violent act. Ryan thought it best not to antagonise him.

"Yeah, I did a few years."

"You ever kill anyone?"

"Never saw combat," Ryan said truthfully. "I joined too late for Afghanistan. Mostly it was training for a war that didn't come."

Phil seemed disappointed that Ryan had no stories to share. He grunted, then took out his phone and started playing Candy Crush.

"How long have you been working for Mr Marsh?" Ryan asked Terry.

"'Bout ten years. He's a good boss."

"A diamond," Phil agreed.

"What is it you do for him?"

Terry laughed. "Whatever he fucking wants!"

That elicited a chuckle from Phil, but his face soon straightened as he concentrated on mastering his game.

Like Paul, they were keeping things close to their chests. There was little point in pressing for further details, so he simply stared out of the window. Within twenty minutes they were on the motorway, following the signs pointing east. Ryan wasn't sure whether they were going to maintain that heading and take a ferry from Hull to the Netherlands, or switch south for Dover. There was little use asking, though.

When they joined the M1 at Leeds, Ryan knew it wouldn't be Hull. Terry was wearing headphones connected to an iPhone, and Phil had barely spoken two words in the last hour. Ryan had tried to engage him in conversation, but Phil simply held up his phone and said nothing. Ryan soon got the picture. With nothing else to do, he tried to get his head down.

He was shaken awake by banging on the side of the van, then the rear doors opened.

"Rise and shine. Time for a burger and a shit."

Ryan shook off the fog of sleep and sat up. "Where are we?"

"Thurrock services," Phil told him.

That put them on the M25. They'd bypassed Harwich, which meant Dover was their destination.

Ryan followed them inside. The food courts were quiet, and it didn't take long to order their food. Ryan had a chicken sandwich while the others stuck to beef burgers, and they all had coffee.

"Did you sleep much?" Terry asked Ryan.

"A couple of hours, I think."

"Try and get some more on the ferry. Once we cross the channel, you'll be driving for at least twelve hours. After that, Phil will take over."

"Hmm. Twelve hours, in a foreign country, in the dark. Sounds fun."

"But you're getting paid for it," Phil pointed out.

"I guess."

"Then shut the fuck up. Once you've done the run a few times, you get to choose the schedule. Until then, you get the shitty jobs while me and Terry get pissed on the ferry."

Terry saluted them with his coffee cup, then drained it and put it on the table. "I'm off for a splash. See you back at the van."

Ten minutes later they were back on the road, and with the midnight traffic light, it wasn't long before they reached Dover. Terry had explained that the two a.m. crossing was one of the quietest and easiest to get on, which was one of the reasons he'd chosen it. On the way back, they would be arriving at the maritime equivalent of rush hour, which meant they were less likely to be stopped by customs.

Once on board, the three men went up to the bar. Terry and Phil ordered pints of lager with brandy chasers, but Ryan had to settle for an orange juice.

"Before you get too pissed," Ryan said as they found an empty table, "wanna give me directions for when we get off?"

"The van's got satnav. Follow the directions and you can't go wrong. I've done it loads of times."

Twelve hours could take them anywhere. They could be heading to Germany, Poland, Spain, Czech Republic, Austria or a host of other countries. And that wasn't even their final destination, just Ryan's stint at the wheel. He hated not knowing, but had to go with the flow.

His companions polished off five pints apiece by the time they'd reached Calais. Terry was boisterous, but Phil looked like he needed medical attention.

"Is he okay?" Ryan asked.

"Phil's fine. He's a sleepy drunk. Once he gets in the van he'll be out like a light for ten hours at least." Terry gave Ryan a knowing wink. "Word of warning, though. Drive with the windows open."

Half an hour later, as Ryan joined the A26, he realised what Terry meant. Both of them were fast asleep, alternating their snores so that it seemed like one continuous sound, and the first breath of foul wind escaped from Phil's ample body. It smelled like something had crawled up inside him and died. Ryan wound down both windows, but had to see the funny side. He'd encountered something similar while on exercise in Germany a few years earlier. His unit had been posted to Bielefeld, and after five days on manoeuvres eating army-issue rations known as MREs—Meal, Ready-to-Eat—they'd gone out to unwind with a few beers and a curry. For the next two nights, the barracks had smelled much like the van.

Ryan missed the army. There had been a camaraderie that you couldn't find on civvy street. The more time he spent working for Marsh, the closer he would get to the likes of Paul, Terry and Phil, but they would never be like a family to him. He doubted any of them would risk a bullet for him, or sling him over their shoulder and carry him out of a battle zone.

If he hadn't beaten the crap out of that corporal, he would still be in the army. In fact, he'd probably have been in the SAS by now. He'd told Marsh at the interview that he didn't know whether he could have passed the selection process, but that had been a lie. Ryan knew he would have aced it.

He still vividly remembered the first time he'd attempted the fan dance, one of the disciplines on the endurance, fitness and navigation, (or "the hills") phase of the selection process. He carried a fifty-pound pack up and down Pen y Fan in the Brecon Beacons twice, starting at the Storey Arms outdoor education centre, over the summit and down to Torpantau railway station, then back along the same route. The muscles in his legs cried out for mercy at the halfway point, but Ryan knew that to give up was to abandon his dream. His breath coming in gulps, he fought through the pain, telling himself that each step was one closer to victory.

The target time to cover the fifteen miles was four hours, and Ryan had done it with over half an hour to spare.

He soon discovered that if the fan dance was hard, the worst was yet to come: the long drag. Forty miles in twenty hours, navigating from one checkpoint to the next with a map and compass. Ryan did it as part of a paid excursion run by an ex-SAS trooper. He shouldered a forty-pound pack, plus water, food and a steel pipe to mimic the rifle he would have to carry on the real thing. Selection was carried out twice a year, once in the summer and again in winter. Having done the fan dance in July, he opted for the December course to make sure he was familiar with both climates.

It almost killed him. The rain was constant, his soaked clothing and pack adding at least fifteen pounds to his burden. It had hurt, too. Blisters developed within a few miles, but he kept it to himself, knowing the tour operator would bin him for health and safety reasons. For fifteen more hours he sucked it up, telling himself over and over that pain was temporary, fleeting, and wasn't worth throwing away his career for. Mental toughness was what got the few successful people through, not merely physical strength, and Ryan managed to get in within the time limit by simply refusing to be beaten

Since then, he'd done the SFBC, the special forces briefing course, a week-long ordeal that gave candidates an insight into what selection entailed. It included tests like map reading, swimming and running in the hills. At the end of it, each candidate was told their likelihood of making it past selection. Ryan had been a solid pass.

Now, the only challenge he faced was getting through the next twelve hours without suffocating on the smell of rotten eggs.

His stint at the wheel was uneventful. He stopped once to fill the tank and take a leak, and Phil woke up, pissed in the petrol can, then went back to sleep without a word.

At four in the afternoon, Ryan woke them.

"There's a services up ahead. Fancy some breakfast?"

Phil simply groaned, and Terry asked where they were.

"We just passed Dijon."

Terry stared at his watch, probably trying to get his eyes to focus. "Looks like we're on schedule. Good work. Now find a place that does a full English."

"In France? Are you kidding?"

"Of course I am. Just stop at the next place."

Ryan pulled into the services and parked up. He got out and opened the rear doors for his companions. Terry bounced out, as if the drinking session on the ferry had never happened. Phil looked like he was close to death.

"You gonna be all right to drive?" Ryan asked him.

Phil groaned and forced himself into a sitting position. He rubbed his head, then inched his way towards the door.

"He just needs coffee and food," Terry said. "He does this every time, and hardly ever crashes."

"What d'ya mean, hardly ever??"

Ryan saw the smirk on Terry's face and knew that he was just winding him up. "Git."

They walked into the building and found a McDonald's restaurant, where they loaded up on burgers and caffeine. Ryan skipped the coffee, planning to get his head down for a few hours while Phil took the wheel. Better to die in his sleep than see it coming, he decided.

They were back on the road forty minutes later. Terry decided that Phil hadn't recovered enough and opted to drive for the first couple of hours, which helped Ryan relax enough to sleep. The humming of the van's tyres aided him, and within minutes of re-joining the motorway, he was out cold.

* * *

Ryan jerked awake to the sound of doors squeaking open, and for a second he struggled to work out where he was. Then the smell of rotten…something invaded his nose, and he remembered he was in the back of the van.

He stood up and stretched, then climbed out.

"*Ciao!*" Terry grinned. "Welcome to Italy!"

Ryan saw Phil in the distance, running awkwardly towards a building that had various brands emblazoned on the wall. "What's his problem?"

"Needs a shit," Terry said.

"No, I mean why doesn't he talk? I can barely get him to grunt in my direction."

"He does. We had a great conversation about football while you were asleep. Don't take it personally, but Phil doesn't like new guys."

"How come?" Ryan asked.

"It goes back a couple of years. This guy Kenny joined the team and he and Phil became good friends. They were inseparable, did everything together. Went to the Etihad to watch City play, best drinking buddies, you name it. They were only a shag away from being lovers. Then one day we discover that Kenny was an undercover cop. It broke Phil's heart. He has a lot of trust issues now, and won't open up to anyone unless he's known them for years."

"That's understandable," Ryan said. "I just don't see why he has to be a dick all the time."

"If you're still around in five years, he might buy you a pint. Until then, just do a good job and earn our trust."

"You, too?"

"Hey, Kenny was a mate of mine, too. It's nothing personal."

It was a fair reaction. Ryan would probably have done the same in Terry's shoes.

Terry locked the van and started walking towards the services. Ryan kept pace with him.

"What happened to Kenny?"

"Dunno," Terry said. "One minute he was with us, the next he was gone. Marsh told us he was a copper and that we should never let our guard down."

Ryan didn't believe for one minute that Terry hadn't been told of the cop's fate. Marsh would certainly have used Kenny as an example to others, and among such a tight-knit group, word must have spread. Another sign of their caution around the new guy.

Ryan was prepared to wait as long as it took.

After a brief pit stop, they were back on the road. They by-passed Milan and continued south with Terry at the wheel.

Ryan didn't try to engage them in conversation. Instead, he waited until the sun rose, then pulled out one of the paperbacks from his holdall.

"What'ya reading?" Phil asked.

"Fair Game," Ryan said. "It's the eighth book in the Spider Shepherd series by Stephen Leather."

"Spider shepherd? He rounds up spiders?"

"No, you gimp," Terry laughed. "Dan Shepherd. He's ex-SAS but his nickname's Spider 'cos he ate one for a bet."

"A big, hairy one," Ryan added. "You know the books?"

"Read the lot," Terry smiled. "Brilliant, all of 'em."

"Can I borrow it after you?" Phil asked.

"Sure."

"It's got some big words," Terry warned Phil, "and no pictures."

"Will you stop making out I'm stupid just 'cos I'm buff."

"Buff as in big ugly fat fucker!"

Ryan tried to keep a straight face so as not to antagonise Phil, but it was a battle he was never going to win.

"Bollocks to the pair of ya," Phil growled. He turned his attention back to his phone and continued his epic quest to crush his candies.

It was six in the evening by the time they reached Bari on Italy's east coast. Terry drove to the ferry port and parked up.

"We've got three hours to kill before we board the ferry. Let's get something to eat."

Terry led them inside one of the terminal buildings. It was a bar-cum-cafe, and he ordered beers for himself and Phil.

"You can have a few when we get on the ferry. Don't want you getting pissed and driving into the sea."

That suited Ryan just fine. While they started another binge, he tucked into a sandwich. As before, their conversation was about football, girls and fights. Ryan tried to turn it to other topics, but they pretty much ignored him. He even tried a couple of jokes, but they still seemed unwilling to let him into their little circle.

Eventually he gave up and said he was going to wait in the van and read. Terry tossed him the keys, and Ryan walked back to the vehicle.

He'd finished his book and was making inroads on the second when they came stumbling towards the van, their spirits high. Terry locked Phil in the back and got into the passenger seat. Ryan put the book back in his bag and tossed it into the cargo hold.

"Where to?"

"Take that road there," Terry said, pointing vaguely out the window.

Despite the poor instructions, Ryan got them on the ferry. It was a 150-metre roll-on-roll-off, and once parked they headed straight for the bar on one of the upper decks. Terry peeled off and joined them ten minutes later. He handed Ryan a key to his cabin.

"Where are we heading?" Ryan asked as he sipped his first cold beer of the trip. Terry had kept hold of the boarding passes and his Italian wasn't good, so he was still in the dark.

"Durres. It'll take about ten hours."

"Where's that?"

"Albania," Phil butted in. "Makes Moss Side look like a fuckin' boom town. When we get there, don't forget to put your clock back twenty years!" He exploded with laughter at his own joke and chugged his beer.

"It's the arse-end of the world, all right, "Terry added. "When we dock we'll drive to Tirana and stay there for a couple of days."

"Then what?"

"We come home, job done."

"We're not picking anything up?" Ryan asked. "We're certainly not dropping anything off."

"We'll drop you off if you keep asking so many fuckin' questions," Phil said, suddenly serious again.

Ryan put his hands up in submission. "Just curious, that's all. It's a long way to come just to head back again."

Silence ensued, until Phil burst into life as he remembered a strip club he'd recently visited. Terry was familiar with it, and the conversation was back on track.

Admitting to himself that he wasn't going to be accepted by them on this trip, Ryan said goodnight and went in search of his cabin. It was on one of the lower decks, just above the water line. There was a porthole, bed, dressing table and a bathroom, which contained a small shower, toilet and sink. Ryan stripped off and took his first shower in a couple of days, then got under the sheets naked.

He wanted to sleep, but one question kept him awake: what was the purpose of the trip? Was it another test? If so, what was the objective? To see if he could drive? Check his tolerance for bodily emissions? They must be bringing something back to the UK, but what, and how? Was it something small enough to carry on their person? If it was, surely it didn't need three of them to make the journey. Terry or Phil could have flown out, picked it up and flown back in the same day, instead of wasting a week on the road.

They must have driven for a reason. Was the package too sensitive to take through airport security? If so, surely there would also be a risk getting it through customs at Dover. That said, he'd never known anyone to be patted down when crossing the channel to France and back. The border security officers were focused on finding drugs, cigarettes and illegal immigrants, and rarely the contents of a traveller's pockets.

Ryan sensed that the method of transport was key. The van was important somehow, and he needed to find out why.

He eventually drifted off as the ferry crossed the Adriatic. When he woke, it was still dark outside. Ryan dressed and went up to the café. There were a lot more people than he expected, mostly those who hadn't bothered to purchase a cabin for the crossing. The majority were asleep at tables, but some were awake. He bought a coffee and took it outside onto the deck. Here, even more people were sleeping.

"You're up early."

Ryan spun to see Terry standing beside him. "I could say the same about you. You knocked a few back last night."

"I can handle my beer," Terry said. "It's Phil that struggles in the mornings."

"So what's the plan?"

"Drive to Tirana, meet a couple of guys, then check into the hotel for a couple of days. You can do what you want while we're there."

"Such as?" Ryan asked.

"Get pissed. Get laid. It's up to you. We're booked into a hotel in a place called The Block. It's where the last dictator used to live. Nice area. Got a casino, bars, nightclubs, restaurants, everything."

"What about you two? What will you be doing?"

"We'll be around," Terry said, sipping his hot drink. "Phil likes the casinos. Reckons he's an expert at blackjack but every time he plays he spunks his dosh. I tried telling him it's fixed but he won't listen. Not the sharpest tool in the box, our Phil."

Ryan decided to try his hand once more. Terry seemed a rounded guy, unlike Phil, who was likely to explode at the drop of a hat. "How come it took three of us to drive all this way when one could have got on a plane? Is this just another one of Paul's tests?"

"No, we're here on business, and that's all you need to know. After you've done the run a few times, we can let you in on it, but until then, you do your share of the driving and that's it."

"Fair enough," Ryan said, and immediately changed the subject. "There's a casino, you say?"

"Yeah, right next to the hotel. You play?"

"Sometimes," Ryan said. "The trick is to go in expecting to lose everything. Anything else is a bonus. But I do know one way you're guaranteed to walk out with a small fortune."

"What's that?"

"Walk in with a big one."

Terry laughed. "I like that one. Tell it to Phil next time he comes out empty."

"No, thanks. I'm not sure he likes me as it is. Not sure I want to piss him off."

"Phil's a teddy bear," Terry said, spitting over the side of the ship. "Once he's a mate, he's a mate for life. As I said before, he don't like new people. He'll come round eventually."

"I hope so. It'll be pretty shitty if all the trips go like this one."

"That it would," Terry agreed. He tossed his empty paper cup over the rail. "Let's go get breakfast. We'll be docking in a couple of hours."

Terry went to rouse Phil from his slumber and they entered the café just as Ryan was sitting down to a bowl of muesli. They ordered a plate of cold meats and bread and sat down next to him.

"Feeling okay?" Ryan ventured.

Phil looked at him blearily through yellow eyes, then put his head down and stuffed some meat into his mouth, chewing noisily.

"I'll drive to Tirana," Terry told Ryan. "It's only a couple of hours. When we meet our contacts, say nothing. They're suspicious of new faces, just like me and Phil."

"Who are they?" Ryan asked, then put his hand up. "Never mind, it's need to know."

"That's right," Terry said. "Once you've been here a few times, I'll let you know what's going on."

After breakfast, Ryan went down to his cabin and packed his bag, then joined the others on the car deck. Phil was waiting by the rear of the van, and Ryan guessed he was getting the cheap seat. He climbed in, and ten minutes later they were on Albanian soil.

Ryan didn't know what Phil or Terry were referring to when they'd described the place. It certainly wasn't London or New York, but it wasn't as run-down as he'd imagined. There were lots of apartment buildings, but they looked quite modern, and the streets were relatively clean.

They were soon on the main highway that linked the port town of Durres to Tirana, the country's capital. This was more like the Albania Ryan had imagined, the two-lane road lined with old-style buildings nestled among their more modern glass-fronted contemporaries. After ten minutes of more of the same, Ryan settled back with his book.

Before he knew it, they'd arrived at their destination. Terry opened the back doors. "Out you get, and bring your bag."

Ryan did as he was told and found himself on a narrow road between two breeze-block walls, beyond which were single-storey dwellings to the right and on the left a four-storey house in the early stages of construction. It wasn't the kind of place Ryan would have chosen to stroll through on his own. He joined Terry as he headed for a green metal gate. "Remember, leave the talking to me."

Ryan nodded. The gate opened before Terry had a chance to knock. The man who emerged looked to be in his forties and had a body much like Phil's, only leaner. He wore a black leather jacket and black jeans, with a T-shirt that had once been white but was now a faded cream colour. His face hadn't touched a razor in a few days. Terry approached and gave the man a one-armed hug, and Ryan could see that the Albanian had a pistol tucked into the front of his trousers.

Phil was next to say hello, then Terry introduced Ryan.

"This is Endrit. Endrit, Ryan."

Ryan shook his hand, which felt like a vice.

Terry put an arm around Endrit's shoulder and they walked away with the Albanian doing most of the talking. They looked back once at Ryan, then continued their discussion. Ryan couldn't hear what they were saying, but Terry seemed to be in conciliatory mode. He reached into his jacket and handed Endrit a stuffed envelope. The man toyed with it for a few moments, then nodded and put it inside his own jacket and held his hand out. Terry gave him some keys and Endrit walked back to the gate and closed it behind him.

"Now what?" Ryan asked when Terry rejoined them.

"A cab will be waiting at the end of the street," Phil told him, and set off walking away from the green gate. "We check into the hotel, then you can do what you like until Friday afternoon."

That gave Ryan just over two days to kill, and he planned to use the time constructively.

If they wouldn't tell him the purpose of the trip, he'd find out for himself.

Chapter 13

John Latimer waved goodnight to Paul Benson as the detective sergeant left the office. The shift had long since finished, but Latimer was using every spare minute of the day to help build a defence for his friend James Knight.

It wasn't looking good.

Forensics had confirmed that the hairs found on the body of Sean Conte belonged to Knight, and along with the shoe imprints, motive, lack of alibi and fingerprint evidence, the case against him looked watertight.

His personal investigation into the shoes had been a waste of time. The size and make had been available in dozens of stores across the country, and he'd requested details from each of them for credit and debit card purchases. It had taken a couple of weeks to get the information, but ultimately it had proven fruitless. None of the sales were to people on the list of suspects Latimer had compiled. These were people Knight had arrested during his career, but if one of them had bought a pair of size-nine Minster Wayfarers, they must have done so with cash.

Latimer had even made a second list containing the names of everyone who had worked with Knight over the years, but a comparison with the shoe list had drawn a blank, too.

The deadline was getting uncomfortably close. Knight was on remand in Brixton and the trial was due to commence in just under six weeks. All the defence lawyer had to offer was to point out that evidence could be fabricated and planted at the scene. That wouldn't explain how Knight's bloody fingerprint came to be on the inside of Conte's wallet.

The autopsy had concluded that Conte had died of blunt force trauma after having been subdued with a stun gun. Toxicology had revealed no foreign substances.

Latimer didn't think Knight was capable of beating someone to death, particularly a helpless man, over a building extension. Sure, the episode had cost Knight his entire savings, but was that enough to make such a level-headed man take such drastic action?

One thing that gave Latimer hope was the lack of tyre tracks. Having visited the crime scene, it was clear that a vehicle had driven into the woods and that Conte's body had been dragged from it to the grave. There were scuff marks in the ground where his heels had dug in, but they ended abruptly a few yards from his final resting place. Someone had taken the time to obscure the tyre tracks. Why go to that trouble, yet leave some much other evidence on and around the body? It pointed to someone setting Knight up, and he didn't have long to find out who it was.

DCI Ingram passed his door. Latimer hoped she would keep walking, but she paused and then stepped into his office.

"Your shift finished a couple of hours ago," she said. "Tell me you're not still wasting time on the Conte murder."

Latimer had told her his theory about the tyres a week earlier, but she hadn't been convinced. As far as she was concerned, the evidence gathered at the scene was just one step short of a full confession.

"I was just researching ways to transfer fingerprints," he told her. "It wouldn't be the first time it's happened."

Ingram sighed. She put her briefcase on a chair and draped her coat over it. "I know you and James were close—"

"—are close," Latimer corrected her.

"Quite. But I fear this…misguided loyalty is only going to lead to disappointment. The evidence against him is overwhelming, John. Surely you can see that."

Latimer could. If he were the investigating officer, he'd be rubbing his hands together right now, convinced that he would secure a conviction. The lack of tyre marks wouldn't be a concern for him.

But he wasn't heading the case, and James Knight was not a killer. Latimer was certain of it.

"The odds do seem stacked against him, I'll admit, but he's a friend, and he deserves the best possible defence. I aim to give him that."

"Even at the expense of your own health?" Ingram asked. "Look at you. When was the last time you had a good night's sleep? And this issue with your wife can't be helping matters."

"What issue?" Latimer asked.

"The court case. I read about it in the paper."

The last thing Latimer wanted was the entire force knowing his problems, but it was too late now. The reporter had come to his home wanting to hear Fiona's side of the story. She'd given him the standard response, that she couldn't comment on it with the trial looming, but he'd been persistent. Eventually he'd left, and Latimer had expected to hear nothing more until the trial was over, but the story made page two of the local paper. It had been a rehash of previous articles including the original social media posts, and the only input from Fiona had been her refusal to comment.

"That's not a problem," Latimer told her. "The other woman hasn't got a case. It's not something we're worried about."

He hated lying to his boss, but he didn't want Ingram thinking he was spreading himself too thin. If she knew how much it was affecting him, she would force him to drop the Knight enquiries.

In truth, the prospect of having to hand tens of thousands of pounds over to an unknown author simply because she wrote a book along the same lines as his wife wasn't pleasant. With that financial sword dangling above his head, he could understand why people did crazy things when money was involved. Latimer had fantasised many times about what he'd like to do to Bethany Ambrose, and none of it was sexual.

"Any luck following up on the tip-off?" Ingram asked.

That had been another thing that made Latimer think Knight was being framed. The email account that the message had been sent from had been created the day before Hampshire police had been told where to find Conte. It hadn't been used since. The email provider had logged the IP address and other details of the device used, but it was a common brand of phone and had been connected to a public Wi-Fi account. The phone hadn't been registered or used again since, and even if the shopping mall still had CCTV recordings, it would take him weeks to go through the footage. He'd be looking for someone using their phone, and that would be fifty per cent of the people on the premises. Trying to pick the informant from thousands of suspects would be impossible.

"No, that's a dead end. Whoever sent the email went to a lot of trouble to remain anonymous, which again makes me think James is being screwed over."

"Or they just value their privacy," Ingram pointed out.

"Perhaps, but given the location of the grave, it's unlikely that anyone would come across it by accident. I think the person who sent the email also obscured the tyre tracks, and they would only do that if they were the killer."

"Then why not pass that to James's defence team and let them put it to the jury," Ingram said as she picked up her coat and briefcase. "And get some sleep," she added as she left his office. "You look terrible."

Chapter 14

As Phil had promised, a cab was waiting for them by the time they walked back to the main road. Terry got in beside the driver and Ryan shared the back seat with Phil, whose frosty attitude gave him the perfect excuse to stare out of the window.

Ryan noted what looked like a laundrette, with garish orange writing above the door, and he memorised the name of the street as they reached the corner. He kept repeating it to himself as they journeyed deeper into the capital, breaking it down into single syllables to make it easier to remember.

It took half an hour to get to the Grand Hotel on Rruga Ismail Qemali, and they'd each been booked into single rooms. As soon as he got to his, Ryan wrote down the name of the street and placed the small slip of paper in his wallet. He hit the shower, changed into a new shirt and slacks and went down to the bar to meet the others. Phil and Terry were already there, their pint glasses almost empty.

"What are you having?" Ryan asked.

Terry polished off his beer. "Not for us. We're hitting the town." He dug into his pocket and handed Ryan a roll of Albanian bank notes. "That's thirty-five grand, about two-fifty in real money. Don't spend it all at once."

"And don't go getting nicked," Phil added as he got off his bar stool. "Be back here at midday on Friday, or you're walking home."

"There's a couple of good restaurants on this street," Terry said as he slipped his jacket on, "and the casino is about a hundred yards on your right as you leave the hotel. If you're looking for company, turn left out of the hotel, walk right to the end of the street, take another left and a right at the roundabout. Best strip club in town." He clapped Ryan on the shoulder. "Have a good one."

The pair left, and Ryan sipped his beer until he was sure they weren't going to return. He threw the barman a hundred lek and left half of his drink. He wanted to keep his head clear.

He stopped at the first restaurant he came to. On such a pleasant day there were plenty of people eating al fresco, but Ryan chose a small table inside, near the back, and picked up a menu. A waitress appeared, her long black hair tied in a ponytail. She smiled provocatively at Ryan, something he was used to. If this were a social trip he'd have happily flirted with her, but he didn't have time for distractions. He ordered the seafood pasta and she sashayed away, glancing over her shoulder to see if he was watching. Ryan saw her head turning and averted his eyes, pretending to be engrossed in a fresco on the wall.

He wished he had his phone. It wasn't as if he had many people to call, but he liked to keep up to date with current affairs. It would also be handy to look up the street he was going to visit that night, but he could always pick up a map from a local shop.

After eating Ryan went for a walk. He found a place that catered to tourists and bought an A-Z map, and after quickly consulting it he made his way to the river. It was a huge disappointment, looking more like an open sewer. Still, he sat on the grass of the sloping bank and ran through the index until he came to the street he was looking for. It turned out to be about three miles south-west of the Grand Hotel, an easy stroll, but he would take a taxi to a nearby street and walk from there. He had no idea what the crime rate was in Tirana, and he didn't plan on finding out the hard way.

Ryan wandered the streets for a couple of hours. He found a clothes shop and purchased a black jersey, then went back to the hotel. There was no sign of Phil or Terry, and he assumed they were enjoying a few beers and a lap dance. Ryan took his book down to the bar at five in the afternoon. He found a quiet table and had a couple of beers while he finished his novel, then went into the restaurant and had a steak before retiring to his room at seven. He set the alarm on his watch for midnight and was asleep in minutes.

* * *

When he woke to the *bee-beep, bee-beep, bee-beep* of his watch, Ryan wet his hair and ran a comb through it, then took advantage of the coffee-maker in the hotel room. By one in the morning, dressed in his new black jumper and black jeans, he was waiting at the kerb in front of the hotel. The late-summer night was cool, but not quite jacket weather. After a couple of minutes, a cab stopped to pick him up. Ryan gave the driver a slip of paper with the name of a street written on it. He'd looked it up on the map and it was a couple of hundred yards from the target address. Traffic was much lighter than when they'd hit Tirana twelve hours earlier, and he arrived at his destination within minutes.

After the taxi drove away, Ryan crossed the street and walked down a narrow road. A couple of minutes later, he was once again at the location where he'd got in the cab with Phil and Terry earlier that day. In the dark of the moonless night, it looked even more unwelcoming.

The house he was looking for was about seventy yards away, down another small road. From where he was standing, Ryan could see the house that was in the midst of construction. It was about twenty yards from the ten-foot green gate where they'd left the van, and tall enough to give him a good view of the surrounding area.

There was no one around, so Ryan walked down the lane and then climbed over the six-foot concrete wall and into the grounds of the new build. The structure was little more than a breeze block shell, and the stairs had yet to be built. Fortunately, a ladder stood, giving access to the top floor. On the second floor, he found a window that overlooked the green gate, but all he could see was what looked like a workshop, and the huge double doors were closed and secured with a padlock. As there were no signs of life, Ryan decided to take a closer look. He climbed back down and jumped the wall into the lane, then walked to the gate. It was made of steel and was too tall to see over, so Ryan moved to his right and grabbed the top of the wall. He peered over the top and saw nothing, so he pulled himself up and over and walked over to the workshop. There were two small windows on either side of the double doors. Ryan looked through one of them and saw the back of the Transit van, its rear doors open.

The only thing he recognised was the licence plate. The side panels had been removed, as had the floor of the cargo area, and the pieces were strewn around the inside of the building.

Ryan doubted they'd come all this way just to have the van serviced. It could only mean one thing; they were going to line the walls with something. Drugs, probably, or even weapons. Customs officials at the posts might be on the lookout for suspicious packages or large amounts of alcohol and cigarettes, but they wouldn't go to the trouble of disassembling a vehicle as part of their inspection routine.

Ryan had seen enough. He climbed back over the wall and walked calmly to the main road, then headed back towards the centre of the city. He hoped to hail a cab on the way, but few seemed to venture out this far. He ended up walking the entire way.

As he neared the hotel, he didn't feel much like sleeping. The only venue that seemed to be open at two in the morning was the casino, so Ryan walked in. The receptionist asked for photo ID and he handed over his driving licence, then she buzzed him inside.

He'd been to casinos a couple of times, and this was much like the others. Slot machines lined the outer walls, while the gaming tables dominated the centre of the room. Ryan navigated towards the roulette table and handed the dealer ten thousand lek. He got fifty chips in return.

Three spins later, they were gone. He parted with another ten grand and fared better, leaving the table half an hour later with thirty thousand in his pocket, a profit of around seventy pounds. As he walked towards the cash desk he heard a commotion at the blackjack tables, and it wasn't hard to spot the man at the centre of it.

Phil was clearly drunk, and like many hardened gamblers, he was blaming the dealer for his losing streak. Ryan saw two huge members of security making their way to the table, and he decided to try to defuse the situation. He jogged over to Phil and put an arm around his shoulder.

"I think it's time to go, mate."

Phil shrugged him off, stood and pushed him in the chest, and Ryan fell backwards onto a small table laden with coffee cups and sandwiches. He picked himself up just as the security team reached Phil. One of them grabbed Phil's arm and immediately regretted it. Phil's punch caught him on the jaw and he dropped like a stone, and the other bouncer went straight in for the knockout. He pivoted on his left foot and his right whipped around and struck Phil on the side of the face. He went sprawling, and the bouncer dropped a knee onto his chest and started pounding Phil's face.

Ryan couldn't stand by and do nothing. Phil had brought this on himself and was getting what he deserved, but they were a team.

Ryan grabbed the bouncer's collar and yanked him backwards. He expected the man to land on his back, but despite his size, he was surprisingly agile. He sprang to his feet and swung his arm in a wide arc, but Ryan saw it coming. He ducked underneath the swing and delivered two quick punches to the man's kidneys, then one to the side of his face. The bouncer staggered, then shook his head and roared as he came back for more. Ryan waited until he was two yards away, then spun ninety degrees and thrust out a leg. The bouncer walked into it and the sole of Ryan's boot connected with his jaw, sending him crashing to the floor.

Ryan didn't stop to inspect the damage. He grabbed Phil and dragged him to his feet, then helped him to the exit. By the time they reached the door, Phil was ready to go back for more, but Ryan kept a tight hold on his jacket and pulled him outside.

"You'll get us nicked, you fuckin' idiot!"

"Get off me!" Phil thrashed around, but Ryan had the advantage of being sober. He pulled Phil towards the hotel, ignoring his protests, and by the time they reached the Grand, Phil had worn himself out. Ryan took him up to the fourth floor and deposited him on his bed. He made a couple of attempts to get up, then abandoned the struggle and closed his eyes. Within seconds he was snoring.

Ryan went to his own room, brushed his teeth and lay on his bed. He now knew the reason for the trip, though what they would be smuggling back to the UK remained a mystery. Terry had hinted that there were regular runs to Tirana, so it was possible that one day he'd discover the nature of the consignment. Given what they'd said on the journey, though, he didn't think it would be any time soon.

Chapter 15

When Kelly arrived at the hotel, Scott could tell immediately that something was amiss. She smiled and kissed him when he opened the door to let her into the room, but then she turned cold, as if a switch had been thrown.

"What's wrong?"

"Nothing," she told him. The smile was there, but devoid of warmth. "I hate meetings, that's all. They sap the life out of me. I'd rather wrestle sharks than sit listening to a presentation for an hour."

Scott had never had that problem, but could imagine how boring it would be.

"Did they say what your next assignment would be?" he asked, hoping the answer might be one that cheered her up a little.

"No, not yet. There are about four or five that are suitable for me, but most are in London. There's nothing in your neck of the woods."

Scott guessed that was why she seemed a little off. Perhaps she was just sad at the prospect of leaving France and ending their brief relationship. He knew he was.

Their love-making that night was tepid, perfunctory, and afterwards she turned over and fell straight to sleep. The next morning, he was barely been able to get a smile from her, and although she perked up as the day wore on, she still wasn't the girl he'd fallen for.

They took the two o'clock shuttle back to France. Scott bought sandwiches in the buffet car.

"When will they have a decision about your next assignment?" he asked.

Kelly shook her head as she munched the sandwich, then swallowed. "It'll be made tomorrow."

"But you're pretty sure it'll be London?"

"It looks like it," she said, and Scott detected a hint of sadness in her voice.

He'd already told her that he never wanted to return to England. A flying visit was one thing, but the mere thought of settling back there set his heart racing. He could hear his heartbeat, and a knot grew in his stomach. He wished there could be some sort of compromise, a way to continue what they had, but the possibility seemed remote. He considered asking her to quit her job, but that would have been selfish. She had her life mapped out, and the next five years would be used to gain experience in the market before branching out on her own. He couldn't ask her to abandon her plan simply because he was besotted with her. He could certainly afford to provide for her, so she could concentrate on starting her own business, but what if things didn't work out between them? What if they grew apart after a few months?

"I really wish we could find a way to make this work," Kelly said, as if reading his thoughts, "but I have to think long-term. I know you can't live in London again, and there's no way I could commute. The only option would be to request a transfer overseas, but these days everyone wants to do that."

He was glad to see she was thinking along the same lines, but they weren't any closer to a resolution. Perhaps the only way forward was a long-distance relationship.

"If you're happy to keep seeing me, we could meet up at the weekends," Scott suggested. "I could travel to London one week, you come visit me the next."

Kelly's face lit up at the suggestion. "That could work," she beamed.

"Then it's settled."

Her expression suddenly changed and her head dropped. Scott sensed bad news. "There's also a possibility I could be sent to Australia."

"What? But...that's fantastic!"

"It is?"

"Of course! I'd love to go there. How long would that be for?"

"A year," Kelly said, suddenly happy again. "It's a role within the Melbourne office, again working for the wine industry. A couple of people have already requested it, though, so chances are I won't get it."

Scott hoped she was wrong. Australia would be the perfect location, even if it was only for a year. "We'll just have to keep our fingers crossed," he said.

The train emerged from the tunnel and soon after they pulled into Calais station. Scott was happier now that they were on French soil once more, but he'd give it up in a heartbeat to be with Kelly. If she could swing the job in Melbourne, he would follow her just as soon as she was settled. If things were still good by the time her placement was up, he might think again about persuading her to quit and start her own business.

A month earlier, he would never have imagined his life turning around so quickly. He'd gone from wallowing in self-pity to having a reason for living, and he would do whatever it took to keep the feeling going. Kelly seemed as keen as he was to make a go of it, and the worst-case scenario was that they only got to see each other at weekends. That was still more appealing than never seeing her again.

"When we get back to Auxerre, I won't be able to stay the night," she said, bursting his bubble. "I've got so much packing to do."

"Surely it's just a couple of suitcases," Scott said.

"You'd think, but I was always a heavy traveller. Kitchen sink, and all that. I've got to see my client tomorrow morning, but I was hoping we could spend the evening together."

"I'd love that," he said, and his heart danced its own jig of approval.

Chapter 16

As Terry drove the van back through France, Ryan couldn't help but wonder what contraband was secreted around and below him. It had to be something that would fetch a good price on the black market, so he ruled out cigarettes. Drugs was the most likely answer.

Terry and Phil had knocked on his hotel room door on Thursday morning to thank him for intervening at the casino. Ryan had shrugged it off, but Phil seemed genuinely grateful. He'd invited Ryan to go with them that day, and had treated him to dinner followed by a few beers and a lap dance at the Candy Club. More beers had followed, and he'd collapsed into bed at two in the morning.

Ryan had been worried that the local police might be called in to investigate the brawl at the casino, but Terry had squared that away. He'd spoken to Endrit, whose mafia connections were enough to convince the casino manager to forget the entire incident. They didn't call the police, and in return the casino didn't burn to the ground.

The three of them had taken equal turns at the wheel on the drive back, and during the obligatory drinking session on the ferry ride to Bari, Terry and Phil had treated Ryan as if he'd always been one of their own. When they'd stopped at one of the services in France, Terry had purchased several crates of beer for each of them, along with a few cartons of cigarettes for Marsh. He'd called it a bonus for a job well done.

All went well until they reached Calais. Terry pulled over near the Eurostar terminal and turned off the engine.

"We're taking the train from here," Terry said, and he and Phil got out and opened the back door for Ryan. He picked up his bag and climbed out.

"No, I mean me and Phil are taking the train. You take the van across on the ferry."

"How come?" Ryan asked as he tossed his holdall onto the passenger seat.

"The boss's orders," Phil said.

Ryan suddenly knew the reason they'd brought him along. He would be the one to take the van through customs in Dover, and if the hidden cargo was discovered, he would take all the heat.

Of course, he couldn't point that out. If he did, they would know he'd been sneaking around the workshop, or at the very least, assume he'd guessed the reason for the trip.

"No problem." Ryan got in the van and started the engine. "Where do I meet you?"

"Ashford International," Terry told him. "I already put it in the satnav. We should be there by five," He handed Ryan a pack of cigarettes and a lighter. "Smoke one of those. If you get stopped, it'll look bad for a non-smoker to have cigs in the back."

The two men threw their bags over their shoulders and walked towards the rail terminal. Ryan lit one of the cigarettes and blew the smoke out without inhaling. It smelled disgusting, but Terry's logic was flawless. Once he'd burned through it, he tossed the butt out the window and pulled away, following the electronic map on the dashboard to the ferry.

All the way across, Ryan wondered how many others had been made to play patsy on the Albania run. There must have been a few over the years, but he'd never seen anything on the news about vans with secret compartments being discovered by customs officers. That was a good omen. Also, it was unlikely Marsh would try it if any of his other shipments had been intercepted.

That thought helped him relax a little, and as he drove off the ferry he was convinced he just had to get out of the port and he'd be home free. He joined the queue at customs, watching as officers picked random vehicles to inspect. He smoked another cigarette as he crawled forward, turned on the radio and found a song he could sing along to. It took his mind off what lay ahead, and he was belting out a Blondie track when the young officer at the checkpoint pointed for him to pull over to the right. Ryan flicked him a mock salute and did as instructed.

"Turn the music off a second," another customs officer said, a man in his fifties.

Ryan hit the button.

"Where have you travelled from?"

"Here and there," Ryan said. "France, Italy, Albania," He'd considered this answer on the ferry, and the truth was the best option. Although his passport hadn't been stamped, there would be a record of the van on the ferry between Bari and Durres. If they checked, it would leave him with some explaining to do.

"What was the purpose of the visit?" He was looking around the inside of the cab, breathing deeply. Ryan knew he was looking for signs of drug use.

"Just a holiday, pick up some booze and fags."

"Can you open the back please?"

Ryan got out and walked around to the back of the van.

"Why Albania?"

"I know someone from Tirana," Ryan said. "I used to work with him. Name's Bashkim," Ryan answered with the name he had read on the hotel bartender's name tag. He opened the rear doors of the van and the customs officer looked inside.

"How many cigs have you got?"

"Twelve hundred," Ryan said, "plus six crates of beer."

The man climbed in the back and moved things around, looking for anything hidden among the cases of booze. He looked at the sleeping bags. "You sleep here?"

"Yeah. Cheaper than a hotel and lets me keep on the road."

"Why two bags?"

"The other one's for my mate. He pulled out at the last minute and I couldn't be bothered taking it out before I set off."

With one last look around, the officer climbed out. "Off you go, "he said. "Sorry to keep you."

"No worries," Ryan smiled, his stomach churning.

The official moved on to the next vehicle in the queue, and Ryan got back in the van and drove out of the terminal. After a week on the road, all he knew for certain was that something was concealed in the frame of the vehicle. He hoped he didn't have to wait too long to discover what it was.

Chapter 17

Karen spotted Bobby Waterstone as he walked along Pitshanger Lane towards his flat. He was late, but that was a good thing. There were fewer people around at midnight, and those at home would be tucked up in bed, not staring out of a window.

She let him get ahead a few hundred metres, then started the car and slowly set off after him.

He was quite a big man, but like her previous victim, it was mostly fat covering his bones. Unlike Sean Conte, though, she wouldn't have to get physical with him. The method she'd chosen tonight called for subtlety and relied on his animal urges.

Waterstone was unsteady on his feet, which was normal for a Saturday night. In fact, he spent most evenings at a nearby pub, and afterwards he always bought a takeaway kebab before walking home. It had been the same routine for the five weeks she'd been watching him.

Five weeks since her last kill.

Time to strike again.

Karen eased up beside him and pressed the button to wind down the passenger window.

"Hi. Could you tell me how to get to Clarendon Road?"

Waterstone walked over to the car and bent over to look inside. He clearly liked what he saw, and so he should. She'd spent hours on her make-up and choosing the right clothes, tight-fitting jeans and a snug woolly jumper. Her hair hung provocatively across one side of her face, and she was giving him her best come-hither smile.

"No problem, darling. I'm heading that way myself."

Karen knew that. Clarendon Road was one street away from where Waterstone lived.

"Go to the end of the street," Waterstone said, "then take a left and then a right at the—"

"I'm hopeless with directions," Karen said. "If you're going that way, get in and I'll drop you off."

Waterstone looked ecstatic, like Christmas and all his birthdays had come at once. He opened the door and got in beside her, a big, cheesy grin on his face.

"Hope you don't mind the smell," he said, holding up his wrapped kebab.

"Are you kidding?" she winked. "Who doesn't love a big portion of hot meat?"

Karen put the car in gear and set off, and her hand crept over his crotch. "Wow! That's a *huge* portion."

Waterstone looked stunned for a second, then started gyrating his hips under her hand. He didn't seem to notice that they'd already turned into the next street, his sole focus the attention he was getting from her delicate fingers. He put his hand on her thigh and she let out a soft moan. When she indicated for the next turn, Waterstone suddenly came to his senses.

"That's the wrong way," he said. "You need to take a right."

"I know," Karen smiled, as she rubbed his hardening cock, "but it feels like we've got some unfinished business."

At the next junction, she put on the handbrake and took a small pill bottle from her pocket. She shook out the contents and popped two into her mouth, then offered the other two to Waterstone.

"What are they?"

"Quaaludes," she said. "Ever tried them?"

He shook his head.

"You should. You'll never have a better sexual experience, I guarantee it."

Waterstone grinned as he swallowed the pills, and Karen turned right, toward the destination she had scoped out over the past five nights. As she faced away from him, she spat the pills from her mouth.

"How do you feel?" she asked a few minutes later as they neared the industrial park.

Waterstone fumbled for words, but none came. He looked groggy, like he'd just gone a few rounds with a heavyweight champion. The combination of beer and the sedative tablets she'd given him had worked wonders.

Karen took his right arm and held it up. When she let go, it flopped by his side. *Perfect.*

She took the hypodermic needle from inside her calf-length boot and took off the protective cap. Waterstone saw it and tried to move, but his body wouldn't obey.

"Hmmmn...harrummnn..."

"Yes, I know," Karen smiled, "I hate needles, too, but it'll all be over soon."

She plunged the hypodermic into his neck and pressed down until the chamber was empty. The sodium thiopental went to work quickly, and Waterstone was soon unconscious. Karen rested his head against the window and set off for the countryside.

She didn't go as far as Hampshire, much as she wanted to. She was constrained by time, but the spot she'd chosen was as good as any. She was on the A40 in minutes, and when she reached the Swakeleys roundabout near Uxbridge, she headed north. The place she'd picked was off a country lane. She drove up to a dilapidated gate and got out of the car, listening carefully. The only sound was the breeze rustling the leaves in the hedges on either side of the lane. She pushed the gate open and quickly got back in the car and drove through, parking up against the hedge so that she couldn't be seen from the road. After closing the gate again, she slowly inched the car around the edge of an open field. The grass came up to the windows, and bushes dotted the landscape.

With her lights off, Karen followed the hedge for a hundred yards until she reached the corner of the field, then turned left. Fifty yards on, she stopped. A small copse stood to her right, and she got out of the car again. As with her last burial plot, it hadn't been disturbed in the days since she'd last been here.

She got to work, dressing in a disposable paper suit and putting men's shoes on her feet. With her mask in place, she opened the passenger door, dragged the unconscious Waterstone into the trees and let him flop into the grave. She'd dug it a few nights earlier, knowing she wouldn't have time to do it this evening.

Karen went back to the car and took an envelope from her handbag. She put it on the seat, then donned the gloves she'd created and took the large sheet of polythene from the boot. She took several hairs from the envelope and went over to the grave, placing them on Waterstone's body. One went under his fingernail, another between his collar and skin. She dotted the rest about his body, then spread the sheet out in the grave. The plastic was huge, twice as long as her victim was tall, and just as wide.

Waterstone groaned, reminding her that her work wasn't complete. She ran to the car and took the knife from under the rubber carpet in the footwell. Waterstone was still motionless when she got back to him. Karen dragged him into the grave, on top of the plastic sheet, and kneeling above him and to the side, put the sharp blade up against the point where she'd injected him and drew the knife across his neck. She jumped back as blood spurted from the wound. His body began to convulse as the red liquid ran down his throat, drowning him.

After a minute, he lay still.

Karen dipped a couple of fingers in the pool of blood that had formed in the hollow of his neck, then grabbed Waterstone's arms and laid them across his chest. The bloody prints were clear, but she couldn't rely on just a couple of sets. They might be obscured when she filled in the grave, so she made sure there were fingerprints all over the knife, too. She placed the murder weapon on his chest, wrapped him in the plastic to preserve the evidence, then picked up the shovel and started filling in the grave. Twenty minutes later, she was done.

Back at the car, she stripped off the protective suit and put it in a black bin liner along with the mask, shoes, gloves and the shovel. She put the bag in the boot, then drove back to the gate and parked behind the hedge, where she picked up a branch and retraced her steps to the grave. From there, she followed the car's tracks, obliterating them as she went. She didn't want a farmer to discover them, or to follow them to the grave. The body had to remain undiscovered for a couple of weeks at the very least.

Returning to the rental car, she paused to admire her own cleverness. She had placed strips strategically on the number plate. The number six now looked like an eight, and the letter *V* had become a *W*. If any security cameras had picked her up in the area where she'd met Waterstone, they would send the police on a wild goose chase.

After closing the gate, Karen drove back to London. She stopped behind a row of shops and dumped the black bag in an industrial waste bin, then drove south. All she had to do now was remove the tape from the plates, hand the car back and get home in time for the next phase of her plan.

Chapter 18

Paul Gardner knocked on the door to Franklin Marsh's office before walking in. "It's on for tonight." He closed the door and took a seat on the sofa.

"What time?" Marsh asked.

"Seven. They wanted to pick the venue but I told them it was our choice or they could sod off."

"Too right. I don't trust those bastards."

Paul didn't trust the Turks, either, but in this business, they often had to deal with undesirables. At least the Turks respected boundaries, unlike the Russians. Erkan Demir had been running his operation in Manchester for ten years now, and though there had never been any violence between the two gangs, it didn't mean they wouldn't screw Marsh over given half a chance.

"I sent Terry to the meet," Paul said. "He'll watch for anyone turning up early."

The place he'd chosen was an abandoned farm north of Manchester. It was one of a few remote locations Marsh used to exchange goods with his customers. Usually it was drugs, but on this occasion, the Turks had requested weapons. Their own supply route had been closed down after an eagle-eyed customs officer had discovered a cache of AK-47s hidden inside a shipment of industrial pipes. The shipment had been allowed through and tracked to its destination, resulting in numerous arrests, but like Marsh, the head of the Turkish mafia never went near his own merchandise. A few lower ranks were sent down, but the men at the top were untouchable.

"Who are you taking with you?" Marsh asked.

"Just Phil," Paul replied.

"Not Ryan?"

"I thought about it, but he's only a couple of months in. I'm not sure I trust him a hundred per cent yet."

"Why? Billy Marsden already gave him the all clear. What more do you want? Is he acting strange, asking too many questions?"

"No," Paul admitted. "If I tell him to hit someone, he doesn't think twice. Terry says the same. And he never asks what you do. It's just…it's too much of a coincidence, the way you met him."

Marsh lit a cigarette and blew a cloud up towards the ceiling. "You checked him out personally. You've been to all the places he worked, you've spoken to people who worked with him, it all checks out. There's no gaps in his employment history bigger than a few weeks. That's not enough time to join the police and train to go undercover."

"I know, everything looks fine…maybe I'm not over Kenny. Still hard to believe he was a copper."

"It's natural," Marsh said. "When something like that happens, you suspect everyone, but you can't let it consume you. If we spend all our time looking for moles, we'll get nothing done. Ryan checks out, that's good enough for me. If you don't want to use him tonight, fine, but I'm not paying him all that money just to slap people around."

"Got it," Paul said. He went to the fridge and took out a bottle of orange juice. "If the Turks like the samples we show them tonight, I'll take Ryan on the exchange."

Paul left the office and walked through the empty nightclub to the rear exit. The Vine wouldn't be open for another six hours, but the cleaning staff were hard at work and the bar manager was stocking the fridges ready for another hectic night. Paul got the barman to lock the door behind him, then drove to collect Phil from the gym. He had to wait half an hour in the café, sipping a coffee, while Phil finished his daily routine and took a shower.

"We going tooled up?" Phil asked when they got in the car.

"No need. We're just showing them samples. If they want more, then yeah, we'll be carrying."

Thanks to traffic, it was a two-hour drive to the farm. When they got to within a mile of it, Paul called Terry.

"Anything?" he asked.

Terry's job was to ensure no one arrived at the rendezvous early to set a trap. Customers were always given the location at short notice. That made it difficult to get people into place if the buyer planned to turn a straightforward deal into a robbery.

"All clear," Terry replied. He would stay hidden until the deal was over and everyone left.

Paul pulled up to the barn half an hour before the meeting was to take place. He and Phil went inside and saw that Terry had laid out the two sample weapons, an AK-47 and a Zastava M57 7.62x25mm pistol, on a bale of straw. As usual, there was no ammunition.

They talked about sports until Terry called at three minutes before seven. "Range Rover. Black." It pulled up outside the barn a couple of minutes later.

Three men got out. Paul recognised two of them: Oguz, the Turkish ringleader's right-hand man, and Ilker, a heavy who was built like Phil. The third man was a surprise. He was dark skinned, though he didn't look Turkish. At least, not like the Turks Paul had dealt with. While they were rough and ready, this man was immaculately dressed in a silk suit and polished shoes. His beard was neatly trimmed, and he strode with a confident gait.

Paul shook hands with Oguz, then offered his hand to the stranger, who ignored the gesture and pointed to the two weapons. "Is this all you have?"

Paul didn't like the man's tone, nor his arrogance, but the deal was worth a lot of money. Marsh wouldn't be pleased if he just told the guy to fuck off.

"These are samples. You'll get the rest once we agree on a price."

The suit reached into his pocket and Paul tensed, but he pulled out a pair of latex gloves. He put them on, then picked up the AK-47 and stripped it down in seconds, examining every component. He put it back together equally quickly, then turned to the pistol. "What is this?"

"A Zastava M57," Paul said. "It's Yugoslavian. Well, what used to be Yugoslavia."

"You mean it's old," the man said, tossing it on the bale. "I need reliable weapons, not this junk."

"They work fine," Paul insisted, wishing he could demonstrate by putting a bullet through the prick's head. "If you want something else, the price goes up. A Glock is going to be two grand, but you can have these for nine hundred."

"I want Glocks," the suit said. "Ten, plus ten rifles. I also need five hundred rounds for the handguns and three thousand for the AKs. What about magazines?"

"Not a problem. How many do you need?"

"Three for each Glock, ten for each rifle."

It sounded like the man was preparing for war. The only reason he'd need that many magazines was if he planned to use all the ammo at once, but that wasn't Paul's concern. His job was to sell the guns, not worry what they were used for. "We can do that." He did a quick calculation. "That'll be forty grand for the AKs, twenty for the Glocks and five grand for the ammo. I'll throw the magazines in for free."

Marsh would have settled for him bringing back a lot less, but Paul was adding a surcharge for the suit's disrespect. He expected the man to haggle, but he did not seem price-sensitive.

"That is acceptable. How long before I can take delivery?"

"Nine days," Paul told him. It would mean another trip to Albania to get the AKs and the ammunition, and the handguns would have to be imported from Austria. They would be broken down to their component parts and shipped separately, then reassembled in the UK before being sold on. That was, if Marsh let the transaction go ahead.

"Let my friend know when they are ready." The suit stripped off the gloves and walked back to the car without another word. Oguz threw Paul an apologetic look and followed.

"What a wanker," Phil offered as the car pulled away.

"Totally," Paul agreed. There was something about the man he didn't like. Not just his arrogant manner, either. As Franklin Marsh's right-hand man, Paul got to meet a few of the major underworld figures, and this guy wasn't one of them. Only one thing came to mind. "I bet he's Al-Qaeda, or ISIS, whatever they are these days."

"Could be," Phil said. "You gonna tell Marsh?"

"I have to. He thinks he's selling to the Turks."

Paul called Terry, who said that the Range Rover had left. Paul instructed him to take the weapons back to their caches spread over the greater Manchester area, from lock-up garages to legitimate businesses.

It was nine by the time Paul, Phil and Terry returned to the Vine, still an hour away from opening. Paul found Marsh doing his usual walk-through, ensuring the nightclub was ready for the late-night crowd.

"How did it go?" Marsh asked as he sipped a glass of single malt.

"They want ten Glocks, ten AKs and a shit-load of ammo."

"Good. Good. Get a decent price?"

"Sixty-five grand," Paul said.

Marsh's eyes widened. "Sixty-five? From the Turks?"

"I don't think the Turks were the buyers. They had a guy with him and he did all the talking. I think Erkan's acting as a middleman, getting a finder's fee from the sale."

Marsh didn't react well to the news. "Who the fuck was he?"

"I dunno. Some Arab. When I mentioned the price, he didn't flinch."

"And you didn't think that was strange? You ask him for at least ten grand more than the guns are worth and he doesn't bat an eyelid. That smells like copper to me."

Marsh turned and walked to his office. Paul recognised it as a bad sign, but had no choice but to follow. Once inside, Marsh poured another whisky but didn't take his usual seat behind the desk. Paul thought it best to remain standing, too.

"He didn't seem like a cop," Paul offered.

"Oh, he didn't? And how the fuck would you know? You thought Kenny was clean and he was a copper. You think Ryan's a copper when he's as pure as the driven fucking snow! What makes you the expert all of a sudden?" Marsh was red in the face by the time he'd finished his outburst.

"If anything, he's more likely to be one of them terrorists than a cop."

Marsh looked like he was about to explode. "You what? You fucking what? Are you telling me you just offered ISIS all the weapons they need to go tear up the Arndale centre?"

"We don't have to go through with the deal," Paul said. "No money changed hands, so if he's a cop, he can get me on conspiracy, that's all. But if we don't go ahead with the deal, even that would be shaky. We could call it entrapment."

"So now you're a legal expert, too, eh? Okay, smartarse, let's say he's not a copper. Let's say he really is Al-fucking-Qaeda. The moment I tell the Turks the deal's off, I lose all credibility. Word will soon get 'round that I can't even supply ten fucking AK-47s! I'll be a laughing stock!"

"That isn't on me," Paul said. "I had no idea the Turks would bring in a stranger. If you're gonna be angry with anyone, it should be Erkan."

Paul's logic had the desired effect. Marsh took his seat and drained his glass before lighting a cigarette. Paul remained standing.

"I'll have to go and see him," Marsh said. "There's no way I'm arming those bastards."

"What will you tell him?" Paul asked. "You can't just say it's because the guy he brought along looks like a Muslim. Erkan is, too. That would really piss him off."

"I know," Marsh said. He was twiddling his cigarette, spinning it around the way he always did when agitated. "I'll give it a couple of days, then say our supplier on the continent was shut down. I'll tell him it'll be a couple of months at least before I can get my hands on any weapons."

"You think he'll go for it?"

"Why wouldn't he?" Marsh said. "Erkan knows what AKs go for, so I'd be stupid to turn down such a great price for no reason."

"What about the Arab, though? He'll just get his guns from someone else."

"Not if we tell the old Bill," Marsh said. "Let Billy Marsden know what happened. He can pass it up the chain as an anonymous tip."

"Will do."

Marsh extinguished his cigarette, then poured himself another shot of single malt. "Sorry for going off at you. You did nothing wrong."

"No worries," Paul said. "I'm gonna shoot off if that's okay. Got an early start tomorrow. That junkie loser Mark Bramley is late on his payments again. Seems he forgot the lesson Ryan taught him. I thought I'd give him an early morning wake-up call."

"Off you go," Marsh said. "And take Ryan with you. Bramley needs teaching a proper lesson, you got me? Tell Ryan not to hold back. If he doesn't, then maybe you'll believe me."

Paul nodded and left. When he got out into the street, he sent Billy Marsden a message to meet him for lunch the next day, then drove home.

Unsure as he still was about Ryan, Marsh had a point. His background checked out. Paul himself had been around to three of his places of work, and at each job they verified that Ryan had been a good employee—the factory incident apart—but hadn't lasted very long. His average stint was a few weeks, but he managed nearly four months on the building site. The men there remembered Ryan as pleasant and funny, though he rarely socialised after work.

Maybe Marsh was right. Maybe Ryan was who he said he was. After almost a year, a copper would have made some mistake by now, or at least have some of the team pulled for their illegal activities, but the recent Albania runs had gone unhindered, and the drugs were still flowing in from Europe.

The nagging doubt wouldn't leave him, though. Ryan had been tested twice and passed both times, yet Paul still wasn't convinced. Maybe it was time for one final attempt to put the matter to bed for good, and today's meeting gave him an idea.

Chapter 19

Ryan Anderson understood why people wanted to work for Franklin Marsh. After ten months in the man's employ, Ryan had saved over fifteen grand in cash, he had a nice apartment, a wardrobe full of designer clothes and girls flocking around him when he visited the Vine nightclub. His looks had a lot to do with it, but being one of Marsh's men was what drew them to him.

He had everything a man in his twenties could ask for. It was just a pity it wasn't legal.

But then, that was why he was there, to find out everything he could about Franklin Marsh's empire and help bring it down. Only it wasn't going as planned. He'd imagined that once he'd got his foot in the door, he'd soon learn everything about Marsh's business, but that hadn't happened. He'd been used as an enforcer, collecting debts and putting rivals in their place, but what he really needed was to gain access to Marsh's inner circle. He needed to be in Paul's position, or at least up there with him, but the prospect looked a long way off.

The most he'd learned about the operation was that there were regular runs to Albania, but what they were bringing back was still a mystery.

His boss wasn't happy.

Malcolm Brigshaw had sold the job as long-term, but with every passing week, he was pushing for more information. Perhaps Brigshaw was getting stick from his own superiors, but Ryan doubted it. Brigshaw didn't seem the type to take shit from anyone.

He'd first met the man while in 2 Para. Ryan had been a 23-year-old corporal, and as he'd told Marsh, he was up for his third stripe and weeks away from attempting SAS selection. That was, until Malcolm Brigshaw had turned up at Colchester Garrison.

* * *

Ryan marched down the corridor to the CO's office and knocked on the door. He heard the instruction to enter and opened the door, coming to attention in front of the commanding officer's desk and offering a smart salute.

"Corporal Anderson reporting as ordered, sir."

"At ease," Lieutenant Colonel James Crofter said, giving a quick salute in return. He was a thick-set man in his late forties, and filled the chair he was sitting in.

"Is this the man?"

Ryan turned his head a little and noticed another man in the room. He was dressed in civvies, a grey suit and highly polished shoes. He looked to be in his fifties, with short, thinning grey hair neatly trimmed. He had a military bearing, confirmed by the regimental tie.

"It is," Crofter confirmed. He didn't seem happy with the other man's presence.

The civilian stood. He was an inch shorter than Ryan's six-two. "Let's take a walk."

He opened the door and Ryan looked at his CO, who waved him out. Ryan stood to attention once more, saluted and turned smartly on his heel. In the hallway, he followed the civilian out into a warm May morning and fell in step.

"How are you, Ryan?"

"I'm good, sir. Mind telling me what this is about?"

"All in good time. My name's Malcolm Brigshaw." He looked around. "This place has changed somewhat over the years."

Ryan said nothing. He wasn't interested in which buildings had been replaced over the years, and he thought mentioning it could send the old man down nostalgia lane without telling Ryan the purpose of his visit.

"I used to be stationed here a few years ago," Brigshaw said, pointing to his left. "My barracks were just there."

"That's nice. Look, if you're here to write a book about the garrison's history, I'm the wrong man."

That brought a chuckle from Brigshaw. "Hardly. Things change all the time, it's inevitable, and only fools wallow in nostalgia. No, I'm here to discuss the future." He looked over at Ryan. "Your future."

"I think that's pretty much set. I get my third stripe in a few weeks, then I'm off to Hereford."

"Ah, yes, I saw your application. And I must say, your record has been exemplary to date. The SAS would have been a good fit for you, I'm sure."

Ryan stopped in his tracks. "What do you mean, 'would have been'?"

"I'm here to offer you an alternative path." Brigshaw resumed walking, not turning to see if Ryan was behind him.

"If there's a new unit that's better than the SAS, then I want to know about it." Ryan was level with Brigshaw once more. Whoever he was, he appeared to have access to military records. Ministry of Defence, perhaps?

"Not new," Brigshaw said. "We've been around for a long time, but we fight on a different front. Rather than storming buildings in a far-off land, we protect our country from domestic foes. We just don't use military tactics to achieve our goal."

"Ah, so you're MI5."

Brigshaw smiled. "The CO said you were a bright lad. Yes, I'm with the security service."

"So what do you want with me? Are you auditioning for the new James Bond?"

"He was Six," Brigshaw said. "But yes, we're recruiting. Tell me what you know about MI5."

"Only what I've seen on TV. Spies running around with guns, going undercover to infiltrate the bad guys."

Brigshaw nodded. "Yep, that's about as far from the truth as you could possibly get. In fact, we rarely venture out into the real world, and when we do, we're seldom armed. Up until now, the footwork was done by agents, which is a bit of a misnomer. People think agents are the ones who are employed by us, but they're actually members of the public who already have an in with the people we're interested in. We call them covert human intelligence sources. Think of them as informers. People like myself, who run the agents, are called intelligence officers."

"I stand corrected," Ryan said. "So what do you want from me? I don't know any villains."

"Well, unfortunately, we do. And our old strategy wasn't effective. We'd throw money someone's way, hoping for intel, but most of the time we were double-crossed. Fed fake leads about incoming shipments, things like that. You see, the people we're after don't take kindly to snitches, so few people took us up on our offer. It was decided that a tactical revamp was required. From now on, the agents we run will be professionals and will work directly for MI5."

Ryan shrugged. "So you're sorted. Use your own guys or get some undercover cops and away you go."

"We thought of that. Twenty years ago, it might have worked, but criminals are a lot more sophisticated these days. Not only can they perform more rigorous background checks, but there's also the chance that an undercover officer might trip across someone he's already had dealings with. No, what we're looking for is someone with a totally clean history."

Ryan could see where the conversation was heading. "You want me to work undercover for MI5?"

"In a nutshell."

It certainly wasn't what Ryan had expected when he'd marched into the CO's office. He'd thought perhaps it might be to discuss his promotion, or his request to try out for the SAS. He never imagined being headhunted to become a spy.

"I'm flattered," he said, and meant it, "but I've worked hard to get where I am. I don't want to throw that all away."

"You won't be throwing anything away. Think of it as a secondment. As I said, we need fresh faces for every operation. Once you've been in the field, you become a liability. You'd spend two years with us, perhaps three, then you can return to the army and pick up where you left off."

"Simple as that? They'd just welcome me back, no questions asked?" The words were out of his mouth before Ryan had time to think. It surprised him that he was actually considering the offer.

"That's the arrangement we have with the MoD," Brigshaw said. "You'd spend a year training, then take on your one and only role. Once that's complete, you'll have a job here waiting for you."

Ryan would be twenty-five, perhaps twenty-six by the time he returned. Still well below the maximum age to join the SAS. As long as he kept himself fit, he should have no problems. There were other things to consider, though.

"If I have to infiltrate a jihadist terror cell, won't they notice my white skin and accent?"

"We don't deal exclusively with Islamic extremists. It's the main focus of our work at the moment, but we're also interested in the people who supply them with weapons. That usually means home-grown organised crime. That's where you come in."

"Okay. What about pay and my pension?"

"You'll get double what you're receiving at the moment, and they'll continue to pay into your army pension. We'll also put a lump sum into a civil service pension for you."

The financial side sounded good, but Ryan wasn't about to commit without more details.

"What would I have to do?"

"Get in with the wrong crowd," Brigshaw said. "We've got our eyes on a few people, career criminals, but they operate at arms' length from the illicit side of their businesses, so we can't pin anything on them. Your job would be to get in at the bottom of one of these organisations and work your way up until you're close enough to the man at the top to get details of his operation."

"And what if they twig that I'm MI5?"

"It won't happen. They can do all the checks they like, but there'll be nothing to tie you to the security services."

Brigshaw seemed certain, but he'd already admitted it was a new venture for the security service. Ryan would have preferred something to measure his confidence against, like a few successful missions that ended with the agent walking away in one piece.

"How long do I have to think about it?" Ryan asked.

"I'll need an answer tomorrow. And I don't need to tell you that this conversation never took place. If anyone asks why you were talking to me, I'm a solicitor, informing you of a great-aunt's will."

They'd walked around the block and were almost back to where they'd started.

"How do I contact you?" Ryan asked.

"Just give the CO your answer. He'll get in touch with me." Brigshaw stopped and turned to Ryan, looking him in the eye. "I wouldn't have asked if I didn't think you could do the job. Of all the people we had to choose from, you were the standout candidate. You're cool under pressure, your decision-making skills are exemplary, and you're capable of looking after yourself. You'd be doing your country a great service."

Brigshaw turned and walked away, leaving Ryan Anderson with plenty to think about.

* * *

The next morning, Ryan went to see the CO. While his roommates had gone to the mess, Ryan had spent the night in his barracks, chewing over Brigshaw's proposal.

His initial reaction was to dismiss the idea. His career was mapped out and everything he wanted was within his grasp. He was confident that he would pass SAS selection, and within a year he'd be badged and working towards his first deployment. He had joined the army to fight, and it was all he'd ever wanted.

Until Brigshaw—if that was his real name—had turned up with his unexpected offer.

The more he thought about it, the more appealing it sounded. Three years wasn't that long, and he'd probably learn a new range of skills in this assignment. The extra money would come in handy, too. He could put it toward a deposit on his own home after releasing from the forces. That, and both an army and a civil service pension to look forward to.

The job didn't sound too difficult, either. Growing up in one of the poorer areas of Leeds, he'd mixed with villains all the time. Most were just brainless thugs, but there were some real bad boys around at that time. Ryan had never got involved in anything like drugs or theft, though. He'd always known he'd enlist and went out of his way to keep his nose clean. He'd been in a couple of scrapes with some of the hard cases, but had given as well as he'd got. People had soon learned not to mess with him.

It wasn't that Ryan was scared to walk into a lion's den. He could look after himself, and hanging around with career thugs would be like going back to his school days. What really concerned him was going in alone. In the army, his mates had his back. Out there, he'd be on his own.

After hours of consideration, Ryan could see no real downside, and he'd fallen asleep with visions of James Bond playing in his head.

Ryan knocked on the CO's door and waited to be ordered inside. After saluting, he got straight to the point.

"Sir, I wish to accept Mr Brigshaw's offer."

Colonel Crofter looked disappointed. "That's your prerogative. I trust he explained the situation fully?"

"I know that I'll be gone for three years at the most, and that I can come back here and continue where I left off, sir."

119

"That's right, though don't assume you'll get that third stripe the moment you return. This little venture will put you back a year, at least."

Ryan could sense that Crofter wasn't enamoured with the whole arrangement, but that was to be expected. If Ryan were running the show, he wouldn't want a civil servant coming along and cherry-picking his best men.

Having to wait another year to make sergeant wasn't that big a deal anyway. He'd apply for the SAS the day he returned and earn his extra stripe there.

"I understand, sir, but I still want to go ahead with it."

The Colonel picked up a pen. "Fine. Report back here at fourteen hundred, sharp."

Ryan left, unsure of what was going to happen next. His secondment could take weeks to process, and though Crofter wasn't the petty kind, Ryan was sure it wouldn't be business as usual until his discharge papers came through.

After a five-mile run and lunch, Ryan returned to the colonel's office, but didn't make it inside. Brigshaw was waiting for him, a smile on his face. He walked past Ryan towards the exit. "Come."

Ryan followed him out into the sunshine.

"I got your message," Brigshaw said. "I'm glad you decided to join us."

"It was too good an opportunity to pass up. So what happens now?"

"We have to decide on your exit strategy."

"What do you mean?" Ryan asked. "Don't I just complete the paperwork?"

"It's not as easy as that. I told you, these people know how to dig. If they find out you just left the army for no good reason, it'll raise flags. We need to manufacture a way for you to be kicked out."

Ryan stopped. "Whoa! There was no mention of that yesterday. I don't want to come back here in a couple of years and find I get passed over for promotion because of a strike on my record."

"Your record will be wiped once your mission with us is complete," Brigshaw assured him. "This needs to be done thoroughly, with no cutting corners. If the man you're after has a friend in the army, it could all go pear-shaped unless everything rings true. Now, I thought perhaps you could steal something, or get involved in a fight with a colleague, anything that will lead to a court-martial."

The notion of being expelled from the army didn't please Ryan, especially if his mother found out about it. He wouldn't be able to explain that it was for the greater good, that he was now working for MI5. In fact, he wouldn't be able to tell anyone.

"I wish you'd told me this yesterday," Ryan sighed.

"Look on the bright side," Brigshaw beamed, "you now have free rein to beat up anyone you want. Surely there's an obnoxious arse that you'd just love to punch in the face."

"Sure, I could name a few, but…"

"Ryan, if you're going to work for me, you have to be ready to let your fists fly without compunction. You're going to be put in situations where you'll be asked to hurt others. If you hesitate or refuse, that's your career over. You need to get your head into the role, starting right now."

"That won't be an issue," Ryan said. "I'm just concerned that it'll come back to haunt me somewhere down the line. What if I come back in three years, apply for the SAS and the guy I hit turns out to be my instructor?"

"Then pick someone who couldn't possibly make it past selection," Brigshaw said. "Or pick a short-timer, someone coming to the end of their service. Either way, it has to look convincing and be bad enough to get you discharged."

The perfect name leapt into Ryan's head. Corporal Sean Murray was a first-class prick who'd made no secret of the fact that he was getting out by the end of the year. Murray thought that his five years in 2 Para was all he needed to start his own security company, offering bodyguards to rich clients. What he failed to realise was that few of his colleagues would ever want to work with him again, no matter how lucrative the contract. Murray was self-serving, always looking out for number one, which didn't go down well within a close-knit unit.

"Say I do this. Then what?"

"You'll go before a court-martial," the MI5 man said, "where I want you to plead not guilty. Once your paperwork is squared away I'll have someone meet you in the Grapes on Mersea Road."

"Will I have to do any time in the glasshouse?"

"I'll see to it that you don't. Crofter will have you confined to barracks and you might get some KP, but that's it."

A few days buttering rolls and cracking eggs in the kitchen seemed worth it for a free go at Sean Murray.

"Okay, when do you want me to do it?"

"No time like the present," Brigshaw told him. "Give me a few minutes to give Crofter the heads-up."

Brigshaw held out a hand and Ryan shook it. The older man's grip was firm, confident.

"Just don't go too far," Brigshaw winked. "If you kill the guy, you're on your own."

Ryan watched him walk back towards Crofter's office, then went back to his room to change before heading to the gym. Murray was always there at this time of day, pumping iron in an effort to maintain his physique. He was a big man, packed with muscle, but not as hard as he looked.

When Ryan got there, Corporal Sean Murray was sitting on the end of a bench doing bicep curls with fifteen-kilo weights. He was talking to two privates, telling them how successful he was going to be once his stint in 2 Para was over.

"I've already got a dozen big clients lined up," Murray told the pair. "They've got projects in Iraq, Afghanistan, Somalia, you name it. Anyone who comes and works for me will earn four times what they get in the paras."

Ryan walked over and stood a couple of feet from Murray. "Bullshit."

Murray looked up at him. "What?"

"I said bullshit. The market's saturated. These days you'll be lucky to get three hundred dollars a day and no expenses. You're getting into the business twenty years too late, so stop filling their heads with crap." Ryan turned to the two privates. "Ignore this idiot. He's only getting out because he can't hack it."

Murray shot to his feet and stood nose to nose with Ryan. "What's your problem?"

Ryan pushed him away. "You're the problem, Murray. All those steroids have addled your brain. You're more concerned with this stupid dream than mucking in with your mates, and you only pump yourself up because you've got such a small prick."

Ryan couldn't have choreographed it better. Murray went to push him in the chest but Ryan deflected his hand and caught him high on the cheek with a vicious right. Murray's head snapped sideways and Ryan followed up with a left that sent blood flying from Murray's shattered nose. Murray staggered backwards and fell over a bench, landing in a heap, but Ryan wasn't done. He kicked the man in the ribs, then got in close and rained blows to his head.

"Enough!"

The voice belonged to Captain Jock Carson, and Ryan obeyed his barked command. He stood up and faced the officer.

"What's the meaning of this?"

"He attacked me, sir," Ryan said as he stood to attention. "It was self-defence."

The captain looked at the two privates, but they avoided eye contact.

"Pick him up," the officer ordered, and the two men each grabbed an arm and dragged Murray to his feet. His face was covered with blood, and one eye was already completely closed due to heavy bruising.

"Anderson, come with me."

Ryan followed Carson along the now familiar route to the CO's office. The captain knocked and went in while Ryan waited outside. A few minutes later, Carson emerged.

"You're confined to quarters. The CO wants this dealt with swiftly, so you'd better get your story straight, sharpish."

Carson marched away, and Ryan walked back to his room, unable to remove the Cheshire cat grin from his face.

* * *

The proceedings were set up a lot faster than Ryan had expected. Two days after the incident, he received notice to attend the court-martial set for three days later. He was offered counsel but refused, saying only guilty men needed a lawyer.

At the trial, he pleaded not guilty. The two privates Murray had been talking to testified as witnesses. They both stated that Ryan had thrown the first punch, something Murray corroborated when it was his turn to take the stand.

When his turn came, Ryan insisted that Murray had actually tried to put his hand on him first, but only his own quick reactions prevented him from doing so. Fearing another attack would come, he'd struck first.

Ryan only had to wait half an hour for the panel to make up their minds. He was brought before them once more, looking sharp in his dress uniform. He stood to attention while they read out the guilty verdict, with the presiding judge recommending an immediate dishonourable discharge.

Murray had grinned as Ryan was led out of court, but Ryan hid his jubilation. Within two hours, he was sipping a cold lager in the Grapes not far from Merville Barracks, his worldly possessions in a bag at his feet.

The pub was quiet. The lunchtime throng was gone and it was too early for the after-work crowd. Ryan was sitting behind a table, looking at the news on his phone, when a stout man walked in, looked around and made a beeline for him. He sat down without asking and thrust out a hand.

"I'm Marcus Hayes," he said. His accent told of private schooling and privilege. "Brigshaw sent me."

"Oh, okay. I was expecting him, that's all." Ryan shook hands, noting that Hayes' grip was strong, not in keeping with the flabby physique. He pushed his pint aside and reached down for his bag.

"No need to waste good beer. We're not in a hurry."

Hayes went up to the bar and returned with a glass of orange juice.

"So what's the plan?"

"Head to Surrey," Hayes said. "My car's outside."

"Surrey? Not Thames House?"

"I see you've done your homework. No, you won't be going there until you've completed the evaluation. We do that outside London."

Ryan paused mid-sip, his eyes narrowing. "Evaluation? Are you telling me that I have to audition for the part? After I just got myself kicked out of the army?"

Hayes didn't seem fazed by Ryan's steely gaze. "Nothing like that. It's a chance for us to get to know you, see what makes you tick."

"And what if you don't like what you see?"

Hayes shrugged. "You get paid for two years, then go back to what you were doing."

That didn't sound too bad, but Ryan was determined not to fall at the first hurdle.

* * *

Ryan needn't have worried. Within hours of arriving at the house in rural Surrey, Ryan knew he was going to fit in.

The main part of the training centre was a detached house set on thirty acres of land. A half-mile dirt road led from the country lane to the front door of the eight-bedroom property, and behind it and to the right there was a separate rectangular building that looked new. Beyond that was nothing but open land for hundreds of yards in either direction. Ryan guessed it was designed that way so that no one could sneak up to the house.

"No security measures?" he asked Hayes.

"CCTV on the access road and in the trees around the property, plus motion sensors that trigger an array of 3,000-lumen spotlights. We've got a couple of men monitoring them twenty-four-seven."

Ryan was impressed by the fact that he hadn't seen any cameras on his way to the house.

A man wearing jeans and a T-shirt opened the front door as the car pulled up. He walked towards the car with his hand outstretched.

"Hi, Ryan. I'm Zack. Zack Bennett."

He appeared to be in his late twenties, but had a seasoned look about him, like he'd seen a lot. His black hair was cut short, and his frame suggested he looked after his body.

"I guess you know who I am," Ryan said as he shook the hand. He looked up at the three-storey house. "This where you train all the spies?"

"Agents," Bennett corrected him. "And yes, this is where training will take place. You're actually the first, but more will be joining us over the coming weeks."

"How does that work? Won't we be at different stages by then?"

"You will, but as each recruit arrives, so does their handler. I'm yours, and it's my job to teach you everything I know."

"Great," Ryan smiled. "So when do I get my Aston Martin?"

Bennett laughed. "I like you, Ryan. But by the time this is over, I guarantee you'll hate me."

Ryan doubted that. Having decided to take on the challenge, he intended to put everything into it. He knew he had the smarts and the stamina to get through whatever they had to throw at him.

"So, if I don't get the car, what about my legend?"

He'd read enough thrillers to know that undercover officers always adopted a false identity, known in the trade as a legend, a fabricated personal history that included bank accounts, work history and criminal record.

"There isn't one," Bennett said as he led Ryan inside. "When you go in, you'll be Ryan Anderson."

"Wait a second. They'll know exactly who I am?"

"That's right. That way, you don't have to remember a lot of fictitious details and you can't trip yourself up. Just tell them everything about yourself. Where you grew up, who your mates were, why you got kicked out of the army, everything. When they run checks on you, it'll all come back good."

Ryan was not impressed with the answer. For one, if he managed to get enough intel to bring down his target, they would certainly look for retribution.

"What about when they come looking for me?"

"They won't. If you do your job properly, they'll all be in prison. Besides, we'll pull you out weeks before we go in and arrest anyone. They won't suspect you."

"But if they do?" Ryan insisted. "Or they go after my family?" He was an only child, but just the thought of putting his mother in danger sent a shiver through him.

"If it ever comes to it, we'll arrange new identities for her. A new home in a different county, or a different country if that's what she wants. But as I said, it won't happen. We've thought this through and we use the protocols that have served us well over the years."

"I thought this was a new venture."

"It is," Bennet said, "but we've been running civilian agents since the Second World War. We know what works, trust me."

"If it worked so well, I wouldn't be here," Ryan pointed out.

Bennett put an arm around his shoulder as they walked. "This is different. We used to use amateurs who were already associated with the target, but now we're handpicking the best. With your clean background, there'll be no reason for them to suspect you."

"But surely MI5 has its own undercover agents—sorry, officers."

"We do, but naturally they have to go in with a false name, history, etc. There've been times when their real life and undercover life have crossed over, and you can imagine how awkward that could be. One guy was two months into an operation in Manchester when he came back to London to visit family. His kids begged him to take them to Stamford Bridge to watch Chelsea play Manchester City, but while he was there, a member of the gang he'd infiltrated saw him. Our guy was supposed to be single, no kids, but there he was with the wife and two sons. Needless to say, the op was blown."

"What did they do to him?"

"Nothing much. They followed him back to his house and checked the electoral roll to see who lived there, saw the names didn't match and gave him a beating. Not bad enough to put anyone away for it, but it served as a warning. We knew we had to revise our strategy."

That wasn't encouraging news, but as Bennett had pointed out, Ryan would be going in clean. He wouldn't have to memorise a new personality, just be himself.

Bennett showed Ryan around the house. The ground floor had two reception rooms complete with sofas and TVs, plus a dining room and a spacious kitchen staffed by two cooks. They went through a door marked Security and saw a dark-haired woman in her thirties monitoring a series of screens. Bennett introduced her as Kate, then left her to do her job.

Upstairs there were eight bedrooms, four with en suites, and two separate bathrooms.

Ryan was given a room overlooking the rear of the property. It had a small double bed, desk, wardrobe and chest of drawers. A flat-screen TV was attached to the wall, and a DVD player and satellite box sat underneath it. As he was one of the first to arrive, he had his own bathroom.

"Dinner is at seven," Bennett told him. "We'll have a chat afterwards, but the real training starts tomorrow."

With a couple of hours until chow, Ryan unpacked his few belongings and took a shower. The house was clearly old, but a lot of work had been done on the interior. The bathroom looked brand new, and the water pressure was strong enough for Ryan's liking.

He went down to the dining room five minutes early and found Bennett sitting at the table next to a familiar face.

"I trust the room's to your satisfaction," Malcolm Brigshaw said as he sipped a glass of water.

Ryan took a seat opposite them. "It's fine," Ryan said. "Though I do have some laundry."

"There's a utility room off the back of the kitchen," Bennett said. "It's got everything you need."

"I'm sure you have a lot more questions," Brigshaw said, steepling his fingers, "so we best get them out of the way now."

There were indeed many questions floating around inside his head, but he knew the answers would come as the course progressed. He decided to just get himself settled in and comfortable.

"Okay. Shopping. Do I have access to a car to go into town?"

"We'll supply anything you need," Bennett said. "Just let us know and we'll pick it up for you."

"So I can't leave here?" Ryan pushed.

"We'd prefer it if you didn't," Brigshaw answered. "Just for now, until you're settled."

That was no real hardship. "What about pay? I don't suppose my salary will show up as MI5 on my bank statement."

"No, that money will be paid into a separate account under a different name. You won't have access to it until your job with us is complete."

"So what do I live on?"

"Whatever you can earn in the next twelve months, though we'll take care of most things. We'll be sending you out to build a legend that covers the training period. You'll find odd jobs here and there, bar work, construction, whatever takes your fancy. You'll register with the benefits office, everything a normal person would do after being kicked out of the army. If you had a year with no work, no income, it would look odd. In between jobs, you'll come back here for further training. While you're away, we'll give you materials to study."

The chef brought in three plates of roast lamb and they tucked in.

"What are you going to teach me over the next twelve months?" Ryan asked Bennett before filling his mouth with meat and broad beans.

"Fieldcraft, mostly. How to spot a tail, how to follow someone without them noticing, dead drops, the usual."

Ryan had expected those things, but there had to be more to it. "Gadgets?" he asked.

"There'll be some, but nothing like the movies. No tie clips that shoot lasers or anything like that. Mostly listening devices and cameras. Some will be for your home, others to wear."

"Like a wire? Won't they check for that kind of thing?"

"These ones are unnoticeable," Brigshaw assured him. "They're sewn into clothing and don't require power packs. We'll show you it in good time, don't worry."

Silence descended as Ryan ran out of questions.

"Nothing else you want to ask?" Bennett said.

Ryan shook his head.

"Well, I'm glad you didn't ask what happens if you want to quit."

"The thought never crossed my mind. I wouldn't have agreed to come along if I thought I'd walk away at some point."

"That's the impression we got from reading your file. You're not a quitter. That was one of the main reasons we chose you."

It was Brigshaw's turn to ask the questions. While they finished their meals, he quizzed Ryan on his upbringing. Specifically, he wanted to know about any dodgy characters he'd hung around with. There'd been plenty, and for two hours he regaled the two officers with his exploits as a youth. He'd never been in trouble with the police, but some of the stuff he'd got up to had been morally questionable.

At nine, Brigshaw excused himself.

"I'd better go, too," Bennett said, "and you should hit the sack as well. We've got a long day ahead of us."

* * *

127

Ryan would always remember every detail of his first day of training. At six, he went for a five-mile run, then showered before breakfast. At eight, Bennett took him through the house once more, asking if he noticed any changes. Ryan picked up on a few, such as the different wall clock in the dining room and the throw over the sofa in one of the reception rooms. When Bennett pointed out a dozen things he'd missed, he felt ashamed, but Bennett assured him that he hadn't been expected to get more than a couple right.

"It's important that you get to know your surroundings, especially if it's a place you visit often. If something changes, there's usually a reason. See that ornament? Take a closer look."

Ryan picked up the female figurine from the mantelpiece and examined it. It hadn't been there the day before. It took a while, but he eventually saw the pin-sized hole.

"That's a camera," Bennett told him. "If you manage to get in with your mark, there's a chance they'll use something like this to monitor you at home. It might not be state-of-the-art like this, but you should be aware of any subtle changes to your environment."

Lesson over, Bennett took Ryan to the outbuilding next to the house. It was kitted out as a gym, with exercise bikes, treadmills and a weight station. These were set up against the walls, and in the centre of the room was a large, square mat.

"This is where we do martial arts. I know you've had some training already, but we'll make you better. You could end up in some hairy situations, so the more you know, the better."

Ryan's schedule included two hours on the equipment each day, followed by another two hours on the mat. He also kept up his daily running routine, and at the end of his twelve-month training programme he was fitter than he'd ever been.

Bennett proved true to his word. Ryan had picked up a lot of useful techniques during his time at the training centre, though after his first ten months working for Marsh, he had little use for them. Most of his confrontations were with low-life drug users who'd made the mistake of owing Marsh money, and none of them challenged Ryan's skills.

Not that his stint on Marsh's crew was a complete waste of time. For the first couple of months, he was given the shitty jobs, like the trip to Albania. He hadn't been able to tell Brigshaw precisely what had been smuggled through the ports in the van's wall cavities, but at least they now knew one of Marsh's methods. It might have been drugs, but Albania was also a known exporter of illegal arms, especially the AK-47s favoured by Islamic terrorists.

Ryan hadn't discovered much more over the last eight months. Once, he'd been told to take a van to a remote part of the East Anglian coast. When he got there, he saw a black inflatable powering out to sea and Terry standing next to a pile of plastic-wrapped packages on the shore. Ryan's job had been to load them onto his van and drive to a residential street in Luton, where he'd been told to lock the van and make his own way back to Manchester. He didn't have a chance to take a look at the merchandise, but was ninety per cent sure the wrappings contained drugs. They were too small to be automatic rifles, though they could have contained ammunition. Given the quantity, though, it was unlikely, unless someone had ordered half a million rounds. He'd passed that on to Brigshaw in the usual manner, but since then he'd been back on thug duty.

Carrying a phone with his boss's number on speed dial was an invitation to trouble, so whenever Ryan needed to make contact or pass on information, he would simply go for a run with his digital Sony Walkman. The device had been modified to work as a phone when he pressed a certain combination of buttons. Ryan would leave his flat on the banks of the Bridgewater canal in Sale and make the call, then set off at a gentle jog. He changed his route regularly, making it difficult for anyone to lie in wait and read his lips as he reported to Brigshaw.

Today's run took him over the railway bridge that led to Oldfield road, then onto Broad Road. A late spring drizzle made the street wet, but it didn't hamper Ryan's progress. As he upped the speed and headed away from the town centre, Ryan gave his boss the latest update.

"Still quiet," he said. "I've had nothing but debt collection for the last few days."

It had been the same for weeks now. Either Marsh's shipments were not as frequent as Brigshaw had assumed, or Ryan was only being used when there was a shortage of bodies.

"What about getting closer to Marsh? It's been almost a year now, and my superiors are anxious to see some results. We've invested a lot of time and effort into this."

You're not the only one, Ryan thought. He'd given up a couple of years of his life to help nail Marsh, and there were times when he thought it might all be for nothing. Instead of the training, the jobs on the building site and the factory, he could have been in the SAS by now. He had to admit, shitting in the factory supervisor's lunchbox had been an inspired idea. It was easy to follow up and verify, and had given him a chuckle every time he thought about the condescending prick putting his hand in to grab a sandwich.

"There's not much I can do on that front," Ryan said. Despite the speed he was travelling, he was barely panting. "I thought taking out one of Marsh's bodyguards would get me that position, but he replaced him from within. I told you before, it'll be some time before he trusts me enough to let me into his inner circle. I rarely even see the man, unless I go to his nightclub."

"Then maybe we need to create another opening," Brigshaw said.

"What do you have in mind?"

"Take out another bodyguard. We can send a few people into the Vine and create a commotion. When Marsh's men step in, we damage one of them."

It was strange to hear a man in Brigshaw's position advocating violence. He worked for the government, and that usually meant rules had to be followed. An undercover police officer would have to tread carefully, ensuring they followed PACE procedures, but Ryan had been given free rein. The only way to fit in with Marsh's crew was to act exactly like them, Brigshaw had said.

Unfortunately, the plan was unlikely to work. "Marsh has bouncers at the club," Ryan said. "His bodyguards wouldn't get involved."

"Then we need to come up with a way to get rid of one of them. Any thoughts?"

"You could give one of them a tug," Ryan suggested. "Have him pulled over in his car and plant some drugs on him, or a weapon used in a recent violent crime. Even a clean gun would do, as long as it gets him remanded."

"That would work. I'll get some people on it. In the meantime, why don't you have a word with Marsh? Tell him you're unhappy with your talents going to waste, that you want more of a challenge."

"It's not easy getting an audience with him," Ryan said. "I can try and grab a word the next time I'm in the Vine, but generally he likes to distance himself from the guys on the front line. He gives Paul Gardner the orders, they're passed to Terry and on to me."

It was always done by word of mouth. Marsh was too savvy to discuss business on his phone.

"Well, see what you can do. I'll get to work on setting up one of the bodyguards."

The call ended, and Ryan switched the Walkman to music mode and continued his run.

Five miles later, he was back at his flat. He showered and dressed in grey slacks and a Lacoste T-shirt that showed off his muscles. He was halfway through a cup of coffee when the doorbell rang, and through the spy hole he could see that it was Terry.

"Grab your coat."

"Where we heading?" Ryan asked.

"Walkden. Some slag owes us money. We're gonna collect."

Chapter 20

Their destination was a semi-detached house in Little Hulton, a council estate on the north-west outskirts of Walkden. The adjoining house on the left had a new roof, repointed brick walls and a neatly-maintained garden with driveway. The target house was the polar opposite. Guttering hung loose from the eaves, the grass was a foot tall and strewn with kids' toys, a fence panel was missing and wheelie bins were being used as garden decorations.

"What I don't get is why Marsh would lend money to people like this. They're obviously skint."

"It's amazing how quickly they find a bit of spare cash after you slap 'em around a bit," Terry said. "No one forced them to borrow money from him."

Ryan didn't believe that to be true. Government cuts to benefits and child support services meant people had a stark choice: borrow from the likes of Franklin Marsh, or starve. Those with young children and no job often didn't have good enough credit to borrow from the mainstream lenders, so their only option was to go to the loan sharks.

Terry hammered on the front door, which shook under the assault. "I know you're in there, Sharon. Open up!"

A child started crying inside the house, confirming that someone was home. A minute later, the door opened.

Ryan was surprised. He'd expected to see...someone different, not the timid young woman who stood before them. She looked to be in her early twenties, with no make-up and her platinum hair tied up in a rough bun to reveal dark roots.

Terry pushed past her and into the hallway. Ryan followed him inside.

"Nicky tells me you don't wanna pay," Terry said, looking from room to room. Nicky was the collector who did the rounds, taking in the money before handing it on to Terry. Nicky's job was to ask for the weekly payments, and if someone was unable to meet their obligations, the heavy boys—Terry included—were sent in.

"I do, I want to," Sharon said as she walked to the living room, "but I just haven't got it." She picked up the screaming baby from the playpen and sat on the sofa, hugging it close to her chest.

The living room was neat, apart from a few toys lying around. The carpet looked clean, and there was no sign of drug use.

"What about the kid's dad?" Ryan said. "When's he home?"

Terry laughed. "Oh, mate, you crack me up. You think this bird knows who the daddy is? What does it say under father on the birth certificate, Sharon? Some soldiers? You've probably had more pricks than a second-hand dartboard."

"My husband left me when I had this one," Sharon said quietly. "A good job, too. All the money went on his smokes and beer." She looked down at the infant. "We're better off without him, aren't we, darling?"

"How much does she owe?" Ryan asked.

"Three hundred."

"Three?" Sharon looked up, startled. "I only borrowed a hundred and I've already paid back two-fifty. How can it be three?"

"Late payment fees," Terry said, "plus interest and my call-out charge. You think I do this for fun?"

Sharon burst into tears. "There's no way I can find three hundred quid. I haven't even got three quid."

"Then I'll do what I came here to do." Terry's grin dripped with malice, and Sharon held the baby tight to her chest.

Ryan had never had any issues doling out a beating to those who deserved it, but Sharon was an exception. She looked like a good mother fallen on hard times, not the usual wasters who borrowed to fund a drug or alcohol habit.

"Let's have a look around," Ryan said. "There might be something worth three hundred in this house."

Terry waved him away, then slowly rubbed his crotch. "Go waste your time if you want. She ain't got nothing."

Ryan was in a bind. He could see what Terry intended to do, but if he intervened it would be out of character. In this organisation, you never gave a sucker an even break. Life wasn't fair, end of. Word would get back to Marsh, and any chance he had of climbing the ranks would be blown.

Brigshaw had warned Ryan that something like this might happen. It was inevitable that at some point, Ryan would be forced to do something he found abhorrent, and he had to remain detached as he carried out his orders. That was easy to say when he was sitting at a comfy desk hundreds of miles away. Ryan was the one facing the dilemma, and he would have to live with the consequences of his actions.

He walked into the kitchen, hoping by some miracle that Sharon had a large screen TV stashed away, but he was disappointed. There was a washing machine that looked a few years old, plus a fridge, cooker, and microwave. They would probably fetch a total of twenty quid second hand.

Ryan opened a few cupboards, but there was no treasure to be found.

A scream came from the other room, and Ryan knew he had to act fast. He began rummaging around in the cupboards, hoping that Sharon had squirrelled some money away, but he came up empty.

A thought struck him as Sharon screamed again and the baby wailed uncontrollably. He took out his wallet. He had just over four hundred pounds. He counted out fifteen twenties and walked back into the living room.

Terry was straddling Sharon, kissing her neck while his hands roamed over her chest. The crying baby wedged between them didn't seem to distract him.

"Tel!"

Terry turned and glared at Ryan, who was holding up the money he'd taken from his wallet. "What?"

"I found it. She had it stuffed in a biscuit jar." Terry stood and took the money from Ryan, who walked over to Sharon. "Think you're clever, eh? Think you could hide it from us?" He slapped her across the face, not hard, but enough to keep her confused for the few seconds he needed. He grabbed Terry and headed for the door.

"Next time, pay up, or I'll let him have you."

Terry lingered for a moment, his hand massaging his stiff cock through his trousers. "Maybe I'll teach her a lesson."

"Do me a favour. That kid's doing my head in. Let's go. You can get a better lay at the club tonight."

Ryan tugged at Terry's sleeve, and the spell was broken. He followed Ryan out into the overgrown garden before Sharon had a chance to wonder what the hell had just happened.

Chapter 21

It was almost eight o'clock in the evening when Karen heard the shouting start. She was in bed, reading a book she'd borrowed from the school library. She couldn't remember what it was called, but it was one of the crime stories she loved. She read a lot of them, because the bad guy always got his comeuppance.

It was unusual to hear raised voices in the house. She'd lived alone with her father, Colin, ever since her mum had left four years earlier, and the only sounds she was used to were the vacuum cleaner and the television.

Unable to contain her curiosity, Karen sneaked downstairs in her nightdress and bare feet and stood outside the kitchen door. The voices were louder, and it was clear her father and another man were angry.

"It worked perfectly fine when I sold it to you!"

"Bollocks!" her father shouted back. "The engine packed in after two days and the garage said it had been patched up just a few weeks ago. You must have known there was something wrong with it!"

Her father had been angry ever since he'd bought the car from his neighbour. He'd been happy with the bargain at first, but once it stopped running, his demeanour changed. He told Karen he'd been conned, and that he wouldn't be making the payments he'd agreed with Dane Edwards.

Karen didn't like Edwards. His son, Tom, went to her school, and he was just like his father. Arrogant, self-obsessed and full of crap.

Karen had forgotten all about the car until that moment.

She had other things on her mind.

The door was slightly ajar, and Karen looked through the gap. Her father was standing with his arms folded tight across his chest, and Edwards was three feet away from him.

"No, I'm not giving you another penny. You can take the car back and fix it yourself."

"We've got a signed agreement," Edwards persisted. "Two-fifty a month for twelve months."

"That was before you tried to rip me off. You wanna do something about it? Take me to court. I'll be happy to show the judge the mechanic's report."

"I'll fuckin' do something about it!" Edwards looked around and saw the knife block. He took one out and held it towards her father. "Give me my fuckin' money!"

Colin Harper backed off, his hands in the air. "Don't be stupid! You stab me, the police will know it was you. You gonna kill me for three grand?"

Edwards hesitated, then slammed the knife down on the kitchen countertop. He pointed an angry finger at Karen's father. "I'll get my money, just you wait and see."

Karen ran from the doorway as Edwards stormed out of the kitchen. She ducked into the living room and heard him walk to the front door and slam it shut behind him.

Karen waited a few minutes. She wanted to rush back to her room, but she needed a glass of water. She always got thirsty in the middle of the night and hated going through the dark house to get a drink. She sat on the sofa for another couple of minutes, then walked into the kitchen. Her father was standing at the sink staring out of the window into the back garden, a large shot of vodka in his hand. He took a big gulp, then topped up the glass.

"Can I have a drink of water?"

Harper spun to see her standing a few feet behind him. "Sure." He stepped to the side to let her get to the sink.

Karen took a glass from the cupboard and held it under the cold tap, praying it would fill quickly so that she could go back to her room.

It was always worse when he had vodka.

The glass was half full of water when he started stroking her long hair.

That was how it always started.

"You look so much like your mother."

Karen tensed, then immediately regretted it. He didn't like it when she was anything but compliant.

"What's wrong?"

"I'm just cold," she lied.

It seemed to satisfy him. His hands crept slowly down her back and came to rest on her buttock.

Karen did her best to stay relaxed. *You like it*, she told herself, over and over. It was the only way to get it over with quickly and painlessly.

It didn't work. As his hand squeezed between her buttocks, Karen clenched. She relaxed immediately, but the damage was done.

His hand flashed across her face, stinging her cheek and spinning her around. She placed her hands on the counter to steady herself, and that's when she saw the knife.

Time seemed to stand still.

It was the knife Edwards had threatened her father with, and his fingerprints were all over it. Karen had pictured herself killing her father numerous times, and in numerous ways. Stabbing him, poisoning him, electrocuting him, but she'd never done it. She knew she would get caught and spend most of her life in prison, no matter what he'd done to her in the past. She'd also considered going to the police, but there were many reports on the internet about children not being believed. That would have left her in a worse position than she was in now, so she'd kept the misery to herself.

Until now. The knife was there, begging to be used, and the prints on it would point the police to Edwards. She would have to make up a convincing story, but after her father was dead, she would have all the time she needed.

She heard her father taking off his belt and knew she had just a few seconds to either act or take what was coming. That thought alone spurred her into action. Karen grabbed a piece of kitchen roll and used it to pick up the knife by the handle, then spun around and thrust it into her father's chest.

Colin Harper stood still for a long moment. He looked down at the knife handle protruding from the left side of his rib cage, then back up to his daughter's face. He tried to say something, but Karen couldn't make it out. He took a step towards her, one hand outstretched while the other tugged at the handle of the blade. When he pulled it from his body, blood spurted over the floor and counter. Karen backed up against the fridge as her father took another step, then collapsed. He landed on his side, then rolled over and looked up at her, his head inches from her feet as he moaned.

Karen looked down at him, feeling shocked but also glad. She'd saved herself from a beating that would have been followed by another rape, and she began to regain her composure as she realised that his abusive days were over.

But she wasn't free yet. She needed to come up with a story that would convince the police that Dane Edwards had been responsible for her father's murder.

I was upstairs in my room and heard them shouting. I looked out of the window when I heard the door slam and saw Edwards walking away from the house. He looked angry. Later, I went downstairs for a drink of water and found my dad dead on the floor.

It sounded reasonable enough in her own head, but she'd read enough crime books to know that blood spatters were a giveaway. She checked her nightdress and saw a couple of tiny spots, big enough for a keen-eyed policeman to notice. That was easily remedied, though. She looked down at her father, who had gone quiet. His eyes were dull, his chest still. Karen knelt down next to him and hugged him, ensuring that a large amount of the blood soaking through his T-shirt got onto her nightdress.

Karen stayed like that for a few moments as she thought about the next step. She would have to call the police soon, but she couldn't do it with a calm voice. A child finding a murdered parent, one they loved with all their heart, would be distraught. That was how Karen had to act: as though her father was everything to her, not the aggressive paedophile he really was. No one could ever learn of his actions. All that would serve to do would be to provide her with a motive. Motive and opportunity were what did for most killers in the novels she read, and she needed to ensure they both pointed towards Dane Edwards.

Karen thought about the saddest moments in her life. There were plenty to choose from. The one that always made her well up was the day she'd learned that her mother was never coming back. As she remembered what that had led to, the tears started to flow. She practised her opening line a couple of times, then used her father's phone to call 999.

"Emergency, which service do you require?"

"My dad's dead!" Karen wailed. "Someone stabbed him!"

"Okay, sweetheart, can you tell me where you are?"

Karen bubbled out her address. "He's not breathing!" she added. "There's blood everywhere!"

The operator asked her to try to remain calm. "What's your name?"

"K…K…Karen."

"Okay, Karen. Can you see if he's breathing?"

"He's not!" Karen cried. "I hu…hugged him but he won't wake up!"

"I see. Is anyone else with you, Karen?"

"No, just me and my dad! Please hurry!"

"An ambulance is on its way. Can you get to the front door and open it for us?"

"Yes."

"Good. Open it now, so we know which house it is. You don't have to go outside, just wait by the door."

Karen did what was asked of her. She left the hall light on and stood inside the doorway so that no one could see her in her night dress. She guessed she'd been asked to wait there because it would be less traumatic than staying with the corpse, and also so that she didn't compromise the crime scene any further.

The first vehicle to arrive was the police car. Two male officers dressed in black jumped out and jogged up the path to her house. The taller one went straight down the hallway while the shorter one took Karen gently by the shoulders and stooped his back so that their eyes were level.

"Where is he?"

Karen pointed to the door on the right. "In…there."

"Okay, you wait here, love."

The ambulance arrived just as the two cops went into the kitchen. By the time the first paramedic got to the door, the tall cop was walking out of the house. They exchanged a few words, then the police officer put an arm around Karen's shoulder and led her into the living room. He sat her down on the sofa and took a seat next to her.

"I'm sorry," he said, and didn't need to elaborate. Karen knew he was talking about her father's passing. She put her hands over her face and forced a sob. The cop waited patiently.

"What happened?" he eventually asked.

137

Karen went through the story she'd concocted, though she made sure it didn't sound rehearsed. She told him how she'd heard the shouting and the door slam, and how she'd seen Dane Edwards walking away from the house. "Dad told me that he wasn't going to give Dane any more money for the car because it was a heap of junk. I think that's what they were fighting about."

The cop asked if she knew where Edwards lived, and Karen gave him the house number. "It's just across the street."

"What happened after Dane left?"

"Nothing. I mean, it went quiet, so I stayed in my room reading. About ten minutes later, I went down for a glass of water and I…I…"

The cop didn't rush her, so Karen composed herself and eventually told him that she'd seen her dad lying on the floor, covered in blood, and she'd knelt down next to him and cradled him in her lap, trying to wake him up. "That's when I called 999."

"Did you touch the knife?"

"No."

"Okay, that's good. What about your mum? Is she out?"

"Mum left us four years ago. Dad said she got another man. I haven't seen her since."

The cop nodded solemnly, then stood and walked out into the hallway before speaking into his radio.

They stayed for over an hour. Karen watched as her father was taken out of the house on a wheeled trolley, and shortly afterwards a young female police officer joined them. She asked Karen the same questions, and Karen stuck to the original story, making sure to avoid embellishment.

"How old are you, Karen?"

"Sixteen."

"I understand that your mum's no longer around. Is there anyone you'd like me to call? Maybe an aunt you can stay with…"

"No, I'm fine. I'll stay here, if that's okay." She hadn't had time to consider the aftermath, and being sent to live with someone wasn't in her plans.

"I'm afraid we'll have to get someone to look after you, just for a while."

Karen didn't like the idea, but if she pushed, the cop might become suspicious.

"Okay, but not my mum, please. I've got a school friend, Jane. She lives at number 30. Maybe I could stay with her."

* * *

Looking back, it had turned out to be a good idea. The policewoman had spoken to Jane's mum, Katherine, and she'd come over to the house and consoled Karen, offering her a home for as long as she needed. She'd been given the spare room and her bed and belongings had been brought over that night. Katherine also helped to arrange the funeral and her father's estate, which amounted to the house and a few thousand in his bank account. The house had been sold, and after the bank took its slice, just over seventy grand was put into a trust fund for when Karen turned eighteen.

Karen had stayed with Jane and her family for four months, until she turned seventeen. Armed with a GCSE A* in art, she'd sent out her CV and portfolio to numerous companies, eventually landing a place at an advertising agency. She'd moved into her own place, a rented one-bedroom flat in London, and stayed there until her eighteenth birthday, when she used her inheritance to put a deposit down on a three-bed semi-detached house. It was bigger than she needed and required some work, but she'd seen the investment potential, even at that tender age. It had been a wise move. She still lived in the house, and it was worth almost four times what she'd paid for it.

As Karen reflected on her childhood, the memories of the abuse had faded, but not the way she'd dealt with it. She couldn't recall the sensation she'd felt when she'd plunged the knife into her father's chest, but her feelings when Dane Edwards was convicted of murder would never leave her. She felt the same with each new kill. She would alter her appearance drastically and attend the trials, sketching the defendant and selling the drawing to the news outlets, but mostly to learn about the court procedures and the evidence offered by the prosecution and defence counsels. She'd picked up a few tips to improve her methods and evade detection, which meant she went into each new venture with increased confidence. What she was really there for, though, was the close of proceedings. Reading about the person she'd framed being arrested was a thrill in itself, but when the jury read out the guilty verdict, she felt a bolt of energy surge through her body.

And it was time to prepare for the next one.

Chapter 22

Ryan didn't know what Paul's problem was, but his attitude suggested it was going to be a long and interesting day.

Their first call that morning had been to collect money from a local layabout named Tom. It wasn't a huge amount, just over a hundred pounds, but the moment Tom opened the door, Paul had gone flying in with his fists before the man had a chance to explain himself. Paul had left him in a bloody pile on the living room floor and gone through his pockets, finding the money he owed, before storming out of the house a couple of minutes after arriving.

"What was that all about?" Ryan asked as he ran to keep up.

Paul ignored him and got behind the wheel of the BMW. Ryan climbed in beside him.

"So?"

"So, what?" Paul said as he started the engine. The tires squealed as he raced away from the kerb.

"What you just did to that guy. That wasn't called for."

"Yes it was. He should have paid two days ago. He won't be late again."

They drove in silence for a few minutes, then Paul sighed. "You're right. I'm sorry. I've just got a load on my mind at the moment."

"Not another girl problem?" Ryan smiled, trying to ease the tension. Paul had a couple of girls on the go at any one time, and it was usually a juggling act to ensure the women never met each other.

"No," Paul said, still serious. "Marsh has set up a buy, but I don't like it."

"How come?"

Paul said nothing, and his face told Ryan he was trying to decide whether or not to open up. That had been the case for some time. Ryan was still doing nothing more than loan enforcement, while Paul would disappear for days at a time on Marsh's bidding.

"You might as well know," Paul eventually said. "You'll be coming with me anyway. We've got a buyer for three dozen AK-47s and ten thousand rounds. We'll be doing the exchange in three days."

"Doesn't sound like a problem," Ryan said, but the confirmation that Marsh was into gun trafficking was huge. He finally had something to report to Brigshaw, and the fact that he was going to the meet meant he would be able to identify the other players.

"It is when the buyer is an Islamic jihadist."

This was absolute gold, but Ryan hid his excitement. "And Marsh is happy to sell to them?"

"As far as he's concerned, if we don't sell them the guns, someone else will. Might as well make a profit from them."

"What about you?" Ryan asked. "You comfortable with this?"

"What do you think? I can't believe anyone would sell arms to those bastards. I'd prefer to wait until they turn up and shoot the fucking lot of them, but Marsh wants this to go through. Sometimes you just can't reason with him."

Though Paul didn't have much in the way of a moral compass, it was pointing in the right direction this time. Ryan was glad it was, otherwise Paul might not have told him about the sale until it was too late. Now he had an opportunity, but he couldn't appear too eager.

"What time will it be?" Ryan asked. "Not another early morning, please. I barely got four hours last night."

"It'll be in the afternoon, but you're going in early," Paul told him. "We always send someone ahead to make sure the buyers don't come mob-handed and that the police don't show up when there's a shit-load of cash and guns on the table. That's gonna be your job."

It just gets better and better, Ryan thought.

"You're gonna have to show me where it is," Ryan said. "I need to check it out and pick the best place for an OP." He saw Paul's look and explained that OP stood for observation post.

"Let's go take a look," Paul said.

Ryan forced himself to relax and enjoy the ride, despite Paul's choice of music. It took over an hour to reach their destination, during which Paul gave Ryan a rundown of the things he'd like to do to the terrorists. Ryan openly agreed with all of them, while all the time noting the passing road signs so that he could retrace the route.

The exchange was going to take place at an abandoned farm. A half-mile dirt road led up to the dilapidated house, and beyond it were two outbuildings. One was a Dutch barn, with no walls.

Paul parked around the back of the house, next to the other building. They got out and Ryan followed him inside. It looked like it might once have been a milking shed, though Ryan was no expert.

"We'll be doing the transaction in here," Paul said.

Ryan scanned the interior, but it was outside where his interest lay. "Let's take a look at the perimeter," he said. He walked back to the entrance and looked around. The ground straight ahead gently sloped upwards, the rise topped with a small cluster of trees. It would be the perfect place to take photos of anyone coming or going. The problem was, if Brigshaw was to put someone in place, it wouldn't do for Ryan to be lying right next to them in case Paul came to get him afterwards. Ryan identified two more spots where someone with a telephoto lens could get decent shots of the players, then turned to Paul.

"I'm gonna have a wander, see the best place to lie up."

"Knock yourself out," Paul said.

Ryan scrambled over the remnants of a stone wall and walked up the hill. When he got to the trees, he noticed several chocolate bar wrappers at the base of an old oak. This was obviously where Marsh's lookout kept an eye on proceedings. It was a good spot, with a clear view all the way down to the main road and beyond. What he was really looking for, though, was the best place to observe the entrance to the shed.

Ryan walked along the crest of the ridge and identified two places where one of Brigshaw's men could dig in and monitor the exchange, then walked back down to the car. Paul was resting against the bonnet, checking his phone.

"Found somewhere?"

"Yeah," Ryan said, pointing up at the trees. "That's where you normally spot from, right?"

Paul nodded.

"Thought so. Whoever was there left a ton of rubbish. They should clean up afterwards."

"You can do that on Thursday," Paul told him. "The meet's at four, so I want you here by twelve at the latest. Make sure your phone's fully charged."

"Will do."

They got back in the car and Paul drove them back into Manchester,. He dropped Ryan off at his flat and leaned out of the car window.

"I'll be out of town on business for the next couple of days, but Terry will drive you up on Thursday morning and drop you off on the main road. I'll pick you up again once they've gone."

"No worries. Need me for anything else in the meantime?"

"Terry or Phil will be round to pick you up tomorrow at eight. There's still plenty of idiots who think Marsh is a soft touch," Paul smiled. "You can put them straight."

Paul drove away, and Ryan went into his flat and changed into his running gear. He hit the buttons on his Walkman as he left the building, then jogged over the railway bridge and into the next residential road.

"I've got something," he said as soon as Brigshaw picked up. "Marsh is going to be selling a stack of assault rifles to a Jihadist group."

"When?"

"Three days from now. I've been assigned a lookout role." Ryan gave Brigshaw the location of the farm and the time of the meet. He described the entrance to the old cow shed and where best to place a photographer.

"You don't think this could be a trap?" Brigshaw asked. "They've been cagey up to now, but suddenly they let you in on something this big."

It did seem a big leap now that Ryan thought about it. But then, they had to let him in on the important aspects of the operation at some point. Marsh wouldn't pay him so much just to have him crack a few heads now and again. Besides, Paul's demeanour when discussing the buyers seemed genuine.

"I'm sure it's the real thing," Ryan said, "and we're only talking about monitoring the deal and identifying the people involved. With a powerful enough lens, your man could be a mile away and no one would know he was there."

"Okay, I'll put that in place, but I'm still concerned with their sudden switch in mood. I want you to meet Marcus at the usual place later today and pick up some gear. We'll be able to keep tabs on you, just in case this is another one of their tests."

The call ended, and Ryan switched the Walkman to a Billy Idol album and upped his pace.

* * *

Paul drove three miles to Phil's flat, a bachelor pad on the outskirts of town. He knocked on the door.

Terry opened it. "He's in the bog."

Paul walked in and sat on the sofa. The living room consisted of the couch, a coffee table and a wall-mounted 60-inch television. Wires led from it to a Sky box and a PlayStation.

He heard the toilet flush and Phil emerged from the bathroom, doing up his jeans. "You all set?" Paul asked.

"Ready when you are."

Terry grabbed a holdall and both men followed Paul down to his car. Terry called shotgun and sat up front, leaving Phil the back seat.

"I bet you anything he's clean," Terry said as they headed to the farm.

"A hundred quid says he's not," Paul said. It was money he'd be happy to lose. This was about proving once and for all that Ryan wasn't an undercover police officer. If that was the case, Paul would never be happier parting with his cash.

But if he was a copper…

"I think he's kosher," Phil said from the back.

"You were the first one to say he was bent," Terry laughed. "What made you change your mind? He giving you one?"

"We've all seen him in action," Phil said, ignoring the dig. "He can't be plod."

"Well, we'll soon find out."

When they reached the road that led to the farm, Paul and Terry got out of the car. Paul opened the boot and took out his own holdall, plus a folding camp bed, a folding chair and a sleeping bag, then he and Terry set off.

"Don't dent my motor," Paul shouted over his shoulder.

Phil got into the driver's seat and revved the engine hard, grinning like a maniac as he disappeared in a cloud of dust.

"Pillock!"

Paul had decided to set up surveillance in the old house. It had a good view of the road from the top floor, and from the other rooms they could see out over the surrounding countryside.

They went in the back way, where a window was broken. The place had been gutted. In the kitchen, only the ancient cabinets remained, the appliances all long gone. The other rooms on the ground floor were all empty, too. They climbed the stairs, each one creaking under their weight. Paul checked each of the rooms in case someone had decided to make it their home, but like the ground floor, it was clear.

He put his gear down in the front bedroom, then made up the camp bed. He and Terry would take turns sleeping while the other kept watch out of the windows.

"How long do you think it'll be before someone shows?" Terry asked. "If they *do* show."

"It'll be hours yet. Ryan has to call it in, then they'll get someone to do the surveillance, then they have to drive here. I'd say it'll be nine o'clock at least."

It would be dark by that time, but Paul was prepared. He'd purchased two pairs of Pulsar Edge Gs night-vision goggles and had a dozen spare lithium batteries for them.

"What if they wait until the last minute?"

"Then we wait, too," Paul said. "I don't think that'll happen, though. They'll want someone in place as soon as possible so that they'll have plenty of time to dig in. They won't leave it 'til Thursday morning."

He hoped not, at least. The onset of summer had brought the first decent sunshine of the year, and the forecast was for more of the same for the next few days. Paul didn't want to waste two of them sitting in an abandoned farmhouse.

Paul began emptying his holdall. He had a carrier bag full of sandwiches, chocolate bars and fruit, bottles of water, bags to crap into, hand sanitizer and three rolls of toilet paper. He hadn't bothered with toiletries as he knew there would be no running water in the house, and two days without washing or brushing his teeth was no real hardship.

He munched on a cheese salad sandwich as he walked the upper floor, checking the view from every window. They would have to keep on the move, going from room to room to make sure Ryan's friends didn't slip past them.

Prove me wrong, Paul whispered to himself as he stared out over the fields to the left of the house. The ground here gently sloped downhill and offered no view of the entrance to the cowshed, so it was unlikely anyone would set up camp there. He would concentrate his efforts on the other three sides of the house.

When he returned to the front bedroom, Terry was on his phone, a cheap Pay-As-You-Go that hadn't been registered. Paul had insisted that they leave their own phones at home, in case they were being monitored by the police.

"Don't waste the battery," Paul told him. "We're gonna need that if someone shows."

144

Terry reluctantly put his phone away. "I'm bored shitless already."

"We've only been here ten minutes."

"Yeah, and we're gonna waste another two days, because no one's coming. Ryan's sound, I'm telling you."

"We'll see," Paul said. "You check the back and the right, I'll stay here." He could tell Terry's heart wasn't really in it, which was why he'd assigned him the rooms less likely to yield results.

Paul unfolded the chair and positioned it a few feet from the window. He had a good field of view, but it would be almost impossible for anyone to see him from the outside.

All they could do now was wait.

* * *

It was seven in the evening when Ryan slipped the gym bag off his shoulder and pushed through the glass doors of the fast food restaurant. He ordered a cheeseburger from a self-service terminal and stood in line waiting for his order to be made up. A couple of minutes later, he took his purchase to a window seat and put his bag on the floor. The man sitting next to him had an identical holdall. Ryan looked out the window at the passing pedestrians who were enjoying the pleasant evening, but none of them seemed to be paying him any attention.

"Don't worry, you're clear," Marcus Hayes said. He dipped a couple of fries in a tiny cup of ketchup and popped them in his mouth.

"I know." Ryan had performed several counter-surveillance manoeuvres on his way to the meeting. It had taken him thirty minutes to be sure he wasn't being tailed, but it was always time well spent. "What have you got for me?"

"Trainers and a polo shirt, exactly like the ones you already own. There's a tracker in the sole of the right shoe, and in the collar of the shirt is a panic button. It works like a glow stick. Just bend it in the middle and it'll start transmitting."

"Why the sudden need for a panic button?" Ryan asked.

"The old man's just playing it safe," Hayes told him. "This deal came out of the blue, and he's not comfortable with it."

"Why not? It's what he brought me in for, isn't it?"

Hayes swallowed a mouthful of burger. "It's the rapid escalation that worries him. All you've done so far is debt collection and that trip to Albania—which he still thinks was a dummy run, by the way—and now they want you in on a weapons sale to jihadists."

"Albania was the real thing," Ryan said. "The van was in pieces. You think we went all that way to get it serviced?"

"Don't shoot the messenger. I'm just telling you how the old man feels."

"Well, tell him from me that everything's fine. If it makes him feel better, he can have a few ARVs on stand by and nick the lot of them once the deal is done." Ryan looked down at his food. "I don't like the idea of those people getting their hands on weapons."

"We can't pull them in on Thursday without compromising you, so we'll just have to keep an eye on the buyers and take them down at a more opportune moment. What bothers the old man is that this is a departure from Marsh's MO. He's never dealt with terrorists before, which makes the boss nervous."

"And he never dealt cocaine until he sold his first kilo," Ryan pointed out. "Besides, that's what the boss brought me in for, isn't it? To find out who's putting weapons in the hands of Al-Qaeda?"

"I guess so," Hayes conceded. He popped the last morsel into his mouth and wiped his fingers on a tissue. "Take care, Ryan. I mean it."

Hayes got up and took Ryan's gym bag with him.

Ryan watched him leave, then finished his own food and picked up the bag containing his tracking gear. As he walked through the town centre, he wondered if Brigshaw's concern was justified. Sure, the news about the weapons sale had come out of the blue, but then that had always been the case. Ryan never knew what the next day was going to bring. He would just wake up to a knock on the door or a phone call and be told what to do. This was nothing out of the ordinary. Also, Paul's reaction that morning struck him as genuine. The man was usually unflappable, but the idea of selling arms to Islamic jihadists had riled him.

Brigshaw was just being overcautious, Ryan decided. His background was clean and he followed Marsh's orders to the letter. There was simply no reason for anyone to suspect him of being MI5.

Still, Brigshaw was the one with the years of experience in these matters, so he would wear the items Hayes had given him.

It couldn't hurt to have a little protection.

Chapter 23

"Welcome to the Vodaphone voicemail service for…"

Scott Davison ended the call without bothering with a message. He'd already left two in the last hour, but Kelly hadn't got back to him.

It was unlike her. She usually picked up within a couple of rings.

He suspected she was probably in a final meeting with her client, ensuring they were happy with the advertising campaign she'd created and handing over any documentation they might need. That was it. It had to be. He was worrying for nothing.

Scott stuck a pod in the coffee machine and waited for it to brew, then took it through to the living room and opened a browser on his phone. There wasn't much of interest in the news, so he put the phone down and sat back with his hands behind his head.

Since arriving back from London the previous day, Scott had done nothing but think about Kelly. Tonight would be their last one together before she headed off for her next assignment on Friday. He hoped the advertising agency would send her to Australia. That would be perfect. He'd give her a few weeks to get settled in and find a place to live, then tie up his own affairs in France and jet out to join her.

If she was told to stay in London, that would be a different matter. He'd told her a long-distance relationship would be fine, seeing each other at weekends, but it wasn't what he really wanted. For one, he hated the idea of setting foot in England again. Secondly, two nights with Kelly just wasn't enough. Even now, when she was just a few miles away, he missed her.

It wasn't as if he hadn't had girls before, but they had been one-night stands. He'd had no desire to revisit any of them. Kelly was different. She wasn't just a twenty-something with zero career prospects, she was a driven woman with a plan. Her energy was addictive, contagious. He'd slept with better-looking women, but none had aroused him as Kelly did.

The phone rang, startling him. He picked it up and saw Kelly's name on the screen.

"Hi," he said.

"Hey. Sorry I didn't get back to you sooner, I was in a meeting."

"No problem. I just wondered what you wanted to do tonight."

"I was hoping you'd suggest a quiet night in at your place," she said.

Scott smiled. "That's exactly what I was hoping you'd say. I'll get some food in. Shall we say, six o'clock?"

"Sounds perfect. See you then."

It was the briefest of chats, but his heart was soaring. Just hearing her voice was the tonic he needed.

Scott warned himself not to mention the idea of her giving up work to be supported by him. Not tonight. In the coming months he might slip it into the conversation, but this evening he didn't want to say anything to scare her off.

He put on his shoes and jacket at the front door. The walking stick was leaning against the wall, a reminder of how far he'd come in the last twelve months. He hadn't used it for a while, but for some reason he hadn't got rid of it.

Scott left it where it was and walked out to the car. His gait wasn't perfect, but it would improve over time. He drove into town and parked near the outdoor market. They always had a great variety of fresh foods, but all Scott could think about was what he was going to get for dessert.

Chapter 24

"I could be shacked up with that Scottish barmaid, but no, I'm here, staring out of the fucking windows."

Paul could hear Terry's mutterings as he crossed from room to room, and he couldn't blame him. He never imagined surveillance could be so dull, so mind-numbing. At least it wouldn't last forever. If no one showed by eleven on Thursday morning, chances were they weren't coming. It was just after one on Tuesday morning, so they had a maximum of fifty-eight hours to sit it out. Even if he managed to sleep three times before the deadline, he could still be staring out into the fields for another day and a half.

It was a depressing thought, and Paul tried to cast it from his mind. He took one last look out the window, then grabbed a plastic bag and went into the toilet. He'd been snacking all day to relieve the boredom and had already gone through half of his supplies. It was time to make room for more, but the idea of shitting into a bag had seemed a lot easier than it actually turned out to be. After a couple of aborted attempts, Paul finally did his business, then double-tied the bag and left it in the bathroom. He vowed to leave the next dump until daylight, as the green-tinted night vision goggles didn't help.

Back in the front bedroom, Paul put his head next to the window frame and scanned the horizon. He saw occasional pearls of light as vehicles passed the farm, but none stopped. Out in the open land, nothing moved.

"I'm gonna get some kip," Terry said as he dropped onto the camp bed.

"Okay. I'll wake you when I get tired."

Paul now had three rooms to cover, but at least it would keep him occupied. He put on Terry's goggles to change the batteries in his own unit, then went on his rounds.

Within five minutes Paul heard Terry snoring, a sound that was likely to drive him mad before too long. He put his jacket over his head and turned on his iPod Touch, selected an album, then put the unit in his pocket so that the light wasn't visible.

He continued his rounds, going from room to room, only stopping for the occasional drink of water. Two hours passed, during which time the only movement he saw in the field was a fox looking for something to eat.

He was back in the front room looking out over the road when he struck gold. A car drove along the main road and stopped two hundred yards from the lane that led to the farmhouse. It was difficult to see anything beyond the glare of the headlights, but when the car pulled away moments later, Paul saw a figure jump over the stone wall and into the field.

"Get up!" he growled, kicking the camp bed.

"What?! What is it?"

"We've got company."

Terry threw on his goggles and Paul showed him where to look.

"Bastard!"

"Tell me about it."

The figure looked like a man to Paul, but it was hard to be a hundred per cent sure at this range. They watched him carry a large bag to the base of the hill, then stop and study the landscape through binoculars.

"Back up!" Paul said, pushing Terry away from the window. He had to be using light-enhancing equipment, and there was a chance he might see them.

Paul manoeuvred himself so that he was kneeling down at ledge height, far enough away from the window as to make himself invisible, but close enough to see what was going on. The man had put down his bag and was now digging behind a small bush. Paul saw him carefully lift off the top layer of grass and put it aside, then spend the next half-hour excavating a hole. He carefully placed the soil on top of some kind of a sheet, and every five minutes the man would stop digging and take the soil back down to the road and spread it out at the base of the wall.

"This guy knows what he's doing," Paul said. "I don't think he's just a copper."

They watched for another two hours as the man worked ceaselessly on his hiding place. He took a folding board of some kind and placed it over the hole he'd created, then covered it with the grass he'd laid aside earlier. Once he crawled into the hole, it was impossible to tell that it was there.

"He's definitely not just poaching," Terry said. "What now?"

"We stay here," Paul told him. "When it's light I'll get Phil to tell Ryan that the deal has been switched to another location. I'll say the buyers were nervous and wanted to do it on their own turf, or something like that. Then we wait for this guy to disappear, and we go pay Ryan a visit."

* * *

"It's off," Ryan said as soon as the call connected. He was jogging through Priory Gardens, a small woodland near his flat. The vehicle pollution coming from the adjacent M60 meant it wasn't the ideal place for a run, but the few people about made a good spot to report in. "Phil told me the buyers weren't happy with Marsh choosing the location. It's all stalled until they can come up with an arrangement that suits both sides."

"Damn!" Brigshaw exclaimed. "I was worried something like this might happen."

"What do you mean?"

"If they suspected you, they would feed you false information and see if you act on it. I said from the start I didn't like this."

"I think you're reading too much into it," Ryan said. "These things happen."

"In my experience, they happen for all the wrong reasons. I'm pulling you out."

"Whoa! Don't be too hasty. We've put months into this. Let's just see what they do."

"What they may do is kill you."

Ryan had never considered that. Being so clean, there was nothing in his background that would make them suspect him, so he'd never contemplated them turning on him. If Brigshaw was right, then he was in a lot of trouble. Then again, people were wrong all the time, no matter how long they'd been doing the job.

"Then put a team on me for the next couple of weeks. I've got the tracker and the panic button, and we can arrange for me to pick up a few more shirts and some decent shoes so that I'm wearing one at all times."

There was silence while Brigshaw considered his request.

"Okay," he finally said. "I'll get a mobile unit to follow you around. They'll be a mile away at the most. But you be careful. You see the slightest change in their behaviour, I want you to run, you understand?"

"Got it," Ryan said, "but I still think you're calling it wrong. When I saw Phil this morning, he seemed fine."

"For your sake, I hope I am. Just keep your eyes peeled. I'll tell Marcus to meet you at the usual place at eight."

The call ended. Ryan completed his run, then went back to his flat to shower. Afterwards, he wore the polo shirt and trainers that Marcus Hayes had given him the day before, then turned on the television. Phil had told him he wouldn't be needed for the rest of the day and he didn't feel like socialising.

At four o'clock, he put a Thai red curry in the microwave and opened a beer while it cooked. He was looking through the TV menu when his phone beeped to announce an incoming message.

Men's clothing sale. 50% off all items.

It had a link to a website, but Ryan didn't need to check it. It was a coded message telling him to call in as soon as possible.

Ryan picked up his Walkman and hit the combination of buttons as he left his flat. He never called from inside, just in case Marsh had installed listening devices while he was out. In the street, he put the earphones in and started walking.

"It's confirmed," Brigshaw said without preamble. "Your cover's blown."

"Wait. How can you be sure?"

"Before I pulled our guy off the farm I had someone else set up a mile away with a zoom lens. Ten minutes after we pulled the first man out, he saw two people leave the farmhouse and get in a car. It was Paul Gardner and Terry Stoppard. They were picked up in Gardner's BMW by Phil Walker. Clearly, they were there to see if our guy showed up."

Ryan couldn't believe it. After all this time, after all the tests he'd passed, they were still suspicious. Not only that, he'd fallen into their trap.

"I'm sorry," Ryan said. "I should have listened to you."

"It was my call to make," Brigshaw replied. "I'm sending the mobile unit in to pick you up now. Just wait where you are."

Ryan hit the button twice to close the call and turned to face the apartment he'd have to abandon.

What he saw made the blood freeze in his veins.

Chapter 25

Kelly was wearing just a T-shirt and jeans, but she looked stunning. Scott held the door open for her and closed it once she was inside his apartment.

"Something smells good." She kissed him tenderly, then walked through to the kitchen, where she put her handbag over the back of a chair and poured red wine into two glasses.

"It's pork tenderloin," Scott said, taking one of the drinks from her.

"Hmmm. Good choice of wine."

Kelly took a seat at the dining table and Scott joined her.

"I heard from the office this afternoon."

Scott tried to read her face, to detect whether it was good or bad news, but she'd have made a brilliant poker player.

"And...?"

Her face lit up. "They want me to go to Australia!"

"That's fantastic! When will you be going?"

"Next week. I have to go back to London tomorrow and spend a few days at the office, then I fly out next Thursday." She held up her drink. "Melbourne, here I come."

Scott clinked his glass against hers. He couldn't have hoped for a better outcome.

"They're paying for the flight, obviously, and I get a hotel for the first three weeks while I sort out my own accommodation. They're giving me five hundred a month toward rent, and throwing in a company car."

"Sounds great," Scott said. "Do you know anything about the project you'll be working on?"

"Not yet. I guess it'll be similar to the one I just completed, but it's a different culture, so the message will have to be tailored to suit the market."

She seemed genuinely excited, and Scott couldn't blame her. Most people would be delighted at the chance to spend a year in the sun doing what they loved. He was pleased, too, for his own reasons. He could see her every day, not just two nights a week.

If she still felt that way.

"Are you still happy for me to join you once you're settled?" he asked.

"Of course! That's why I was hoping for this posting."

Scott almost skipped back to the stove to take his asparagus off the heat and plate up.

The meal was good, one of the best he'd made, and afterwards they opened a second bottle of wine and trawled the internet for places to stay in Melbourne and the tourist sites they would visit together.

Scott's mood dipped slightly when they discussed life on the coast; he wasn't sure how he'd feel in beachwear. The scars from his numerous operations would be with him forever, a constant reminder of a life he'd rather forget. That grim thought led to others, the most crucial being: could he ever tell Kelly the truth? If he did, how would she react? Could she handle knowing that the man she'd fallen for was a fabrication? If he was going to reveal his secret, it would have to be sooner rather than later. Better to lose her now, while there were few memories to haunt him, than ten years down the line.

But Scott couldn't do it. If he did, it would mean becoming the man he was before, and that wasn't the life he wanted to live. He was now Scott Davison, and would be forever more.

"What are you thinking about?" Kelly asked.

"Nothing."

"Really? You look serious."

Scott smiled. "Just wondering how the good folk down under will react when they see my pasty-white body the first time we hit the beach."

"I wouldn't worry about it. Within a couple of days, you'll look like one of the locals. Your only concern is keeping me happy…and satisfied."

"That," Scott said, running his hand up her thigh, "will be my pleasure."

Chapter 26

John Latimer pulled in behind the marked police car and turned off the engine. The hedges on either side of the narrow country lane stood six feet tall, giving the place a claustrophobic feel. He and DS Paul Benson got out as a uniformed officer approached their vehicle and Latimer flashed his ID.

"Where is it?" he asked.

"Through the gate and you'll see a small copse to your right. SOCO is already there."

The two detectives walked into the field and immediately spotted activity near a small cluster of trees. Benson made a beeline for them, but Latimer stopped him.

"Notice anything?" the DI asked.

Benson looked around. "No."

"Exactly. I bet you a tenner that the body was driven right up to the trees and then dumped in the grave."

"That would make sense. Easier than carrying it all the way from the road. Or, the victim could have walked to the trees and been killed there."

"I doubt it. The tip-off we got. It's similar to the one Hampshire received when Sean Conte was discovered." Again, it had been an anonymous email with detailed instructions on how to find the body.

"You think it's the same person?"

If it was, they had a serial killer on their hands. Once the press got hold of it, the pressure to find the culprit would intensify. It would also mean that James Knight was innocent. There's no way he could have committed a murder while on remand in Brixton.

"No one drove across this field in the last few weeks, you can tell. Which means they would have driven around the perimeter of the field. So where are the tyre tracks?"

Benson looked around. "None, just like last time."

"Come on." Latimer led him through the overgrown grass to the trees, where white-suited scene-of-crime officers were painstakingly gathering evidence. He showed his ID once more, asked for the officer in charge, and was directed to someone named Carrick.

"What have we got?" Latimer asked her. She looked to be in her forties, with mousey hair tied up under her white plastic hood.

"The jackpot, by the looks of it. IC1 male, laceration to the neck. We've got the murder weapon, prints and hair follicles. If the killer's in the system, you'll have this wrapped up by the end of the week."

Latimer wasn't so certain. "Mind if I take a look?"

"Sure, but you know the drill. We've isolated a couple of footprints, so steer clear of them."

She handed the detectives rubber gloves and plastic coverings for their footwear, then went back to cataloguing the find.

As they approached the body, the smell got worse. The stench of decay. Latimer put a handkerchief to his mouth and nose and stood over the body as it lay in a two-foot-deep hole. The scene was all too familiar. The hands of the corpse had already been bagged to preserve any evidence, and the gash in the throat was filled with congealed blood. Latimer could see bloody prints on the dead man's bare forearms.

"Any ID on him?" Latimer asked Carrick.

"A wallet with driver's licence, debit card and a couple of credit cards. His name's Robert Waterstone, lives in Ealing."

Latimer copied down the details from her clipboard. "How long do you think he's been there?"

"Hard to be precise," Carrick told him. "Two weeks, give or take. It's been a hot old summer, which tends to accelerate the decomposition process."

Latimer made a mental note to see if there had been any missing person's reports for the victim. If he had family, they could help to determine his last known movements. "How long before we have DNA and prints ready for comparison?"

"Some time tomorrow. If you leave me a number, I'll get back to you as soon as we have something."

Latimer gave her his card, then he and Benson walked back to the car.

"Still think it's the same person?" the DS asked.

"I'm sure of it. They left a treasure trove of evidence, but obscured the tyre tracks. That, and the emailed tip-off, tells me it's the same guy."

"Which is good news for James Knight," Benson said.

"Only if we catch the killer. All we have at the moment are similarities, and all the evidence in the Conte murder still points to James." Latimer slipped off his gloves and put them in his pocket. "Let's go find out all we can about Robert Waterstone."

* * *

Determining Waterstone's last movements proved more difficult than Latimer had hoped. He was single and lived alone, so there was no one to report him missing. Being a self-employed builder, there were no work colleagues to worry about his absence, either. House-to-house enquiries had turned up very little, but one neighbour noticed that he went out almost every night. Based on the victim's physique, the officer predicted it was to the pub. His guess was spot on. The landlord of a bar in the area identified Waterstone as a member of his darts team, and confirmed that he'd last been in a couple of weeks earlier, on a Saturday. He hadn't been that good a player, so when he didn't show for the last two matches, they weren't concerned. No one in the pub knew of anyone who would want to hurt Waterstone, and he'd never caused any trouble there.

Unfortunately, there was no CCTV to go through. None of the cameras covering the area stored their recordings for more than ten days. Not that it would have been much help. Regulars at the pub said Waterstone was known to head to a kebab shop on the way home, and the uniformed officer who'd tracked him to the pub also spoke to the takeaway owner. He confirmed that Waterstone had purchased his regular meal two weeks earlier, but hadn't been seen since. That shop was on the edge of the CCTV coverage area. There were no more cameras between the takeaway and Waterstone's house, so unless he was abducted immediately after buying supper, it would have been useless anyway. All Latimer could do was wait for the forensic evidence to be processed and see if they could find a match.

It was just after one in the afternoon the day after the body was discovered when he was given the details he was waiting for. Sipping his fifth decaf of the day, he looked at the single sheet of paper that had been handed to him by a civilian member of the force.

The DNA from the hair follicles found under Waterstone's fingernails matched no one on the PNC, nor did the fingerprints.

Damn!

It was time to cast a wider net. He forwarded the details to Interpol, then sent a request to the ministry of defence to check the armed forces databases to see if the suspect was or had been a serving member.

Latimer was ready to head home for the evening when he heard back from Interpol. It wasn't good news. That left the MoD databases as his only real hope of identifying the man responsible for Robert Waterstone's death, and they were notoriously slow in processing requests.

The clock ticked over to seven as Latimer grabbed his coat and headed for the door. He strapped on his backpack and helmet as he walked to the parking area, where he unlocked his bike and climbed on.

As he cycled towards the gates, Latimer continued to consider the similarities between this case and the one that saw James Knight sitting in a cell in HMP Brixton. The shallow grave complete with murder weapon, the abundance of physical evidence, the lack of tyre marks leading from the burial site, the anonymous tip-off via an email address that hadn't been used before or since. He'd presented these to DCI Ingram in the hope that Knight might be released on bail, but she had been unreceptive. While she admitted that it appeared to be the work of the same person, it didn't prove Knight's innocence, and there would be hell to pay if Knight's DNA was found at the latest crime scene.

With his mind on the case, Latimer almost barreled into the elderly man who was standing in his path. Latimer squeezed the brakes and almost went over the handlebars.

"You trying to get yourself killed?"

"I have the utmost faith in your riding abilities, Detective Inspector Latimer. Mind if I have a word?"

Latimer was unnerved. He didn't know the man, yet the stranger seemed to know him. He got off his bike in case an attack was imminent and sized the man up. He was dressed in a long, dark woollen coat and wore a trilby on his head. The way he stood suggested he wasn't about to launch into action.

"What about?" Latimer asked.

"The request you sent to the MoD this afternoon."

That caught Latimer off guard. The only person he'd told about the request was DCI Ingram. "How did you know about that?"

"Walk with me," the man said, and Latimer had little choice but to follow.

Chapter 27

"Welcome to the Vodaphone voicemail service for oh…seven……"
Scott hung up and threw the phone on the bed in frustration. It had been sixteen days since Kelly had left to go back to England, and he hadn't heard a word from her in all that time.

If she'd had a change of heart and decided not to see him again, that was fine, but it was the silence that was destroying him. No text message to say "Thanks for the fun time but I think we should move on," or an email to wish him all the best for the rest of his life. Just…nothing.

He didn't think he could face another sleepless night, tossing and turning while wondering whether she'd had an accident and was lying in the bottom of a ditch somewhere. Maybe she was knocked down crossing the street, or slipped in the bath…

He didn't want to do it, but he'd already waited too long. He had to have closure. He picked up the phone again and sat in front of the laptop in the living room to look up the name of the company she worked for. He dialed the contact number for the London branch.

"Pressley Mainwaring, Diane speaking, how may I help you?"

"Hi. I'd like to speak to Kelly Thorn please."

"One moment, please." Unnecessarily loud elevator music boomed in his ear as he waited for the call to be connected. "I'm sorry, "the same voice said, "but we have no one of that name here."

He realised he'd made a rookie mistake. "She was recently transferred to your Melbourne office. Could you give me a contact number there?"

The receptionist looked up the number and read it out. He thanked her and hung up, then called the Australian branch. Halfway through dialing, he hung up. They were ten hours ahead, so it would be close to midnight in Melbourne. He would have to wait until late in the evening to call.

He knew that sitting staring at the walls would drive him mad, so he put on his jacket and opened the front door.

Scott almost jumped out of his skin when he saw the man standing inches from the door, his hand out ready to ring the bell. It was a man he'd hoped never to see again, a man who'd caused him so much pain and stolen his future from him.

"Hello, Ryan," Malcolm Brigshaw said.

Chapter 28

Ryan hadn't heard the Transit van pull over. The phone conversation through the earphones he'd been wearing had drowned out the sound, and now Paul Gardner was standing next to the vehicle, a pistol in his right hand. It was hanging down by his side, but his finger was already inside the trigger guard.

"Get in," he said.

Ryan feigned surprise, hoping to buy some time. "What's up, mate?" He raised his hands to straighten his collar and set off the panic button, but Paul advanced with the pistol up, aiming at Ryan's face.

"Don't move a fucking muscle. Hands out and get in the fucking van."

Ryan had no option but to comply. Paul was only about four yards away now, and at that range it would be difficult to miss. He was sure he'd get an opportunity to activate the alarm at some point, so Ryan held his arms out by his side and walked to the back of the van. Paul moved with him, ensuring Ryan was never close enough to him to strike.

The van's back doors were open, and inside Ryan saw Phil, his face like thunder as he toyed with an eight-inch blade. Ryan turned to Paul, who gestured with the gun. He didn't look as angry as Phil, but Ryan didn't mistake that for compassion. Paul was always cool. The only time he'd seen him lose his temper had been a couple of days earlier, when he'd set up this whole episode, and he realised that that had been for show.

Ryan climbed in and sat on the floor, and Paul got in and sat opposite him.

"You fucked up, Ryan," Terry shouted from the driver's seat as he started the engine.

"Shut it!" Paul screamed back. He pointed the gun at Ryan. "Strip."

"What?"

"You heard him!" Phil said, jabbing Ryan in the shoulder with the blade. The strike drew blood, but Phil didn't seem concerned in the slightest.

Ryan rubbed the wound and his hand came away bloody.

"Get on with it," Paul said.

Ryan put his hands on his collar and located the panic device at the base of his neck. He cracked it as he pulled the garment over his head and tossed it aside, then slowly removed his trainers, socks and jeans. He had to give his back-up team time to get to him.

"Everything," Paul said, pointing the gun at Ryan's groin.

Ryan removed his underpants and put them on top of the pile.

"The watch, too."

"What is this?" Ryan asked as he undid the clasp and discarded his timepiece.

Paul ignored the question. He opened the back door and threw Ryan's belongings on the road. Terry jumped out and locked the back doors, then got back behind the wheel and set off.

"What the fuck are you playing at?" Ryan shouted, still playing the innocent. This wasn't good. Brigshaw now had no way to track him, and he couldn't take Paul and Phil out, not in the confines of the van. If he attacked one, the other would do him some serious damage.

He could only hope that the team looking out for him found the pile of clothes quickly and radioed back so that they could check CCTV, but even that wouldn't guarantee a speedy resolution. He'd checked out all cameras in the area around his flat, not wanting to be seen talking on one when making his reports. There were none along the route he'd taken, so anyone looking for him would have to scan all traffic on the nearby main roads, and that could take hours.

Somehow, he didn't think he had that long.

"I'll ask you again, what the fuck are you playing at?"

"You know exactly what's going on, Ryan. If that is your name."

"Of course it is. You know it is. You told me yourself, you checked me out, all the places I worked, everything."

"Yeah, and you did a good job convincing those people to lie for you," Phil chimed in.

Ryan gave him a look of astonishment. "Are you saying I paid those people to lie about me? Seriously? There must have been seventy people working at that factory, more on the building site. You think I paid them all off?"

"I don't know how you did it," Paul said, "but you fucked up when you told your people about the arms deal with the jihadists."

"What people!" Ryan threw his arms up in frustration. "I wish you'd make sense."

Phil grabbed Ryan's neck and put his mouth close to his ear. "Paul and Terry were there," he growled. "They saw someone dig in a couple of days before it went down, and just after I told you the deal was off, the guy suddenly leaves. You gonna tell me that's a coincidence?"

Ryan turned his head as best he could, struggling against Phil's vice-like grip. "Maybe it was Paul that told the cops. He said he hated the idea of selling to the Muslims."

"There was never gonna be a sale," Paul said. "I made it up."

Ryan had suspected as much, but couldn't go down without a fight. "Then one of you is trying to frame me," he said. "I'm better than you in every way, and you're jealous. Jealous that Marsh'll see how good I really am and give me one of your positions. That's it, isn't it?"

"Nice try," Phil said, squeezing harder.

"Was it you?" Ryan grimaced. "You've never liked me, have you? You've got motive, you had the opportunity…yeah, I bet it was you."

"You even sound like a copper," Phil said, and banged Ryan's head against the van's internal wall.

"Enough!" Paul snarled. "We'll get to the truth eventually."

The ride took forty minutes, and Ryan knew the search for him would be well under way. One thing on his side was that the van they were using was the same one he'd travelled to Albania in. He saw the panel where a bored Phil had once carved his name into the metalwork. It was one of several vehicles Marsh and his men used, and Brigshaw had the licence plate numbers of all of them. All the intelligence officers back at Thames House had to do was check the CCTV to see if any were in the vicinity of his street and then follow them on camera.

It sounded simple enough.

In theory.

The van stopped, and Ryan heard doors slam shut before Terry opened the back of the vehicle. Paul backed out, his eyes always on Ryan, then gestured with the gun. "Out you get."

Phil poked Ryan once more with the knife to ensure his compliance, and Ryan reluctantly climbed down.

They were inside what looked like a three-car garage. There wasn't a lot of room, and it was freezing. Ryan saw two people standing in the shadows at the back, and a wooden chair was sitting on top of a large sheet of plastic wrap in the middle of the empty space.

Ryan knew what was coming, and it wasn't going to be pleasant, but he just had to hold on until help arrived. He didn't have to make it easy for them though.

When Phil grabbed his arm to move him forward, Ryan twisted and struck him in the middle of the chest with the flat of his hand, knocking the air from his lungs. Phil staggered backwards and hit the wall, and Ryan spun to face Paul.

He was a fraction too slow.

* * *

John Ward spun the grey Peugeot Traveller's wheel to the right. The vehicle leapt across two lanes of oncoming traffic and drifted into Britannia Road. He kept his foot to the floor as two of his companions checked their weapons one last time.

"Two hundred yards," the fourth member of the team shouted from the back.

Ward barrelled down the street as the distance was counted down, then stamped on the brakes when it got to five yards. The two armed occupants jumped out, their weapons by their side and eyes scanning.

"Here!" one of them said, ran to a pile of clothes in the road, picked them up and ran back to the van. "They must have taken him. Call it in."

The man in the back abandoned the tablet showing the location of the tracker and got on comms to update the office.

"No sign of Ryan. Looks like they stripped him and dumped his stuff in the street. Check CCTV for any vehicles leaving Britannia Road in the last few minutes."

"On it."

Ward executed a smart three-point turn and roared back up to the main road. At the junction, he paused. "Come on…left or right?"

After what seemed like an age, he got a response. "Left. A white Transit." The operator read out the index of the vehicle as Ward made the turn.

"Where next? Put it on speaker."

They were now in the one-way system, but a choice soon presented itself. "Do I go straight or right?"

"Wait one."

Drivers behind leaned on their horns as Ward stopped in the middle of the road. He ignored their protests, waiting for confirmation.

"Straight on. They're on the M60."

Ward gunned the engine. "North or south?"

"North."

He flew across the roundabout and onto the slip road before bullying his way onto the motorway. "We'll be at junction seven in one minute. Stay on or get off?"

"Stay on," the control room said, "I'll see if he gets off at junction eight."

"Hurry," Ward shouted. "We'll be there in less than two minutes."

"He stayed on. Checking junction nine…"

Ward stayed in the inside lane in case he had to leave the motorway. It was slow going, stuck behind a procession of lorries, but it gave the team back at the office time to work out the route to follow.

Ward had never met Ryan Anderson and had only been assigned to the case the previous day, but he felt like his guardian angel. It was his job to pull Ryan out of danger, but so far he'd been a step behind. He had to get to him soon, otherwise a brave young man could lose his life. Franklin Marsh wasn't the type of man to give people a warning and send them on their merry way.

"We have a problem," control said. "The cameras at nine are out. I'm checking ten."

"Hurry," Ward said, "I'll be at nine in a couple of minutes. I need an answer."

He slowed as much as he could, but the marker for junction nine soon appeared in front of him. "I need an answer," he said once more.

There was nothing from control beyond "wait one", but time was fast running out. He had to commit. Another reminder showed up on the gantry above the motorway, a large white arrow pointing the way to Trafford Park. Moments later, the exit was upon him.

Talk to me, Anderson.

* * *

Ryan knew the second he opened his eyes that he was in trouble. His ankles were bound to the legs of the chair with tape and his arms secured behind its back. More tape strapped his chest to the back of the chair and went under his seat and over his thighs. He could move only his fingers, toes and eyes.

The men who had been standing in the shadows were now bathed in the light of the single fluorescent unit hanging from the ceiling. One of them was tall and blond. Ryan remembered him as George, the bodyguard he'd taken out when he'd first encountered Marsh months earlier.

Marsh himself was also there.

"I must say, you surprised me," Franklin Marsh said as he blew out a cloud of smoke. "Everything about you looked kosher, but thankfully Paul here thought you were too good to be true, didn't you, Paul?"

Paul was standing off to Ryan's right and he nodded.

"So, what's your real name?" Marsh asked.

"Ryan Anderson."

The blow to Ryan's cheek came from nowhere.

"This is how it works." Marsh dropped his cigarette on the ground and crushed it with his foot. "I ask you a question, and you give me an honest answer, otherwise the boys are going to have some fun with you. Got it?"

Ryan nodded.

"Okay. What's your real name?"

"Ryan Anderso—"

This time the strike arrived from the left, a solid blow to the temple from Phil's meaty fist.

"One more time."

"My name is Ryan—"

Paul's fist connected with Ryan's nose and blood splattered as bone and cartilage shattered.

"He's not getting it," Marsh said. "Take off one of his toes."

Phil gave Ryan an evil grin as he knelt in front of him, a pair of bolt cutters in his hand. Ryan shouted for him not to do it, but fire erupted from his feet as the metal blades made short work of his little toe.

Phil held up the bloody appendage. "One down, nine to go."

"Name!" Marsh barked.

Ryan shook his head violently, knowing that they would never accept the truth.

Marsh nodded, and Phil went to work once more, taking the small toe from Ryan's other foot.

"We can do this all day," Marsh said. He lit another cigarette. "If you don't want to give us your name, how about who you work for?"

"I work for you!" Ryan spat blood. "This is all a big mistake. Someone set me up!"

"Nice try, but I've known my boys for years. I've only known you two minutes. You should just tell us everything and this'll all be over."

Ryan knew that didn't mean walking away with a telling off. He was going to die, unless a miracle happened.

"I can't tell you anything if it's not true!"

"Suit yourself. Paul, get the hammer."

Ryan watched Paul pick up a sledgehammer in his right hand. He tested the weight against his left hand, then swung it up over his head and brought it crashing down on Ryan's right knee.

Ryan had never experienced pain like it. It was like a lightning bolt shooting up every nerve ending and coming together for an enormous explosion in his brain.

Ryan cried. He didn't even try to stop himself, he just let the tears come and wailed like a baby. Maybe they would take pity on him and stop the torture, or at least give him time to recover before they inflicted more torment.

It wasn't to be. Paul brought the hammer down on Ryan's left knee, smashing the cap into thousands of pieces. Another surge of pain racked his body, and Ryan screamed, an animal sound he didn't know he was capable of.

Marsh waited until he was almost coherent before moving to stand in front of him. "You can end this now by telling me the truth, or I can get Phil to cut your balls off. What'll it be?"

Ryan tried to squeeze his legs together, but any effort he exerted brought a fresh wave of agony.

"Better make your mind up quick, "Marsh said. "Phil's been begging me to let him do this all day, and I can't wait to hear your scream when he does. You cost me a fortune, you little shit. I can't do the Albania run anymore because of you, and that was one of my biggest earners. Do you realise how many shooters and how much cocaine you can fit in the shell of a Transit? A shit load, that's how much. And now I'm gonna have to come up with a new way of getting them across." Marsh grabbed Ryan's cheeks and squeezed. "But the biggest disappointment is knowing you lied to me. You treated me like an idiot, and for that you're gonna pay, big time. After Phil chops your cock off, we're gonna use a hacksaw to cut your feet off, then your hands, and we're gonna cauterise them so you don't bleed to death. We kept the last one alive for forty hours. Nearly two fucking days! Think about that."

Ryan could only shake his head. He wanted to speak, to protest his innocence, but the words wouldn't come. Perhaps it was the shock, or the futility of the situation. He'd undergone basic interrogation resistance in the army and a more intense course during his training with Brigshaw, but it hadn't prepared him for the real thing. Marsh was going to hurt him for the fun of it, not to get information. Whether he was MI5, National Crime Agency or the police, it didn't really matter. They knew he'd betrayed them, and it was pointless denying it. The pain was going to come, again and again, and there was nothing he could do about it.

"Please…" Ryan managed to say, but Marsh didn't seem in a merciful mood. He stood back so that Phil could take over.

"No…please…"

Ryan could offer no more resistance. His body was in preservation mode, shutting down to protect the vital organs.

Phil stood before him with a look of pure malevolence, then everything got confusing. Phil's demeanour changed, his eyes widened, and there was a loud crash somewhere in the room, but Ryan couldn't make out where it had come from. There was shouting, then Ryan's entire body tensed as a loud bang filled the small space. He knew it was a gunshot, but didn't feel the bullet hit his body. Then his vision was filled with people he didn't recognise. They were shouting and holding guns, and Marsh was standing with his hands in the air.

A face appeared in front of Ryan's. It was a man, and he was talking, but Ryan couldn't hear him. He just knew it was a friendly face. Then everything went black.

Chapter 29

The room was bathed in a dull light, like a cinema just before the curtains are raised. Ryan saw several LED bulbs recessed into the ceiling and knew he wasn't in his own apartment. So where was he? All he could remember was darkness. He heard a beep from the side of his bed and turned his head to see a contraption with lights and moving graphs.

A hospital?

The floodgates opened. The small garage…Marsh…his toes…the sledgehammer…

The machine gave shrill warble and he turned to see the heart rate monitor spiking.

Ryan almost jumped out of his skin when a hand grabbed his arm.

"It's okay," a familiar voice said. "You're safe now."

Ryan looked to the other side of the bed and saw the chubby face of Marcus Hayes smiling at him.

"Glad to have you back," Hayes said. "You had us worried for a moment."

The monitor's high-pitched alarm continued to fill the room, and Ryan flinched when the door flew open. He didn't need a machine to tell him how hard his heart was pounding, but it wasn't Marsh or one of his men come to finish him off. Instead, a nurse ran in and silenced the alarm with the press of a button. She adjusted a drip, and Ryan immediately began to feel drowsy.

"You can't go exciting him," she berated Hayes. "He needs his rest. You should leave and come back in the morning."

Hayes tried to stand, and Ryan threw a hand in his direction, managing to grab hold of his suit jacket at the second attempt.

"Stay. I need to know what happened."

Hayes looked at the nurse, who glared back, clearly unhappy at having her authority questioned.

"Five minutes," she said, "then he needs to sleep."

She closed the door on her way out.

"How bad is it?" Ryan asked when she was gone. He tried moving his legs but got no response. At least there was no pain, just a heavy fog behind his eyes.

"The doctors are optimistic," Hayes told him. "It's only been five days—"

"Five days?"

"Yeah. You weren't in good shape when they found you. They've had you sedated since you arrived, and have operated on your legs twice. They seem confident you'll be back on your feet in a few weeks and fully recovered within a year."

Ryan was struggling against the drugs to stay awake. "Did you say a year?"

"They had to do reconstructive surgery on the joints of the tibia and femur, and you've got brand new synthetic knee caps. The doctor said you should be walking without a limp this time next year."

"I'm supposed to go back to Two Para," Ryan said. "How long before they let me back in?"

"Well, we'll see."

Something in Hayes's reply told him that wasn't going to happen. It would take some time to get back to full fitness, a lot longer than twelve months. That was just to walk properly again, and then he had to learn to run once more. To be fit enough to go into battle would take another two years at least, and even then the doctors might not sign him off. If he couldn't get back into his old unit, any hopes of joining the special air service were over. He was three weeks past his twenty-fourth birthday, and his dreams were over before they'd begun.

Anger flushed through him. If Brigshaw hadn't approached him, he'd be in the regiment now, perhaps already deployed abroad. Now he was facing life outside the army, a prospect he wasn't prepared for.

"What took them so long to find me?" Ryan asked. "I thought they were supposed to be minutes away. I stalled them for at least three minutes."

"I checked the log," Hayes told him. "From the beacon activating to the team finding it was one minute, thirty-six seconds. They missed the van leaving your street by about ten seconds, and from then on, they were playing catch up. When you're in those situations, time plays tricks with the mind."

"So how did they find me?"

"Pure, blind luck," Hayes smiled. "The team leader had a choice to make: stay on the motorway, or get off. He got off, which was the right call. If he'd stayed on, it would have been at least another fifteen minutes before they got to you. I'd hate to think what state they would have found you in."

Ryan didn't want to even think about it. Marsh's last order had been to castrate him, and Phil had looked eager to carry out his orders.

Escaping with his tackle intact didn't make Ryan feel any better, though. He was still angry, mostly at Brigshaw for getting him into this in the first place.

"At least tell me you got Marsh."

"We did," Hayes said. "Marsh, Paul Gardner, Phil Walker and George Atkins. They'll be going down for some time. They're charged with kidnapping and grievous bodily harm with intent. That gave the police grounds to search Marsh's home and businesses, so hopefully we'll be able to pin more on him. Tax evasion, for one."

It was the outcome they'd worked towards, though the manner in which they'd achieved it had come at a huge personal cost. Two missing toes and a year of rehab hadn't been part of the bargain, and now that Marsh was behind bars, Ryan was effectively unemployed.

"So, what happens next?"

"At some point, you'll be asked to give evidence at their trial. That'll be done via video link and your face and voice will be obscured, obviously. In the meantime, we're moving you to a safe house in London to begin your recuperation. You'll be paid your normal salary until that's complete, and Brigshaw mentioned a little something as compensation for your injuries. I'll let him fill in the details. He'll be along in the morning."

"Tell him not to bother," Ryan said wearily. "I don't want anything to do with him. If he hadn't come up with this stupid idea, I wouldn't be in this mess. I'll speak to you only from now on."

"I'll tell him," Hayes sighed, and checked his watch. "I'd best be going."

"Hang on. What about security? Marsh will be looking for me. If I'm silenced…"

"Not going to happen. They'll be looking for you in the Manchester hospitals, not here in London, and we signed you in under a false name. If anyone asks about a male your age being admitted for trauma to the knees, the hospital is under instructions to deny knowledge. This place is the best private medicine has to offer, and discretion is guaranteed."

Ryan yawned as the drugs in his system began to win the battle.

Hayes tapped him on the shoulder. "I'll see you tomorrow. Get some rest."

Ryan had so many more questions, like who had fired the shot he'd heard, but fatigue overcame him. He drifted off to sleep, and fell almost immediately into a dream that he later suspected would haunt him for years to come.

Chapter 30

"Hello, Ryan," Malcolm Brigshaw said.

"My name's Scott Davison now, remember?"

"Of course. Mind if I come in?"

Ryan hesitated. There was no conversation he wanted to have with this man. He'd said all he wanted to say the day Brigshaw had visited him in hospital against his wishes.

"It's important," Brigshaw pressed, "otherwise I wouldn't be here."

Ryan sighed, then stood back and opened the door fully. Brigshaw walked inside and made straight for the living room.

"You still dress like a spymaster, I see." Every time Ryan saw him, he was wearing the long wool coat and trilby, regardless of the weather.

Brigshaw took his coat off and draped it over the back of the sofa, then placed his hat on top. "It's a double bluff. No self-respecting spy would dress like a spy, so anyone dressed like me couldn't possibly be a spy."

Brigshaw smiled, but Ryan didn't reciprocate. Instead, he went to the kitchen and put the coffee machine to work. "How do you take yours?" he shouted through to the other room.

"Milk and half a sugar."

While the machine chirped and gurgled, Ryan wondered what could have forced Brigshaw to leave his comfortable desk to visit him. If it was to convince him to go back to work for MI5, then it would prove to be a wasted journey.

Ryan poured the drinks, then took them through and put one on the table in front of Brigshaw, who had taken a seat on the sofa. Ryan chose to stand.

"How are you holding up?" Brigshaw asked.

"I thought this wasn't a social visit."

Brigshaw looked thoughtful for a moment. "Then I'll get straight to the point. When was the last time you visited London?"

It seemed a strange question, but there was no harm in telling the truth. "A couple of weeks ago. I stayed overnight at the Radisson. With a friend."

"What date?"

"The fourteenth. It was a Friday."

"And what did you do while you were there?" Brigshaw asked.

"Not that it's any of your business, I watched a movie in the afternoon, then we ate and spent the rest of the night in our room. What's this about?"

"It's about Robert Waterstone."

"Never heard of him," Ryan said truthfully, and took a sip of his coffee.

"Perhaps, but you've met him. Remember that day in the supermarket car park. The builder who confronted you over the handicapped parking space?"

Ryan would never forget it. The video had gone viral, and he suspected that was how Marsh's men had managed to track him down months later. "Yeah, I remember."

"The builder was Robert Waterstone. There was a name and shame campaign on Facebook and plenty of people recognised him. The story even made the London Standard."

"I never knew that. Once the video was in my feed every day, I quit social media. So what happened? Did he finally get a parking ticket?"

"He was murdered," Brigshaw said.

Ryan felt...nothing. No remorse, no joy. He'd rarely thought about the man whose actions had led to Marsh finding him again, so news of his death barely registered. "You couldn't have put that in an email? You had to come all this way to tell me in person?"

Brigshaw stared at him. "He died on or around the fourteenth. Your DNA was found at the crime scene."

"What! That's impossible!"

"They also found your fingerprints on the murder weapon."

Ryan flopped into an armchair, unable to believe what he was hearing. How on earth could his fingerprints be on a weapon? "This can't be happening," he said. "When I was in London, I dropped my friend off at her office, then watched an Avengers film alone. When she was finished, we met at the hotel, had a meal together, then went to bed."

"That's not how the police see it." Brigshaw took a sheet of paper from his pocket and unfolded it. "Do you have any footwear that match this shoe print?"

Ryan took the paper and studied it, but it wasn't familiar. Then again, he wasn't one for studying the soles of his shoes. "I'll take a look." He went through to the hallway and picked up his black leather shoes, but the sole was devoid of any pattern. He tried the trainers next, his heart pounding as if it knew what was coming. When he turned them over, they matched the printout perfectly.

He turned to find Brigshaw standing behind him.

"They match, don't they."

Ryan nodded. "I can't...this doesn't make any sense. I know for a fact that I didn't take my trainers to London."

"So how do you explain it?"

As far as Ryan was concerned, only one thing made any sense. "Marsh must be setting me up."

"I thought that, too," Brigshaw said, "but how would he know what footwear you use? He could only know if one of his people was in this apartment, and if they had access to you, why frame you for murder? Why not just kill you?"

"Maybe he wants me convicted so that I'm sent to the same prison as him and he can finish me off personally."

Brigshaw made a non-committal face and walked back into the living room. Ryan followed him, still unable to believe what he'd heard in the last few minutes.

"Obviously, the police want to speak to you. I held off giving them your location, but I can't stall forever. Not even MI5 officers have immunity from prosecution for murder."

"I didn't murder anyone!" Ryan said, and immediately realised how defensive he sounded. How else to react, though?

"I believe you," Brigshaw said, "but you have to turn yourself in. Speak to them, explain your side of the story."

"My side is that I'm innocent. Don't you think they've heard it all before? 'It wasn't me, I'm being framed!' They'll have me banged up for life before they can stop laughing."

"I'm sure it won't come to that. If you can—"

"You were sure I wouldn't get hurt when I took the job, but that didn't turn out too well, did it?" Ryan picked up his coffee. It was now tepid, but he emptied the cup anyway. "Twice they got me. Twice!"

"I was going to say, if you have an alibi, we can explain the rest away. Who is this friend you mentioned?"

"Her name's Kelly," Ryan said, aware that Brigshaw was avoiding the subject. "I met her a few weeks ago. She works for an advertising agency."

"Give her a call, ask her to join you in London to give a statement."

"I've been trying to get in touch with her for the last two weeks. She was transferred to Melbourne, but I haven't heard from her since. I was going to call her new office tonight."

"Do it. She can probably make a statement at her local police station and they'll forward it on. They might want her to travel back so that they can question her, though."

It wasn't what Ryan wanted. If she turned up, she would soon learn his real identity. Would she be willing to forgive him, especially after dragging her all the way across the world to defend him against a murder charge when she'd only been in her new role for a matter of days? Ryan doubted it. She'd likely get straight back on the plane and he'd never see her again.

He had to do this without her.

"Okay, I'll speak to the police, but I'm not going to the station. I'll meet him on my terms."

"That's fair enough, but do it soon. If we drag this out, he'll chase it up the ladder and eventually I'm going to have to tell him about your Scott Davison legend. When that happens, they'll come for you."

"I will...and thanks...for coming to see me first."

"It was the least I could do."

Brigshaw picked up his coat and put his hat on. "I'd better be going."

"You can stay if you like. I'll be cooking soon."

Thanks," Brigshaw said, "but I have to get back to the office." He took a rolled-up envelope from his inside pocket and put it on the table. "That's everything the police have. Forewarned and all that."

Brigshaw patted Ryan on the arm as he passed. "For what it's worth, I'm truly sorry...about everything."

Ryan said nothing. He opened the door and closed it behind his former employer.

Back in the living room, he sat on the sofa and picked up the envelope Brigshaw had left. He tore it open and took out the contents. The first few sheets contained crime scene photographs, the one on top being a shot of the corpse. There were pictures of the murder weapon, a knife with a blade caked in dried blood, images of shoe prints, blood traces on the victim's arm. Ryan put them aside and looked at the reports. The fingerprints were of excellent quality, though no match had been found on the police national computer.

Brigshaw had been able to match them, though.

To Ryan.

One thing he knew for sure was that he hadn't committed the murder. He could visualize almost every moment of his trip to London, and that meant he was being framed. The only person who would want to do that was Franklin Marsh.

The fact that the gangster was sitting in a cell in Strangeways, and would be for the next two years, didn't preclude him from orchestrating the killing. It simply had to be one of Marsh's people, though how they managed to get his fingerprints on the knife was a mystery. They had to have picked up something he'd touched, like a glass in a restaurant or café, then used tape to transfer the prints to the murder weapon. They certainly hadn't been in his home, because he had hidden cameras and an app on his phone that let him know if there was any movement in the house when he wasn't there. So how did they know what style of shoes he wore? Ryan tried to think back to all the occasions when he'd been out, either alone or with Kelly, but he couldn't recall seeing anyone taking an interest in him.

The final sheet in the file was a photograph of a middle-aged man with bicycle clips on his ankles about to put on a cycling helmet. At the top of the page it had his name, Detective Inspector John Latimer, and his home address.

Ryan knew that if he wanted answers, he had to pay Detective Inspector Latimer a visit.

Chapter 31

Karen Harper wished she could watch the video again, but it had long since been purged from the internet for some reason she could not imagine. She still had the print account of the incident, though, tucked away in her pile of Evening Standards by the workroom door. Like millions of others, she'd seen the recording of the confrontation in the supermarket car park. If ever someone had motive, it was the guy on crutches.

The guy who turned out to be Scott Davison.

She'd watched as the fat builder had levelled a verbal volley at him, an expletive-filled tirade that the man on crutches had done nothing about. How could he, though? He was barely able to get back to his car afterwards. She had no idea how he managed to drive it, though she suspected it had been retrofitted with controls for the disabled.

At that point, she knew she had the perfect pair, the victim and the murderer.

He'd almost got away from her.

A few days after seeing the video, Karen arranged a lunch date with a friend, Phillip, who worked for a parking enforcement company.

He placed two coffees on the table and sat opposite her. "How's work?" Phillip asked, as he always did. It was his way of turning the conversation to how much he hated his job, and she was sick to death of listening to it.

If you hate it that much, quit and find something better!

"Not bad. You?"

"Don't get me started," he said, sipping his drink.

Karen wished she hadn't, but she needed his help.

"I was spat at twice yesterday, and the boss doesn't give a shit. They're supposed to make sure their employees are safe when they're working, but all they care about is profit. I should write to the papers, I should."

"You really should," Karen said, jumping in to change the subject. "But before you do, could you do me a huge, ginormous favour?"

"I'm afraid I'm skint, if that's what you're gonna ask."

"No, nothing like that. In fact, I could put a few quid in your pocket."

Phillip perked up. "Yeah?"

"Yeah. You see, a few days ago I was coming back from a restaurant and some guy hit my car and then ploughed into a van. I got out to exchange details but he just drove off! I was wondering if you could look up the guy's details on your computer."

"Why didn't you just call the police?"

Karen looked ashamed. "I'd had a few glasses of wine with my dinner. I only planned to have one, but then…you know. If I called the police, they'd have taken my license."

"You could have called them the next day," Phillip said.

"I could, but then how do I explain not calling them at the time of the accident? They've heard all the excuses before, and I'm not a very good liar," she lied.

Phillip looked unsure.

"Please," she begged taking his forearm in both hands. "I need to claim on the insurance but I need to speak to the other driver first."

"What if he asks where you got his details from?"

Karen stalled, as if coming up with an answer, but she'd already anticipated the question. "I'll just say I was driving past and noticed his car in the driveway, and had noted the license plate just after he hit me."

Phillip shook his head slowly. "I don't know…"

"I'll give you fifty quid."

"Fifty?"

Karen dug into her bag and pulled out five tens. She handed them to him before he could change his mind. "If you could also get me the details of the van owner, that would be great. I'd like to let him know who hit his vehicle."

While he studied the money in his hands, Karen took out the two license numbers and handed them to him. "If you could get them to me tomorrow, I'd really appreciate it."

The following day, she had everything she needed on Scott Davison and Robert Waterstone.

Her first port of call was to Scott's house, a detached property to the west of London. She'd checked the place out on Google Earth and seen that the windows were the old sash variety, so she armed herself with a set of brochures from a double-glazing company. When she got there, her heart sank. Even at a glance, she could see the house was uninhabited. The curtains hadn't been drawn, and the living room was completely empty. She tried around the back, but the kitchen, too, was lifeless.

Disappointed, she went home to wait for the next opportunity to arise. That came in the shape of James Knight and Sean Conte. Their story was in the Evening Standard, and the challenge of framing an ex-police officer was too much to resist.

It took her some time to find the addresses, but eventually she tracked them down on the council website, going through all planning applications in the area mentioned in the article until she hit the jackpot. Google Earth's Street View showed that Knight already had double glazing, so she got her hands on some solar panel leaflets instead.

The news story had mentioned—and pictured—Knight's wife, Jenny. Karen watched her leave for work, then half an hour later, knocked on Knight's door.

Knowing how most people, herself included, reacted to cold callers, Karen launched into a pitch as soon as the door opened.

"I can see from the double glazing that you're conscious about your heating bills. That's why I want to offer you the very latest in solar technology at an absolute steal. We're having a sale at the moment, offering sixty per cent off all of our products, with no deposit and three-year, interest-free payments starting three months after installation. If you're not completely satisfied by then, we'll uninstall them free of charge and you won't pay a penny."

It had taken her hours to type up the contract, similar to one she'd received through the post from the real solar panel company, improving it to create an offer few could refuse.

She was relieved when Knight invited her inside, but her task had only just begun. She needed an excuse to visit the upstairs bathroom to get hair samples from his comb, but she'd already thought that through.

"Can I get you anything?" Knight asked. "Tea, coffee, water?"

"Coffee would be great, thank you. Would it be okay to use your toilet?"

"Sure. It's just there, in the hallway."

Karen had been hoping to be shown upstairs to the bathroom, but had anticipated this, too. She went into the room Knight indicated and locked the door, then took the toilet paper from her jacket and trouser pockets. She'd brought about a hundred sheets with her, and she used the toilet brush to stuff them around the u-bend, along with a couple of sanitary towels. After that, she waited a few moments, then flushed. She was pleased to see the water rising, then staying in the bowl.

Karen went back into the living room with a startled look on her face. "This is so embarrassing. I think I blocked your toilet."

She led Knight back to the scene of the crime and stood outside the toilet door while he investigated. While he was plunging away with the toilet brush, she took out her phone and snapped a few photos of a pair of shoes that were sitting in the hallway, getting shots of the top, profile and sole.

"Yep, that's proper blocked," Knight said as he washed his hands. "I'll get a plumber round to fix it."

"I'm so sorry," she said.

"Heavens, don't worry about it. You just happened to be the one who flushed. It could have been me, or my wife. So, shall we...?"

Karen took the hint and they returned to the living room, where she explained the benefits of the solar panels and how much he could save each year. She drank her coffee as fast as she could and made a show of the empty mug.

"Can I get you another?"

"Oo, yes please. Is that a special roast? It's delicious."

"I don't know. My wife buys it."

"I'd love to know the blend."

Knight was back a few minutes later with a fresh brew and the name of the manufacturer.

"She buys it from a shop in the high street," he told her.

"I'm going there right after we're done," Karen smiled.

She asked questions about his current bills, what energy saving steps he took, then did a calculation that showed Knight could expect a seventy-six percent reduction in fuel bills.

"The panels will pay for themselves within forty-seven months, according to my calculations, and with a twenty-year guarantee, you'll be quids-in for at least another sixteen years."

"So what's the catch?" Knight asked. "If an offer looks too good to be true, it usually is."

"No catch," Karen said, handing him a copy of the doctored contract. "Everything I mentioned is in here. Feel free to read through it. It's plain English, no hidden surprises."

Knight took it and started reading, giving Karen to chance to make her move.

"Do you mind if I use the toilet again? I'm afraid the coffee's going right through me."

"Sure, it's in the hallwa...actually, better use the one upstairs. It's the first door on the left."

She left him to study the document and went upstairs. The bathroom was nice, with a shabby-chic décor. Thankfully, Jenny Knight wasn't the most house-proud. There were plenty of hairs to choose from, and after discounting the longer ones likely to be the wife's, she selected a few short grey ones and put them in a bag, which went in an inside pocket.

When she returned to the living room, Knight handed her the contract. "It says here that projected savings are only twelve percent a year, and given the price you quoted, I'll still be out of pocket after twenty years."

"Ah. That's the manufacturer's estimate," she said, seeing the deal going south and hoping to help it on its way. The last thing she wanted was him signing the contract and the panels not being delivered. That would give him cause to remember her. "I've known one customer who did save over seventy percent."

"It also says there's a twenty per cent deposit to be paid within fourteen days."

"Would that be a problem?" she asked.

"Coming into my home and lying to me is a problem," he said, his pleasant manner evaporated.

"I'm sorry," Karen said, gathering her things. "I'm new to this, and I haven't been able to make a sale yet. I was desperate."

"Then just tell people the truth. Better still, consider another career."

Karen looked sheepish. "I think I will." She headed for the front door. "Thank you for the coffee."

Knight let her out and closed the door behind her, and she walked to the next street where she'd parked her car.

Back home, she copied the prints from the back of the clipboard and set to work making the gloves she would use to kill Sean Conte. The feeling she'd have when she got to read about Knight's arrest would make it all worthwhile.

It was by complete happenstance that she'd bumped into Scott Davison soon afterwards. She'd been working on an intricate brooch for a customer who'd relocated to France, and after delivering it in person, she'd stopped in town for something to eat. She'd recognised Scott the moment she set eyes on him. He'd been sitting alone outside a café, his head stuck in his phone, and she knew that fate had delivered her to this spot. With no way of knowing where he lived, or whether he was just on holiday, she'd taken a window seat in a restaurant opposite and ordered a small salad. An hour later, Scott had paid his bill and left, hobbling away with the aid of his walking stick. She'd given him a head start, then followed him to his car. Fortunately, there'd been a taxi rank nearby, and after finding a driver who spoke good English, she'd instructed him to follow Scott's Citroen. Once she knew where Scott lived, she made a note of the address and flew home to London.

The first thing Karen did was look to see if the house was a holiday apartment. If it was, Scott could leave at any moment and she might never find him again. After hours of searching, she saw no trace of it being a temporary let, so she formulated a plan.

She would have to get Scott to travel to London around the time she planned to kill Waterstone, and for that, she would need a new passport. It had taken a couple of weeks to find the right person, then another three to get the document in the name of Kelly Thorn. Once she had that, it was just a case of coming up with a reason for spending a few weeks in Auxerre, and work seemed the perfect cover. Her normal MO was to pose as a saleswoman, peddling various wares, but that wouldn't work due to the location. Instead, she would have to worm her way into Scott's life.

Armed with everything she needed, she'd flown back to France and checked out Scott's place. The same Citroen was in the driveway, so he hadn't moved house. It was just a case of waiting near his home each morning until he left to go into town. She'd then followed him to the café, where he'd met his friend and talked over coffee. Not wanting to make a move while Scott had company, she'd once again waited in an adjacent café until she saw Scott's friend drain his cup and make no move to get a refill. When Scott went to the toilet, she walked over and found a seat close to his, and minutes later, she was in conversation with him as Kelly Thorn.

The sad thing was, she actually liked Scott. He was moody at first, sure, but such a bad accident was bound to leave a mental impression. He was otherwise kind, and over the days and weeks that followed, she'd grown to really like him. Not as much as he liked her, that was clear. She could see the puppy-dog look he always gave her, and it nearly broke her heart to lie to him about Australia.

But someone had to take the fall. It was the way it worked.

Seeing the news report about the discovery of Robert Waterstone's body meant the search for Scott would be well under way by now. She was tempted to send another email with his whereabouts, but that would be counterproductive. The police would wonder why anyone would send them that information, and probably deduce that the sender was at least an accomplice. No, best to let the police work it out for themselves. Once they contacted Interpol, Scott's days would be numbered. She could only foresee one problem, and that was if the police checked Scott's movements. His passport would show that he'd travelled to France the morning Waterstone died. There was nothing she could do about that except hope that the police couldn't establish an exact date of death, and as Waterstone was in the pub most nights, it was unlikely that anyone would remember the precise day he last popped in.

It was time to move on to the next one, though this time there wouldn't be months of preparation. On reflection, the previous killings were too similar. Fingerprints *and* DNA were overkill, and the police would surely detect a pattern if she continued in the same vein. Her fifth victim wouldn't be buried in a remote location, she wouldn't send an anonymous email to tell them where to find the body, and she wouldn't leave prints on the murder weapon. No, just motive, DNA and opportunity were called for.

Armed with only a notepad, pen, and the laminated ID she'd created on her laptop, Karen drove to within half a mile of John Beckett's house and parked up.

His home had been easy enough to find, thanks to the article she'd read in the Evening Standard. It had mentioned the street Beckett lived in, and through public records she had found his house number. It was a seventies terrace with a tiny front garden and wood cladding on the upper floor. Karen prepared her best smile and knocked on the uPVC door.

The man who answered looked older than he had in the newspaper. His dark hair was peppered with grey, suggesting he'd worn some kind of product in it before his photograph had been taken. His skin looked sallow, and the eye bags were more pronounced. For someone in his late fifties, he looked a lot older.

"Hello, mister Beckett," Karen beamed. "I'm Sally Hanson from the Herald. I was wondering if I could do a follow-up story on the scam you were involved in."

Beckett gave her a tired look. "There's not much more I can tell you," he said. "They covered everything last time."

"Yes, I read the story in the Standard, but I'm here for the human interest aspect. They didn't really touch on that last time."

Beckett hesitated, then opened the door and walked down the hallway. Karen closed it behind her, then followed him into the living room. It was packed with ornaments and photographs, most of them of Alice, the wife he'd lost three years earlier, according to the Standard's piece.

Beckett clearly enjoyed his cigarettes. The room stank of stale smoke, and the sofa was covered in a nicotine-stained throw. She took a seat anyway, pretending not to be disgusted by the pervading odour.

"Can I get you anything?" Beckett asked. "Tea? Coffee?"

"Coffee would be wonderful. Milk, one sugar."

"It's instant, I'm afraid. I know most of you youngsters prefer the Starbucks blends these days."

"Instant's fine," Karen assured him.

Beckett left the room, and moments later Karen heard the kettle start to boil and a teaspoon clink against cups. Karen spotted a pair of boots near the living room door and quickly took photos of the soles and top, then picked a few hairs from the back of the armchair that faced the television. She placed them in a small plastic bag and stuffed it in her pocket before Beckett returned with the drinks.

"So, what do you want to know?" he asked as he sat in the armchair and sipped his coffee.

"What we want to get across to our readers is the devastation these scams cause. How has it impacted you personally?"

Beckett spent five minutes on his story while Karen pretended to take notes in shorthand. Beckett had been sucked into a land-for-sale scam, where people were cold-called and invited to purchase land that they could sell on to developers. The pitch had been professional, the returns mouth-watering. After Beckett handed over his life savings, he discovered the plot he'd purchased turned out to be protected greenbelt, with zero chance of getting planning permission. He'd basically bought a field two hundred miles away that he could do nothing with other than growing crops —and he was no gardener, let alone a farmer.

Karen nodded sympathetically at the appropriate times, and once he'd finished, she asked what he hoped to see happen to the fraudster, Roger Hamilton.

"I want my money back, first and foremost," Beckett said. "He took everything. I retired early to look after my wife, and now I have nothing. No income, no job, nothing. After that, he should go to jail so he doesn't do it to anyone else."

He'll get more than that, Karen thought.

She thanked Beckett for his time, then put her notepad in her bag and let him lead her to the front door.

"When do you think it'll be in the paper?" Beckett asked her as she stepped out of the house.

"We do a human-interest section once a month, and I'm hoping this will be selected for the next edition. If not, it'll be the month after."

By which time you'll have other things on your mind.

On the way back to her car, Karen felt little sympathy for Beckett. Anyone stupid enough to hand over their life savings to a voice on the phone deserved to be taken for a ride.

And anyone evil enough to prey on the vulnerable deserved what they had coming.

Like John Beckett, Roger Hamilton hadn't been hard to find. A quick search of the Companies House database gave her his address, and she went there straight from Beckett's house.

It took her just an hour to get to Hamilton's home on the country lane in leafy Surrey. She knew the way, having been there twice already. She thought it prudent to see if she could get to Hamilton before going to get what she needed from Beckett, and his home looked the perfect place to take him out. No CCTV cameras, its own driveway and five-foot-tall, well maintained hedges all the way around the property.

On both her previous visits, one during the middle of the day and the other first thing in the morning, she'd looked for other vehicles parked outside the house, but on both occasions there had only been the two-year-old Jaguar.

It was the same this time, but that didn't confirm that Hamilton lived alone. He could share the car with his partner, or his other half may not drive. There had been no mention of a Mrs Hamilton as director of his company, though, and married couples often appointed the spouse as a director or company secretary, drawing dividends rather than salary to make it more tax efficient. It could be that Mrs Hamilton wanted nothing to do with his illegal operation, so Karen thought it best to visit as many times as possible to see who was actually staying in the house.

Hamilton's place was near a layby that was used by walkers making the most of the hiking trails. Karen parked there and got out of the car, then walked back along the lane. As she passed Hamilton's house, she noticed the driveway was empty.

That meant he had to come back at some point, but she had no way of telling how long that would be. Preparation, though, was her strong point. She took a folding chair from the boot of her car and set it up so that she had a good view of the Hamilton residence, then put out the small folding table and her picnic bag. She placed a Thermos of coffee and a bag of sandwiches on the table, then sat back and pretended to enjoy the view across the field to the hills beyond.

It was a beautiful day, the sky cloudless, the breeze just subtle enough to take the edge off the heat and keep her comfortable. An elderly couple with a dog walked past, offering her a smile. She returned it happily, just a city girl making the most of the gorgeous weather.

It was an hour before she saw Hamilton's car approach the house. She waited until it pulled through the stone gate posts and into the driveway, then stood and stretched. From where she was standing she could see the top of Hamilton's head as he got out of the car.

Alone.

Karen watched him put the key in the front door and open it, walking in without calling to anyone inside.

She'd seen enough. She still had some shopping to do, but within the next few days, she would have another kill under her belt.

Chapter 32

John Beckett stared at the boxes of Losartan and Amlodipine on the table in front of him. They were sitting next to the half bottle of whiskey and the photograph of Alice, his wife of over thirty years.

It should have been forty years, then fifty, but God had decided to cut short their time together.

No, that was wrong.

There was no God.

How could there be? He and Alice were good people. They never crossed anyone, rarely had a bad word to say to each other, they went to church regularly and had been faithful throughout their marriage. So why would God rip his life apart like this? Why let the thieves, murderers, liars and conmen prosper while he had to spend the rest of his life mourning the only woman he'd ever loved?

Why?

If Alice had still been with him, she would have seen through Hamilton's lies immediately. She was—had been, he corrected himself—a strong, clever woman, and she would have told Hamilton where to go. But, no, God had to rip her from him in such a painful manner, leaving him vulnerable to the snake oil salesman. Not only had God taken the only thing he ever loved, He'd also introduced the conman into his life. God had piled misery upon misery, and for what? To test his faith? What kind of God did that? What cruel entity would look down from above, see that John and Alice Beckett were good people, and punish them for it?

Shouts erupted from the house next door. Beckett had tuned them out over the years, but now they got his attention. It was the woman who made all the noise, the Filipina with the split personality. Whenever Beckett met her in the street she was kind and polite, but when she was alone with her English husband she would explode in anger several times a day.

If ever God needed another soul, why not take Rose instead? Why take Alice, who was so full of love, when there was a hate-filled monster living right next door?

Because there is no God, he reminded himself.

Beckett went to the kitchen and returned with a glass and a small bowl. He poured himself a generous shot of Macallan 18-year-old triple-cask single malt. The bottle had cost him a week's income support, but he no longer had a need for money. He took the plastic strips of hypertension drugs from the packets and slowly emptied them into the bowl, one by one, all the time looking at the photograph of his wife.

Won't be long now, he told her, but was that really the case? If there was no God, where was Alice waiting? *Was* she waiting?

He would soon find out.

Once all the pills were in the bowl, he took a handful and put them in his mouth, washing them down with the smooth whisky. After a few minutes, the bowl was empty. John Beckett had one last shot of amber, then closed his eyes and waited for the inevitable.

Chapter 33

Karen's only dilemma had been how to gain access to Hamilton's home. She had the option of a forced entry, hitting him with the stun gun the moment he opened the door, but that was risky. He might have it on a chain, or keep his weight behind the door, offering a small profile that would be difficult to hit.

In the end, she'd decided on the official approach. She'd spent a day on her computer creating an identity card that was guaranteed to get her through the door, and as she pulled her car into Hamilton's driveway, she took it from her handbag and put it in her inside pocket.

Karen was dressed conservatively in dark pants and jacket over a plain white blouse. Her hair was once more coloured dark with a temporary dye that would wash out in minutes. Confident that she looked the part, she picked up her clipboard, got out of the car and walked to the house. It was a large red brick structure with marble columns framing the entrance.

Karen knocked on the door, and Hamilton opened it a couple of inches and peered out through the crack. "Yes?"

Given the way he was standing, Karen was glad she'd made the effort to adopt the Independent Office for Police Conduct role.

"Kate Hooper," she said, taking the leather wallet from her pocket and showing him the laminated card. "May I have a word?"

Hamilton scrutinised the ID. "What's this about?"

"I'm with the IOPC," Karen said. "We're investigating complaints about the officer leading the investigation into your case. There have been suggestions that evidence has been manufactured to secure convictions. I'd just like to ask you a few questions, if that's okay."

As she'd expected, Hamilton was happy enough to open the door and let her in. Karen gave him a smile as she stepped over the threshold and into a large hallway. The house was just as impressive on the inside. An oak stairway clung to one wall, and doors led off to three rooms on the ground floor. Karen followed him into the living room, all the time looking for clues that he might not live alone. She saw none.

The view out through the large conservatory onto the vast rear garden was stunning. However he made his money, Hamilton sure knew how to spend it.

"Can I get you anything?" he asked.

"No, thank you."

Hamilton gestured for her to take a seat on one of two huge sofas facing a large fireplace, coal and logs ready to be lit, but she told him she wouldn't be staying long.

"So, what do you need from me?"

Karen handed him the clipboard and asked him if any of the technical information seemed familiar. It was a diagnostic dump she'd taken from the internet, absolute gobbledegook to anyone but the most computer-savvy.

As Hamilton looked at it with a furrowed brow, Karen took the knife from the leather sheath tucked into the back of her pants and thrust it up under his ribs.

She expected his face to contort in shock, not for the clipboard to smash her in the face. Karen stumbled sideways and tripped over the solid wood coffee table, landing in a heap next to the sofa. Her eyes watered, mixing with the blood pouring from her nose. She shook her head and got to her feet, just as Hamilton pounced on her, the knife still sticking out of his chest. She had clearly missed the heart, and now her intended victim was trying to turn the tables. Hamilton grabbed her around the throat with surprisingly powerful hands, a ferocious, animal-like growl emanating from him.

It was all going wrong, and Karen began to panic. She flapped at Hamilton's head, but it was just out of reach, and her vision clouded as he maintained his powerful grip on her neck, his face red with the effort. Karen clawed at his hands and punched his arms, but to no effect. She was blacking out and flailing wildly when her hand hit the handle of the knife. Hamilton winced in pain but continued to strangle her, and Karen grabbed the knife and used the last of her strength to twist it. Hamilton's grasp weakened, and she pulled the knife from his chest and stabbed him in the side of his neck. He released her, both hands going to the new wound, but despite applying pressure, blood spurted between his fingers. Karen plunged the blade into his abdomen, again and again, and when Hamilton put his hand out to stop her she sliced through two of his fingers. He staggered and fell to his knees, doing his best to stem the flow of blood and failing miserably. He knelt on the floor for what seemed an age before finally collapsing to the carpet, his fight over.

Karen panted, trying to regain her composure, but the scene before her was a nightmare. There was blood everywhere, and some of it was hers.

That hadn't been part of the plan.

Get inside, stab him, leave, burn your clothes. That was how it was supposed to go down, not like this.

Think, woman, think!

Cleaning up the mess would do no good. Any semi-competent forensic team would find traces of blood in the carpet, even after the most thorough of washes, and her DNA was bound to be under Hamilton's fingernails. She would have to cut his hands off and take them with her, but what about the blood?

Start a fire, a voice in her head told her.

That was it. If she burnt the house to the ground, it would surely be impossible to identify the blood spatters. But she had to act quickly.

Karen put on two pairs of latex gloves—*bit late now*—one on top of the other, and went through the conservatory and out into the garden. There was a shed at the bottom, a big structure made of the same red brick as the house, and it was unlocked. She went inside and saw what she was hoping to find. A petrol-powered lawnmower It didn't take long to find the petrol can, and when she lifted it up it felt almost full. It would have to be enough. On the wall she saw a set of power tools, the kind with interchangeable attachments. This one had a sander, drill, and most importantly, an electric saw. Karen put the saw together and checked that the battery contained a charge, then took her haul back to the house and dumped the items next to the body.

Think it through, she told herself. Once it was done, there was no going back.

Karen sat on the sofa and pictured the process. First, she needed something to take the hands away in. A couple of plastic bags, wrapped double, from the kitchen would do. Then she had to leave Beckett's hairs in a place that wouldn't be affected by the fire. The only thing she could think of was inside Hamilton's mouth. His wounds would indicate a struggle, and it was feasible that his mouth might get close to the attacker's head. She also had to leave footprints using the brand of boots Beckett wore.

Okay, bag the hands, hair in the mouth, leave footprints, douse the body and set it alight.

That wasn't sure to get rid of all evidence that she'd been there, though. The fire might not burn hot enough, or it could fizzle out.

Karen went into the kitchen and searched for more accelerants, but discovered something even better: the hob was gas-powered. She found some plastic bags in a cupboard and took them through to the living room, then went to the front door. She opened it a crack, and after confirming that there was no one around, Karen quickly ran to her car and took the holdall from the boot. Back in the house, she removed the change of clothes she'd brought along and put them on a sideboard far away from Hamilton's body. She'd assumed she would get blood on her from the knife attack, and how right she'd been. Karen put on the boots she'd purchased and went into the back garden once more. At the bottom of the property was a large wooden fence, and in order to make it look like Hamilton's attacker climbed over it to gain access to the house, she jumped into the flower bed. The imprint was deep and clear.

Karen wore the boots back to the house, then switched to her own footwear once more. The trail of mud she'd left on the carpet might not survive the imminent fire, but she'd left a strong enough clue near the fence.

The next step was to leave Beckett's DNA at the scene. Karen took the small plastic bag from her pocket and plucked two hairs from it, placing them in Hamilton's open mouth. She tried to close it afterwards to protect the hairs from the fire, but it flopped open again. The only way to get it to stay closed was to turn him on his front.

Karen then picked up the electric saw and took Hamilton's left hand in hers. The blade buzzed into life, but slicing through his lower arm was far more difficult than she'd imagined. She placed the severed body part in the plastic bag, then removed his other hand and put it with the first. She tied the bag tight, then put it in another bag and secured that one, too, before putting it in the holdall.

All that remained was to change and then light the place up. She put her holdall by the front door and stripped naked, removing the outer set of gloves, then went and got the clothes from the living room, giving the body a wide berth. Once dressed, she emptied the petrol can over the corpse and laid a trail to the kitchen, where she turned the knobs on all six burners. The smell of gas was immediate. She ran back to the living room, dripping petrol to the door leading to the hallway, then threw the empty can aside.

Karen patted her pockets.

Shit!

She didn't have a lighter or any matches, and there was no sign that Hamilton was a smoker, either.

The fireplace!

Karen ran back into the living room. The coal fire was stocked with kindling and coal, and next to it was a box of extra-long matches. She grabbed it and retreated from the room once more. After another check outside to ensure no one was around, she dragged two matches along the strip of sandpaper down the side of the box and waited until the flame took hold, then dropped them on the carpet.

The fire caught immediately, a yellow line snaking towards Hamilton's dead body. Karen watched until it reached him and flared up, then walked out of the house, closing the door behind her. She threw the bag into the boot of her car along with the other pair of latex gloves, then got behind the wheel. With one last look at the house, she started the engine and did a three-point-turn, then drove out into the country lane.

There were bound to be cameras of some kind in the small village nearby, so Karen headed in the opposite direction, using the satnav to avoid major roads. Seven miles from Hamilton's home, Karen found a country pub and pulled into the car park. It was two in the afternoon, so the lunchtime rush would be over, which was perfect. She went inside and asked to see a menu, telling the barmaid that she'd heard great things about the food here and had put aside a day to try it out.

"I'm sure you won't be disappointed," the barmaid said, as she poured Karen a glass of lemonade. "You should try the chicken stuffed with black pudding. It melts in the mouth."

Karen had gone with the recommendation, and it had been spot-on. The smashed potato with bacon and cabbage was to die for.

After her meal, Karen left a large tip—yet another reason for the staff to remember her if the police should come calling—then got in her car and drove around looking for somewhere to dump the evidence in the boot. She eventually came across a small wood that looked thick enough to hide her activities from passing motorists, and used the small shovel in the holdall to excavate a hole. She dumped the bag in it, as well as the spade, then used her hands to fill the hole in again. Her final act was to get piles of dead leaves and scatter them on top to hide the disturbed earth. Back at the car, she used wet wipes to clean her hands and dropped them out of the window half a mile down the road.

It was done. The only clear evidence they would find would point to John Beckett, and this time she wouldn't have to wait weeks for the police to identify the main suspect.

Chapter 34

Ryan Anderson presented a calm exterior, but inside his stomach was churning. If Brigshaw had told the policeman about his Scott Davison legend, the next few minutes were going to be interesting.

Ryan made it to the head of the immigration queue at Paris Gare du Nord rail terminal and handed over his passport with a steady hand. The Asian lady behind the desk glanced up to compare him with the photograph in the document, then scanned the passport and handed it back with a smile that flashed across her face for barely a second, her interest already on the next person in the line.

Twenty minutes later, Ryan was on his way back to London once more. He still didn't feel comfortable, despite clearing the first hurdle. French immigration could have tipped off the British about his imminent arrival, resulting in a swarm of police waiting for him at St. Pancras International.

His other main worry was bumping into one of Marsh's people. Although their patch was Manchester, they sometimes did business in the capital. Ryan had even been down as part of Marsh's entourage to watch a heavyweight boxing match, so he couldn't rule out coming across one of the gang in town on a social visit. Ryan didn't want to happen across one of them by accident; he wanted to plan each confrontation. He'd spent the last year worrying that the gang he'd infiltrated might find him once more, but now it was time to go on the offensive.

He wanted payback.

The fear he'd felt for the last year had turned to anger. If Marsh would just serve his sentence—lenient as it was—and let it go, Ryan could do the same. By framing him for murder, Marsh had pushed too far, but Ryan was no longer vulnerable, unable to defend himself. A few months ago, Ryan might have gone into hiding, but now his legs were almost completely healed. He'd returned to running a couple of weeks earlier and he would step up the intensity until he was back to his former fitness. By that time, Marsh, Phil Walker and Paul Gardner would be out of jail, but in the meantime, he would deal with whomever had set him up.

Franklin Marsh's short sentence had been an insult to Ryan when he'd first heard about it, but now it was a blessing. Four years for conspiracy would mean two spent inside, and one of those had already passed. This time next year, Marsh would be a free man, and Ryan would be waiting for him.

Ryan tried to put such thoughts behind him. He was here to find out how he'd been framed for murder, not to wallow in the past or dream about the distant future. He needed a strategy, and so far, he had a few bones to throw Latimer's way.

He checked his watch and saw that it was still far too early to call Kelly. He'd taken the night train to London rather than wait for the morning. He wanted to speak to Latimer as soon as possible, and the best time to catch him would be on his way to work the following day. He would book into a hotel that night, one that would accept cash and not ask for ID. He'd also purchased a new, unregistered pay-as-you-go phone in Paris, along with forty euros of credit. He didn't want to make it any easier for Brigshaw to track him. He would get what he could from Latimer, then start his own investigation, and he didn't need his old boss climbing all over his back.

At London St. Pancras station, Ryan went through customs unchallenged and out into the night. After an hour on the subway, constantly changing trains to see whether he'd picked up a tail, he declared himself clean and walked down a street in Earl's Court looking for a place to stay that night. The fourth hotel he tried accepted his story that he'd been mugged and lost his wallet, and that he'd borrowed money from a colleague until he could get back home to Durham.

The room was what he'd expected for £60 a night, but the shower worked and the bed wasn't too uncomfortable. Ryan set his alarm for five and got his head down.

* * *

Ryan jogged past Latimer's semi-detached house just before six in the morning. The sun would be up in a few minutes, but it was already promising to be another scorcher. It was a quiet street, which meant he would stick out like a sore thumb if he just waited for the detective inspector to emerge. Fortunately for Ryan, that wouldn't be necessary. The house was in a cul-de-sac, with only one way out. He continued on to the junction with the main road, and from there he could see the house where the policeman lived. Across the road was a bus stop that served several routes, the perfect place to wait out in the open.

Ryan sat in the shelter and pretended to be engrossed in his phone, glancing up every few seconds to see if any lights came on at Latimer's place. It was six-thirty before a small yellow glow came from the frosted bathroom window.

He had to wait another hour as buses and commuters came and went, but eventually Latimer left his house and climbed onto his mountain bike. Ryan pulled a scarf up over his face so that only his eyes were visible, raised his hood over his head and dodged between vehicles to get to the other side of the road just as Latimer reached the junction. The policeman had to give way to traffic, which gave Ryan his opportunity. As Latimer scanned the road for a gap to ease into, Ryan walked up to him and stood by his front wheel.

"I'm Ryan Anderson. We need to have a word."

Latimer looked stunned, and Ryan quickly nipped the idea of an arrest in the bud.

"I just want to talk. If you try to detain me, it'll turn out badly. For you."

Latimer hesitated, then shuffled his bike over to the kerb. "Okay, talk."

"Not here. Get off the bike and come with me."

Ryan waited for him to dismount, then set off towards a park two streets away, feigning an exaggerated limp. He kept Latimer in his sight all the way, just to make sure he didn't use his phone or signal anyone.

When they got to the park, Ryan led Latimer to a bench and they sat down.

"You spooks never heard of offices?" Latimer asked. "Isn't this a bit clichéd?"

"I have a feeling that if I went to the station with you, I wouldn't be coming out in a hurry. So, tell me about this murder I'm supposed to have committed."

"It's hard to hear you with that scarf over your face."

"Get used to it," Ryan told him.

"I'm sure your boss filled you in. Robert Waterstone was killed a couple of weeks ago, and you're the prime suspect."

"Because my prints were on the knife."

"And your DNA was at the scene," Latimer added.

"Which could have been planted there."

"I'll grant you that," Latimer conceded, "but the fingerprints?"

"Whoever did this picked up something I used and lifted the prints somehow. That's the only explanation I have. One thing I need you to clear up. What time was he killed?"

"We can't pin it down, but the autopsy suggests it was on or shortly after the fifteenth, which was the last time he was seen alive."

"Then I have a cast-iron alibi," Ryan said. "I was in London with a friend, Kelly Thorn, on the fourteenth. We were together from five in the evening until we returned to France the next day."

He didn't mind giving Latimer his vague location; the cop would probably want to verify his movements in order to rule him out of the inquiry. It also meant blowing his Scott Davison legend, but he could always ask Brigshaw to arrange another ID so that he could disappear.

"I'd like to speak to her," Latimer said.

"Me, too." He'd meant to call her that morning, but when he'd woken he'd been so focused on meeting Latimer that he'd forgotten. It would have to wait. "She's currently in Australia. I've been having trouble getting hold of her for the last couple of weeks."

"Sounds convenient. Your one alibi can't be contacted."

"She's real. You can check with Eurostar and French immigration. They'll both have records of her arriving on the fourteenth and leaving the next day. I was travelling with her under the name Scott Davison."

"Why?" Latimer asked. "Why the false name?"

It wasn't something Ryan wanted to go into, but the more information he gave Latimer, the better his chances of clearing his name.

"Does the name Franklin Marsh ring any bells?"

192

"Sure. He went down last year…wait. You were the guy he put in the hospital?"

"I wouldn't put it so mildly, but yeah, that was me. And six months later, he sent his men after me again. I was in a safe house here in London when six guys broke in and attacked me. My legs were about a month away from healing properly, but they smashed my knees again and I spent another six months recovering. Now I think he's setting me up for this murder."

Latimer shook his head slowly. "This makes no sense. Why kill some random guy? Why not someone you know? At least then we could pin motive on you."

"I did know him, apparently. You remember a video that went viral in the winter? The builder and the cripple, they called it?"

"I remember."

"That was us," Ryan said. "I was the cripple, Waterstone was the builder. We believe Marsh's men saw the video and tracked me by the licence plate on my vehicle. They paid me a visit a few days after it hit social media. That's why I moved to France."

Ryan couldn't tell whether Latimer was buying his story. He didn't look sceptical, though, which was a bonus.

"I want you to look at Marsh's known associates and see if any of them travelled to France in the last two months. If they did, that's your starting point."

"If I do that, someone's going to ask why I'm searching for them, and then I'll have to reveal that we had this conversation. I think it would be better if you came in and made a statement."

"No way," Ryan said. "Once I'm in the station, you'll never let me go. Check out Marsh's men, and don't forget Kelly Thorn. Once I get in touch with her, I'll tell her to give you a call."

Ryan rose, but Latimer grabbed his arm. "How do I get I touch with you?"

"You don't. I'll call you."

Ryan shrugged off the grip and jogged deeper into the park, his gait uneven, before Latimer could say anything else. He looked around once to see whether the detective was following him, but Latimer was still sitting on the bench, as if mesmerized. Ryan found a block of public toilets and ran around the back. With no one to observe him, he took a black holdall from the backpack and opened it up, then dumped the backpack inside it along with the hoodie, scarf and jogging pants. Underneath he had jeans and a grey wool jumper. A minute later, he was walking back along the same path, his fake limp gone. Latimer was pushing his bike towards the exit of the park, his phone to his ear. He was obviously calling in the encounter, but any description he gave would now be obsolete.

When Ryan reached the exit, Latimer was still on his phone, looking around as he spoke. Ryan could hear what he was saying, and it sounded like his sole focus was on finding Ryan, not following up the leads he'd given to the detective.

He'd expected as much. Ryan walked away and pulled his own phone from his pocket. He dialed a number and it was answered almost immediately.

"We have to meet."

Chapter 35

The place Ryan had chosen was a pub just a few minutes' walk from Piccadilly Circus. It was convenient enough for Brigshaw to reach from Thames House, and busy enough for Ryan to disappear into the crowd if necessary.

Ryan arrived by tube. He'd dumped his bag back at the hotel and eaten breakfast, leaving enough room to swallow his pride. He was going to do the unthinkable: ask Brigshaw for help.

He navigated his way through the ticket barriers and headed for the exit that led to the Shaftsbury Memorial statue, commonly known as Eros.

He saw the flick of a high, blonde ponytail from the corner of his eye, and it made him pause. He'd seen something similar before, but the hair had been dark. Ryan turned and watched as the woman made for the barriers that led to the Piccadilly line.

It looked a lot like Kelly, but it couldn't be. She had dark hair, almost black, and was thousands of miles away in Australia.

Or was she? It might explain her reluctance to answer her phone.

"Kelly?"

Several heads turned when he shouted the name, but not the blonde. She reached the turnstiles, presented a card to the reader and took a step forward, but the barrier didn't open. When she looked back at the sensor and tried again, Ryan got a look at her face.

It was definitely Kelly.

"Kelly!" he shouted again as he moved through the crowd to get to her. He tripped over a suitcase being dragged by a Japanese tourist and landed heavily on his front, instinctively doing all he could to protect his knees. When he got back to his feet, the blonde had moved through the barrier and was following the masses toward the trains.

Ryan reached the turnstiles, then cursed. He'd only purchased a one-way ticket to get to Piccadilly, and the machine had swallowed it when he went through the barrier. He considered jumping the gate, but two transport police were watching him, probably because of all the noise he was making. Ryan cursed again, then fought his way through the oncoming surge to get to the ticket machines. He found an empty one and purchased a ticket that would give him a days' travel to all zones, then ran back and inserted it in the barrier. The gates opened, and he barged his way to the platforms.

Now he only had to discover which way she would be going. He heard the sound of a train approaching the westbound platform, so he tried there first. It was packed. Fortunately, he was tall enough to see over most people's heads, but there was no sign of a blonde woman in a black jacket. Then again, Kelly was a few inches shorter than him, so she might be obscured by one of the larger passengers.

Ryan pushed his way through the crowd as the train came to a stop. The disembarking swarm pushed Ryan toward the exit. He did his best to see whether the blonde got on the train, but it was impossible to tell.

As the doors closed, Ryan gave up. He let the tide of commuters carry him off the platform, then he ran across to the eastbound side. A train was already waiting, having disgorged its passengers, and those on the platform were fighting their way aboard. Ryan jumped up to see over the heads, and on the third attempt he spotted a blonde ponytail as it slipped through the door four carriages away. He got on at the nearest open door just before it closed, then stood by the door as it pulled away. He considered going from carriage to carriage through the connecting doors, but that was not only dangerous, he might be reported by a fellow traveller. If the police then got involved, his day could be ruined.

When the train stopped at Leicester Square, Ryan got off and moved down three carriages, all the while looking at the people getting off ahead of him.

There was no sign of Kelly.

He waited until the very last moment, then got on the train again, in the carriage next to hers. He made his way to the end and looked through the window. The blonde with the black jacket was standing with her back to him, her head down.

When the train reached Covent Garden, she made no move to get off, but as it approached Holborn, she eased her way closer to the door. Ryan did the same, and as soon as the doors opened, he rushed out and toward her carriage. The blonde was one of the first off, and Ryan easily caught up with her.

"Kelly!" he said as he grabbed her arm.

The woman turned, shock written all over her face. "Get the fuck off me!"

Ryan immediately let her go. "I'm sorry, I thought you were someone else."

The woman backed away, now angry more than anything, then turned and walked to the exit.

Ryan watched her leave.

What the hell are you playing at?

Of course it wasn't Kelly. She was probably already in bed, asleep, preparing for another day in Melbourne.

Feeling foolish, Ryan crossed to the westbound platform and caught the next train back to Piccadilly Circus. He was still thirty minutes early, which was plenty of time to get a window seat at a nearby café to keep an eye on the pub. It wasn't that he didn't trust Brigshaw, but once the old man's superiors got wind of the problem, they might decide to cut ties and hand him over to the police.

He needn't have worried. Brigshaw arrived alone five minutes early and went straight inside the Red Lion. Ryan didn't see any suspicious vans pull up, or road sweepers mysteriously appear and concentrate on the same patch of pavement. Still, he gave it another ten minutes, and when he was convinced that Brigshaw was alone, he jogged over to the pub and walked in. The place was almost empty, it being a little early for the lunchtime crowd.

Brigshaw was sitting at a table in the corner, with a glass of neat brandy and a pint of lager. Ryan sat opposite him.

"Enjoy your coffee?" Brigshaw asked as he pushed the beer Ryan's way.

"You saw me in the café across the road," Ryan said. "I didn't even see you glance my way."

"Skills you could learn if you ever decide to come back." Brigshaw smiled.

Ryan was tempted to openly dismiss the idea on the spot, but he needed the old man's help. Better to let him think there'd be something in it for him if he co-operated.

"Once this mess is cleared up, I'll think about it. I still have a few trust issues, as you can imagine."

Brigshaw nodded once. "Understandable." He took a sip of his drink. "What did you learn from Latimer?"

"I got the impression he just wants to pin this on me. I told him about the Marsh operation and that he's probably the one behind it, but after I left him he was straight on the phone sharing my description."

"It's possible that he'll still follow up on what you told him," Brigshaw said. "Naturally, he'll want to sit you down and get your story on tape. It's his job, after all."

"That may be, but I can't sit around hoping he believes me. I need you to cross reference all of Marsh's known associates and see if any of them travelled to France in the last couple of months."

"Should be simple enough. Anything else?"

"Yeah. I need you to look into Kelly."

"You do realise you could come in and do this all yourself?" Brigshaw pointed out.

"I could, but Latimer knows I work for you. He'll probably have people stationed near the office in case I show."

Another nod from Brigshaw. "What in particular am I looking for as regards Kelly?"

"Printouts of her movements, her work history, family, everything you can find. Oh, and she booked the hotel when we came here a couple of weeks ago. Get a copy of the registration, too. If I can hand Latimer a file with all her information and proof that we travelled together, he might believe she exists. As it is, he seems sceptical."

"I'll have something for you by the end of the day. Do you have a home address, date of birth, anything like that?"

"No, we never got round to discussing any of that," Ryan said. "Just get details of the passport she used on the fourteenth and fifteenth and work from there."

That information would also prove that it hadn't been Kelly that he'd seen that morning. It would show that she'd travelled to Australia, where she was waiting for him to join her.

Ryan sipped his beer, though he didn't really want it. He needed a cool, clear head for the next few days. "I'm also going to need a new legend."

Brigshaw reached into his inside pocket and pulled out a small envelope. "I assumed you would. Passport, pre-paid credit card and some cash."

Ryan opened the package and looked at the passport. It was two years old and had a couple of stamps in it, one for the Philippines and one for the US. The name in it was Richard Altman, and he suspected the photo they'd used had been through Photoshop a few times. The hair was over his ears and the beard thick and black, just as they were now.

"I haven't really had the chance to say this properly, but I'm sorry for everything you went through."

Ryan looked up at him and stuffed the envelope in his pocket. Brigshaw looked sincere, but that didn't change what had happened. The hardest part was knowing his dream of ever joining the SAS was well and truly over. After a year of light movement, it would take a phenomenal amount of work to get his muscles back to their best, and even then they would not be as effective as he would like. He could certainly make it back into 2 Para, but could he take the next step?

"The pain was one thing," Ryan said, "but having my future torn from my grasp…"

"You could always have a future with us," Brigshaw reminded him.

Ryan shook his head. "You said it yourself. One job, then I become a liability."

"As an undercover operative here in the UK, perhaps, but there are other options to consider."

"If you're going to offer me a desk job, forget it."

"On the contrary, it would be a field role, but you'd be based out of the country."

"You want me to work for Six?" Ryan asked.

"Not directly. When we started this project two years ago, it was one of several initiatives that had been put forward. Another was a joint project between Five and Six. As you know, the sharing of intelligence between the two agencies hasn't always been at its best. We trip across someone who is planning an attack on British soil, only to find that they've been on Six's radar for some time. In another instance, Six tracked an arms shipment to our shores, only for us to lose them because the information didn't reach us in time. While we're handling local threats, Six are dealing with the foreign aspect of the same investigation, and we're just not meshing. It was decided that a joint task force would be created that would widen our jurisdiction and allow us to function both here and abroad, with one central command overlooking the entire operation."

"And how's that working out, or did you plan on making me your Guinea pig again?"

"It's going very well, actually. They currently have people in five countries, and they're looking to expand…once they've found the right people."

The right people being me, Ryan thought. It was certainly something to consider, though. His army career was in tatters, and his choices in Civvy Street were limited. Whatever he ended up doing, he was sure it wouldn't be a patch on the SAS.

"I'll think about it," Ryan said, taking another sip of beer.

"You do that," Brigshaw said. He polished off his brandy and stood. "I'll get that information to you this evening. Where should I drop it off?"

"The Savoy," Ryan said, patting his jacket pocket. "I'll be having dinner there, compliments of Her Majesty's civil service."

Chapter 36

John Latimer was just finishing the washing up when the doorbell rang. He wasn't expecting visitors, especially at eight in the evening, so he assumed it was the Mormons or Jehovah's Witnesses doing their late rounds. Fiona got up to answer it, but Latimer told her to stay where she was.

The last person he expected to see when he opened the door was Jenny Knight. Her long, dark hair, usually flowing over her shoulders, was tied up in a bun, and she looked like she hadn't slept in days.

"Hello, John."

"Jenny. I…what can I do for you?"

"I need to talk to you. Can I come in?"

Latimer held the door open. "Of course."

Jenny offered a weak smile as she walked past him and into the hallway. He led her through to the living room, where Fiona was typing away on her laptop. She stopped when Jenny walked in.

"Hi, Fiona. I'm sorry to come round so late, but I really need to speak to John. It's about my husband."

"It's no problem at all," Fiona assured her. "Can I get you a tea?"

Jenny nodded, and Fiona went through to the kitchen.

"Have a seat," Latimer told her, and Jenny took a spot on the sofa.

"As I said, it's about James. He couldn't have killed Sean Conte."

"I know how you feel," Latimer sighed. "I just can't believe it, either."

"No, I mean it's impossible. He has an alibi."

"He hasn't," Latimer told her. "I've been through this with him. He was home alone that afternoon, and you were at work."

Jenny looked down at her hands and spoke softly. "That's because he didn't want anyone to know about the affair."

Latimer eased himself into his armchair. "What affair?"

"Her name is Anabelle. He told me all about her when I last went to visit him in Brixton."

"I think we really need to speak about this at the station."

"No!" Jenny exclaimed, then composed herself. "No. James doesn't want anyone to know. I can't go on record with it. I promised James I wouldn't."

"But it could mean his release."

"I told him that, but he insisted that I don't tell anyone."

Latimer sat back in his chair. "How long have you known about this other woman?"

"I've had my suspicions for a few months, but James only confirmed it when I went to see him a couple of days ago. I asked if he'd been seeing someone, and he admitted he had. He believes you're doing enough to clear his name without this coming out, but I told him, 'If that's the case, why are you still locked up?' He couldn't answer that."

Latimer had no answers, either. He'd been to see Knight two weeks earlier and told him that he hadn't found anything to point the finger at anyone else. Knight's mobile phone was shown to be at his house all afternoon, but he could have left it at home.

The only positive he had about the case was the similarity to the Robert Waterstone murder. Again, a plethora of evidence had been found linking the body to the killer, who denied having anything to do with it. Ryan Anderson was sure he was being set up, just like James.

He'd spoken to Anderson the previous day. In the meantime, he'd circulated his name, but hadn't been able to come up with a photograph. His request to the passport office had drawn a blank, either because Anderson hadn't applied for one, or because Brigshaw had blocked it. What he had been able to do was obtain a list of Franklin Marsh's known associates, and once he knew which ones weren't behind bars, he'd looked into their travel arrangements. Two of them had taken the ferry to France, but that had been early on the fifteenth, the day Waterstone was last seen, so they could be eliminated. Before leaving the office, he'd also had people look into Kelly Thorn. Hopefully, there'd be better news when he got to work the following morning.

None of that helped James Knight, though. Even if Ryan Anderson had been set up, it didn't automatically follow that James had been, too.

"If I'm to use this to prove James didn't kill Sean Conte, I'm going to need Anabelle's full name and address. We'll need to speak to her."

"James wouldn't tell me," Jenny said. "Perhaps he knew I'd come straight to you with it."

"Then I'll have to go and see him first thing in the morning. He can't sit on this, and he knows it. The phrase 'it may harm your defence if you do not mention when questioned something which you later rely on in court' should be familiar to him."

Fiona returned with a tray of drinks and put them on the coffee table.

"I was just telling John that James was having an affair," Jenny said.

Fiona sat down next to her. "I'm so sorry."

"Don't be. I can't blame him. Since I hit menopause seven years ago, I've had no interest in sex, but I could hardly expect James to go without. I asked him if he planned to leave me, but he swore that wasn't his intention."

"Still, it must feel awful, what with everything else."

An awkward silence fell over the room. Latimer hadn't for one moment considered the emotional impact of Jenny's discovery, but it was the first thought in Fiona's head.

"You're more than welcome to stay the night," Fiona offered. "I can break out a bottle of wine and you can let it all out."

Jenny shook her head. "I'm okay. I just wanted John to know so that he can get James out of that hell hole. You can't begin to imagine how they treat police officers inside."

Latimer could. He'd heard all the stories, and none of them were pleasant.

He excused himself and went upstairs to the spare room he used as an office, where he logged onto his computer and made an online request to visit James Knight the following morning. He couldn't promise his friend a way out, but the news that there had been a similar murder and the prime suspect was sure he was being framed might give the man hope.

Chapter 37

James Knight looked a broken man.

John Latimer watched his friend being escorted to the table by a prison officer. As he was only on remand, he was allowed to wear his own clothes, but they seemed to be falling off him. He'd always been thin, but he appeared to have lost so much weight in the few weeks he'd been detained at Her Majesty's prison Brixton.

Latimer pushed a paperback across the table, but Knight barely looked at it.

"Either you found the real killer, or Jenny went to see you," Knight said, once the guard had walked away to take his position against the wall.

"She did," Latimer acknowledged. "Why didn't you tell me about Anabelle from the beginning?"

"Simple. I didn't want Jenny to find out. When she came to see me yesterday, she asked if I'd been having an affair. It was a shock, I can tell you. I thought I'd covered my tracks pretty well, but there's no accounting for women's intuition, eh?"

"Indeed. Fiona knows if I put half a sugar in my coffee at work."

Knight managed a half-laugh. "I was stupid to try to hide it from her."

"So, who is she?"

Knight clearly didn't want to share the details, but Latimer's look said he wasn't going anywhere until he had the truth.

"I met her at the golf course. She's a widow. Her husband died a few years ago and left an insurance policy that paid off the house, so she has a lot of spare time. Initially, it was just a smile in passing, then one day I was in the clubhouse and she sat next to me at the bar. It just went from there."

"And?"

"And, we started arranging to meet at the course twice a week. At first, we played and had a drink afterwards, but soon we were skipping the golf and going straight to her place."

"Okay. Now that it's out in the open, I need to speak to Anabelle. If she can verify that you were with her on the afternoon Conte disappeared, it'll go a long way to proving your innocence."

"It won't," Knight said. "With all the evidence pointing to me, she'd be taking a huge risk. If they don't believe her, they could charge her with perjury. Worse still, they might consider her an accomplice. No, she's best left out of it."

Knight was right. With the mountain of evidence against him, introducing an alibi at this stage would appear an act of desperation.

"If we can't use Anabelle, there may be another glimmer of hope. We discovered the body of a builder a few days ago. He'd been buried out in the countryside for a couple of weeks, and the killer left plenty for the forensics team to work on."

"That sounds familiar," Knight said.

"It does. I spoke to the main suspect and he also swears blind he has an alibi." Latimer didn't mention that Ryan Anderson hadn't been able to contact his, though. Saying so would put a dampener on things, and he needed Knight thinking at his critical best.

"Has he been charged yet?" Knight asked.

"No."

Latimer explained how Anderson had approached him on his way to work the previous day, and the names he'd asked Latimer to investigate.

"If it is Franklin Marsh, it doesn't help me," Knight said. "I never had any dealings with him."

"I know, I checked the list of people you've arrested. None of Marsh's men are on it."

"Then we're back to square one," Knight said.

"Maybe not. The MO is the same in each case. I think we're looking for the same man, someone who has been in contact with both you and the other suspect, Ryan Anderson. I need you to think back over the last few months. Is there anyone that could have had access to your shoes, or your hair?"

Knight sat back in his chair and crossed his arms, something Latimer remembered him doing every time he was deep in thought. He didn't need to remind him that every person, no matter how inconsequential they seemed, had to be considered.

"Okay, the gas man came round and took a meter reading about five weeks ago, and I had a plumber take a look at the downstairs toilet. Some girl selling solar panels blocked it up."

"That's it?"

"That's all I can remember," Knight said. "If you ask Jenny, she'll have the details of the plumber. He left his card. The other was British Gas."

"What about the woman?"

Knight shook his head. "Too small. There's no way she could take Conte down."

"Best to rule her out anyway."

"If you say so. She left a brochure. It's in a drawer in my study."

It didn't look good. Latimer knew the chances of Knight and Anderson both using the same plumber, solar or gas company were remote in the extreme, especially as Anderson had been living in France for the last few months. Still, he had to follow them up and rule the men out.

"I'll get back to the office and work them up. Do you want me to bring anything on my next visit?"

"Another couple of books would be good. The library here isn't that great."

"Will do," Latimer said. "If you need anything else, call me."

Knight picked up the novel and walked to the officer, who checked the book for contraband, then led him through a door and back into the prison population.

Latimer walked out to his car and called Jenny Knight. She answered on the seventh ring.

"Sorry, John, I was at my desk. I didn't want to take a call in front of my colleagues."

That was understandable. "I just spoke to James."

"How is he?"

"He's doing good," Latimer lied. Jenny had seen him just the day before, but he doubted James had let on how hard he was taking it. "He mentioned a couple of people that visited the house recently. One of them was a plumber. I need to know who it was so that we can rule them out."

"I can't remember the name offhand, but I've got his card at home. How urgent is it?"

"The sooner the better," Latimer told her.

"Okay. Give me an hour. I'll have to speak to my supervisor, but it shouldn't be a problem."

Latimer thanked her and hung up, then drove to the station. Jenny called just as he was walking through the door. He jotted down the name she read out.

"Can you also go into his study and look in his drawers. James said there was a brochure about solar panels. I need the name of the company."

He heard rummaging around, then Jenny came back on the line.

"It's called Regency Renewables. Their office is in Kentish Town."

Latimer asked her to read out the address, then promised once again to do whatever he could to get James back to her.

The words sounded hollow even as he said them.

Following the discovery of Robert Waterstone's body and the similarity to the Conte case, DCI Ingram had given Latimer permission to consider them linked. That meant he could now investigate during office hours, and his first stop was to send DS Paul Benson to the headquarters of British Gas to find out who was recorded as reading Knight's meter in the last six months.

Latimer's task was to speak to the plumber, Gary Welsh. He called and arranged to meet Welsh between jobs, and they settled on the car park of a supermarket on the Old Kent Road.

He was putting his jacket on to leave when DCI Ingram put her head around his door and asked for a word.

"Of course." Asking her to come back later would not have been a good career move.

Ingram closed the door and sat down opposite him. "There was a house fire in Surrey two days ago," she said. "It looked like a gas explosion, but a body was discovered in the living room and the fire chief said there were signs of an accelerant."

"Do you want me to take the lead?" Latimer asked.

"No, I just wanted to make you aware. His name was Roger Hamilton."

"Doesn't ring any bells."

"He was due to face trial for fraud, something to do with selling land for development that can't be built on. The autopsy revealed the cause of death to be multiple stab wounds. When the body was examined yesterday they found a hair inside the victim's mouth. Naturally, anyone known to Hamilton was questioned, especially the people he'd ripped off. They came up with a match for the hair."

"That's good," Latimer said, not understanding what it all had to do with him.

"It's far from good. The hair belonged to John Beckett. He died two days before Hamilton was killed."

"Two days? So he couldn't have killed him. Unless Hamilton had lain undiscovered for some time."

"We checked his credit card transactions. He used the card two days ago to pay for his car service."

"So how did Beckett's hair get in his mouth?"

He knew the answer before Ingram had a chance to reply. Someone had planted it there. Either that, or Hamilton had sucked the head of a two-day-old corpse before stabbing himself to within inches of death and then setting fire to himself. Not one of the more common ways to commit suicide.

"We don't know yet," Ingram told him, "but forensics are going back over the remains of Hamilton's house."

"Someone obviously tried to frame Beckett. Do you think it could be the same person who killed Conte and blamed it on James?"

"Not to mention Waterstone and Ryan Anderson," Ingram added. "If we can link all three murders, it clears Knight and Anderson."

"It also means we have a serial killer on our hands."

No force wanted that. The aim was to find the killer after the first murder, not the third or fourth.

"Is there anything that points to a third party in the Waterstone case?" Ingram asked.

"No, but I'm working on the theory that someone visited Knight's house in the weeks leading up to Conte's death in order to get the physical evidence. I was just on my way out to check on some leads."

"Okay. Keep me updated."

Latimer signed out a car and drove to the supermarket. By the time Latimer got there, Welsh was already parked near the car wash, as agreed. Latimer pulled in next to the plumber's van, which was empty. He had to wait ten minutes for Welsh to emerge from the shop with a sandwich and a can of cola.

"How can I help London's finest?" Welsh asked after Latimer introduced himself.

"I understand you did a job for James Knight. A blocked toilet in Merton Park. It was some time in the last few months."

Welsh scratched the back of his head. "Old guy? Thin?"

"That's him," Latimer said.

"Yeah, I remember. A load of toilet paper and sanitary towels got stuffed down the bog. The guy thought it strange because his wife hadn't used pads in years. Only took me about ten minutes."

Knowing he had the right man, Latimer asked him where he'd been on the fifteenth of the previous month, the day Conte had last been seen alive.

"I was in Crete. Go there every year. I can email you a receipt if you like, or you can check with the airport. I flew EasyJet."

"A receipt will be fine," Latimer said, though he would check with the airline as soon as he got back to the office. Welsh might have purchased the tickets, but that didn't mean he used them.

After seeing Welsh's driving licence and noting down his address, Latimer drove to Kentish Town and the offices of Regency Renewables. It was a small showroom off the high street. Inside, he found a selection of display panels and two desks. Only one was occupied, by a man in his forties wearing a light grey suit over a pink shirt.

Latimer introduced himself, and the man gave his name as Derek Jones, the managing director. Latimer asked how many salespeople the company employed.

"Just myself and Adrian. He's out on a sale at the moment. Oh, and my wife, Elaine. She does the accounts."

"Does Elaine ever go out on sales calls?"

Jones laughed. "No chance. Her only interest in the business is knowing how much money comes in so she knows what she can spend."

Latimer felt a tingle run through him. "So she wouldn't have visited a home in Merton park in the last few weeks?"

"Definitely not," Jones said.

"How would someone get hold of one of your brochures?"

"They could pop in, or request one from the website or over the phone."

"Then I'm going to need a list of everyone you've sent one to in the last twelve months. How long before you can provide me with that?"

"Give me a moment," Jones said, and sat behind his computer. A couple of minutes later, the printer whirred and three sheets of paper sat in the tray.

Latimer knew this information had to be key to the investigation. He could think of no reason why someone would masquerade as a salesperson other than to gain access to Knight's house. If it had been merely to steal something, Knight would have mentioned it. The woman had to be there to get Knight's hair samples.

Latimer thanked Jones and walked out into the street. He was so engrossed in the discovery that he didn't notice the figure emerge from the adjoining shop doorway.

* * *

Ryan had barely slept. One line from the conversation he'd had the night before with the advertising agency in Melbourne kept playing over and over in his mind.

"I'm sorry, but no one by that name works here."

It was what he'd expected after receiving the details of Kelly Thorn's movements. The last time her passport had been used was the day he'd travelled back from London with her.

She'd lied about the job in Australia.

If she wanted to break up, why not just tell him? Why go through the ruse of moving to the other side of the world?

Those questions had troubled him for some time, before the obvious hit him.

She hadn't left France.

He'd called Brigshaw first thing and asked him to track Kelly's phone, but it couldn't be found anywhere. Which meant it had been turned off.

She'd certainly gone to lengths to cover her tracks, even as far as disposing of her old number, which was a throwaway, unregistered. Why do that? Why not just block his number? It would take a lot of effort to update everyone on her contacts list and let them know her new number. Why go to all that trouble?

The questions kept coming, and Ryan could make no sense of any of it.

At eight he showered before heading out for breakfast. He found a café and ordered a full English, and while he ate it he thought about the information Brigshaw had given him the night before. Apart from the news about Kelly, there was a page that related to Franklin Marsh. Two of his men had driven to France and returned to England three days later, but they couldn't have been involved. They'd taken the ferry to Calais the day he and Kelly had returned on the Eurostar, so unless they had time-traveled, they couldn't have planted the evidence.

So who had set him up?

The only people who had been in his apartment over the last few months had been Marcus Hayes and Kelly, and if it was an MI5 plot to have him put away, why was Brigshaw helping him now?

That left Kelly, and the very thought of her killing anyone was ludicrous.

Or was it?

What did he really know about her? That she lived in London and worked for an advertising agency. That was it, really. She'd mentioned her parents but no siblings. In fact, most of their conversations had been about the future, as if she'd deliberately avoided talking about the past.

What if everything she had said was a lie?

The more he thought about it, the more ridiculous it sounded, but there was only one way to find out.

He finished his meal and took the tube to Oxford Circus. The advertising agency Kelly worked for was just a few minutes' walk from the station, and when he got there just before nine there was a steady trickle of people entering the building, which was home to several businesses. Ryan saw that Kelly's firm was on the third floor. When he got off the elevator, he asked the middle-aged woman behind the reception desk if he could speak to Kelly Thorn.

"I'm afraid we have no one by that name," she told him.

"Are you sure? You haven't even checked."

"Yes, I'm sure," she said, bluntly. "I've worked here for over twenty years and I'm responsible for updating the staff contact list, not to mention routing hundreds of calls every day. If we had someone named Kelly Thorn, I'd know about it."

Ryan knew there was little point asking to speak to a manager. This woman obviously knew everyone in the company, and if she said Kelly didn't work there, he would have to accept it.

He walked slowly back to the elevator and pressed the button, then took his phone out and called Brigshaw.

"What else did you find out about Kelly?" he asked as soon as the old man answered.

"I just asked the analyst for passport usage and that's all he sent me. Why?"

"She lied to me. She didn't work for the advertising agency, in London or Australia. Can you check to see if she has any connection to Marsh? Maybe he told her to get close to me and get physical evidence to plant at the murder scene."

"Call me back in five minutes."

The phone went dead just as the lift pinged and the doors opened. He let two people out and rode to the ground floor, then out onto the street.

How could he have been so stupid? His training dictated he do a thorough check on anyone who tried to get close to him, which should have involved a call to her employer at the very least.

That said, he was no longer with MI5. Sure, he could have called Brigshaw and asked him to run a full background check on her, but he'd cut his ties, he was out, never to go back. He'd checked that the company she claimed to work for existed, and that should have been enough. It was a lot more than most ordinary people would have done.

But you're not most people. You were hiding from a brutal gangster, and alarm bells should have been ringing the moment she sat down with you at the café in Auxerre.

Ryan knew that if he continued to beat himself up about it, he'd accomplish nothing. He took out his phone and called Brigshaw back.

"What have you found?"

"Kelly Thorn is a single mother, two children. A boy aged eight and a daughter, three. She lives on a council estate in South Acton and hasn't worked since she left school nine years ago. We haven't seen any obvious link to Marsh, but we're still digging."

"No, you've got the wrong Kelly. Check the address against her passport."

"That's what we did," Brigshaw said. "This is the Kelly Thorn that travelled with you from France to London and back."

"What about her finances? Have you checked her most recent transactions to try to pin her down?"

"We did. She only has a debit card, and it was last used in Lidl, Shepherd's Bush, two days ago."

None of this made any sense. There was no way Kelly was a mother, never mind one who'd been on benefits all her life. And how could she get back from France without her passport showing up?

He had to prove Brigshaw wrong once and for all.

"Give me her address."

Brigshaw read it out. "You can't go there alone," his former boss cautioned. "If she does have links to Marsh, his men could be in the area, or even in her house."

Right now, Ryan felt angry enough to take anyone on, but as always, Brigshaw was right. Charging in might tip them off, and there'd be no way he could take them out one by one after that. He needed someone else to visit Kelly and verify that it was her.

"I need you to arrange something, and quickly."

He spelt out what he needed, and Brigshaw told him it would be with him in an hour. They arranged the meet at a coffee shop in Piccadilly Circus, and Ryan set off on foot.

He was just finishing his coffee when Marcus Hayes entered the establishment and sat down opposite him. He handed Ryan a phone and a pen.

"You'll be able to track him with that," Hayes said, pointing to the phone. "It shows his location based on his mobile phone. As long as it's on, you'll know where he is. If you can convince him to check out Kelly, get him to put the pen in his top pocket." He clicked the top of the pen and a red light flashed three times, then went off. "That's now recording." He clicked it again. "Now it's off."

"How do I view the footage?" Ryan asked.

"It uses Bluetooth. Just put it next to your phone and connect."

It sounded straightforward enough. Ryan picked up the phone and it asked him for his fingerprint. He pressed his thumb on the screen, then clicked the Tracker app. It showed a red dot moving north on the A4200.

"He's out and about," Ryan said. "I've got to get moving."

He clapped Hayes on the shoulder and thanked him, then walked out into the street and hailed a passing cab. He told the driver to head to Camden Town, which was a couple of miles north of John Latimer's current position. If the policeman deviated, Ryan would plot another intercept course.

Ten minutes later, Latimer's marker remained stationary in Kentish Town. Ryan gave the cab driver the new destination.

"What's your game? You got money for this fare?"

The driver clearly thought Ryan was looking to run off without paying. To ease his mind, Ryan took two twenties from his pocket and pushed them through the gap in the Perspex separating the driver from his passenger. "I'm tracking my son's phone. It was stolen this morning."

The cabbie's demeanour changed instantly. "No worries, squire. It's just you see all sorts these days. Just this morning one of them city bankers tried to pay me with dodgy twenties. I told him where to get off."

Ryan just lowered his head, looking at his phone in the hope the driver would take the hint.

It didn't work.

"Thieving bastards these days, they'll nick anything not nailed down. Good job you had a tracker on it. You should call the police, get them locked up."

"I'm not sure they'll be interested in something as trivial as phone theft. They'll probably just tell me to claim on the insurance."

"Yeah, probably."

The red marker was still in the same place, and now the phone's green dot that represented Ryan's location was closing in. Ryan instructed the driver to take a right, then got him to pull over around the corner from Latimer's location. He told him to keep the change from the money he'd given him and got out before the cabbie had a chance to say anything.

Ryan walked to the corner of the street and zoomed in on Latimer's location. It showed him inside a building, so Ryan put his hood up and strolled around the corner, glancing into all the shops he passed.

Latimer was in the third one, a business that sold solar panels. Ryan ducked into the next doorway and waited for the policeman to come out. A few minutes later, Latimer walked past him, moving towards a black Ford. Ryan pulled the scarf up over his face and fell in step a few paces behind him, and when Latimer unlocked his car and got behind the wheel, Ryan jumped into the front passenger seat.

"We need to talk," he said, enjoying the policeman's shocked expression. "And no, I'm not ready to hand myself in just yet, so hands where I can see them."

Latimer slowly gripped the wheel. "You're not doing yourself any favours," he said.

"Yes, I am. I'm ensuring you investigate this case fully rather than relying on evidence that has clearly been planted."

"That's what I'm doing," Latimer insisted. "In fact, I've just discovered a vital piece of information."

"What's that?"

"I think the person we're looking for is female. Either she's the killer, or she's working with him."

Ryan was stunned. He'd been hoping he was wrong about Kelly, despite the new information he had on her, but this seemed to cement her guilt.

"Do you have a suspect?" Ryan asked.

"Not yet. I was on my way to speak to someone about her, to get a description. His name's James Knight. I think she framed him for murder, too"

"No need," Ryan said. "I have her address. Let's go."

"Wait. Who is she?"

"Her name's Kelly Thorn. She was my alibi, but she disappeared. I tried the place she worked but they've never heard of her, and her passport wasn't used to leave France, even though her last debit card transaction took place in London two days ago. You need to go to her place and verify that it's her."

"How do I do that?"

Ryan handed Latimer the pen Hayes had given him. "Click the top and it starts recording after the light stops blinking. Put it in your top pocket, with the clip facing outwards. I'll be able to see her face."

"And if it's her?"

"You can ask her where she was on the fourteenth and fifteenth," Ryan said.

"What if it isn't her?"

"Then you'll probably want to know who was using her passport."

Ryan directed him to Harlech Tower on the South Acton estate. Kelly lived on the eighth floor, and Ryan accompanied Latimer as far as the piss-stained lift.

"I'd better wait here. If, as I suspect, she's working for Franklin Marsh, one of his men might be up there. I don't want them knowing I'm back in England. She's in eight-oh-three."

Latimer nodded and took a deep breath before getting into the elevator.

"And don't even think about calling in back-up to pick me up," Ryan said as the doors slid closed. "If I spot anyone, I'm through helping you."

Ryan walked outside and over to the next tower block, where he went into the bin area to keep an eye on Kelly's building.

* * *

Latimer was glad to get out of the elevator, but the eighth-floor landing didn't smell much better. Boiled cabbage came to mind. He found 803, clicked the top of the pen, and when the light stopped flashing, he knocked on the door.

The woman who answered looked to be about thirty, with dark hair tied up in a rough bun. Not exactly beautiful, but a pleasant face despite the dull look in the eyes. "Yes?"

Latimer showed her his warrant card. "Kelly Thorn?"

"Yeah. What do you want?"

"A word. Can I come in?"

"What's it about?" she asked, giving the impression that letting him in was the last thing she wanted to do.

"I'm leading a murder investigation and your name came up. Now, we can do this here or down at the station."

"I've got my kids with me," she said

"Then it should be an easy choice." Latimer raised an eyebrow, and she sighed before stepping back and letting him into the flat. As she walked to the living room, Latimer noticed the tattoos on her arms and the back of her neck. Funny how the unemployed complained about never having enough money but could always afford to cover themselves in ink.

The hallway was cluttered with plastic bags and shoes, and she led him into the living room. For someone on benefits, she was doing well for herself. The TV on the wall must have been fifty-five inches.

She plonked herself down on the sofa and lit a cigarette. A young boy wandered into the room, his head stuck in a phone.

"Get back to your room."

"I'm hungry."

"Then get some crisps and disappear."

The child left, and she blew a cloud of smoke at the ceiling and looked at Latimer. "So?"

"How do you know Ryan Anderson?"

She shrugged. "Never heard of him."

"Really? You didn't spend time with him in France recently?"

She laughed. "I've never been as far as Manchester, never mind France."

"Then why does your passport say you went there on the fifteenth of last month?"

Her face dropped, and she played the end of her cigarette across the floor of the ashtray.

"She said she was desperate. Her boyfriend used to beat her and she had to leave, but couldn't apply for a passport because he always got to the mail first. She said he was going to kill her one day."

"Who did?" Latimer asked.

"I don't know. She came up to me while I was shopping and asked if I'd have a coffee with her, no questions. Even gave me twenty quid just to talk for half an hour."

"Then what?"

"She told me she had to get a passport, but couldn't get one in her own name. She asked if I ever went abroad, but I told her there's no way I could afford it. She said she'd give me fifteen hundred if I applied for it, and another fifteen hundred when I gave it to her. I was desperate for the cash, so I said I'd do it."

"And you used your own photo, or hers?"

"Mine. She looks like me. I mean, it's spooky. We could be twins. Only, her hair is blonde."

"What if you ever wanted to go abroad in the future?" Latimer pressed.

"I asked her that, and she said she only needed it to get away from her boyfriend. She said when she got to Europe she'd apply for a passport in her own name and she'd post mine back to me, but she never did."

Latimer had all he needed. If Anderson verified that this was the Kelly he knew, then she must be lying. Either that, or Anderson was.

"I just need to take a quick look around," he said.

"Have you got a warrant?"

Latimer stared at her. "Seriously? You've just admitted a crime that could see you go down for a couple of years. Do you really want me to make this official by getting a warrant?"

Kelly sighed and gestured to the door. "Go crazy."

Latimer walked from room to room. He was only interested in knowing whether she had any male guests that could be Marsh's men, but the place was empty apart from the boy in his bedroom and a little girl asleep on Kelly's double bed.

He went back to the living room. "Did this woman give you a name, contact details, anything?"

"No, nothing." She put out her cigarette. "Am I going to be in trouble?"

"I don't know. If it turns out you're hiding something, then yes. If not, worst case scenario, you'll have to jump through hoops to get another passport."

He walked out of the flat and back to the lift. The policeman in him wanted to call it in and have Anderson arrested so that they could continue their discussions under caution, but the man had been right so far. Betray his trust, and he might run into a dead end.

He descended in the lift alongside an old woman who didn't seem to notice the smell, then hurried out into fresh air. He saw Ryan strolling towards him and took the pen from his top pocket.

"How soon before you'll know if it's her?" he asked.

Ryan already had his phone in his hand. "A minute or two." He took the pen and ran his finger over the phone's screen, then stared at it for a few seconds. "It's not her. Looks a lot like her, but Kelly doesn't have tattoos, and her hips aren't as big."

"This one claimed she applied for a passport and gave it to a woman who looked just like her."

"I believe her," Ryan said. "Does she know who it was?"

Latimer shook his head. "But she said the woman was blonde. Does that fit?"

Ryan remembered the blonde he'd seen on the tube, the one who'd looked just like Kelly. "The girl I knew had dark hair, but that can easily be changed these days."

"Then it's not all bad," Latimer said. "Whoever your Kelly is, she's now a person of interest in this case, perhaps two other cases we're investigating. I need to go and see James Knight and get a description of the woman he told me about. If it matches, you could both be in the clear."

"You do that. In the meantime, I'll run this woman's passport through facial recognition and see if we can find a match through the passport office database."

Ryan turned to walk away, but Latimer grabbed his arm. "We can't keep up this cloak and dagger crap. I need a way to contact you."

Ryan looked down at the hand on his arm, and Latimer released his grip.

"Give me a minute." Ryan walked away and made a call. After a hushed conversation, he returned. "Call this number," he said, and Latimer put it in his phone as Ryan read it out. "Don't bother trying to trace it. The phone has a marker on it. One attempt to find out where I am, I disappear forever."

"I won't," Latimer promised.

"And I don't want anyone trying to pick me up. We're close to finding her, and you're going to need my help."

"Ryan, I believe you. It's time to start trusting me, too."

"At the moment, I'm not ready to trust anyone. I'll be in touch."

Ryan walked away, and Latimer took his phone out and called DS Benson.

"Paul, I need you to arrange an emergency visit with James in Brixton. I'll be there within the hour."

"Will do."

"And I need a photo of Kelly Thorn, 803 Harlech Tower, Acton. Get the one from her passport and send it to my phone."

"On it," Benson said, and hung up.

Latimer got in his car and drove south. He was crossing Battersea Bridge when his phone chirped to indicate an incoming message, and the next time he was stopped by a red light, Latimer checked it. It was the photo he'd requested.

At the prison, Benson had again come through. Latimer was escorted to a private room, and James Knight was brought in a few minutes later.

"I hope this is worth it," the prisoner said. "I had to miss exercise."

"I pray it will be. Take a look at this."

Latimer held out the phone and Knight studied the picture on the screen.

"Is that the woman who tried to sell you the solar panels?" Latimer asked.

"The face looks familiar, but the girl who came 'round was blonde."

Latimer beamed. "That's just what I wanted to hear. Tell me everything you can remember about that day."

Knight puffed out his cheeks and exhaled slowly. "Well, I can't remember the exact date. She knocked on the door and said she was with this company, I can't remember the name. Regency something."

"Regency Renewables."

"That's the one. I'd been considering getting solar panels for a few years, actually, so I let her in and we had a chat. At some point she went to the toilet, and when she came out, it was blocked. She went again, later, but used the upstairs bathroom."

"Did she have time to get a good look at your shoes at any point, perhaps take a picture?"

"Possibly. It happened weeks ago. I remember she left me with a brochure to look through, but I have no idea how long she was gone. It could have been two minutes or five, I can't be sure."

"What would you say if I told you Regency Renewables don't employ any female salespeople?"

Knight's face lit up. "Then she must have been there to gather evidence. I mean, she wasn't there to steal. I'd have known if she took anything."

Latimer took the phone back and clapped Knight on the shoulder. "I'll be in touch, mate. Hang in there."

"Do you know who she is?"

"Not yet, but we soon will. We'll have you out of here in a couple of days."

As Latimer left, he prayed his prediction would prove true.

Chapter 38

Ryan had called ahead, and when he walked through the doors of Thames House, Marcus Hayes was waiting for him at the reception desk. Ryan had checked the area around the entrance beforehand, but there was no sign of a police welcome.

"We've re-activated your old account," Hayes said as they walked to the elevator. "Between you and me, I think Brigshaw wants it to stay in use."

"That's a conversation for later," Ryan said. He didn't want to commit to anything right now, and whatever he told Hayes would surely get back to the old man.

The office hadn't changed in the two years since he'd last been there. He recognised a few of the people and they acknowledged him with nods, then Hayes escorted him to one of two hot desks.

"Your password has been reset to 123456. Once you log in, you'll have to change it and confirm biometrics."

Ryan sat down at a terminal and entered the default password, then changed it to something new, ensuring Hayes wasn't looking over his shoulder. He then put his right thumb on the pad attached to the CPU by a USB lead.

He was in, but a little rusty on the system. He had to ask Hayes how to access Kelly Thorn's file, then put it in facial recognition and run a comparison against the passport office's database. Ryan knew that things like a change of hair colour wouldn't fool the software. While that processed, Hayes took him to see Brigshaw. Halfway to his office, Ryan's phone rang.

"It's me," Latimer said. "I've just spoken to James Knight. He remembered a blonde visiting his house selling solar panels. I went to the company and they said they didn't have any female sales staff, so that's how I suspected the person we were looking for was a woman. James said the photo of Kelly Thorn was a great likeness. If we can find out who paid Kelly for her passport, we could have our killer."

Ryan wasn't so sure. He'd spent a lot of time around people for whom violence was just an everyday activity, like eating or breathing. Kelly simply wasn't like that. If anything, she was working for Franklin Marsh, either willingly or under duress.

"I'm running a search for her now. I'll get back to you as soon as we have a hit."

Ryan put the phone away and followed Hayes into Brigshaw's office.

"Ryan," Brigshaw said, standing. "How's the search going?"

"Just started. Hopefully it won't take too long."

"Good. Good. Marcus, some coffee, if you will."

Hayes left, closing the door behind him, and Ryan took a seat.

"Are you still convinced Franklin Marsh is behind this?" Brigshaw asked.

"He has to be. Who else would want to frame me?"

"I don't know, but you have to face the fact that it might actually be the woman masquerading as Kelly Thorn."

"Impossible," Ryan said.

"Perhaps, but I want you to go into this with an open mind. You've been under a lot of mental strain over the last year, and if it does turn out to be her, there's no telling how it might affect you."

"I was 'under strain'," Ryan said, making air-quotes, "because I was almost killed—twice—on an operation you sold as safe."

"It was safe, but you insisted on sending someone to check out the weapons exchange with the jihadist group. I warned you against it."

"So now it's my fault?" Ryan said, his voice rising.

"Not at all," Brigshaw said. "I was running the operation and I made the call. What happened to you will be on me, always. If I could go back and overrule you, I would, but I thought the man in the field, the one closest to the action, would know the lay of the land better than I ever could. I was wrong. I'm sorry."

"That still makes it sound like I was taking unnecessary risks, when all I did was try to achieve our objective: bring Franklin Marsh down."

"I didn't mean it to come out that way. All I'm trying to say is that there could be some emotional backlash if it turns out Kelly was behind this. I'd like you to reconsider the help we offered."

Ryan knew he meant the psychiatrist. The counsellor, as he'd liked to be called, had been assigned to Ryan while he was still recovering in hospital the first time. The only good thing about their sessions had been the soporific effect of the counsellor's voice, which ensured Ryan fell asleep within minutes of him starting to talk. After half a dozen meetings, Ryan asked Hayes to cancel any further sessions.

"Talking about it isn't going to change what happened," Ryan said. He'd never put much stock in mental-health warriors.

"That's true, but it can often help you come to terms with it. There's always a danger that it'll consume you, and you'll cease to function rationally. I've seen it happen."

"Not to me," Ryan insisted. "I was in a dark place a year ago, but I'm fine now." It was an outright lie, but there was no way he would willingly submit to further scrutiny. All he needed was something to focus his mind, something other than alcohol and Netflix. "Tell me about this joint operation between you and Six," he said, keen to change the subject.

If Brigshaw noticed his tactic he didn't let on. "We've been working on Operation Broadfoot for some time now—"

Hayes returned with a tray of drinks and put it on Brigshaw's desk. "Your search should be done by now."

"Really?" Ryan said. "I thought it took hours."

"A couple of years ago, maybe, but technology has moved on."

Ryan picked up his cup and stood. "Sorry," he said to Brigshaw. "I need to get on this."

"By all means. We can discuss it later."

Ryan returned to his desk and signed back into the computer. The search wasn't quite finished, but it had already thrown up half a dozen matches. He looked through them and stopped on the third picture.

It was Kelly. At least, it was the Kelly he knew. Her real name was Karen Harper, and she lived in Richmond.

"Is that her?" Hayes asked. Ryan hadn't noticed him standing so close to his shoulder.

"Let's see."

Ryan queried the immigration database to see when her passport had been used. There was a trip to France about six weeks before they'd met, then another, two days before she'd introduced herself. The most telling was the flight to London on Saturday the fifteenth, the day he and Kelly had travelled back to France. She must have dropped him off at his place, then gone straight to the airport. She was back in France early the next morning, according to the database. Why make that journey if she was just passing information and his hairs to Marsh's people? Why not meet them while he was in the cinema?

Because she killed Waterstone.

"That's her. That's Kelly."

"Call Latimer, let him know."

It was as if Hayes could sense what he was thinking, and it was a good call. He couldn't trust himself to face her alone after what she'd done. Better to hand her over to the police and let them prove the case against her. That said, he wanted to be there when she was arrested, to see what she had to say for herself.

Ryan took out his MI5-issue phone and dialed.

"Latimer."

"I've found her. Meet me in Richmond Park Road, Richmond. And come alone."

Chapter 39

Karen Harper checked the bottom of the boot against the picture on her phone, but it wasn't a match.

This was infuriating.

She put the boot back on the shelf and continued looking, but she was sure she wasn't going to find the right pair. This was the third shop she'd been in, and none of the shoes she'd looked at had a sole that matched the one belonging to failed author Bethany Ambrose.

She's probably had them re-soled with a generic pattern.

She should have known better than to photograph the boots when there were other shoes next to the front door, but she'd been drawn to them somehow. They were old, which suggested they were used often.

Too often, it appeared.

Karen walked out into the street and found a coffee shop, where she ordered a decaf latte.

She wanted to go ahead with the next kill, but something told her it was a bad idea. The fiasco with Hamilton could have ruined everything, just when she was on a roll. Maybe it was a sign that it was time to stop, or cut back at the very least.

Yes, time to sit back and re-evaluate. The Hamilton episode a few days earlier had been rushed, and she knew it. She should have stuck to her modus operandi, using both hair samples and fingerprints to point to someone else, but no, she had to go barging in and leave blood at the scene. It was reckless, stupid. She'd changed tack because the police might eventually link the murders, but that was easily solved. She could move to another city, even another country. Scotland, Wales, Northern Ireland. By moving around, it was unlikely the deaths would show any pattern.

Of course they would. That's why it's called the Police National *Computer.*

If she were to continue, it would have to be outside the UK. Her language skills were terrible, so it would have to be an English-speaking country, like Australia or Canada, perhaps even the US. Yes, somewhere big, where a provincial murder was unlikely to make the national headlines. Where a small-town sheriff could take the credit for an easy bust.

It shouldn't take too much to get a green card. She had a highly-paid skill, and in the land of the dollar, money spoke volumes. Her house was paid for outright, so she could sell that and have at least half a million in the bank to back up her application. While she waited for that to come through, there was nothing to stop her taking a three-month vacation and testing the water.

Karen felt a new sense of purpose. She would cease her activities here in the UK and wait for an opportunity in America, where—

Her phone played a doorbell chime that alerted her that someone was at the door to her house. She had bought the app after seeing an ad on TV. She wasn't expecting a delivery, so it must be a cold caller. She was tempted to ignore it, but better to let a stranger know they were being watched than have them feel comfortable that the house was empty. She opened the app, and her heart almost stopped.

* * *

When Latimer cruised down Richmond Park Road, he spotted Ryan easily. He was wearing the same hoodie, only this time his head was uncovered. He could now see that Ryan had a full head of black, shoulder-length hair, with a dark beard that covered most of his face. Latimer pulled alongside him and turned the engine off.

"What's the suspect's name?" he asked as he got out of the car. The rear passenger door opened, and a uniformed Carole Ingram joined them on the pavement.

"I said to come alone," Ryan said, adopting a stance as if ready to flee.

"If John is going to make an arrest today, he needs a backup, and as the suspect is female, I thought I'd tag along. Much more fun than the meeting I was about to attend with the chief constable." She held out her hand. "DCI Ingram."

Ryan shook reluctantly. "This doesn't mean I'm coming to the station," he said.

"If this pans out as you believe, that won't be necessary. John has updated me on the case, and it seems this woman is of more interest to us than you at the moment. So, who is she?"

"Karen Harper," Ryan said. "She lives at number forty, but I did a walk-past and it doesn't look like anyone's home."

"Then let's take a look."

Ryan led them to Harper's house, a semi-detached with a one-storey extension built onto the side. There was no car in the driveway.

"I see your limp's gone," Latimer said to Ryan.

"I knew you'd circulate my description the moment I left you, so I did it to throw you off the scent. I was standing next to you when you called it in."

One smart cookie.

"I'd like you to wait out here," Ingram told Ryan once they reached the front door. "We have to avoid cross-contamination. As you were the prime suspect in this case, her lawyer could argue that allowing you access to her home invited the planting of evidence."

"That would be a bit rich, considering what she's done."

"That may be," Latimer said, defending his superior's stance, "but this is an unusual case. If we're to get a conviction, we need to do this by the book. We can't afford to give her a way out."

Ryan folded his arms and looked ready to argue, then relaxed his posture. "Fine. I'll wait here. But if she's in there, I want to talk to her before you take her away."

"That we can do," Ingram agreed. "Once she's under caution you can ask her questions through me."

With Ryan satisfied, Latimer rang the bell. There was no answer. He tried again, but still no one came to the door.

"Can you break in?" Ryan asked. "I mean, legally?"

"Only if we have reason to believe she's on the premises," Ingram said.

Ryan looked up. "In that case, I just saw a curtain twitch. Up there, the one with the small open window. Of course, it could just be the wind."

Latimer looked at Ingram, who shrugged. "That's good enough for me."

Latimer moved his boss aside and aimed a kick at the front door. It held fast. He stepped back and tried again, but with no success.

"Allow me," Ryan said. Latimer made way for him, and with one kick the door flew inwards.

"Nice work," Ingram said. "Now, please wait here."

Both officers put on blue latex gloves and Latimer took the lead, shouting a warning that the police were on the premises and the occupants should identify themselves. He checked the ground floor while Ingram crept up the stairs.

The dining room was clear, as were the living room and kitchen. Latimer checked the toilet, but it was empty, too. The only other room on the ground floor was off the kitchen. He opened the door and walked into a workroom, with a large bench up against the outer wall. It seemed an odd set-up, so Latimer went over for a closer look.

There was a microscope with what looked like a tiny vice underneath it, and to the right of that was what appeared to be wooden guttering screwed into the bench. An assortment of tools lay on the left side of the work surface. None of it looked suspicious.

There was a pile of correspondence on another bench, and Latimer flicked through them. Most appeared to be invoices, and it soon became clear that Karen Harper was an engraver. She made a tidy sum doing it, too.

There were a few items on the table that Latimer wouldn't have associated with engraving. Plaster of Paris was one, and another was a litre tub of latex. Perhaps she was making casts of her work to sell as replicas.

The one thing he didn't see was a clear sign that Karen Harper was a killer. He would have to get the forensic team in to go over the entire place and see if she'd left any incriminating evidence. He went to the door, and as he got there, Ingram appeared. Latimer stepped aside to let her in and lost his footing on the head of a broom. He fell backwards, but thankfully crashed into a pile of old newspapers. They fell around him as he ended up on his backside.

"You okay?" the DCI asked as she leant down to help him up.

"Fine. Just getting clumsy in my old age." He stood and wiped the back of his trousers, then bent down to start picking up the newspapers. The first one he grabbed made him straighten up slowly. The newspaper had been folded open on the third page, and the picture above the article was of a familiar face. He passed it to Ingram.

"Look at this."

The DCI took the paper from his hand and stared at the photo of James Knight. "This is about his dispute with Sean Conte," she said.

"I know." Latimer checked the other editions and saw that most showed the front page. Only a few were folded open to reveal the inside stories. He checked one that had been folded on page nine. It had a picture of a man standing outside court.

"Roger Hamilton. Wasn't he the guy who was murdered in the gas explosion?"

"He was," Ingram said, taking the paper from him. She read for a few moments, then handed it back. "It mentions John Beckett as one of his victims."

The connection between the killings was staring Latimer in the face. "It wasn't random."

"She picked these victims for a reason?"

"I'm sure of it. What's the first thing we ask ourselves when a body turns up?"

"Who are they, who would want to hurt them, do we have—"

"Exactly. Who would want to hurt them? We'd suspect anyone with a grudge against the victim, and if their DNA and fingerprints were at the scene, we'd look no further."

"Just like James Knight and Sean Conte," Ingram said.

"James and Conte, Hamilton and Beckett." Latimer got down on his knees and sorted through the papers, looking for other examples.

"What about Ryan? What's his connection to Waterstone?"

"A viral video," Latimer told her. "He was...wait, here it is." He passed her another edition. "A piece on their confrontation in a supermarket car park. She saw their stories in the Evening Standard and knew the first person the police would suspect was the one the victim had a disagreement with."

"Okay, get a SOCO in here and turn the place upside down. We need...John? Are you all right?"

Latimer got up slowly with a newspaper in his hand, then ran past her.

"John!"

Latimer wasn't stopping. He belted out of the house to his car. By the time he got there, Ryan was right next to him and DCI Ingram was running to join them.

"What is it?" Ryan asked.

Latimer thrust the newspaper at him. "Get in."

Ryan was still reading when Ingram caught up and got in the front passenger seat.

"What the hell's going on?" she demanded.

Ryan handed her the newspaper and climbed into the back seat. The car shot forward and both passengers struggled to put on their seat belts as Latimer threw it into the turns.

When they reached the main road, Ingram looked at the story Latimer had been reading. It had a picture of a woman in her thirties by the name of Bethany Ambrose. Towards the bottom of the page, another photo.

Of John and Fiona Latimer.

* * *

Karen couldn't believe the image on the screen. She knew the man standing at the door because she'd studied the photograph in the newspaper for hours. His name was John Latimer, husband of one of her intended victims, Fiona Latimer. To his left was a cop, a woman, but what shocked her more was the man standing to Latimer's right.

Scott Davison.

What was *he* doing there? He was supposed to be in France, or a police cell, one of the two. The last place he should be was outside her front door.

Somehow, they knew about her. She'd messed up, big time, probably when she'd killed Hamilton.

The phone began to tremble in her hand, and she realised she was shaking.

Shit! Shit! Shit!

Karen tried to picture a way out, but there was none. Scott being at her house meant the Kelly Thorn ID was blown, and she obviously couldn't use her own. She was trapped, with no way out of the country.

She hadn't thought far enough ahead to anticipate this. She'd expected every kill to go smoothly, but in her rush to satisfy her urges, she'd broken protocol and ruined everything. She'd told herself that the change in MO was to throw the police off the scent, but she realised it was because she simply couldn't wait for the next fix. It wasn't excellent detective work, but her own impatience that had led to her downfall.

She watched the scene on her phone, trying to decide whether to reply over the intercom. She could tell them she was out, but that would tip her hand. They didn't know that she could see them. She kept her hand off the reply button, hoping to give herself some time to formulate a plan.

She watched Latimer kick at the door, twice, then Scott had a go.

This was no social visit. As they walked into her house, Karen heard Latimer shout "Police!" The newspaper hadn't mentioned him being a cop — otherwise she would never have picked his wife as the target.

Her life was over, that much she knew. She would spend the rest of her life behind bars, locked in a cell with a succession of lowlifes, eating when ordered to, sleeping to a strict schedule. No more shopping, nights out, takeaways and Netflix box sets, constantly watching your back…

Karen couldn't live like that. In fact, it was no life at all. Better to be dead than have your soul slowly sucked out of you, year after year, decade after decade.

She would end it herself, on her terms.

But how? The drugs she used on the victims were at her home, and that was now off limits. An overdose would have been a nice and peaceful way to go, just fall asleep as if pleasantly drunk, never to wake again. That was now out of the question. She had to think of another method, one that would be quick and relatively painless.

The only thing she could think of was a bullet between the eyes. She'd be dead before the sound of the shot reached her, and it was a good alternative to a chemical demise.

The only trouble was, she didn't have a gun.

But she knew who had plenty.

Chapter 40

"C'mon, pickup!"

Latimer's call to his wife rang out and went to voicemail once more. He decided to leave a message this time.

"Fiona, as soon as you get this, get in the car, drive to the station and call me from there."

He hit the button on the steering wheel to end the call and leaned on the horn as a van cut into his lane without indicating.

Ingram was on her radio, ordering units to Latimer's house. She also gave instructions to find out which car Karen Harper was driving and put a Be On Look Out onto it.

"Maybe your wife went out and left her phone at home," Ryan said.

"Never. She works from home, and it's always right next to her laptop." Latimer pounded the wheel in frustration as another traffic jam developed near a set of road works. It was eight miles from Harper's house to his, but it had already taken him twenty minutes, and there were still three miles to go. Not even the blue lights in the grill of his unmarked car helped when the vehicles ahead were not moving.

They inched forward for a few metres, and the oncoming lane suddenly cleared. Latimer swung the wheel to the right and hit the gas. He drove straight toward a lorry and flicked on the siren, then took a right and nipped down a side street. He paralleled the A205 for half a mile, then rejoined it. They were past the obstruction and he was able to put his foot down once more, but it had cost them precious time.

A call came in over the radio. The first of the armed response vehicles was two minutes from Latimer's home.

"Tell them to wait for us to arrive," Latimer said. "We'll be there in a few minutes."

Ingram relayed the instructions.

"Ask if Fiona's car—"

He was cut off by the sound of his phone ringing. The display on the dashboard told him the caller was his wife.

"Fiona, thank God. Where have you been?"

* * *

Karen pulled into the driveway and got out of the car, taking her purse with her. She still had the IPOC identification, though she wasn't really dressed for the role today. She could only hope Fiona Latimer wasn't as sharp as her husband, but she would only need the policeman's wife off guard for a few seconds.

Karen reached the door and took the ID from her inside pocket. From her purse she took the pepper spray she always carried with her and held it behind her back. After taking a deep breath and letting it out slowly, she rang the bell.

The woman who answered looked every bit like her photograph. Fiona Latimer offered Karen a smile. "Hello."

"Hi," Karen said, holding up her ID. "Kate Hooper, IOPC. We're investigating a case that your husband's involved in. Can I come in?"

Fiona looked almost panic-stricken. "Of course." She held the door open and Karen walked in. She waited while Fiona closed the door, and when she turned, Karen emptied half the can of pepper spray into her face.

Fiona screamed, her hands over her eyes. She collapsed to the floor, her back to the door, but Karen kicked her shin and told her to get up. A phone rang somewhere in the house, almost drowned out by the sound of Fiona wailing like a maniac. Karen grabbed her by the hair and dragged her through to the kitchen. She let go and Fiona fell to the floor. Karen left her there while she went through the drawers until she found what she was looking for. Armed with an eight-inch blade and a roll of tape, she took hold of Fiona's hair once more and pulled her to the living room.

The mobile phone next to the laptop began to ring, but Karen ignored it. Instead, she turned Fiona onto her front and knelt on her, holding the sharp point of the knife to her cheek.

"I need you to stop struggling," Karen said calmly. "Put your hands behind your back and lay still."

"Why are you doing this?" Fiona cried. "If you want anything, take it. My purse is in the hallway!"

Karen pushed the blade into her cheek and enjoyed the flow of blood. "If you don't do as I say, it'll be your eye next."

Fiona stopped moving, tears running down her cheeks.

Karen took her right wrist and wound tape around it, then crossed it over the left and secured them together.

The phone rang again, and after eight rings, it stopped.

Karen pulled Fiona to her feet and pushed her onto the sofa.

"Please, my eyes hurt so much."

"It only lasts thirty minutes. By that time, this'll all be over."

The phone was ringing again. When it stopped, there was a short beep. Karen picked the phone up and swiped it open. There was a voicemail message waiting. Karen ignored it. She looked through the list of most recent calls and saw four from John in the last few minutes. She clicked the entry to expand it, then hit the call button.

"Fiona, thank God. Where have you been?"

Karen smiled. "John Latimer, I presume."

"What have you done with my wife?" The anger in his voice came clearly through the phone.

"She's fine, but not for long. So tell me, where did I trip up? Was it Hamilton?"

"Let me speak to Fiona," Latimer said.

"Sure. Why not." Karen held the phone close to Fiona's face. "Say hello to your husband…for the last time."

Fiona screamed Latimer's name, and Karen moved away from her. "Where did I go wrong, John? What gave it away?"

"Killing people and thinking you could get away with it. That's where you went wrong."

"Really? Then how come I wasn't arrested ten years ago when I killed my father? And why is James Knight sitting in a jail cell right now? No, I got greedy, that's all. I should have left a couple of years between each one, but I just couldn't wait. You don't know how it feels to kill a man and know you're going to get away with it."

"You didn't get away with it, you sick bitch. You're gonna spend the rest of your days behind bars."

"I doubt that very much," Karen smiled to herself. "In case you hadn't guessed, I'm at your home. Don't take too long."

She hit Call End and put the phone back on the table, then took hold of Fiona's arm and lifted her to her feet. "Come on, it's nearly over."

* * *

Latimer hit the brakes as soon as he pulled into his street. Marked units had blocked the road, and several armed officers were already in position near his house.

The trio got out of the car and Ingram immediately took control of the scene.

"Any sign of movement in the house?" she asked a sergeant carrying an MP5 carbine.

"We haven't made contact with anyone inside. We were told to wait for you."

"Okay. Let's start clearing the neighbouring houses and—John, wait!"

The order fell on deaf ears. Latimer strode toward his house, only one thing on his mind. Ingram shouted for him to stop once more, but he ignored her.

At the top of the driveway, he stopped in mid-stride. The front door opened slowly and Fiona walked out, closely followed by Karen, holding a carving knife to his wife's throat.

"Give it up, Karen. There's nowhere to go."

"Back off, John. You know I'll do it."

Latimer had no choice but to comply. He walked slowly backwards, his hands raised. "Look around you," he said. "You can't escape. Just give me the knife."

"As long as I'm holding all the cards, I can do what I want," said Karen.

She spoke calmly, which Latimer knew was a bad sign. The ones that were wound up like a clock spring could be anticipated, spoken to, but Karen seemed in total control.

Karen was still advancing on him, forcing him out into the middle of the road. Fiona shook uncontrollably. Her face was red with tears, and her lips silently begged him to do something.

"Tell me what you want," Latimer said.

Karen looked around. "First, tell the police to back off, then arrange a helicopter to take us to the airport. I want a private jet waiting, with ten million in cash and a gun, like these guys are carrying."

"You know I can't do that," Latimer said.

Karen smiled, but it was devoid of warmth or humour. "I know. I was just kidding. What I want is for these guys to shoot me. I'm not going to prison. There's no point. Why should the taxpayer have to support me for the next forty years when you can end it all with a bullet that costs less than a latte?"

"That's not going to happen."

"It is if I stab your wife in the back. Maybe I'll hit a kidney, or sever her spinal cord. Do you think she'd still love you if she has to spend the rest of her life in a wheelchair and you could have prevented it by giving one simple order?"

"It doesn't work like that," Latimer told her, "and you know it. I can't force anyone to shoot you."

"Then you and I have a problem."

* * *

"Cuff me," Ryan said to Ingram. They were standing outside the police cordon, and both could see the situation was heading towards a deadly climax.

"What?"

Ryan held his hands behind his back and turned away from her. "Cuff me."

"I'll do no such thing," Ingram said. "Whatever you're thinking, it's not going to happen. I'm not putting a civilian in harm's way."

"I'm not a civvy," Ryan said. "I'm sure John told you who I am."

"It makes no difference. You're not under my command."

Ryan spun round to face her. "Then for fuck's sake, make a decision. Order your men to fire, or prepare to watch John's wife die."

He could see how conflicted Ingram was, and didn't envy her the position. Whatever she decided to do, it would come under great scrutiny and no doubt hang over her for the rest of her career.

"What do you have in mind?" she asked.

Ryan told her, and Ingram considered it before nodding solemnly. She called over the nearest officer and asked for his cuffs. Ryan turned so that she could apply them, then he felt a tug in his waistband.

"Good luck," she said.

Ryan strode out between the police cars, toward Karen Harper. As he got to within five yards of her, he stopped and turned slowly, showing open palms. He turned again and continued towards her until he was standing next to Latimer.

"Let her go, Karen. Take me hostage instead."

Karen laughed. "And why would I do that?"

"Because I'm the reason you're here. I'm the one who figured it all out. If it wasn't for me, you'd be out having a cappuccino right about now. If you really want to die, do it hurting the man who put you in this position in the first place."

His eyes met hers, and he kept his face free from emotion.

"Turn around again," Karen told him, and Ryan did as she said.

"Open your hands and spread your fingers." Again, he followed her instructions.

"Tell me why you're doing this," Karen said. "You don't know this woman. What's it to you?"

Ryan faced her once more. "Because you broke my heart. I really thought we had something, but you lied every step of the way, and it destroyed me." He hung his head. "You might as well finish the job."

"We were only together for a few weeks," she scoffed. "Don't you think you're overreacting?"

"That may be, but you turned my life around. I had a new purpose, something to get out of bed for each morning. Now it's gone."

Silence descended. Even the birds in the trees halted their song to await the next development.

"Aren't you curious?" Ryan asked. "Don't you want to know how I discovered the truth?"

"Tell me."

"Let Fiona go and take me instead. Then I'll tell you."

Ryan stared at her, his face blank, until she relented.

"Okay, turn around and walk backwards...slowly."

Ryan did as she asked, inching towards her until he felt a hand in the middle of his back. He saw Fiona stumble to his left and the knife was immediately at his throat. As he was a few inches taller than Karen, she grabbed the hair at the back of his head and pulled down so that his back was slightly bent.

Just what Ryan wanted.

"So, what gave me away?" Karen asked.

Ryan reached into his waistband and took out the key to the handcuffs. "Actually, you made three mistakes. The first was to tell me you were being transferred to Australia. Surely you must have known I would check up on you once you failed to answer my calls."

"I guessed you'd try to get in touch, but my plan was that you'd be arrested before you became really suspicious. I guess I didn't know you that well. What's the second thing?"

"You used a false passport to travel to London with me. I managed to convince Latimer to check into it, and we found the real Kelly Thorn."

"Bravo," Karen said. "What's the third?"

"You didn't do your homework into me."

Ryan's hands came up and grabbed her wrist, pulling it away from his neck. In the same movement, he ducked under the knife and twisted her arm violently, popping it from her shoulder. The blade fell from her hand, and the armed officers rushed in and threw Karen to the ground. Ryan was pushed out of the way for his own safety, but he knew the threat had already been neutralised.

He walked over to the Latimers, who had retreated behind the police cars. John was standing over Fiona, who was being treated by paramedics.

"You okay?" Ryan asked.

"She'll be fine," John said. "Thanks. That was a really brave thing to do."

"Don't mention it."

In truth, he'd done it for his own selfish reasons. Ryan wanted Karen alive. If she were dead, too many questions would remain unanswered. At least now there was a possibility that she would talk, if only to get a reduction on her inevitable sentence.

He looked back and saw two uniformed cops leading a handcuffed Karen away, she twisting and jerking despite her injury. A third cop dropped the knife in a bag as evidence.

Ryan removed the cuffs still attached to his right hand and took them over to Ingram.

"That was a bold move," she said. "I just hope it doesn't cost me my career."

"It won't. I'll have my boss speak to the home secretary and square it away."

Ryan wasn't sure whether Brigshaw had that much pull, but Ingram deserved to be covered for making such a ballsy call. Besides, the incident had been resolved without loss of life, so there was no need for anyone to come down hard on her. The only thing that might cause a problem would be an accusation of police brutality relating to Karen's injury. Given that Karen was determined to die that day, though, he thought it unlikely her complaint would get far.

Ryan declined the offer of a lift, preferring to walk.

He had a lot of thinking to do.

Chapter 41

John Latimer pulled up in the street outside the Knight residence and turned off the engine. The decent spell of summer weather was at an end, and storm clouds lurked menacingly on the horizon.

"Looks like we'll have to cancel our golf game this weekend," James Knight said from the passenger seat.

They were approaching the last Saturday of the month, the time they usually got together to play eighteen holes and catch up on the latest events.

"I wasn't expecting to play anyway," Latimer told him. "You and Jenny have got a lot of catching up to do."

Knight looked pensive, and Latimer guessed it was because of the extra-marital affair. That was sure to put a dampener on Knight's homecoming.

"You coming in?" Knight eventually asked.

"No, I have to get back to the office. Give me a call in a couple of days and we'll all get together. Maybe you guys can come over for dinner."

"I'd like that." Knight put his hand on the door release, then hesitated. "I want to thank you, John. For believing in me."

"What are friends for?" Latimer smiled.

"I mean it. No-one else would have lifted a finger to help. They would have taken one look at the evidence and made their mind up."

Before Latimer could respond, Knight opened the door and climbed out. He walked down the path and rang the doorbell, and Latimer waited until Jenny answered before starting the engine and pulling away. In his rear view mirror, he saw them hugging on the doorstep before Jenny led Knight inside and closed the door.

At the end of the street Latimer indicated left, but before he could make his turn, he saw a now familiar figure standing on the street corner. The bearded man approached and Latimer rolled his window down.

"Any chance of a lift?" Ryan asked.

"Hop in."

Ryan climbed in beside him, and Latimer set off again.

"I never did get to talk to her," Ryan said. "Has she spoken at all?"

"Plenty," Latimer told him. Karen Harper had been taken to hospital after the arrest. Her arm had been seen to and she'd been declared fit enough to be discharged into Latimer's custody. For the next two days, she'd sung her heart out. She'd confessed to the murders of her father, Sean Conte, Robert Waterstone, Roger Hamilton and Paul Eccles. That murder had taken place two years earlier, and while there were similarities, there was enough of a difference that it hadn't been flagged when Latimer had looked for similar killings. For one, the deceased had been found in his home in Essex, not buried in a remote location. As with the others, though, Karen had seen a news report in the Evening Standard and chosen the victim because of a grudge he had with a neighbour.

"Did she mention me?"

"Only to say how she'd found you, and how she got your shoe prints, hair and fingerprints."

She'd also said that she regretted the episode with Scott—she hadn't been told his real name—and that under other circumstances they would have been a good fit, but Latimer didn't think it was something Ryan needed to hear. Better that he believe she was a psychopath and that he was lucky to have escaped her clutches. It was unlikely that it would come out at her trial, or that Ryan would attend.

"Is the trial date set?" Ryan asked him.

"Not yet, but it shouldn't be too long. I'll be in touch regarding your testimony, and we'll arrange for you to appear by video feed."

They rode in silence for a while, until Latimer asked Ryan where he wanted to be dropped off.

"The Savoy would be good, but any tube station is fine."

"The Savoy? You staying there?"

"Just for a few days," Ryan told him. "So Kelly—sorry, Karen—picked your wife because of a dispute over a book?"

"That's right. And by the way, Fiona asked me to convey her thanks the next time I see you."

Ryan waved it off.

"Bethany Ambrose accused Fiona of stealing her idea and copying her work, but it's all bullshit. In fact, we sent an email in response to her solicitor's letter a few days ago, and got a reply to say that the firm was no longer representing Ambrose. That's two lawyers she's been to, and neither want anything to do with her. I think it's all going to fizzle out."

"I hope so. You're good people. You don't deserve shit like that."

Latimer looked over at Ryan. "What about you? Back to MI5?"

Ryan's face gave away his surprise for a brief moment.

"Brigshaw told me," Latimer said. "About Franklin Marsh, the beating, your convalescence, everything. What are you going to do now?"

It was a few moments before Ryan responded. "To be honest, I don't know."

"We always need good men in the police."

Ryan shook his head. "No, I won't be settling in England. If I met someone special and settled down, I'd always be looking over my shoulder, wondering if Marsh or his men were coming for revenge. I couldn't put anyone through that."

"So, what, back to France?"

Ryan shrugged. "Maybe."

The way he said it suggested it wasn't going to happen. Latimer had a feeling Ryan wasn't going to let anyone know his next destination.

Latimer had considered his own future following the recent episode, but only briefly. He was too young to retire, and the only person to have seriously threatened him or his wife had been remanded in custody. With her confession and the evidence gathered from her home, it was unlikely that Karen Harper would ever be released to pose a threat again.

When they reached the Savoy, Latimer pulled up outside the entrance, then offered Ryan his hand.

"Thanks for what you did for Fiona. We both appreciate it."

"It was nothing."

"Maybe not for you," Latimer said, "but I couldn't have lived with myself if anything had happened to her. If you're not busy in the next few days, we'd like to invite you round for dinner one evening."

"Sure," Ryan said, and Latimer got the impression he was genuine this time.

Half an hour later, Latimer was back at the station. The moment he entered the building, his phone rang, and when he checked the caller ID he saw that it was DS Benson.

"Yes, Paul."

"A call just came in. A body has been found on wasteland near Longbridge Way. Looks like he's been through a mincing machine."

"I'll be with you in two minutes."

Latimer hung up and made for the stairs. The Robert Waterstone pictures had already been removed from the notice board, ready for the next case. Sadly, the wall never stayed bare for long.

Chapter 42

"You scrub up well," Brigshaw said as he took a seat opposite Ryan.

"It feels good to be back to normal," Ryan said, running his hand over his smooth face. His hair was back to its normal one-inch length, and his jeans and hoodie had been swapped for chinos and a Ralph Lauren polo.

They were sitting in the restaurant at the Savoy. Brigshaw had chosen the venue and ensured they had a quiet table in the corner. They ordered drinks and waited until the server had gone before getting down to business.

"Have you made a decision?"

"Tell me more about the role," Ryan said.

"As I said before, we'll be dealing with people who have a base both here and abroad. Your work will take you all over the world, from Europe to the Far East and all points in between. You'll be expected to gather intelligence and send it back to us so that we can match it up with operations running locally."

"What about back up?"

"A team of two will go with you everywhere. They're seasoned professionals, been in the business for years."

"Which begs the question, why not just use them?"

"Because they're operational support," Brigshaw said. "They currently work for Six, but they'll be transferred to Operation Broadfoot in the coming weeks."

"Catchy name. What about rules of engagement?"

"You'll be totally autonomous. We supply the objectives, you fulfil them. How you do that is up to you, just as long as you don't go creating an international incident that comes back to bite us."

"Weapons?" Ryan asked.

The waiter arrived with drinks. Brandy for Brigshaw, a bottle of lager for Ryan.

"Whatever you need," Brigshaw said when they were alone again. "Within reason."

Ryan took a swallow from his bottle. "What if I get caught in some God-forsaken shit hole. What then? Disavowed?"

"We don't leave our people behind. If diplomatic efforts fail, we'll send someone in to get you."

"Even if it might cause one of these international incidents you're so keen to avoid?"

"I promise we'd do everything we can," Brigshaw assured him.

He seemed sincere, but Ryan knew that any such decision would rest with politicians, and he'd trust a pack of wolves before he put his faith in the government.

His only alternative was to re-join 2 Para and hope to pick up where he left off. It would take a couple of years to reach peak fitness, by which time his chances of joining the SAS would be slim. Apart from the physical aspect, the Special Air Service needed men who were mentally strong and stable, and there was no telling what long-term damage his run-in with Marsh had caused. The army shrinks would no doubt want to thoroughly evaluate his state of mind, and if he failed to meet their standard, he'd be out. No more army, and Brigshaw probably wouldn't be interested in damaged goods.

"How long do I have to think about it?" he asked.

"I think a week should suffice. And in case you were wondering, there will be a mental assessment before you are cleared for operational duty. It's standard, I'm afraid."

"And if I fail that?" Ryan asked.

"Then we'll work with you to see if we can resolve your issues. I'm not one for throwing an asset on the scrap heap at the first sign of trouble. If that was the case, we wouldn't be having this conversation."

Ryan finished off his bottle and put it on the paper coaster. After a moment's thought, he picked it up and held it in the air, catching the waiter's eye. "What kind of people will I be up against? People like Franklin Marsh?"

"Good heavens, no," Brigshaw smiled. "These guys make Marsh look like a rank amateur."

Ryan couldn't help but laugh. "Thanks. That fills me with a lot of confidence."

Brigshaw polished off his brandy. "I'll leave you to your thoughts. You know where to find me." He patted Ryan on the shoulder as he left.

Ryan watched him go, then settled back in his chair. The waiter brought his refill, and Ryan knew it wouldn't be the last of the night.

Epilogue

The early evening sun cast long shadows over the square as the target emerged from the bank. In her hand was the same briefcase she'd entered with, and she strode confidently to the Mercedes parked in the side street.

"She's on the move," he said into the microphone sewn into his collar. He climbed aboard his motorcycle, a powerful Suzuki, and fired up the engine.

The target, Lorena Vasquez, reached the car and the rear door was opened by her driver. She slid in elegantly and he closed it before getting behind the wheel.

"Mobile in a few seconds. Everyone on station?"

"Roger that."

"Good to go."

He liked that. The team had only been together for a few weeks, but already they functioned like a single organism.

"They're moving. I'm on their tail."

He pulled out behind the German car, keeping half a dozen vehicles between himself and Vasquez.

And the item she'd picked up.

"I see you now," Sophie Harris said. She was tasked with watching the feed from the traffic cameras dotted around the town, just in case he lost visual.

"I'm on San Martin," David Hunter announced.

The road paralleled the street he was on, meaning Hunter could intercept Vasquez if he was forced to abandon the chase for any reason.

"She's still heading for home," he told them. "Remember, we make the move in the tunnel, not before." There really was no need to remind them; they'd been over the plan time and time again.

"That's affirmative," Hunter said.

He followed the Mercedes through relatively light traffic, its gleaming white chassis easy to spot. It turned right on Bartolomeu Mitre as expected, heading for the Rua Mario Ribeiro that would take Vasquez west to her home.

"On Bartolomeu," he told the team, and they acknowledged his call.

Two minutes later, they reached the junction with the freeway. The Mercedes pulled up at the red lights, indicating to turn left. He was just four cars behind now. Almost time to make his move.

The lights changed to green, but the German car didn't move. Drivers behind beeped their annoyance, but the Mercedes stayed where it was.

"Something's up," he said.

"I see them," Sophie announced. "I'm looking right at the driver. He seems to be talking to the rear passenger."

Cars began to edge around Vasquez's car, leaving him vulnerable. If he went with them, he would be out of position. If he stayed where he was, they'd spot his bike. He was about to move when mercifully the lights changed back to red.

"If he doesn't move the next time they change I'm gonna—"

The Mercedes shot out into the junction, the driver throwing the wheel to the right as he hit the gas. Cars skidded to a halt to avoid a collision, leaving the road blocked.

"They're on to me," he said, giving his own engine plenty. He snaked his way through the stalled vehicles and was soon doing eighty as he weaved in and out of traffic in an effort to stay with Vasquez.

"Alpha Two, where are you?"

"On your six," Hunter replied. I see you."

He didn't bother looking behind. Instead, he maneuvered around a painfully slow bus and almost ran into the back of a taxi. He hit the brakes at the last second, then jerked the handles to the right and mounted the pavement, scattering pedestrians. It was a hundred yards before he could get back onto the road, by which time the Mercedes had gained a big lead.

It was going to take a lot to rescue this mission, but he wasn't going to fail.

It wasn't in his nature.

Ryan Anderson spun the throttle to the stop and a grin slid onto his face.

THE END

If you enjoyed Ryan Anderson, you'll love Tom Gray! Check out the million-copy bestselling series starting with Gray Justice.

AUTHOR'S NOTE

If you would like to be informed of new releases, simply send an email with "Motive" in the subject line to alanmac@ntlworld.com to be added to the mailing list. Alan only sends two or three emails a year, so you won't be bombarded with spam. You can find all of Alan's books at www.alanmcdermottbooks.co.uk.

Printed in Great Britain
by Amazon

49575252R00144